SUMMERTIME

A NOVEL

for anyone who
remembers the heat
and joy of a special
summer.

David P Fleming

DAVID L. FLEMING

Illustrations by Rob Fleming

Texas Christian University Press

FORT WORTH

Library of Congress Cataloging-in-Publication Data
Fleming, David L., 1951-
  Summertime.

  I. Title.   II. Title: Summertime.
PS3556.L437S8   1986   813'.54   85-20827
ISBN 0-87565-060-0
ISBN 0-87565-061-9 (pbk.)

Design by Whitehead & Whitehead
Illustrations by Rob Fleming

AUTHOR'S NOTE

In Texas, 1956 marked the seventh year of a drought which researchers at the University of Arizona called the worst in 700 years. The drought began in 1950, with rainfall rates eleven inches below normal, and continued through 1956, when the rainfall rate dropped almost eighteen inches below the normal thirty-two. Reservoirs dwindled. Crops burned in the fields. Cities and counties began lengthy disputes over water rights. On May 28, 1956, President Eisenhower signed the Soil Bank Plan into law, giving some farmers in the Southwest a chance to cover their losses for the year and hope for better weather in the future. The Guadalupe River, which flows near the Central Texas setting of this story, dropped from an average of 500 cubic feet per second to only seven in June. On July 1, 1956, all but five of the 254 counties in Texas were designated disaster areas. By the end of the summer, many farmers, already in debt from previous dry years, either lost their farms or were forced to leave them for jobs in the cities and towns. In 1957, the drought broke. The year was marked by record rains.

For the family; lest we forget.

Monopoly

W<small>E HAD JUST FINISHED</small> eating supper and Mama and Carol were in the kitchen cleaning up. Father and Gerald had gone outside. I was in the bathroom. It was hot in there and I was getting tired of counting the tile squares around the bathtub when the telephone rang. I heard Carol answer it. I started listening. I couldn't tell what she was saying, but the way she was talking made me mad. I knew she must be talking to one of her dumb boyfriends. I couldn't see why she needed boyfriends when she had me and Gerald around to talk to and do stuff with. Then I heard her saying "Please" in a voice so pitiful it would have made me cry not to give her what she wanted, but I knew she only wanted to go somewhere with some dumb boy, so I was glad when I heard Mama say no.

School was out and it was summertime. I didn't mind school too much, but Gerald hated it. He had been in the eighth grade at the junior high and all the teachers there were old and mean. Carol had just graduated from high school the week before. Father was glad. He said, "That's one less. One more to go."

"You mean two," I said.

He shook his head and looked at Gerald who was trying to get his shirttail out of his zipper. "I think just one more," he said, and Gerald got mad.

Me and Rebecca, who lived at the bottom of the hill, made the highest grades in Mrs. Hood's fifth-grade class. Rebecca's were higher than mine, but mine were second. She studied more, and besides, her father taught at the college in San Marcos. He made her do a lot of stuff that Father never would make any of us do. I didn't mind if Rebecca got higher grades though. Carol said one time that girls were always smarter than boys at that age. Gerald said that was just a lot of baloney, but I believed Carol.

Carol was nice and she was the prettiest girl I ever saw. She was as tall as Father's shoulder and she had blue eyes and hair as yellow as sunlight. In the summers she always tanned a dark brown, and when she wore her white shirt there was no one prettier anywhere. She had been the Sweetheart of the Class of 1956. There was a picture of her in the paper with some dumb guy standing beside her and smiling a dumb smile. Gerald said he was smiling because of where he had his other hand and I got mad and tore the boy out of the picture. Mama got mad at me, but it was all right because Uncle Raisin brought a copy of the paper over. He said that Carol's picture was the only good thing he had seen in the paper all year. The paper was always full of news on the drought and how people weren't going to make it if it didn't rain soon. Father said one time that even if it did rain, all the dirt would wash away.

By the time I got out of the bathroom, Carol was off the telephone. I went down the hall to the kitchen and stood in the doorway. Carol was drying dishes while Mama washed them and they were arguing. Carol was saying things like, "I don't see why not." Mama was saying, "Because. And that's a good enough reason." Then Carol said something else. Mama was starting to get mad. I turned and walked back down the hall, through the living room, and out the screen door.

Gerald was sitting on the edge of the low, concrete porch, letting his legs hang over. He was barefooted as usual, and every now and then he would dig into the dirt under his feet with his toes. Father was sitting with his back to the house in the red lawn chair. His old hat was pushed back on his head and his shirt was unbuttoned halfway down. When I came out the door, he took the cigar out of his mouth and looked at me.

"You *have* to let that door slam ever' time you come out of it?" he asked.

"No sir."

"It's already loose at the top. You want to break it all the way and let the house fill up with flies?"

"No sir."

"Well, think about things like that," Father said.

I went over to the edge of the porch and sat down near Gerald. From somewhere I could hear a redwing blackbird whistling and the breeze made a dry sound in the elm tree at the edge of the yard. It was already dropping yellow leaves even though it was only the first week in June.

"What are you doing?" I asked Gerald.

"Waiting for a train. What does it look like?"

"I just asked."

"Don't, next time."

"What's your mama doin'?" Father asked, blowing out cigar smoke.

"She's doing the dishes and talking to Carol," I said.

"Sounds more like she's *fightin'* with Carol."

Even sitting on the porch, we could hear them inside yelling at each other. Mama sounded sharp and Carol was saying the same things over and over.

"What does she want?" Father asked.

"Who? Mama?"

"No. Carol. Sounds like she wants somethin' she ain't gettin'."

"Some dumb boy called her and she wants to go somewhere with him."

We stopped talking and listened for a minute. Mama was banging pots and pans around like she always did when she got mad. To me, that sound was worse than fingernails on a chalkboard. Carol was saying she didn't see why not.

"Who was it?" Father asked. He was sitting with one boot propped up on the other knee and every now and then he would rub his ankle like it was sore.

"I don't know," I said. I didn't want to talk about it. I

didn't like Carol to go anywhere and I was glad Mama was making her stay home.

"Probably Mark," Gerald said.

I turned and looked at him. "Maybe not," I said.

"You know it was," Gerald said. "Why do you always have to act like such a queer?"

"I'm not."

"That's the first thing a queer always says."

"Shut up."

"That's the second thing."

"I *mean* it."

"That's the third thing," Gerald said.

"Make him shut up, Father," I said, mad.

"All right. That's enough," Father said.

Gerald shot me the finger where Father couldn't see him. "Father," I said.

"Mark seems like a good enough fella," Father said.

"He's too *old* for her," I said, because I had heard Mama say it one time. Mark was twenty and Carol was just eighteen.

Father took his cigar out of his mouth and looked at me with one eye closed against the smoke that blew back around his head. From inside the house the telephone started ringing again. Both Mama and Carol got quiet.

"What makes *you* such an authority?" Father asked.

"He's in love with Carol himself," Gerald said.

I jumped at Gerald like I was going to kill him, and I hit him before he could get up. He was off balance and fell into the yard.

"Well, look at that," Father said.

"You asked for it!" Gerald said, getting to his feet.

I turned and jumped up on the porch to run in the house. Mama opened the door before I could get there. Gerald caught up with me and slugged me in the back. It took all my breath away and filled my chest up with needles.

"What in the world's going *on* out here!" Mama yelled, still mad from fighting with Carol.

I wanted to cry, but I couldn't get my breath. I turned and pointed at Gerald. He was backing away and watching Mama's face.

"Has everybody turned into a bunch of wild Indians?" Mama cut a look at Father. "Don't you think you could make the boys behave while you're just sitting there smoking?"

"They weren't doing anything much," Father said with a little edge on his voice. He started to say something else, but he stopped and looked out into the yard.

Mama looked at me. "Are you all right?"

"I think my back is broken."

"It should be," Gerald said.

"Shut up, Gerald!"

"Stop it, both of you," Mama said.

"All right now," Father said, looking at Gerald who picked up a rock and threw it at the driveway.

"I came out here to tell you that Rebecca called and wanted to know if she could come over for a while. Her parents have some company."

"They *always* have company," Father said.

"We would too, if this family knew how to act right."

Father let that pass, but Gerald threw another rock. A little cloud of dust rose off the driveway where the rock hit.

"Well?"

"Yes ma'am," I said.

"Well, see if you can't straighten up before she gets here," Mama said, still holding the screen door open. She was staring at Father. Father turned and looked at her. I think she was waiting for Father to say something, but he didn't. She turned and went back in the house.

"Mama slammed it that time," I said.

"Shut up," Father said, and Gerald laughed. "You too," Father said, looking hard at him like he wanted to rap his head with his knuckles.

"I wasn't saying anything," Gerald said.

I went over to the edge of the porch and sat down again a little farther from Gerald. He picked up another rock and threw it. I picked one up and threw it at the dust too. My cloud was bigger than Gerald's. I stuck my chin out at him.

"Queer," he said.

"I guess this heat is gettin' to ever'body," Father said behind us.

5

"Be all right if it would rain," Gerald said. Sometimes he acted like he didn't know anything about the farm. Other times he seemed to know almost as much as Father about things.

"Yeah," Father said and smoked. "But that's the problem. It don't rain durin' a drought."

"Why not?" I asked.

"I don't know," Father said slowly, smoking, his eyes sharp and far away like hunters' eyes. "The clouds are all wrong for it and nothin' happens to make them change." Then Father's voice got lower and he said, "One thing's for sure. If it don't go to rainin' around here pretty soon, things on this farm are going to change."

Gerald turned around and looked at Father. He was waiting for Father to say something else, or maybe he was just watching Father smoke. Father didn't say anything else, but he was doing plenty of smoking. I could tell from the way he was puffing on that cigar that the butt wouldn't be worth stealing so me and Gerald could smoke it later.

From out on the road we could hear the sound of a truck roaring up the hill. The sound was muffled by the bend in the road, but I could tell the truck was really working. When it broke the top of the hill, we turned and watched it go by. Worthless, our crummy dog, came out from somewhere and barked at the noise twice, then went back around the corner of the porch. The motor was clattering and the tail pipe was loose. The truck was loaded with old, beat-up furniture. A green piece of canvas had come loose and was flapping across the back of the truck like a flag.

"Wonder where they're going," Gerald said.

Father took the cigar out of his mouth and said, "Top of the next hill, probably."

"They're moving in to that old green house?" Gerald asked, surprised.

"Think so," Father said. He cleared his throat and spit out into the yard. "I believe Wheeler sold that place."

"They sure had trashy looking stuff," I said.

The door opened and shut softly and Carol came out on

the porch. A while before supper she had washed her hair and now it was dry and shiny and soft. The wind tried to blow her ponytail when she came out on the porch.

"Oh brother," Gerald said, looking at her and then away.

I smiled at her and she smiled back. She went over to Father's chair. Father was looking out toward the road again and did not turn around until Carol got behind his chair and put her hands on his shoulders.

Before she even said anything, Father shook his cigar and said, "Don't start in on me. It's too hot, and I wouldn't cross your mama for nothin'."

Carol moved her hands on his shoulders. "It isn't like I go out every night or anything, Father. You know that."

"Yeah, I know it, Carol, but don't start on me about it."

"After all, I have graduated now. And my grades were all good. You know I work hard around here."

"I know it, Carol. Now just don't start on me."

Gerald looked around and said, "Might as well tell her to go ahead and finish, 'cause she's already started."

Carol narrowed her eyes and said, "Mind your own business, Gerald."

"What did your mama say?" Father asked.

Gerald turned around and picked up another rock. When he threw it, I looked out toward the road and saw Rebecca walking along the edge of it. She looked small.

"She said I stayed out too late after graduation, and since that was only last Friday it wouldn't hurt me to stay home tonight."

"Reckon it wouldn't," Father said.

"Oh Father!" Carol said, a little mad. She pinched his shoulder, and Father smiled.

"Go on, now," he said. "I told you not to start. You may feel like scrappin', but it's too hot for me."

"Why don't you ask Ricky if you can go?" Gerald said and laughed.

I started to get up, but Father said sharply, "Boy, don't even *think* about it. You kids are goin' to get me in trouble yet, and I'm tellin' you it's too hot for trouble."

I looked at Gerald as hard as I could. Sometimes he went too far and I really hated him, especially when he said things about Carol or teased me when I wet the bed.

"Here comes Rebecca," Gerald said. He looked at me, then he picked up a little rock and threw it at the driveway.

In a minute Rebecca walked into the yard. She was wearing her jeans rolled up at the cuff and a white shirt with lots of little pink flowers on it. It was a good shirt, and Rebecca had worn it so much that the little pink flowers were getting hard to see. Her hair was in two braids and there was a little pink ribbon at the end of each braid. She was carrying her sandals. Her mother always told her to wear them, but she never did.

"Hello, Mr. MacAllister," she said.

Father looked at her and nodded. Carol was standing beside him now and leaning on his chair a little.

"What are y'all doing?" Rebecca asked, walking up to the porch.

"Gerald's waiting for a train," I said.

"Shut up," Gerald said. "Who's at your house?"

Rebecca sat down close to me. "Some people Daddy knows," she said.

"From the college?" I asked.

"Yeah," she said, looking at her feet. "All they do is sit around and talk or play cards."

"That's all we ever do," Carol said. She looked at Father.

"I can't help that," he said.

"Yeah, but I like it when y'all do it," Rebecca said.

"I'm going to college when I grow up," I said.

"Ha ha," Gerald laughed.

"Are you going to be like my father?"

"I hope not," Father said, and we all laughed, even Rebecca. Her father was a little strange. He hardly ever talked to me or Gerald when we went down to see Rebecca. I didn't think he liked living in the country.

Mama came outside then to see what everybody was doing. Father told Gerald to get one of the other lawn chairs for her. They were out in the yard under the elm. Gerald picked one up and carried it over his head to the porch. Two brown leaves fell out of the seat and blew away. Gerald set the chair on the porch beside Father. Mama said hello to Rebecca, then looked at the chair.

"My, I'm not used to such treatment around here."

Gerald made a face and came back over to the edge of the porch. Mama sat down in the chair. She was rubbing lotion on her hands. Carol stood up straight and walked around behind Mama, heading for the door.

"Where are you going?" Mama asked her.

"In the house," Carol said in her mad voice. "If that's all right."

"Fine," Mama said. She watched Carol go in the house. She was still rubbing lotion on her hands.

"What was that row all about?" Father said in his low voice.

"I imagine she told you all about it," Mama said.

"Guess so," Father said.

Gerald kicked around at the dirt under his feet for a few minutes. There weren't any rocks close enough to get without standing up and going for them. He stood up and stepped back on the porch. "I'm going in too," he said.

After a while, me and Rebecca got up and went in the house too.

"What's with everybody?" Mama said as I pulled open the door.

"Too hot," Father said. He took one final puff on his cigar and threw the butt out into the yard.

We went into the kitchen. The sun was going down beyond the cotton fields and the sky was all red. I got a glass off the draining rack and I turned on the water and watched it come out slowly. It used to come out with bubbles, but now it just ran clear and slow out of the faucet. Rebecca stood by the cabinet waiting for me.

"Want some?"

"Okay."

She took a little drink and gave the glass back to me. Her lips were wet. Standing close to her, I could smell her. She had a sweet smell that wasn't perfume like some of the girls at school wore. I could smell where some of them had been even if the hall was empty. I could never smell Rebecca until I was beside her. Then she smelled like new hay or pine trees.

"It tastes kind of funny," she said.

"The well is getting low. It takes all night for the windmill to fill the tank. Father says it might go dry."

"What would you do then?"

I put the glass back on the rack and wiped my mouth. "I don't know. I don't think the well will go dry. It never has in all the time since Grandfather had it dug."

"We got a letter from the people who own the co-op well saying not to use very much water. Daddy thinks we will end up carrying water from town. He wants to—"

"Wants to what?" I asked, standing by the cabinet.

"I don't know. He thinks he wants us to move."

I looked at the floor. The faucet dripped once behind me. The sink smelled like dishwashing soap.

"Where to?" I asked.

Rebecca looked at me with her brown eyes. "I don't know. He was just talking about it the other day."

"Oh. Father does that all the time. He's always saying he ought to do this or that. He never does any of those things. That's just the way they talk."

"Yeah," Rebecca said.

"What do you want to do?"

"I don't know." She shook her shoulders. "What would *you* like to do?"

"Let's go upstairs."

We left the kitchen and went down the hall to the stairs. Rebecca stopped and put her sandals on the last step and we went up. The stairs were not very high, and they turned in the middle. Upstairs there was another hall. Carol's room was on the right, and the spare room was on the left. At the end of the hall was the room that me and Gerald shared. It was a good room, with two beds on either side of the big window and our dresser drawers, bookcases, and the table under the window where we kept the old radio Grandmother had given us.

Carol was in her room playing some records. She had a magazine in her lap, and she was sitting on the edge of her bed turning the pages hard like she wanted to tear them out. I stopped by her door.

"Rebecca's here," I said.

Carol looked up and stopped turning the pages. "I saw her. Hi, Rebecca."

"Hi. Your hair sure looks pretty, Carol."

Carol smiled then and she did look pretty. "Thanks. I washed it this afternoon."

"I wish my hair was blond like yours," Rebecca said, touching one of her braids.

"Come on," I said.

We went on down the hall. Gerald was on his bed reading a Superman funny book when we walked in. He was lying on his back looking up at the pages. I sat in my chair at the table and looked out the window. The sky was getting a little darker, but it was still plenty light even though it was after eight. I could just barely hear Mama and Father talking from the porch below us. Rebecca sat down on my bed near me and said something to Gerald. Gerald didn't answer.

"Guess what," Rebecca said.

I leaned back in the chair and looked at her. It was hot in the room. Gerald looked at her.

"What?" I said.

"I saw Amy in town the other day."

Gerald went back to reading.

"You did?" I said, but I really didn't care about Amy. She was the kind of girl who never went barefooted. On the playground, she would follow some of the older boys around and giggle. Sometimes she would hang around with Rebecca when Rebecca sat with me at lunch.

"Yeah," Rebecca went on. "She was coming out of J C Penney's with her mom."

"What did she say?"

"She asked me if I had seen you since school was out," Rebecca said, cutting me a look.

Gerald laughed from his bed and turned a page. For a

minute it was very quiet upstairs. I could hear the breeze in the elm tree, and past that, the slow creak of the windmill as it turned. Carol's record player changed records.

"What did you tell her?"

"I told her I had."

"Yuck. You should have told her I died."

"That's a terrible thing to say."

"Amy is a terrible girl," I said.

"Don't ever say that about dying," Rebecca said.

I looked at her and Gerald did too. Rebecca was always saying things like that, and her face when she said them was so strange that me and Gerald always looked at her to see if it was phony. It never was. Gerald said one time that she was too serious. Another time he said it was because of her father that she acted strange and that it was up to me and him to show her how normal people acted.

"All right," I said.

"Don't worry," Gerald said. "People like Ricky live forever."

"Read your funny book," I said.

"Don't get too tough or Amy will be sending flowers."

"I wouldn't want to live forever," Rebecca said.

"Why not?" I asked.

"Just think about it. If you lived forever, then you would always see people you loved die. You would meet them and love them and they would die, but you wouldn't. Think how hard that would be if it happened over and over again."

Me and Gerald were watching Rebecca's face again. She reached up and scratched her shoulder and looked past me out the window. It was getting darker outside. Rebecca's eyes were far away.

"How long can you stay?" I asked.

"As long as you will let me, I guess," Rebecca said and looked down at her feet. Gerald was watching her face again.

"How long will the company be there?"

"'Til late, probably," she said.

"You can sleep with me tonight," Gerald said without looking at her. Then he laughed.

I pushed away from the table and got up. Rebecca was looking at something on the floor. Gerald gave me a quick look to see what I was going to do, but I didn't care about him anymore. I went to the bookcase by the desk and started looking around in it. We had lots of funny books, some fossils, puzzles, and two piggy banks in the bookcase. Gerald's piggy bank was cracked. The crack had Scotch tape over it. Nothing looked any fun.

Carol came to the door. "It sure is quiet in here," she said.

"Until now," Gerald said, without looking at her.

"We were just talking," Rebecca said.

"About Ricky's girlfriends," Gerald said.

"Shut up," I said.

Gerald made a pooty noise. Carol said, "You have girlfriends, Ricky?"

"No."

"What about me?" Rebecca asked.

I looked at her. Everybody was looking at me, and it made me mad. "Not you either," I said.

The screen door slammed down under us. Mama and Father were coming inside. In a minute, I heard the television come on. It was dark outside now, but it wasn't much cooler. Carol was sitting on the end of Gerald's bed where he couldn't reach her with his foot. I was sitting on my bed and leaning against the wall with my knees drawn up. Rebecca was sitting on my bed too. She had her back to me.

Carol slid a funny book to the floor that was in her way. Gerald looked around the one he was holding and said, "Hey, watch that."

"What difference does it make?" Carol said. "Most of them are already on the floor."

"Just the ones I want to be on the floor."

"Oh good grief."

"Such language," Gerald said. "Why can't you sit some place else? Like on the moon."

"I like it here," Carol said. "Despite the smell."

"I saw your picture in the paper," Rebecca said.

"The funny paper," Gerald said.

"What are you going to do now that you've graduated?" Rebecca asked.

Carol leaned forward with her elbows on her knees. Her hair hid part of her face from me. "I don't really know yet," she said.

"She's going to haunt old houses," Gerald said.

"Oh, be nice, can't you?" Carol said.

"What's in it for me?"

"You may live 'til morning."

"I'm not impressed."

"Are you going to college?" Rebecca asked.

I looked at Carol. I didn't see what the big deal was. Just because she graduated from high school didn't mean she had to change her life all around. She could stay on the farm and do things like always.

"I thought about it," Carol said. "But I don't really think college would do me any good."

"She means she's too stupid to go to college," Gerald said.

"Then what?" Rebecca asked. Sometimes, watching them, I imagined that Carol and Rebecca were sisters.

"Who knows? I'll probably get a job, or I might even get married."

"Why?" I asked.

"Why not?" Carol looked at me.

"Because it's dumb," I said.

"Your mother and father got married," Rebecca said, not looking at me.

"Yeah, and look what it got them," Gerald said.

"What is *that* supposed to mean?" Carol said, looking at Gerald.

"Get a mirror and I'll show you."

Carol reached over and slapped Gerald's thigh. Gerald tried to hit at her with his funny book. She dodged him and her ponytail flipped back and forth.

"Cut it out," she said. She straightened up and looked at me. "Anyway, I'm not getting married tonight."

"Too bad," Gerald said.

It was quiet in the room for a few minutes. Rebecca was looking at the floor again. Carol and Gerald always acted up when someone else was around. Any other time they would barely talk to each other.

"Let's do something," Carol said.

"Kill yourself," Gerald said.

"You're so lucky not to have any brothers," Carol told Rebecca. She smiled.

"What about me?" I asked.

"Hey," Carol said. "Let's play Monopoly."

"Too hot," Gerald said, reading again.

"Can I be yellow?" Rebecca asked.

"I wanted yellow," I said.

"That's why I want it."

Rebecca got up and followed Carol down the hall to her room. We always played on Carol's bed because it was full size and we could all sit around the board. I slid to the edge of my bed and stood up.

"You comin'?" I asked Gerald.

"I guess so," he said, making it sound like a fate worse than death.

Carol already had the box out when we got there. She opened it and spread the board on her bed. Rebecca went around and got on the bed by the yellow places where the fat policeman was blowing his whistle. Yellow was my favorite color, and she knew it. I started to sit by her at the head of the bed, but Gerald said, "Watch it. I get to sit by Boardwalk." I went around to the foot of the bed and climbed on. Carol put out the trays with the money in them and Gerald slid them over to himself.

"Now wait a minute," Carol said.

"I get to be banker," Gerald said. "I said first."

"Keep an eye on him, Rebecca," Carol said.

"For what?" Gerald said.

"You cheat."

"— to you," Gerald said, making a pooty noise.

"Are you going to play right?" Carol asked.

"Sure sure sure. Let's start. Give me the dice."

"Banker rolls last."

"Since when?"

"Give me that blue one," I said.

Gerald grabbed the spool up and put it down for himself. "Blue is for boys. Take this red one."

"The yellow one is mine," Rebecca said.

"Wouldn't you like a red one?" I asked.

"Wouldn't you?" She smiled and tried to touch me, but I jerked away, pretending to be mad.

Carol moved the box and sat down across from Rebecca. She curled her long, brown legs under her.

"Look out for the bank," Gerald said, pushing her shoulder.

"I am," Carol said. "Why do you think I sat here."

"Just to bug me."

Carol acted like she was going to kiss Gerald, and he nearly fell off the bed. Rebecca laughed in that way she had. It was a high fast laugh, and it always made me laugh to hear it.

"Come on," I said. "Where's the money, Banker?"

"I'd get it if I could keep this whore off me."

Carol slapped Gerald in the side and I was glad. "You'd better watch it," she said.

"You watch it," Gerald said, trying to count out our money and keep one eye on Carol.

Carol put down the brown spool for hers. We had lost the pieces that came with the set a long time ago. Gerald took them to school with him and there was a strange guy named Ernest in his class who said he could eat metal, so Gerald gave him the little race car and said, "Eat that." Ernest ate it and Gerald kept on giving him the little pieces until they were all gone.

"It's a good thing this money is all different colors," I said, taking mine from Gerald.

"I like the tens," Rebecca said, holding them like a yellow fan.

"I like the five hundreds," Gerald said.

Carol put the Community Chest and Chance cards on the board and gave the houses and hotels to Gerald. "Where are the deeds?" she asked.

"I've got 'em," Gerald said. "Pass the dice."

Carol gave the dice to Gerald and told him to put the deeds out where she could see them. Rebecca arranged her money neatly in separate stacks and tucked them under the edge of the board on her side. I just spread mine out in front of me.

Gerald shook the dice. "Highest throw goes first." He rolled the dice on the board and they turned up a double six.

"Read 'em and weep," Gerald said to Carol.

"I don't believe it."

"See? I don't need to cheat with luck like that. Your roll."

When we were finished, I came after Gerald with a ten, Rebecca with an eight, and Carol was last with a three.

"Beauty before age," Gerald said.

"Just start," Carol said.

Gerald rolled the dice across the board toward me. They stopped just at the edge and he leaned forward to read them. It was a seven. "Too bad we're not shooting craps," he said as he moved his spool. I picked up the dice and watched him move. He stopped on Chance. We all waited for him to pick up the card. When he did, he read it and flipped it at Carol.

"More money," he said.

"Let me see," I said.

Carol read the card out loud. It said for the bank to pay him a $50 dividend.

"What's that?" I asked.

"Money," said Gerald. "Roll."

I rolled the dice and counted a nine. I leaned over by Carol and picked up my spool and started counting the spaces off.

"Connecticut Avenue," Gerald said, trying to hurry me. He always wanted it to be his turn. "Want it?" He shuffled through the cards while Rebecca picked up the dice and rattled them in her hands.

"Sure," I said. I gave Gerald a hundred and a twenty and he flipped the card across the board toward me. It hit my knee.

"Keep your feet off my bed," Carol said to Gerald.

He looked at her. "*Your* feet are on the bed."

"Mine aren't filthy."

Gerald slid his feet a little closer to the edge of the bed and looked at Rebecca. "Roll," he said.

Rebecca shook the dice hard for a minute and looked at me. She rolled the dice out on the board, and we all looked. It was a six.

"Oriental Avenue," Gerald called before Rebecca could count it out. She touched all the places anyway which made Gerald wrinkle up his face.

"Want it?"

"I'm collecting those," I said.

"I want it," Rebecca said.

Gerald laughed and looked at me as if Rebecca had just hit a high fly and I had dropped it. He started shuffling through the cards again. I looked back at Rebecca. She was carefully pulling a $100 bill out from under her edge of the board.

"I was collecting those," I said.

"Me too."

Carol gathered up the dice and Gerald said, "Look out!"

"Shut up," Carol said. She shook the dice and let them roll across the board. Gerald was watching.

"A seven! Chance!" he said.

"Move over," Carol said, sliding her spool along and deliberately knocking Gerald's off the board. She reached forward for one of the Chance cards. Her shirt opened a little and I could see the rounded tops of her bosoms.

"It says to advance to the nearest utility. Ha ha."

"Big deal," Gerald said, snatching up the dice and rubbing them between his hands as hard as he could and blowing on them.

"Slow down, buster. I'm buying the Electric Company."

She counted out the money, but Gerald wanted to roll. "Buy it later," he said.

"Now, or give me the bank," Carol said.

I was looking at Rebecca. I thought she was having a good time, but when Carol and Gerald were fighting and she thought I wasn't looking at her, she had a strange, kind of sad look on her face that made me think something was bothering her. She was staring at the board as if it were a hundred miles away, and her eyebrows were wrinkled together. Her braids were hanging forward off her shoulders.

"There!" Gerald said suddenly, flipping the card at Carol. Rebecca raised her head and looked right at me.

"Now," Gerald said. "Let's really see some dealing."

He threw the dice and one of them slid off the edge of the board. It was a six. So was the other one.

"Doesn't count," Carol said.

"What!"

"Oh shut up. You know it doesn't count when the dice roll off the board. If you don't like it, quit throwing them."

"Crap!" Gerald said, taking the dice back. He shook them hard, but he let them roll out of his hands a lot easier. It was a four and a one. He was mad. That put him right on Carol's property.

"Four times five is twenty. You owe me twenty dollars," Carol said. She laughed and held out her hand.

"I'm giving it to you in fives," Gerald said. "Because I hate pink."

Carol took the fives and started to put them with the rest of her money, then she stopped and counted them. There were only three fives. "All right, cheat. Where's my other five?"

Gerald gave her the other five and looked at me. "Roll, queer."

"Stop calling Ricky a queer," Carol said.

"Yeah," I said.

"Shut up and roll. Queer."

I looked over at Rebecca. She was looking at the board and not saying anything. Carol was looking at her too. I rolled the dice. It was an eight. "Community Chest," Gerald said before I could move. I picked up one of the yellow cards. It said I was to get $25.

"What for?" Gerald said. "Let me see that card. Lousy queer."

"I said to stop calling him that," Carol said.

Gerald frowned and threw the card back on the board. He counted out a twenty and a five from the bank and handed it to me. "Don't spend it all in one place," he said.

Rebecca was looking at the board. "Everybody has property but you, Gerald," she said.

"Just wait 'til it's my turn again," he said, looking hard at her face. He looked over at me for a minute, then down at Rebecca's roll. It was a three. "Ricky's crummy place," he said.

I laughed. Carol was just watching. "That will be eight dollars," I said.

"Wow. Moneybags," Gerald said.

Rebecca carefully counted out the money and passed it across to me. I thought she was still acting strange, but she didn't say anything. The way she looked reminded me of how she looked last winter when we were down at the tank lying on our stomachs on the cold ground watching the ducks. The ducks were green-looking with red and yellow on their heads and we had never seen any like that before. Then it had started to rain and I had jumped up and started running back to the house without waiting for her. I thought she would be right behind me, but she wasn't. She was way back and just walking slowly through the rain. I waited for her at the shop. Her hair was wet when she got there. She had the funny look on her face and didn't answer when I asked her why she hadn't run. She said she had to go home and went to the house to call her mother. I stayed down at the shop. When her mother came, she ran out and got in the car. Her mother turned the car around in front of the shop. I could see Rebecca sitting there, but she didn't look at me or wave. She got like that sometimes.

Carol picked up the dice and rolled. Something happened, but I wasn't paying attention. I was thinking about something, then I looked at Rebecca. She was looking at me with her brown eyes.

"I'm just glad school let out," Gerald was saying. "If I had had to sit in those classes one more day, I would have burned the school down."

"You say that every year," Carol said.

"It's true every year."

I saw Carol put a deed card down next to her money. Gerald was shaking the dice and blowing on them.

"Mrs. Hood isn't going to teach there next year," Rebecca said.

I looked at her. "How do you know?" I asked.

"My father told me. He said it was in the paper that she had quit."

"Roll," Gerald said.

I shook the dice and rolled. "Why?"

"My father said her husband was real sick."

"Want a railroad?" Gerald asked.

"Yeah."

"What's wrong with him?" Carol asked.

"My father said he had been to Korea and gotten messed up over there."

I was looking at Rebecca. She looked at me. I thought

maybe she was just worried about Mrs. Hood. She had been a good teacher. She let me and Rebecca sit next to each other.

"The war," Gerald said. "Roll, Rebecca."

"There always has to be a war," Carol said.

"I hope there's one when I'm old enough to go," Gerald said.

"What an awful thing to say. Shut up. And get your feet off the bed."

"They're not on the bed."

Rebecca rolled. She got an eleven and Gerald whistled.

"Too bad. It just puts you on Free Parking."

"Why don't you let people do their own moving?" Carol asked.

"Too slow. Roll."

Carol picked up the dice and shook them and let them fall. She had a five. She moved her spool by me. Leaning over like that, her face was close to mine. I could smell her. She smelled different from Rebecca, but nice.

"Want it?"

"Why not?"

"If you got the money, honey—"

"I'm not your honey."

"Thank God," Gerald said, finding the deed. "I would hate to be Ricky."

"Shut up," I said. I looked sideways at Carol.

"What a tough guy."

"You're the one who's tough," Carol said. "Tough to look at."

"Ha ha. Here. Old Kentuck'. And I hope you choke."

Carol gave Gerald the money and slipped her card under the edge of the board. Gerald made a show of putting the money up. I looked at Rebecca. She was leaning forward with her chin on her hand looking at the board.

"You sure are quiet tonight, Rebecca," Carol said, using her natural voice. When she talked to Gerald her voice became sharp and lower.

Rebecca looked at her. "I'm all right," she said.

Carol looked at me like I had done something. Gerald

rolled. One of the dice tumbled up on the Community Chest cards. A nine. He moved his spool quickly by leaning all the way across the board.

"Wait a minute," I said. "That was ten."

"Shut up, queer."

"It should be on the B & O. You owe me twenty-five dollars."

"Crap! This is a stupid game. Here. Roll!"

"I'm rolling," I said, picking up the dice. I rolled a four. That put me on Marvin Gardens. Rebecca looked hard at me.

"You want it?" Gerald asked, picking up the cards.

Rebecca was looking hard at me. I knew she would want the yellow ones. But she knew I liked yellow too.

"Want it?" Gerald asked again.

"Yeah," I said. Rebecca looked down and picked up the dice. I gave Gerald the money and he threw the card at me. "Quit throwing them," I said.

"Serves you right," Carol said.

"Why?"

"Roll, Rebecca," Gerald said.

"Why?" I said again.

"Never mind," Carol said.

Rebecca rolled. It was a seven. "Ventnor Avenue," Gerald said. "Want it?"

"No."

"Take it, Rebecca," Carol said. She looked at me again. I was starting to feel bad.

"Yeah, take it. Serves the queer right," Gerald said.

"What did I do?"

"Okay," Rebecca said. She carefully counted out the money and Gerald handed her the card. She slid it under the edge of the board and put her chin back in her hand.

"Hold on," I said. Carol picked up the dice and started shaking them. "What did I do?"

"You took Rebecca's color," Gerald said. "Queer."

"She took one of mine."

"Wow," Gerald said, rolling his eyes.

"Ricky!" Mama called from the bottom of the stairs.

"Just a minute. Be quiet," Carol said.

"Rick-y!"

"What."

"Don't what me, young man. It's ten-thirty. I think you should take Rebecca home now."

"Can't you take her in the car?" I called. Carol was looking at Rebecca.

"No sir, I don't think so when it's just to the bottom of the hill."

"I can walk by myself," Rebecca said.

"No you won't," Carol said. She cut me a look.

"All right," I called.

"So much for that," Gerald said. "I didn't even get a single piece of property."

"That makes you the loser," Carol said, letting the dice roll out of her hand onto the board. It was a double six. "Wouldn't you know?" she said.

"Loser, nothing," Gerald said. "The winner is the one with the most cash at the end of the game. That means me."

I piled my money on the board along with my deeds. Rebecca was doing the same.

"Cash includes property," Carol said.

"I still have more," Gerald said, lifting his stack of money. On the bottom was about ten five hundred dollar bills.

"Why you little cheat," Carol said. She slapped him in the side again.

"Watch that," Gerald said.

"Ricky?" Mama called again.

"Coming!" I looked over at Gerald. "Are you coming with us?"

"Why should I?"

"I don't know."

"You scared to walk back by yourself?"

"No."

"Then why should I come? I'm tired."

"You're not coming?" I asked, not looking at Rebecca.

"I can go by myself," Rebecca said.

"Nope," Gerald said.

"No, you can't," Carol said. She looked at me.

"Come on," I said.

"It's really all right," Rebecca said.

"Same with me."

We got off the bed, and I looked hard at Gerald, wanting him to come with us. I didn't want to walk back up the hill in the dark by myself.

"We'll see y'all later," I said, looking at Gerald.

"Don't let the wolfman get you," Gerald said, stacking the money.

"Oh shut up," Carol said.

"Or Frankenstein."

"Come on, Rebecca," I said.

Gerald was laughing, and Carol was saying things to him. I went out into the hall with Rebecca right behind me. The light over the stairs was burned out, but the steps were lighted from the kitchen light downstairs. Rebecca touched my arm before we started down the stairs.

"You really don't have to walk with me, if you don't want to," she said.

"I want to."

We went down the stairs. I slid my hand along the banister. Rebecca's feet barely made a sound. From behind us I heard the rattle of hotels hitting the floor and Carol yelling at Gerald. At the bottom of the stairs, Rebecca bent down and picked up her sandals. Father came out of the bathroom scratching his head.

"You taking Rebecca home?" he asked.

"Yes sir."

"Well, watch out for monsters," he said.

"Mac!" Mama said, coming out of the kitchen. She put a hand on Rebecca's shoulder. "Now you see where Gerald gets it from," she said.

"Don't blame that on me," Father said, going into their bedroom just off the hall.

"You be careful," Mama said. "If any cars come by, be sure to get well off the road. You know how the drunks come around that curve sometimes."

"All right," I said. I started walking away. Rebecca followed me.

"Tell your mother any time you want to come up, it's fine with us."

"I will," Rebecca said.

The lights were off in the living room. Out in the front yard was a rectangle of light from our room. I felt like throwing a rock through the screen and maybe hitting Gerald on the head, but I just crossed the yard. Rebecca was walking beside me carrying her sandals. The night was warm as bath water all around us. I thought maybe Worthless would be lying around close by, but as usual he was off somewhere being worthless. Father said one time that if Worthless didn't die pretty soon, he was going to shoot him. He was only kidding though, because Carol found Worthless and it was her dog.

When we were out on the driveway and away from the house, Rebecca said, "Look at all the stars."

I looked up. The sky was clear and deep as a lake and the stars were like spilled sugar on a black tablecloth. Behind all the brighter stars was the Milky Way, hanging like an unravelled rope. Gerald used to say that God put those stars there with a giant shotgun. "Yeah. One he could shoot the Russians with," I said. He said I was stupid. Carol said there was nothing prettier than the sky on a summer night. "Except you," I said, and Carol had hugged me so tight I couldn't breathe.

"You know what I would like to do?" Rebecca said. She said it like it wasn't something happy. I looked at her light face in the darkness, but I couldn't tell what she was thinking.

"What?"

"I'd like to stand on my head and push off the earth and fall into those stars feet first. Then I could dance across the sky and all you would have to do to see me would be look up there."

"If you were on those stars," I said. "You'd be so far away that I couldn't see you at all."

"Yeah. I guess you're right."

We came to the end of the driveway. The south wind was blowing over the fields and it felt like the air that comes out of the oven when I pull open the door to check the toast. Everything looked different to me and spooky in the dark. Even the mailbox looked like something with a big head and only one leg.

"Besides," I said, turning my back on the mailbox. "All I have to do is look down the hill. I can see the lights of your house from our window upstairs."

"You know what I do sometimes?"

"What?"

"I sit on our front porch and look up the hill waiting to see your light go out at night."

"Why do you do that?" I asked, looking at her. Our shoulders touched as we walked.

"I don't know. It makes me feel good. I don't feel so alone."

"You were by yourself?"

"I'm always by myself."

"No you aren't. Your mother and father are there," I said.

"Sometimes I wish I was your sister."

We were walking down the middle of the road. The gravel and tar were still warm. I was trying to keep my feet on the yellow line.

"Then Gerald would be your brother," I said.

Rebecca laughed. "But then I could always be around you."

"You already are," I said. "We sat by each other at school and on the bus, and we go to each other's house any time."

"But every night I'm by myself."

I looked at Rebecca out of the corner of my eye. She was walking along with her head down. Little hairs around her face had come loose and were blowing softly. From somewhere out in the cotton a whippoorwill called. I turned and looked, then looked back at Rebecca.

"You want to spend the night at our house sometime?" I asked.

"I don't know, Ricky. It's funny, but I feel more at home at your house than I do at mine. Your parents are nice and —"

"Mama gets a little rough sometimes," I said.

"Yeah, but y'all all fit together. Even though you're each different, you're a part of each other. I don't know."

We were past the edge of the hill now, and it seemed darker without the house lights behind us. A dog was barking way off along the dry creek down where Mr. and Mrs. Ketchum lived. I wished Worthless was with us.

"Hold my hand," Rebecca said.

"Sure."

I reached out and took Rebecca's hand. It was small and dry, and she was holding mine tightly. I felt older holding her hand. I always felt that way. At school or on the bus or in the house or pasture, whenever Rebecca held my hand I felt older.

"Are you scared?" I asked.

"Not with you."

"Me either," I said.

We walked along. It wasn't that high a hill, but sometimes it made me tired, especially if I was carrying a bag of stuff back from the store or we had been down to the creek by Mr. Ketchum's place before it dried up. Then it seemed like a steep hill and we would walk back and forth across the road like drunks, trying to make it less steep.

"You know what I wish I had?" I said.

"What?"

"A harmonica."

"Why?" Rebecca asked, holding my hand. She held the sandals in her other hand against her side.

"I saw this guy in this movie the other day and he was playing one."

"Lots of people play them, I guess."

"Yeah, but this guy was pretty neat. He was a cowboy and he would play that harmonica whenever he was thinking."

"What was he thinking about?"

"That's what this other cowboy asked him. He was playing it around the fire one night and the other cowboy was listening real close. Then he said, 'What are you thinkin' 'bout?' The neat cowboy quit playing and said, 'A girl I knew once.' But there were other neat things too."

"Did he ever see the girl again?"

"I don't know. I just thought the harmonica was neat."

At the bottom of the hill we passed a house that Mexicans used to live in. There was still an old car with no hood on it parked under a hackberry tree in the yard. Me and Gerald had been through the house. There wasn't anything in it much. Now, in the dark, the house was all black and the windows were blacker, like closed eyes. I thought how weird it would be if someone was inside watching us walk along. I wished Gerald had come with us. I hated having to walk past an empty house in the dark.

Across from the empty house was the little store where me and Gerald bought our candy and soda water. It was owned by an old man named Mr. Norman who lived all alone in the house next to it. Mama said one time that his wife had died and he had no kids. He was a kind of crazy old man who was hard of hearing. He chewed tobacco and spit in a coffee can that he carried around with him. He liked me and Gerald and gave us jobs to do sometimes. Then he would give each of us an orange Nehi and some jawbreakers. Gerald could break his when they were as big as a dime, but mine had to be as little as a pearl before I could crunch them. The store was closed up and dark now, but there was a light on in Mr. Norman's house and that made me feel better.

As we were passing the store, Rebecca said, "Ricky, what if I did have to move?"

"You don't really think you will, do you?"

"What if I did?"

"I don't know. It would be funny not to see you around all the time."

"I don't think I could bear leaving all of y'all," Rebecca said.

"Are you going to move?"

We passed Mr. Norman's house. Up ahead, on the same

side of the road were the remains of the old gin that had caught fire about the time I was born. It had never been rebuilt. There were newer gins in town, Father said.

"I don't know."

"When will you know for sure?"

"I don't know."

"Your father was just talking," I said. "Like I told you. My father does that all the time. Why would he move?"

"It's different with him at the college. We've already moved twice since I was little."

I walked along beside Rebecca, still holding her hand. For her to go away was too strange for me to really think about. Me and Rebecca had been friends since the first grade when she had gotten on the bus crying that first day of school. She got on the bus and sat near the front crying. A Mexican kid named Demos whose family worked for the Ketchums started teasing her. Me and Gerald were sitting in the back because Gerald said that was the best place to be when the bus hit a bump. All of a sudden Gerald got up and walked down the aisle and got Rebecca and brought her back to our seat. Then he went back and sat by Demos for a few minutes. Rebecca and me were friends from that second on. Gerald said it was about right for him to do all the dirty work and me get all the glory.

Rebecca's house was just a little ways ahead of us. The porch light was on and there were two strange cars in the driveway. I could see Rebecca's face better now. She looked at me. I felt very close to her. I thought someone else should have been there to see how I felt, like jumping over a fence when I'm all by myself or hitting a snake in the tank with a rock on the first try.

"Maybe we won't move," Rebecca said. "Anyway, I hope not. I just don't know what I'd do."

We stopped in the driveway while Rebecca leaned against one of the cars and put on her sandals. Rebecca never wore shoes unless she had to. I looked in the windows of Rebecca's house and I could see her mother and father and some other people sitting around the dining room table. They each had a glass in front of them with ice in it and something dark like tea. Mr. Brown was talking and smiling more than I had ever seen him do. I didn't like the way the other people looked. If Father had been there, he wouldn't have liked them either. He would have said a little honest work wouldn't have hurt them any. Father never trusted any man whose hands weren't rough.

"Well, I guess I'll see you later," I said, looking back up the road. After looking at the lights, I could barely see anything.

Rebecca put her foot down and wriggled into the sandal. "Are you afraid?"

"I might run all the way."

"I'm sorry Gerald didn't come with you. It would have been better."

"Only going back," I said.

We stood out by the cars a little while. I didn't want to have to walk back in the dark and Rebecca didn't seem to be in a hurry to go in the house. Finally, she said, "You know what else Amy said?"

"What are you talking about?"

"Amy. When I saw her with her mom. You know what else she said?"

"What?"

"She said that if I wasn't around she would be your girlfriend."

"Amy said that?"

"Yeah. She said that as long as I was around no other girl had a chance."

I didn't say anything for a minute. I could hear the people inside the house laughing. Rebecca looked toward the house, then back at me.

"Did you hit her?" I asked.

Rebecca didn't laugh. "No," she said.

"Amy's crazy," I said. "Nobody thinks as crazy as she does except herself. She makes me sick," I said.

"How come you said I wasn't your girlfriend?"

"When?"

"Tonight. In front of everybody." Rebecca was twisting her feet inside the loose sandals.

"I was just mad," I said.

"It didn't make me feel very good."

"Is that why you were so quiet?"

"I don't know."

"Well," I said. "Forget about Amy. Amy is too stupid to even think about."

"Amy doesn't bother me," Rebecca said. "It makes me mad when I think about what she said, though. Promise me that if I move, you won't start doing things with Amy."

"Oh Rebecca. That's dumb. Me and you have done everything together since the first grade. In all that time, you are the only friend I have ever had. Amy could never be like you."

"Promise me."

"I promise."

Rebecca looked toward the house. Her eyes reflected the light like she was crying. I couldn't tell if she was or not. It was hard to tell with Rebecca. She didn't cry like other people. When she cried, she didn't make a sound. I didn't know why she should be crying now. It bothered me a little and I wished I was already back at the house.

"I'm going in now," Rebecca said. "I'm sorry you had to walk down here with me. I'm sorry you'll have to go back by yourself."

"I'll be all right," I said, beginning to feel bad. It was never easy to leave Rebecca.

"Thanks anyway. Goodnight, Ricky."

"Yeah," I said like Father did when somebody thanked him for something.

Rebecca turned and went straight to the house and up on the porch and across to the front door. She did it so fast I thought she was running, but she wasn't. She was just walking fast. At the door she stopped for a minute. I could see her outlined in the screen door. Then she turned and ran across the porch and down the steps. The porch was wooden and the noise her sandals made on it caused Mrs. Brown to say, "Hush everybody! I think I heard someone on the porch!" Mrs. Brown was always real scary. But before she had even finished saying that, Rebecca ran up to me and put her arms around my neck. I could feel one of her braids against my cheek and I could smell her very close.

"I'm sorry I took your yellow," she said. She turned loose of me and ran back to the porch just as Mr. Brown got to the door.

"What is it, Marvin?" Mrs. Brown called from the next room.

"It's just Rebecca," he called back, letting her in. She never turned to look back at me.

"Thank goodness," I heard Mrs. Brown tell the others. "I was afraid it might be a prowler or something."

The porch light went off, and I was all alone in the darkness. For a minute I just stood there looking at the house and thinking about Rebecca. Every time she went home I thought of a hundred things I wanted to tell her. Finally I turned around and walked out of the driveway.

When I got back to the house I was going to fix Gerald for not coming with me. I had done plenty of stuff for him before when I didn't feel like it. On the road I looked both ways hoping for a car to come along and light the way with its headlights, but there wasn't a car within a hundred miles of Rebecca's house. I walked down the middle of the road, looking quickly on both sides of me.

I started getting scared. I could think of all the terrible stories I had heard and the scary movies I had seen on the television. I remembered everything anyone ever told me about the devil, and I got even more scared because I knew I had not been as good as I should have been. There were so many things the devil could get you for, and once he got you it was forever. I knew that at any second I would turn and there he would be all red and scaly with sharp, bloody horns and smoke all around him and fire in his eyes and big, white teeth like a tiger's and claws on his hands—.

"Hey."

I was just passing the store when something moved on the steps and said something. I started shaking and trying to say help. I must have jumped as high as a mailbox.

"Hey. Take it easy." It was Carol. She laughed a little.

"It's not funny, damn it, Carol," I said.

"I wasn't trying to scare you," she said, walking out to the road. "Who do you think I am? Gerald?"

"What were you doing then?" I asked, calming down.

"I came to walk back to the house with you," she said.

When she was beside me, she put her arm down around my shoulder and we started walking back up the road. The breeze blew the tail of her shirt against my side.

"I wanted to go out tonight, and now I am," she said. She bent over and kissed the top of my head.

"Look at all the stars," I said.

"It's a beautiful night," she said.

"Not as beautiful as you," I said.

Carol laughed. We walked up the road talking. It really was a beautiful night.

Rabbits

W<small>E CLIMBED UP</small> the bank of the washout and looked through the dry grass and broomweed to where the house stood on a bare patch of black dirt just the other side of the fence. From our level, we could see the foundation posts like little legs under the house. Behind the house were some sheds and two pens. A tall, metal cistern was rusting at one corner of the house. The house itself wasn't much. Me and Gerald had been in it lots of times when Mexicans weren't living in it. It only had about five rooms and the long porch across the front. There was no ceiling in the house at all, just rafters and the roof.

"Here comes another one," Gerald said.

I turned toward the road and saw the truck coming up the dusty driveway. We could hear it squeaking and clattering, and the dust rose up behind it and followed it up to the house, then covered the house.

"They're moving in, all right," Gerald said.

The two men in the truck got out and began to untie the load.

"I wonder who they are," I said, brushing dirt off my elbow where it had begun to stick.

Gerald edged forward up onto the dry grass. "Look at those beat-up, old trucks," he said. A grasshopper crackled near his hand and landed. He moved his hand quickly and mushed it. He brushed it away from him. It was turning in the grass and spitting black juice.

We watched the men unloading the truck. The south breeze blew the dry grass back and forth in front of our eyes. From somewhere high up behind us, an airplane growled lazily in the sky; it worked like the tractor does when Father drops the sweeps and they start to dig in and the big wheels filled with water start to spin in the dry dirt. Then black smoke comes out of the exhaust and Father gives more gas, at the same time working the sweeps up through the clods. I turned and looked at the grasshopper again. It was still turning on its side with its head down and spitting black juice.

"They might be movin' in for good," Gerald said, chewing his bottom lip.

I looked back through the grass, keeping my head down. The men were coming out of the house, looking thin in outline, with cowboy hats pushed straight down on their heads. One was a little shorter than the other.

"They sure look trashy," I said. "They must be cedar choppers."

"What would cedar choppers be doing out here?"

I looked through the dry grass.

"Where are they going to find any cedar out here?" Gerald asked, turning and looking at me over his shoulder.

"How should I know?"

"Then shut up," Gerald said.

We heard a loud screeching and turned back to the house. The two men were pulling a long, cloth-covered settee off the truck. They were both on the ground pulling, and the back legs were screeching along on the metal bed of the pickup. Something small like a rag fell off the back end of the truck, but neither of the men saw it. It began to blow away.

"Somebody ought to be in that truck," Gerald said. "They're going to pull the legs off that settee when it hits the tailgate."

We watched. When the back legs came to the tailgate, the settee stopped. One of the men shouted something and the other turned loose of the settee and went up to the other end of it. He lifted it out of the groove between the bed and the tailgate. They went behind the truck carrying the settee to the

36

front steps. The first one shouted again, and after a second the door swung open. They went inside.

"Did you hear what he said?" I whispered.

"Yeah."

Someone had come out on the porch. The breeze blew the plain, cotton skirt out behind her like a sheet on the line.

"A girl," I said.

Gerald moved up in the dry grass. "Yeah," he said again.

I raised my head a little. "It must be the mother," I said.

"What do you mean, the mother? That ain't no mother."

I looked again. She was too young to be the mother.

"She's going to see you," I whispered.

"Shut up."

I moved along the edge of the washout until I could see her better. She wasn't very tall, and she was as thin as the men were. When she stepped off the porch, the wind blew her hair. It was long and light-colored, but that was all I could tell about it. She walked slowly along the side of the house to the back. There were three windows on that side of the house. She stopped by each one of them, cupping her hands beside her face and standing on tiptoe to look inside. The screens had holes in them that I could see from where we were, and they were rusted red.

"What's she doing?" Gerald said.

The two men came out of the front door and stepped off the porch to the truck. One of the men climbed up in the truck and lifted a table down to the other one. The girl came back to the front with her arms crossed. She stopped and watched the two men carrying the table. A boy about four or five years old came out the door just as the two men got to it. He acted like he didn't know what to do, so he just stood there in the middle of the doorway doing nothing. One of the men shouted again and the girl jumped up on the porch and jerked the kid out of the way. The two men turned the table sideways and took it on in the house.

"Listen to that guy, will you?" I said.

"Yeah."

"Somebody get this goddamned kid out of my way!" I said, changing my voice to make it sound more like the tall man's. "I'm surprised he didn't kick the little kid right off the porch into the yard."

The girl was putting the little boy back on the edge of the porch and the little boy was jumping off into her arms again. They were having a good time. When the two men came out again, the boy stopped and watched them walking to the truck. Then he jumped suddenly and surprised the girl. She barely caught him and the little boy must have bumped her chin because her head flew back like when Matt Dillon socks somebody on "Gunsmoke." Gerald started laughing when he saw that, but I didn't. It reminded me of me and Carol. Then the girl set the kid down and slapped him so hard he went backwards against the porch and fell and sat there in the dirt crying. The girl just looked at him and rubbed her chin.

"What a punch!" Gerald said.

"Let's go," I said.

"And miss all this action?"

Gerald backed up and slid down the bank of the washout in the crusty, black dirt. I was already at the edge and slid down beside him. He picked up clods that rolled down and threw them at the dry clay of the bed. It was always dry except after a rain. Then there were pools that sometimes lasted three weeks. But it had been a long time since there had been any water.

"My elbow itches," I said.

"There's forever something wrong with you. They ought to send you back for a refund."

"Shut up," I said.

The wind blew in the dry grass above us. It was starting to get hot in the washout. Way up high in the sky a buzzard was floating along looking for something dead.

"Nobody's sending me anywhere," I said.

"Then shut up about it," Gerald said, throwing little clods of black dirt at the yellow clay of the bed. Then he said, "I wonder if those people are plannin' to stay from now on."

"I hope not," I said.

"Why?"

"You saw them."

"So what?" Gerald said. He threw a clod against the far bank and some loose dirt rolled down. The banks were always caving in.

I thought about the girl and the little boy and when she hit him. I scratched my elbow where the dirt had stuck and lay down against the bank with my eyes closed. I could see red in my eyelids. The man started yelling again and the wind carried it over to us.

"Listen to that guy, will you?" I said.

I opened my eyes and looked at Gerald. He was sitting with his arms across his knees, turned sideways to me. He chewed his lower lip for a minute, then wiped his mouth on his sleeve.

"So what?"

"He scares me," I said.

"Everything scares you."

"It does not."

"Then who peed in his pants 'cause the lights went out the other night?"

Gerald looked at me, then turned away again and started chewing on his lower lip, making it turn bright red like girls' lips. I wouldn't have wet my pants if Gerald hadn't grabbed my throat in the dark and growled like a dog. He had been waiting for me when me and Carol got back to the house. I made such a racket that Father got out of bed and came upstairs and popped Gerald with his belt. Father had been really mad because he was tired and had been asleep. It served Gerald right, but now he was mad at Father.

Gerald stood up and looked toward the house for a minute, then spit in the dirt beside me.

"Let's go back," he said.

The Mexicans were in the field chopping cotton, and Father was in the pasture mowing broomweed and sunflowers. When we came up from the washout, we could see him and the tractor going around the second tank. We ran through the part that he had already cut, looking for rabbits' nests. The grass and weeds were green still and smelled sour and itchy. The stubble was sharp under our bare feet. Father was circling and the dust rose and followed the tractor as he made the turn. He saw us then, but didn't wave. We went through the grass and stubble, looking.

Then I saw the rabbits. They were little cottontails, and they were running away from the tractor and the noise and the cutting and the dust.

"Over there!" I yelled.

We ran after them. Gerald went to the right and I went to the left so we could cut them off. Father was circling. The dust rose. Gerald turned too quickly and fell down. The rabbits cut away from him. I only saw two of them. Gerald got up and dusted his pants.

"Where are they?" he said.

I was running. I cut back to the right and almost fell. Then Gerald was running. He ran in front of me until I cut to his side and then away. Father was going away from us. The stubble was sharp. We were running. I fell, cutting to the left. Gerald jumped, rolled, and caught one. I was up.

"Where's the other one?"

Then I saw it. I stumbled and caught it. We both had one now. Mine kicked and twisted in my hands. It was small and brown. Gerald got up with his. We looked around for more and found another one with its head cut off. There was red blood on its fur. The white fur of the belly was showing and it had blood on it. Father was circling again. The dust rose in the hot air. Gerald bent down and touched the red fur with one hand.

"Look here," Gerald said.

"No."

"Put your hand here."

He turned the little body so that the stump of the neck was pointing up. He looked at me with a grin, then dropped the body back on the ground. He had blood on his fingers.

"Come on," he said, wiping the blood on his pants. "Let's go put these in a cage."

We walked along the fence to the gate and crawled through and walked up the dirt road to the sheds where the wagons and the old corn-picking machine were parked. The gray cat was sitting in the shade watching us. His tail moved back and forth and his eyes were half closed as if he were trying to make up his mind whether to sleep or not.

"I bet that cat would like to get hold of this little rabbit," I said.

"Chew its head off," Gerald said.

The workshop was in the last shed. It was longer than the rest and had a workbench with two vices and an old forge where we sometimes melted lead. Near the forge was a big anvil that had ENGLAND stamped on its side. Gerald said King Arthur used to hammer swords on it. In one corner of the shop was a stack of old boards and rusty iron and other stuff that Mama had thrown out of the wash-shed. There was a beat-up cage there too, that Father had built for us when we had the ducks. The ducks had died.

"This will be perfect," Gerald said, pulling the cage out of the pile with one hand while holding his rabbit in the other. Gerald had strong hands.

We put our rabbits in there. Gerald's was bigger than mine. They huddled together in one corner and trembled like they were scared. Gerald tapped the wire and they ran to the other corner.

"You're scaring them," I said.

"So what?"

"I don't want you to scare mine."

"Yours is too little to live, anyway," Gerald said.

I thought of the one with its head cut off. "No it isn't," I said, but it looked very small and afraid.

"I wonder if they're hungry," I said after a while. "What do they eat, carrots?"

"Sure. There's carrots all over the pasture. What we need to do first is get them some water. Go get a lid and put water in it."

"You do it."

"I told *you* to, you little—" and he made a noise like a pooty.

"I'm not."

Gerald looked at me. "Okay," he said. "Let them die."

I stood up then. "Don't let them get away."

"Who you tellin'?"

Carol was outside throwing bean hulls and snaps over the fence. I went to the trash barrel looking for a lid or a small can. A lid would be better. I found one, a blue and white one with oily mayonaise all over it. Carol walked over with the basket in her hand to see what I was doing. I told her about the rabbits and she followed me down to the shop after I got the water.

Gerald stood up when he saw us coming.

"Carol wants to see my rabbit," I said.

"Yours died. Give me the water."

"Liar," I said.

Carol reached in the cage and lifted my rabbit out and held it very carefully in her hands. She rubbed his little head with her fingers. It seemed to like Carol. She held it close to her cheek and said words to it. She called it "little rabbit," and she was sitting on the dirt floor of the shop in her jeans.

"Look at mine," Gerald said. He lifted his out and it was small, but bigger than mine, and Carol held them both. They seemed to be glad she was there.

"They're both very cute," Carol said. "They're both so tiny and soft."

"Mine's not cute," said Gerald, reaching for his. "Mine's no sissy."

"I didn't mean it was," Carol said, still holding mine and shaking back her yellow hair and looking at Gerald.

"Ricky's can be cute because it's so little, but not mine," Gerald said.

Carol said, "Well, I think it's cute anyway."

"Well, it's not," said Gerald. "And I don't want you saying it is when it isn't."

"Don't you boss me, mister," Carol said.

"Drop dead."

"What's wrong with you?"

"Nothing is," Gerald said. To me he said, "Why did you have to bring her down here, anyway?"

"I wanted her to see my rabbit."

We were all quiet then, sitting on the dirt floor of the shop and looking at each other. Gerald turned a little away from Carol and looked at her over his shoulder. He looked at the way she was holding the little rabbit. He was chewing on his lip.

"I think they're both cute as can be," Carol said, moving toward Gerald.

"Shut up, Carol, so help me."

"As cute as can be," said Carol, leaning toward him.

I stood up on my knees. "Watch out for my cute little rabbit," I said.

"Sissy queer," Gerald said.

Carol held my rabbit in one hand and tried to touch Gerald's with the other hand, but Gerald turned his shoulder on her. Then he got up and went out the wide door of the shop holding his rabbit against his chest. Carol watched him go and she frowned and made a face. Then she smiled at me and said, "Here." I took my rabbit and held it carefully. It wiggled in my hands and I could feel its heart beating fast.

"I guess I'd better get back to the house," Carol said, standing up.

"Carol?" I said. She stopped. "You don't think they'll die, do you?"

"Maybe they won't," she said.

"Gerald said they would."

"Maybe they won't," Carol said again. "Just take good care of them and we'll see. Okay?"

"All right."

Carol walked out of the shop. As she passed Gerald, she said, "So long, cutie."

"Phooey," Gerald said.

Carol picked up the basket she had been carrying and went back up to the house. I went to the wide door of the shop. Gerald turned and looked at me.

"I'll be glad when she moves away," he said.

"I won't."

"Who cares about you?" Gerald stood up. "Come on. Let's get some string and let them play."

We went back into the shop and Gerald found some string on one of the shelves over the workbench. It was the white kind of string that breaks easily. He unrolled a handful of it and we went out the back door of the shop and around to the side that was in the shade. No grass was growing there, but the dirt was soft and it was cooler.

We had just finished tying a piece of string to one of their back legs when Rebecca came around the corner of the shop looking for us. She was wearing a straight, brown dress with a thin brown belt and shoes and socks. Her hair was in a ponytail that bounced around when she turned her head.

"Hi Ricky," she said, coming over to me and sitting down. She stripped off her shoes and started taking her socks off. "Hello, Gerald."

"Chow," Gerald said.

"Where have you been?" I asked.

Rebecca put her socks into her shoes and pushed her feet out in the dirt. Her legs were brown and a little thin.

"To town," she said.

"You sure go to town a lot."

"Rabbits!" she said then, leaning forward and pulling my rabbit toward her. "Where did you get them?" She pulled my rabbit over to her and picked it up. "It's so cute," she said then. Gerald looked at her and made a pooty noise. Sometimes Rebecca was a lot like Carol.

"Mine's not cute," Gerald said, but Rebecca was used to Gerald and she never minded what he said, except once when Gerald called her a skinny little piece of ass, which was something he heard a guy in town say. Rebecca had looked at him with her strange face for a minute or two and Gerald tried to laugh it off. Then Rebecca started to cry, and I went up to Gerald and pushed him. He just stood there like he was listening to the television from the kitchen. He wouldn't fight or say anything. I put my hand on Rebecca's shoulder and after a while she stopped crying, but she went home and didn't talk to us for over a week.

"What are their names?" she asked.

We hadn't thought of names.

"Mine's name is Rex," Gerald said.

"That's a dog's name," I said.

"Shut up."

"Rex means king," Rebecca said.

"How do you know that?"

"I read it someplace, I guess." Rebecca was always reading.

Gerald was happy. "How about that?" he said. "Ain't no king gonna be called cute."

"What about yours, Ricky?"

"I don't know."

"Is it a boy or a girl?"

"His is a girl," Gerald said. "It suits him."

"Shut up," I said, because Rebecca was there.

"Watch out, queer."

"How can you tell whether they are boys or girls?"

We looked at Rebecca.

"Turn it over," Gerald said.

Rebecca turned the little rabbit over in her hand. It didn't like it and started kicking and trying to turn back over.

"That's a girl, all right," Gerald said.

"How do you know?" Rebecca asked, holding my rabbit against her to settle it down. The string hung out between her fingers.

"Like cats," Gerald said.

"I don't think you can tell," I said.

"Shows what you know."

"Maybe it is a girl," Rebecca said.

I looked at her. She had a chigger bite above her ankle.

"It's a girl, all right," Gerald said again.

"Let's name it Becky," Rebecca said.

"I don't know."

"Why not?"

"That's a great name for her," Gerald said.

Rebecca held the rabbit up to her cheek and looked at me with her sharp, brown eyes.

"All right," I said.

"Come here, Rex, old boy," Gerald said. He pulled the string toward him and the rabbit tried to pull the other way. Gerald laughed and slid him along, then scooped him up. He started to say something, but Mama was calling him.

"Oh yeah," Rebecca said. "Your mother told me to tell you she wanted to see you for a minute."

"What for?"

Rebecca shrugged.

"Oh rats," Gerald said, getting up.

"Want me to hold your rabbit?" I asked.

"Not on your life. I'm putting him in the cage."

Gerald went in the shop, and I looked at Rebecca. "What did you go into town for?" I asked her.

She made a soft place in her lap and put the rabbit there and patted its head very softly. "Stuff," she said.

"Like what?"

"What difference does it make?" Rebecca looked at me with her sharp eyes.

"I just wondered. Is your mother here?"

Rebecca looked down. "No. I told her to let me off at your mailbox as we went by and that I would walk home in a little while."

"You aren't going to stay?"

"I can't."

"Why not?"

Rebecca looked down at the little rabbit and patted its head. She was whispering something to it. I looked over at the barn and watched a blue pigeon fly in the big window where Father and the men unload the hay. The window was in shadow and dark. Sometimes I thought I could see something standing back there in the dark looking out. I shivered without thinking about it and looked at Rebecca.

"Do you still feel bad?" I asked, remembering the other night. Rebecca knew what I was talking about. She always did.

"Not really."

"The other night I thought—"

Rebecca looked up quickly and looked back down again. "The other night I was scared," she said.

"When? Walking down to your house?"

"I felt different when I woke up in the morning."

I was looking at her. She was acting funny again. She looked hard at me.

"You want some gum?" she asked, reaching in a side pocket of her dress. "I got some at the store."

"Sure."

It was Juicy Fruit. I opened it and put the paper in my pocket. Rebecca was talking to the rabbit again. I watched her.

"Does that mean you aren't moving?" I said.

"Maybe."

I waited for her to say something else, but she wouldn't.

"Why won't you talk about it?"

Gerald came out of the shop and Rebecca got up quickly. So did I. She gave me the rabbit without looking at me.

"You take good care of Becky," she said.

Gerald laughed, then watched us. Rebecca reached down and got her shoes and socks.

"I have to go now," she said.

She went around me, touching my shoulder with hers as she passed. I turned and watched her. She was walking straight away and she did not look back. The wind was blowing her skirt out behind her as she walked. I thought I could smell her.

Gerald came up and stood beside me. "What's going on?" he asked.

"I don't know."

Just before dinner, Father came in on the tractor and stopped outside the shop. Me and Gerald were sitting in there watching our rabbits. Father turned the tractor off and got down and stood taller than it did. He came into the shop, taking off his straw hat and wiping his face with the sleeve of his shirt. I liked to watch him do that. Then he looked at the sleeve and saw how wet it was and put his hat back on his head. His chin seemed to stick out more when he had his hat on.

"Now what?" he said.

"Look at our rabbits," I said.

"I'm more interested in shear pins," Father said. He went to the shelves nailed to the wall beside the workbench and shoved bolts and nuts and sacks of screws and nails around, looking for the shear pins. He took a box down and held it away from him, looking at the label, then he opened it up. He walked over to where we had the cage. Gerald watched him closely, looking at his face, then down at his hands. I could tell he was still mad at Father.

"This one's mine," I said.

"The runt," said Father. "Suits you."

"I'm no runt," I said.

"You don't talk like one," Father said, taking shear pins out of the box in his hand. One fell on the ground beside Gerald. He looked at it without moving and Father stopped and looked down at him. I thought Gerald would pick it up, but he didn't, and Father went on looking at him.

"*Boy,*" Father said.

Gerald looked down into his lap. I started to get the shear pin, but Father moved his boot.

"Pick that up," he said to Gerald.

Gerald reached over and picked up the pin and handed it up to Father. Father looked at him and took it.

"The other rabbit yours?" he said to Gerald.

"Yes sir."

"Guess I ran over the nest," Father said, closing the box. He turned back to the shelf. I looked at Gerald and felt quiet. "Reckon that's what happened?" Father said.

"Yes sir," Gerald said, looking down into his lap, chewing on his lip.

Father went back outside and I could hear him doing something to the mower. Gerald didn't say anything and I didn't look at him. I looked at the rabbits. They were crouched on different sides of the cage, just sitting there like us.

Uncle Raisin drove up just as we were sitting down for dinner, which made Father say, "Right on time, as usual."

"You can stop that before it even gets started," said Mama. "He can come by any time he wants."

Mama got up and went to the door and Father said, "He does."

I looked at the empty chair beside me and got scared because I knew Uncle Raisin would sit beside me. Father and Gerald sat across and Mama and Carol sat at either end. Carol sipped her iced tea and asked Gerald to pass the sugar bowl. He told her she could get it herself or do without. Father rapped him on the head with knuckles like hammerheads and

Gerald passed the sugar, but he put his finger in it for revenge. I tried to move my chair over a little.

Mama and Uncle Raisin came back. Mama looked like a little girl when she stood beside Uncle Raisin because he was so tall. He had to bend down to get through the door without bumping his head. He was fat, too. He looked like the picture of the giant in my storybook. That's why I was scared of him. Father said one time that Uncle Raisin used to eat live chickens when he was growing up, and that he would hide the feathers in his pillow.

They came into the dining room, then Mama went back into the kitchen to get another plate and a glass of tea. Uncle Raisin said hello to all of us at once, then walked around and sat down beside me. I could feel the floor shaking when he walked behind me, and the chair squeaked like a saddle when he sat down on it. He squeezed my leg with one of his giant hands and leaned over me. His face was red and rough-looking, like an outlaw's.

"What do you say, Mr. Richard?" he said.

"Nothing."

"Ha ha ha," Uncle Raisin laughed, then he cut a look at Carol and made her smile. Gerald was watching him. Father was eating as fast as he could.

Mama came out of the kitchen carrying a plate with silverware on it and a glass of tea. She came around and leaned over me to put them down in front of Uncle Raisin.

"That's what I want to see," Uncle Raisin said, still laughing.

Father got another helping of beans before Uncle Raisin could reach for the bowl. I looked across at Gerald. He was watching Uncle Raisin and sitting up straighter.

"How are things, Mac?"

"Dry," Father said, eating.

"Raisin said he sold some drawings of the boys at a show in Austin," Mama said.

"Really?" Carol asked. Her yellow hair was tied back with a strip of rag. I could see the freckles by her ears.

"Yep," Uncle Raisin said, turning the bean bowl up on

edge to get what was left. His hairy arm kept brushing my shoulder.

"That right?" Father said, eating fast.

"Sure did," said Uncle Raisin. He pointed to a pencil drawing of me and Gerald fishing that was hanging on the wall behind the table. "I sold ten of those. Prints, of course."

"Why don't you do one of me?" Carol asked. She put her hands behind her head and made a kissy-face the way Marilyn Monroe does.

"I can't show that kind of drawing at a county fair," Uncle Raisin said and laughed. He was raking fried squash off onto his plate. I was watching him.

"I don't like that," said Father, tearing a piece of bread in half.

I looked at Mama, but all she did was take another bite. If Gerald had said something like that, she would have gotten mad, but she always acted different to Uncle Raisin. He was her little brother, but he wasn't little. Mama told us that when he was born, he was so wrinkled that Grandfather Clark had called him a little raisin and that name had stuck even after he outgrew it.

"I was only kidding," Uncle Raisin said. Then he said to Carol, "I'm doing a portfolio of your little brothers. Those drawings are getting pretty popular."

"Really?" Mama asked.

"What's a portfolio?" I asked.

"Never mind, Ricky," Mama said. Father looked at me.

"If they sell, it means something extra."

"You spoil my boys and I'll give you something extra," said Father.

I looked at Gerald and he looked at me. I switched my fork to my left hand so Uncle Raisin wouldn't bump me, but the squash wouldn't stay on my fork.

"Was that necessary?" Mama asked.

"I was only kidding," Father said, eating.

"I'm not going to spoil your boys, Mac," said Uncle Raisin. "I just want to follow them around and do some more sketches of them around the farm, working and so on."

"They don't do much of that," Father said.

Gerald's fork stopped on the way to his mouth, then went back down to his plate. Uncle Raisin laughed, eating. Gerald looked at his plate. Carol looked at him a minute and went on eating.

"You goin' into art full time?" Father said.

"May have to. I know one thing," Uncle Raisin said, looking around the table to see what was left. "There's nothing in farming for me."

"You gettin' out?" Father looked up.

"You bet. I already set up a lease with Daniels. Let him worry about it."

"Oh Raisin, no," Mama said.

"*Daniels* leased your land?"

"That's right," Uncle Raisin said, cutting a look at Mama. "But not for this year. For next. He says the seven-year drought cycle will end this year. He claims that next year it's going to rain all day and all night."

"Wouldn't that be wonderful," Carol said.

I looked over at her. I had a dream sometimes about Carol running around outside in the rain. I couldn't remember whether it was a good dream or a bad one.

"What will you do?" Mama asked.

Uncle Raisin shrugged. "Don't really know, Jean. Thought maybe the pictures would help and maybe I could find something in town. I'm tired of being in debt all the time."

"Did Daniels pay you or are you goin' shares?" Father asked.

"Shares. Had to. He's like everybody else. No cash."

"That man was never like everybody else," Father said.

"But the farm," Mama said.

"The farm will still be there," Uncle Raisin said. We all thought he was going to say something else, but he just started chewing on a piece of bread. Mama took a quick look at Father. All of us looked at Father. Father was watching Uncle Raisin. The muscles in his jaw were working. Then Father looked at Mama and down at his plate. It was empty. Mama looked at me.

"What's the matter with you?" she asked.

Everybody looked at me. "The squash keeps falling off my fork."

"Then eat with your right hand like a human being."

I looked sideways at Uncle Raisin's arm. He had his elbow on the table. I looked at Gerald. He was eating again. I changed hands, and Uncle Raisin's arm brushed mine.

"Don't squirm now, Ricky. Eat your dinner."

"Good dinner," Uncle Raisin said, wiping his mouth and reaching for his glass of tea.

"I don't like to be drawn," I said because Uncle Raisin kept bumping me.

"Eat your dinner," Mama said again. Father was watching me and sipping his tea.

"Why not?" Uncle Raisin asked.

"Because he finds out how stupid he looks," said Gerald.

Carol poked Gerald and he tried to hit her back. Mama told them to stop it. "I don't know what happens to this family when company is around," she said. She was looking at Father. Something was different and it was bothering me.

"I don't look like that, really," I said. Father grinned at me quickly, then stopped.

"That's no way to talk about your uncle who is a good artist," Mama said. Mama never seemed to eat at the table. She played with her food and watched all of us eat, especially Uncle Raisin. Gerald said one time that Uncle Raisin was the clean-up squad.

"No. Now, he may have something there," Uncle Raisin said, putting his glass down on the table. The ice clinked. "There is something about Ricky that never gets down on paper, and I've noticed it myself. Whenever I get to his face, I start to mess up somewhere."

"Because it's so horrible," said Gerald. Father looked at him. He was listening to Uncle Raisin.

"His face is fine," Uncle Raisin laughed. "But he is right on the border of being something else, I think, and that makes his face hard to get just right."

"He hasn't learned how to sit still," Mama said. I looked at her and she smiled, but I didn't.

"I don't know what it is," Uncle Raisin went on. "Unless it's his age. How old are you now, Mr. Richard?"

"Ten," I said after a while, but only because Mama was giving me the behave look.

"Yeah. What I thought. Hard age to draw."

"That doesn't make any sense," Father said.

"Maybe not to you, but to an artist who works with a thing's insides as well as its outsides, it makes a lot of sense."

That was the last straw. Father was looking across the table at Uncle Raisin like he wanted to rap him on the head. Uncle Raisin laughed and his face turned very red.

"Oh, well, never mind," he said. "I guess I should just keep my ideas to myself."

"I guess so, too," Father said, and Mama didn't say anything.

Carol was looking at me. She had started to drink from her glass of tea and had raised it to her lips, but now she was just holding it there as if she had forgotten all about it. Her mouth was half-open and she was looking at me without blinking. Then she blinked and looked down and sipped her tea.

After dinner, Mama made me dry the dishes, which I hated to do more than anything except wash the dishes. It was Gerald's turn to clean off the table, but that was nothing. He was through in about five minutes and went outside to see what Father and Uncle Raisin were doing. He was still mad at Father, but he liked to listen to him talk to Uncle Raisin. I could see them down at the shop through the kitchen window while I dried the plates Mama gave me, still hot from the water she rinsed them in. Mama used the hottest rinse water of anybody I ever knew. I had to get dishes out of the pan with a fork or something, and if the water ever splashed on my hand, it left a red place.

"What does lease mean?" I said, after a while.

"It means you rent your land to somebody else."

"Is it still your land?"

"Yes," Mama said. "But you can't do anything with it. The man who leases it has control over it."

"Is that bad?"

"No. It's just the way things are."

I picked up the bowl the beans had been in and started drying it. The big glass bowls were the easiest to dry.

"Why didn't you want Uncle Raisin to lease his land?" I said.

"That farm used to belong to Grandfather Clark. I grew up there. I just don't want to see anything happen to it."

"What's going to happen to it?"

"Nothing."

"Then why did you think something would?"

Mama was washing a pan. She was going around and around the top edge of it with her dishrag. When she was through washing it, she put it in the rinse water.

"I didn't," she said. "I just don't want anything to happen to it. Raisin can do with it what he wants. I just hate to see him quit the farm and start working in town."

"Why?"

"He's too big for town, that's why," Mama said and I laughed. After a minute, Mama smiled. She was washing the frying pan. It was heavy and black and easy to dry. "What did Rebecca want this morning?" Mama asked.

"Nothing. She just stopped by."

"Oh? She told me she had something very important to tell you."

"Like what?"

"She didn't say, but I don't think she was kidding about it."

"She doesn't kid very much," I said.

"She didn't tell you anything earth-shaking?"

"Nope."

"Maybe she forgot," Mama said. She felt around in the dishwater, then she squeezed the dishrag and went to wipe off the table.

I took the frying pan into the pantry under the stairs and hung it on a nail. For a minute I stood in the edge of the dark pantry and thought. Rebecca never kidded very much, but she never forgot anything at all.

Mama always took a nap after dinner and she made me and Gerald take one too, but she never minded whether we went to sleep or not. She used to when we were little. Sometimes Carol would come into our room and read to make sure we took a nap. If I looked at her or talked to her, she would nod her head at my pillow and say, "Go to sleep, scamp." Now that we were bigger, Mama just wanted us to go upstairs and be quiet so that she could rest. Sometimes Father would rest after dinner too, if it was too hot to do anything else.

We sat on Gerald's bed and played cards for a while. We played poker with money from the Monopoly game. Gerald talked tough when he played poker. "Look here, partner," he said. "You want a card or not?" Then, when he won a hand, he would lay the cards out on the wrinkled bedspread and say, "Read 'em and weep."

I lost all my money and didn't want to play anymore. "Let's go spy on Carol," I said.

We got off the bed and sneaked along the wall down to Carol's room. Gerald stood flat against the wall and I got down on my hands and knees beside him and we looked around the door jamb and saw Carol sitting on her bed reading *The Saturday Evening Post*. Her back was against the headboard and her knees were drawn up with the magazine propped on them. We couldn't see her face, just her legs and arms and the top of her head. Her radio was going on the dresser by the bed. It was turned down low, but I could hear Gogi Grant singing "The Wayward Wind."

We watched her for a while, but she wasn't doing anything

except reading, so we went back to our room. I sat in my chair and looked out the window. Gerald started raking through his stack of funny books with the toes of his bare foot.

"Let's do something," I said.

"Like what?"

"I don't know. I'm tired of just sitting here."

"Then go do something else," Gerald said.

"What?"

"Go drown yourself."

Gerald picked up a Superman funny book and turned the pages without reading. He let it fall back onto the stack. "All right," he said, finally. "But be quiet going down the stairs."

We left the room and went down the hall. Carol was still sitting on her bed reading when we passed. Gerald made a pooty noise when he went by. Carol raised her head as I passed. She looked at me and stuck out her tongue.

Outside, the sun was bright and hot, and we stood around on the back porch for a while, thinking of something to do. Worthless was lying in the shade next to the cistern and he never even opened his eyes when we walked by him.

We went down to the barn. The ground was hot and the metal gate we climbed over was like fire. The pen around the barn was bare and dry and dusty and some cows were in the shade of the barn. The cows were lying down, flicking their ears at flies and chewing their cud. The barn itself was very high and had been painted red a long time ago, but most of it was worn off now and the boards were a dirty brown color like hogs.

One time Gerald had climbed across the rafters and crawled out the vent so that he was on top of the roof, but then he got scared and wouldn't move or come back down and Mario, the Mexican who worked for Father sometimes, had come along and seen Gerald up there and went to get him. Mama saw them and spanked Gerald hard when he got back to the house, scared and crying. Then, the next day, Gerald got up there again and got scared again and wouldn't move and I had to get Father to get him down. Father had whipped him hard and wouldn't let him eat at the table with us. Gerald had

gone upstairs and was lying on his back not blinking or sleeping when I went up. Then he did it again. He crawled halfway
out along the peak of the roof and got scared and wouldn't
move. I started to go to the house to get help, but before I
went, he started moving and went all the way to the edge and
looked down and spit. Then he backed up and climbed down
and sat in the hay a long time chewing his lip.

In the front and on the sides of the loft were the big open
doors where Father and the Mexicans lifted bales of hay off the
high wagons. The bales were very heavy, and when we helped,
it took both of us to stack one. Father and Mario could each
lift a bale with one hand and swing it up into the loft. We
watched them doing it one time as if they were in a race or con-
test. They laughed and made jokes and told each other they
were getting old. Uncle Raisin could throw two bales at once,
one in each hand.

Under the loft, it was half open and shady but hot. There
was one long room where we put corn each year. The long
room was empty now except for towsacks and corn shucks and
some rusty baling wire. Father said there wouldn't be any corn
this year, and he was right. It came up a little early in the
spring, then it wilted away. Father let the cows clean it up and it
didn't take them long.

Me and Gerald went to the side where a small half-door
opened on to a walkway that went all the length of the long
room. The half-door was more like a gate than a door, but it
was enough to keep the animals out. Once, our old milk cow
got in there and ate all night and bloated and died. Father was
as mad as I have ever seen him. He took us down to the barn
and wanted to know who had left the door open. I kept telling
him it wasn't me and started to cry, so he looked at Gerald.
Gerald said it wasn't him either, but he wouldn't look at Father.
He just chewed on his lip. Father let it go, and the next week
we got a new cow with one twisted-down horn. She was mean
and stubborn and wandered off all the time and kicked when
Gerald milked her. One time she went through the fence and
wandered all the way to Mr. Ketchum's by the creek and
stomped on all his cantaloupes. Mr. Ketchum liked Father and

Mrs. Ketchum was always nice to me and Gerald because she didn't have any kids of her own, but Mr. Ketchum had a bad temper. When he got mad there was no stopping him. He was always getting into fights with people. He liked to drink beer too, and Father said that was a bad combination. Father had some fast talking to do that time, and when he came home with that stubborn cow, he let it be known that any time we wanted to leave the door open into the corn, just go ahead.

In the middle of the walkway was a ladder that led to the loft. It was old and wooden and boots had worn the rungs out in the middle so that they looked like the bottom half of a smile. Gerald went up the ladder first. I followed him.

The heat in the barn from the sun on the rusty tin roof made the hay smell thick and heavy in a sweet, dead-grass kind of way. It reminded me of the smell behind the tractor when Father was mowing weeds, with the noise of the tractor and the cutting sound and the dust rising in the hot air. The hay in the barn now was mostly last year's hay. Me and Gerald would have to clean it out before any new hay could be stacked. Father started to have us do it one day before school was out, then he changed his mind. He said there wasn't any hurry.

For a while we looked for pigeons' eggs but didn't find any, just broken shells. Then we started playing pirates and chased each other all over the loft and swung on the big rope with the pulley clanking up near the rafter it was tied to. We had sword fights with swords made from pieces of the old picket fence. Sometimes Gerald hit my hand when we had the sword fights and I would cry and he would stop and wait and say things until I got mad and ran at him with the sword and we would start fighting again.

Then it got hot. We sat near the big window to rest and watched the pigeons fly away and come back and fly away again when they saw we were still there. Heat waves came off the shiny tin roof of the house and shop and sheds and off the fields. Father was mowing again. He was cutting weeds around the tank and at the edge of the field where the Mexicans were chopping cotton. He would still have to cut the narrow piece of pasture that ran up to the top of the next hill where the new people were moving in. Mama didn't like for him to cut that part because the washout twisted around through it and she was afraid he might run off into it and turn over. Mama always worried about stuff like that.

Gerald sneezed about six times. Sometimes he had hay fever. We had stirred up a lot of dust.

"I bet if you jumped out of this window, you would break your legs," I said.

"I've done it before."

"Liar. You would be dead."

"I'm still alive ain't I?"

"That just proves you didn't do it."

Gerald sneezed and leaned toward me. "I jumped out this window," he said.

I looked down again and could see the black dirt of the lot and the neck and head of one of the cows. It scared me to look over the edge, and I didn't believe Gerald had jumped without me being there to see him.

"Do it now," I said.

"Don't feel like it."

"You never did do it."

"Queer," Gerald said.

"I am not, and you're a liar or you would do it now."

Gerald looked at me and sneezed. His eyes were a little red and his nose was red and runny.

"I don't have to prove anything to you," he said.

I looked at Gerald, then looked back down at the ground. Maybe he had done it, but I wasn't sure.

Gerald got up without saying anything and crawled back through a long, dark, hot tunnel we had made between the old bales of hay. The tunnel led straight back with one turn to the wall where a crack was that we could breathe near and see out of. The crack was in the back wall and we could see the tank behind the barn. Sometimes the Mexicans swam naked there in the late afternoons just before dark and we would watch them. It was strange watching them. Sometimes just the boys swam there and sometimes Ignacio and Ernestina would come up and swim by themselves. Most of all it was strange to see

Ernestina. She swam in her underwear to begin with, but she usually took it off while they were swimming. She was brown all over and had bosoms and dark hair between her legs. Sometimes she and Ignacio would just stand next to each other in the tank with the muddy water up around their shoulders and kiss. Gerald would say they were doing it and that would scare me. Watching them made me feel like someone was sitting on my chest and my face would be hot. Sometimes I would be shaking all over. In church on Sundays after watching them, I would be scared because I knew God knew we watched them doing it. One time Brother Dowell was yelling something and scaring me and the sun came suddenly through the stained-glass windows and threw a streak of red light across my lap.

Gerald came back with his cigar box. Mine was back there too, but all it had in it was a wooden pistol that Father had helped me carve, some matches and a candle, and a valentine that Rebecca had given me at school that said she was my true love forever. Sometimes Rebecca was silly, but she was nice too. One day after she had given me the valentine, Mrs. Hood was gone and the substitute we had gave Rebecca a thirty on a test for using ink instead of pencil. Rebecca had started to cry and the teacher got real mad at her and told her to leave the room. Rebecca wouldn't do it because she was crying so hard. Then the teacher took her by the hand and pulled her out of her chair and dragged her out of the room. I was worried and mad and went out of the room too, but I didn't see Rebecca or the teacher anywhere. I walked outside and looked around, but I couldn't find them, so I went back in. The teacher was in the room. She grabbed me by the arm and asked me where I had been. I told her I had to go to the bathroom and I knew she wouldn't mind since she was gone anyway, but she minded and made me stand in the hall. The only other person in the hall was a big kid named Floyd who had gotten into trouble too. He was always getting into trouble. He had bowlegs and arms like a monkey. Then I saw Rebecca come out of the restroom. I watched her walk slowly up the hall with her eyes on the floor, and she looked small and sad. When she saw me by the door she walked fast past Floyd and came to me and I hugged her and she started to cry again. I told her it was all right, that I would take care of it. She went in and I stood in the hall wondering what I could do to the teacher to pay her back. After a while I looked over at Floyd, and he shot me the finger.

Gerald opened his cigar box in front of the big window where it was the coolest. His had some matches and a candle in it too, but he also had some cigar butts that Father had not smoked all the way. Sometimes Father just chews on his cigars instead of smoking them. He can look at Mama and tell whether it is time to just chew or whether it is all right to smoke. Sometimes he doesn't look at Mama at all but goes ahead and lights up his cigar at the supper table and blows thick clouds of smoke into the air.

We moved over until we were out of sight of the house but still near the window, and Gerald brought out an old butt about three inches long. He gave me a shorter one. He put his in his mouth and leaned back against the hay. He acted like Father.

"Get off your butt and hand me my butt," said Gerald, making his voice deep. We both laughed.

"Boy, do as I say," I said, making my voice deep.

Gerald squinted at me. "Ricky, don't whine," he said, making his voice deep.

We laughed. I was looking at Gerald. The cigar burned my mouth.

"Dadgummit, Ricky, you wet the bed again," said Gerald, making his voice deep.

I looked away from Gerald. I looked down. "Shut up," I said.

Gerald got a match out and lit his cigar. He could smoke them pretty well. I could too, if I did it slowly, but I felt bad. Gerald always made me feel bad with that, even though I hadn't done it in a long time.

"Want a match?" Gerald asked.

"No."

"Here. Light up."

"All right."

Changing the subject was the only way Gerald ever said he

was sorry. A pigeon came back and flew away again. Or it could have been a new one. I couldn't tell.

"Be careful you don't drop any ashes in this hay," Gerald said. "This old barn would burn up in ten minutes, I bet."

"It would be some fire," I said, crawling to the edge and knocking the ashes down into the lot.

"It would be as big as the great Chicago fire, I bet," Gerald said, smoking.

"That was a big one."

"Yeah, but you don't know anything about it."

"Yes I do," I said, watching my cigar burn.

"No you don't."

"We read about it in school."

"That's not what really happened," Gerald said.

"It was in the book, Gerald."

"Yeah, but that was a lie."

"Books don't lie."

"Sure they do."

"No they don't."

"Sure they do."

"They don't, Gerald," I said.

"Okay, smartass. What did the book say?"

"It said a cow kicked a lantern over and started a barn on fire."

"That's a lie," Gerald said.

"The book said it."

"That's what I mean," Gerald pointed his cigar at me. "That's what I'm tellin' you. The book lied."

I watched the ashes burning on my cigar. "What really happened, then?"

"Okay. The story says a cow kicked over a lantern and the fire got so big the whole city burned down. Right?"

"I guess so."

Gerald sneezed. "Now, if you were milking the cow and she kicked over a lantern, what would burn?"

I thought of the milking stall. There was nothing but the dirt and cow mess. "I don't know," I said.

"Well, there you are. There ain't nothin' to burn, so how's the cow goin' to start a fire that could burn down a whole city?"

"The book said that's what happened."

"It's a lie, I'm tellin' you!" Gerald shouted. Sometimes the cigars made him dizzy and he talked crazy. "No cow ever started that fire."

"What started it, then?"

"Not no cow."

"What, then?"

"Okay. The way I figure it is this. The fire started in the barn, all right, but not from the cow kickin' over the lantern. Another thing. What's the lantern doing sittin' on the ground, anyway?"

"I don't know."

"The whole thing is stupid."

"Tell it, then," I said.

Gerald crawled to the edge of the window and looked toward the house and flicked off the ashes on his cigar. He crawled back and leaned against the hay. My cigar was so short it was beginning to burn my fingers.

"The way it really happened is this," Gerald said. "That lady whose cow it was never milked her that night."

"How do you know?"

"You want to hear this or not?"

"Tell it," I said. Gerald told good stories, but he took too long.

"Okay. Well, this lady, see, whose name was Mildred, never milked that cow. She was supposed to, but she never did."

"Why not?"

"It was cold that day. It gets cold early up there and the wind was blowing real hard down out of Canada. The wind always blows up there."

"We milk when it's cold," I said, watching the ashes on my cigar.

"Yeah, but that ain't the reason she didn't milk that cow. The reason was this man came to her back door and knocked on it. She was coming out with the milk bucket in her hand and the lantern in the other and this man knocked on the door."

"Who was it?"

"It was some drifter named Sam who was passing through Chicago on his way to San Francisco. But he was flat broke and needed money to catch a train down to St. Louis."

"I thought you said he was going to San Francisco."

"He was, but you have to go through St. Louis first. Anyway, Sam was walking down this street and he saw this barn that looked like a good place to sleep, so he went inside. It was warm and dry in there, you know, and he was glad he'd found it until he saw the cow."

"He milked the cow."

"Just a minute. He could tell the cow hadn't been milked, so he thought he would go around to the house and ask if he could milk her for some money or some food. That's why he knocked on the door."

"What did he say?"

"He said, 'Howdy, ma'am. I'm just travelin' through and sure would like to milk that cow of yours if you would let me.'"

My cigar was burning my fingers. I crawled to the edge and threw it down into the dirt. I watched it a second, then crawled back. Gerald was smoking his slowly to make it last.

"Mildred was surprised," Gerald said when I came back. "She said she guessed it would be all right and kinda smiled like this. Then she gave Sam the bucket and the lantern and he went out to milk."

"Then the cow kicked the lantern over," I said.

"I told you that ain't what happened. Why do you keep saying it did?"

"I read the book."

"Only idiots believe everything they read in books."

"Tell it, then," I said.

"Well, Sam went out there and milked that cow and filled the bucket up, but first he hung that lantern on a nail like any smart person would. When he finished, he carried the milk and the lantern back up to the house, and Mildred let him in."

"What did he say?"

"He said, 'I'm mighty grateful to you, ma'am.' Then he stood by this table and watched Mildred strain the milk. She

65

had black hair and big tits and Sam watched her real close. He was thinking he had done the right thing this time. Finally, he was real tired so he sat down at the table. Mildred kinda felt sorry for him and kinda liked him too. She told him just to rest while she fixed him some cake and a sandwich.

"So he sat there awhile with his arm on the table and then he ate and she sat there watching him. When he finished eating, he started telling her his life story and all like that. Finally, he told her that all he really needed was enough money to catch the train to St. Louis. She wanted to help him, but all she had in the world was twenty-six dollars. But ol' Sam knew he couldn't take that, so he told her how much he appreciated the offer, but that she could just keep that twenty-six dollars."

Gerald stopped and looked at his cigar. I knew he was thinking of what came next, so I tried to catch him. "Then what?" I said.

"Then Sam asked her why a pretty girl like her wasn't married. She said she was but that her husband was real mean. He stayed drunk all the time and got into bad fights. Then he would come home and beat her. Sam was surprised. He couldn't believe anybody could beat up on a girl like Mildred.

"Sam asked her where her husband was now and she said she didn't know. Sam was thinking maybe Mildred could come to San Francisco with him and they could do all right out there in the West. So he asked her. For a minute she looked real happy, but then she looked all around and said she could never do it because her husband would follow her and beat her to death. Sam tried to make her say yes, but she was scared. Then she said she would think about it during the night. Sam said that was all right with him.

"It was getting pretty late about then so Sam asked if he could sleep in the barn and Mildred said that would be fine. She wanted him to sleep inside by the fire, but she thought her husband might come in and kill them both."

"Was Sam scared?"

"No, but you know. What else could he do? So he took the lantern and started to leave. She stopped him by the door and thanked him real sweet-like, then kissed him."

"He shouldn't have taken the lantern," I said, thinking of Carol.

"But he did. It had snowed real hard while they were in the kitchen, but it had stopped now."

Gerald went to the edge of the window and knocked the ashes off his cigar down into the lot. His cigar was getting pretty small.

"Then what happened?"

"Well, Sam went out to the barn and climbed up in the loft. He hung the lantern on a nail again and kinda fixed himself a place to sleep in the hay. He laid down, but he couldn't sleep. He just kept thinkin' about Mildred back there in that house and how her husband beat her and all.

"Well, time went by. Then all of a sudden the barn door banged open, powwie! Sam raised up and tried to see, but it was all dark under the loft. He could hear the cow moving around, but that was all. Sam got up. He asked who it was and looked around. Then this voice said, real deep, 'Come down outta dat loft and face yer death like a man!'"

"It was the husband," I said.

"Yeah. And he was drunk and plenty mad. But Sam just called down, 'Come up and get me, doodoo brains!' Then Sam stepped back in the shadows and waited for the guy to climb the ladder. He came up hollerin' and cussin' and when Sam saw him, he thought he never had seen such a big man in all his life."

"Like Uncle Raisin," I said.

"Bigger than that. He was practically a damn giant. Sam knew he was in plenty of trouble now. When the man got up in the loft, Sam rushed him, trying to knock him out, but the man just stuck out his hand like this and stopped Sam dead. Then he just shoved him back and Sam flew into the wall so hard—"

"The lantern fell off?"

"Shut up. He hit the wall so hard a pitchfork fell off a hook. Sam grabbed it up and held it in front of him. The big guy just laughed and walked across the loft toward Sam. Sam tried to stab him, but he just laughed again and knocked the pitchfork out of the way. Then he picked Sam up again and threw him across the loft. Sam hit the floor near the edge and he was kinda unconscious, just lyin' there when this big guy walked over just laughin'. He stood over Sam and Sam woke up and knew he was done for.

"Then bam! Sam heard a shotgun go off and the big guy stepped back with half his left shoulder gone. Then bam! there was another shot and this time half his face was torn away. Sam got up and looked down into the barn, but he couldn't see anything. Then bam! another shot and the big guy started spinning around until he got near the edge and fell off.

"Sam grabbed the lantern and climbed down from the loft. When he got down there, he saw Mildred holding a shotgun and standing over the body of her husband."

"Was he dead?"

"What do you think? Sam held the lantern up and saw that Mildred's face was covered with bruises. 'I'm glad I did it,' she said. 'Me too,' Sam said. Then she started to cry and say how she would never be able to go anywhere because she had murdered her own husband. But Sam told her to go with him. This time she said she would. Sam told her to go get her stuff and he would do the same. He took the lantern and climbed back up into the loft to get his stuff.

"He was almost ready when he heard a noise. He turned around and saw that big guy standing there all shot to hell and bloody and everything. Sam just about froze. Then, quick as a flash, he grabbed that lantern and threw it at the big guy. It blew up and covered him with fire. 'Burn in hell!' Sam hollered, then he went to the edge of the loft and jumped."

"How high was it?"

"High as this."

"Was he hurt?"

"Course not. But that big guy was. He was stumblin' around settin' fire to everything he touched. Sam ran out the door and up to the house. When Mildred and him came back out there was fire everywhere. They just had time to get to the station and catch the last train to St. Louis before the whole city burned down."

Gerald puffed the last of his cigar. "And that's how the great Chicago fire started."

"I never heard of all of that," I said, thinking about it.

"Now you have," Gerald said.

He stood up and went over to the window and threw the cigar butt down into the lot. Something moved in the back of the barn, and I looked around and then back at Gerald.

"Tell it again, Gerald," I said.

"Forget it," he said.

He turned and picked up his cigar box and crawled into the tunnel with it. I sat by the window thinking of the story until he came back. Mama came out the back door carrying a wash basket. She took it into the wash-shed beside the house and went back in.

Gerald came back out of the hay and sat down beside me. For a minute, we didn't say anything. Gerald had his own kind of smell and I could smell him. He was starting to sweat under his arms like Father did. We sat and looked out at everything, at how hot and dry everything was.

Then Gerald looked down and said, "Why don't you jump?"

I thought about Sam. "Why don't you?"

"I already have."

"Show me."

"Okay, queer."

Gerald turned around and let his feet out over the edge.

"You don't have to, Gerald," I said.

"Just watch."

He let himself down until only his arms were still inside the window. Then he looked around to see where he would land and let go. He fell all the way down when he hit the dirt. He rolled over and got up, dusting his pants.

"Nothing to it," he said.

"Did it hurt?"

"Nothing to it," he said again. "Come on."

I started to, then got scared.

"Come on," Gerald said.

"I'm scared."

"There's nothing to it."

I thought of Sam, then hung my legs over the edge. I got scared again and climbed back in. Gerald laughed.

"I can't," I said. I wanted him to say I didn't have to. There was a noise from the shadows at the far end of the loft. I was up there all by myself.

"Chicken," Gerald said. "I'm going to check on the rabbits."

"Wait for me," I said, but he was already walking away.

After supper, I went into Carol's room. She was sitting at her dresser brushing her hair. The big light in the ceiling was on and the little lamp with the pink shade that Carol kept on the dresser was on. The light from it made Carol look funny and pretty at the same time. There wasn't anybody in the world as pretty as Carol was.

"What are you doing?" I asked, walking up and leaning on the dresser. It had three skinny mirrors on it. The one in the middle was the biggest.

"Brushing my hair."

"How come?"

"To make it shine."

I looked at Carol in the mirror and she was watching herself brushing her hair. I looked at me. I didn't look much like Carol. My head looked bumpy and my mouth was too long.

"What are you doing?" Carol asked.

"Nothing."

"Do you always say 'nothing' when somebody asks you what you're doing?"

"I don't know."

"Why don't you?"

"Just don't," I said, watching her. "Let me brush your hair."

"You don't know how."

"Yes I do."

"All right."

She gave me the brush and I walked around behind her and caught her hair at its yellow ends and brushed it very carefully. I could smell her hair and her shoulders. She watched me in the mirror.

"What are you doing?" she asked.

"Brushing your hair."

"Well, brush all of it, not just the ends."

I stopped and looked at her in the mirror. She was waiting. I put the brush at the top of her head and brushed all the way down. Her face wrinkled.

"Not so hard," she said.

She watched me in the mirror and didn't say anything. I could hear Gerald down in the kitchen washing dishes. He always made a lot of noise when he washed dishes because he hated it so much. Carol watched me and folded her hands in her lap.

"Ricky, you didn't let Uncle Raisin bother you at dinner, did you?" Carol asked.

"I didn't really know what he was talking about. He scares me."

"You don't really look funny when he draws you."

"I look different. I don't like it."

"That's just because you're changing every day."

"No I'm not." I made Carol wrinkle up her face.

"Stop that. What are you so touchy about? Do you think everything is going to stay the same forever?"

"Why not?"

"Because it doesn't, that's why."

I looked at Carol's face in the mirror. I thought she was trying to tell me something bad, something that she had been keeping a secret until now. I didn't know what it was.

"Are you going to brush my hair or not?"

"I don't know what you're talking about," I said.

"That's what I'm afraid of."

I put the brush down on her dresser and looked at the lamp with the pink shade. It was quiet in the room and Carol didn't say anything. I could hear crickets outside and a car far away on the highway. Gerald was banging plates around in the sink downstairs. For some reason I thought of the noise I had heard in the barn. It was probably just a rat.

"All right," Carol said in a low, soft voice like the sound the gas heaters make in the winter. "Let's just forget about it."

"About what?" I said. "You mean about you going away?"

Carol grabbed my shoulder and turned me around. Her eyes were blue as blue. I looked at her, then looked down.

"Who said I was going away?"

"That's what you were getting at, isn't it?"

"No," she said.

"Okay," I said, still not looking at her.

After a minute, she picked up the brush and held it out to me. Pieces of her yellow hair were caught in it.

"Brush my hair and don't be silly anymore," she said.

I took the brush without looking at her and walked around behind her and looked at her in the mirror. Her eyes were wide open and blue and her lips were red. She smiled and picked up a file off the dresser and started filing her nails. Something broke downstairs, and Mama started yelling at Gerald.

"Tell me what you did this afternoon," Carol said.

"Nothing."

"Tell me about your rabbit."

I told Carol about my rabbit and the name Rebecca had given it. I watched Carol's face while I told her about it and sometimes I looked at my own face, but when I did I knew that wasn't really me at all. Then I told her about the Chicago fire, but I changed some stuff at the end. Gerald was passing by the door and he heard it. He made a pooty noise and went on to our room.

Later, when we had gone to bed, I raised up on my elbow and looked out the window. At the bottom of the hill there was a single light on. I watched it for a minute. The limbs of the elm tree waved back and forth and hid the light sometimes. Then it went out.

The New People

THE NEXT MORNING, after Gerald had milked and let the cow out of the pen to graze, we crossed the pasture to the washout and ran up through it, keeping low enough that the new people could not see us. When we got to the place where we had hidden the day before, we stopped for a few minutes and watched the house. It looked like all of them were on the front porch, which was narrow and ran across the whole front of the house. The side nearest to us was sagging and some of the boards were missing on the very end. No one was sitting on the end nearest us. One of the men was sitting at the foot of the steps and the other was sitting at the top. The little boy was between them on the steps, playing with something that I couldn't make out. The girl was sitting on the edge of the porch, hanging her legs off the side. The two women were sitting in chairs back up against the wall.

We watched them for a while, but they were just sitting there talking. Two trucks were parked at the far end of the house. The tailgate was down on the blue one and the front door was open on the other one.

"Look at them," Gerald said. "Just sittin' around like they didn't have nothin' else to do."

"Yeah," I said.

One of the men spit out into the yard. The little boy stopped playing and looked up. He looked down again and went on playing.

"Look at them," Gerald said. He watched them for a few more minutes, then slid down the bank and started off up the washout. I slid down too and followed him.

"Keep down," he said, without looking back.

He was running hunched over, so I did the same. The washout twisted around and went uphill toward where our land stopped. The house was about fifty feet from where the washout was blocked by a ragged fence. It was shallow near the fence and we had to crawl. We crawled, then Gerald stopped and waited for me to come up behind him. Past Gerald I could see where the washout twisted on behind the house. The other people who had lived there had used the washout for a trash dump.

"Whatever you do, be quiet," Gerald whispered when I came up beside him.

I was scared that we might get caught. I shook my head and we crawled up to the bank and stretched out flat at the very edge. We could hear them talking from where we were.

"What do you think about it, Carl?" the man at the top of the steps was saying.

"Beats the hell out of me," Carl said. "Too late and too dry to do any plantin' at all. Might get some stock, but you'd have to feed 'em, for sure."

"Hell," the other man said. He was the oldest, I thought, and his face was rough. For some reason I thought of the mean guy in Gerald's story. He would have had a face like that. The man lifted his boot and kicked the little boy in the back. He didn't kick him hard, just enough to make the little kid drop what he was playing with. It was a tin can with rocks in it.

"Now don't start no row," one of the women said. We couldn't see them very well from where we were. Carl reached over and picked the can up from the bottom step and gave it back to the little boy.

"Put them damned rocks back in that can, Bo," the oldest man said. "I don't want to come out here a-trippin' all over 'em."

"Rocks," the little boy said.

"Damned rocks," the man said.

"Now, Wilbur," one of the women said. Her voice was kind of whiny and high.

"Now what," Wilbur said, turning around. His shirt was

open and his hair was long and needed to be combed. The woman didn't say anything. "Don't call my name 'less you got somethin' to say to me," he said.

"Man over there has some nice land," Carl said.

"Huh?" Wilbur said, looking. "Bunch of damn cotton fields."

"He'll have a good crop if it rains."

"Then I hope it don't," Wilbur said. "Show him right. Thinks he's so big with his fancy place. I seen him out shreddin' yesterday when we come in from town. You can tell a lot about a man by the way he sets his tractor."

"Wheeler said his name is MacAllister. Somethin' like that," Carl said. "Been farmin' a long time. Used to be his father's place."

Me and Gerald both got lower in the grass. I didn't like the way they were talking. I wanted Gerald to come away from there.

"Oh forget Wheeler," Wilbur said like he was mad. "Wheeler'd say anything. Then turn around and sell decent folks like us some damn nigger shack."

The little boy got up off the steps and went out into the yard to get some more rocks. He walked along until he saw one he liked. He squatted and picked it up and dropped it in the can. He rattled the can. He was only wearing his underwear and the seat was almost black.

"Man's got to make do," Carl said.

"Like hell."

"This ain't no bad place. Plenty of breeze. Couple of good fields once this drought breaks."

"Listenin' to you, you'd think a man could take a cowturd and make it a cake."

"Rocks," the little boy squealed, shaking his can. Gerald looked at me and made a face like he thought the kid was crazy.

"Shut up, Bo," Wilbur said. Then he said, "A man don't have to make do with nothin' if he don't want to."

The man called Carl didn't say anything. He pulled out his

knife and was shaving part of the bottom step. The girl got up off the porch and went to see what the little boy was looking at. He picked it up by the tail. It looked like a dead lizard. He put it in his can and shook the can.

"Least here there ain't nobody pushin' us around," Wilbur said. "Not like that son of a bitch in Gonzales."

"You were right to move away," Carl said.

"Had to," one of the women said.

"On your back day and night for what ain't none of your fault," Wilbur said.

"I still say you had no call to beat the man near to death," one of the women said.

Wilbur craned his neck around. "You shut your damned mouth, now," he shouted. "He had it comin', plain and simple. He's just lucky I didn't kill him. That was one man that had it comin'."

Carl stopped moving and looked out toward the road. The little boy and the girl turned around and looked at Wilbur. They were very still and quiet. The girl reached up and pulled a piece of hair out of her face. Gerald was watching her.

"The world owes a man a livin'," Wilbur went on. "He don't have to take nothin' he don't want to."

"Guess not," Carl said. He said something else I could not hear.

"You're damned right I can," Wilbur said. "Anytime I want."

Carl looked back toward the house and said, "How much longer you goin' to be?"

A woman answered him, then Carl spit.

"A man don't have to take nothin' he don't want," Wilbur said again. "You take that MacAss over there with all his land. Who's to say I shouldn't have land like that too? But what do I get? Bunch of damned hillside gullies!"

"It ain't that bad," Carl said, looking over his shoulder.

"Don't tell me they ain't that bad. What the hell—you think I ain't got no eyes in my head?"

"Carl just meant—" one of the women said.

"The hell don't tell me what Carl meant. I know good and

goddamned well what he meant and he's wrong. All I got me is hillside gullies and that other son of a bitch got *half* the county. That ain't right. Ain't nothin' right about that."

"Guess not," Carl said.

"Now who's to say I shouldn't have land like that?"

"Not me," Carl said.

"You're damned right," Wilbur said. "Not you nor nobody else neither."

Wilbur spit and everybody was quiet. I was scared. The girl and the boy had moved over toward us and that scared me. What the man had been saying scared me too. I got as low as I could. I could hear the wind in the dry grass and feel my heart beating.

"Hold this a minute, will you?" one of the women said.

"Hold it yourself or put it down on the porch," Wilbur said.

"Ruby Lee," the woman called, then. "Ruby Lee, I'm goin' to need some help in here, girl, if we plan to have that kitchen clean before dinner. You hear?"

"All right, Ma," the girl said.

I was glad, but then the little boy put his hand inside the can and squealed like a pig and pulled his hand out of the can and threw the can up in the air. It hit the ground and rolled in our direction.

"Bo, cut out that noise," Wilbur said.

"Rocks," the little boy said, pointing at the can.

"I'll get it," the girl said. She walked toward us.

I got down so low that my chin was in the dirt. I punched Gerald with short punches to make him leave. The girl started to bend down, but hit the can with her foot. It rolled closer to us, close enough for me to see the freckles on the girl's skinny face as she walked up to it again. Then she bent to pick up the can and looked right at us. I think she made a little surprise sound, but I didn't wait to hear it. I slid backwards as fast as I could and slipped down into the washout and started crawling. I didn't turn around, but I knew Gerald wasn't behind me.

"Ruby Lee!" the woman shouted again. It made me move twice as fast toward the deeper part of the washout. Then Gerald was scrambling along behind me, and we both scrambled until we could run. Then we ran. In the deeper part of the washout sunflowers lined the steep dirt banks and little patches of Johnson grass tried to grow. Me and Gerald ran right over them.

We followed the washout as it twisted down off the hill toward the tank that Grandfather had had dug a long time before we were born. We were running bent over, but in most places the cut was deep enough that, with the sunflowers, we were completely hidden. Closer to the tank, the washout opened up and flattened out. The bed was made of thick black dirt and clay that was soft and cool under the top crust.

"That girl saw us," I said, when we slowed down to a walk.

"I was there," Gerald said, chewing his lip.

We stopped by the tank to throw rocks in the water. If we threw them high enough, they sounded like bullets when they hit the water. The tank was going dry and all around the edges the black mud was cracked and covered with something that looked like gray powder. The cows had tracked the mud all up trying to get to the water to drink.

I was still throwing rocks, but Gerald began to walk away. I threw one last rock, high and spinning, and ran after him. I had the hard feeling in my stomach like someone had hit me there. I stopped running when I caught up with Gerald and we both walked along looking at the ground. The way the mowed weeds smelled made me thirsty.

"I'm scared, Gerald," I said.

"You're always scared."

"We shouldn't have gone up there," I said.

"We were on our own land," Gerald said as we walked along.

The hard feeling in my stomach wouldn't go away. "I bet she tells," I said.

"So what?"

"That man," I said.

We were walking through the part that Father had mowed. The stalks and leaves were already dry and brown. A piece of stubble, hard and sharp, went into my foot. I stopped and looked. There was a spot of blood on my heel. I felt like crying, but Gerald didn't stop. I limped after him.

"That man scares me," I said because Gerald hadn't said anything about him.

"He didn't scare me," Gerald said. "He sounded like a regular tough guy to me."

"But those things he said, Gerald. He was talking about Father."

We walked along and Gerald didn't say anything. He was chewing his lip again. I thought maybe he was still mad at Father. When Gerald got mad, he stayed mad a long time.

"So what?" he said finally.

We didn't see Father until after we had climbed over the gate and were walking up toward the sheds.

"Hey there!" he called.

He had the tractor backed up to a pile of cedar posts by the end of the shed. He was standing on the pile, kicking and lifting the posts off the top with his boot. We walked up beside the tractor and looked at him. The tractor smelled of oil and dirt and it was hot. I raised my heel and scratched it. It had stopped bleeding.

"Where you two been?" Father asked, a little like he was mad.

"Down in the pasture," I said.

"Well climb up here and help me move these posts," he said, taking off his hat and wiping his forehead. His face was dark brown except for a white line near his hair left by his hat. We climbed up on the pile and began rolling the smaller ones off the top.

"I'm looking for a short, stout one," Father said. "It's time we pulled up those posts where the old loading chute is."

Father got down and stood by the tractor. We rolled posts off the top. Gerald found one about a foot thick on its bottom end. I lifted and pushed until the post was clear on my end. He had put down his end and was looking off up the hill. When I had it clear, he bent down again and I bent to lift my end of the post. We both lifted, but I had to drop my end. When it hit, it shook Gerald, knocking itself loose from his hands and causing him to fall backwards off the pile. I laughed while he was getting up.

"You lousy queer!" Gerald said. "What are you trying to do, kill me?"

"It was too heavy," I said.

"You lousy craphead," he said, coming around the pile. He grabbed me before I could get away. First he twisted my arm, then he caught me in the death clinch. He was starting to hurt me.

"Come on," I said, whining a little.

"All right," Father said. "That's enough of that. We've got work to do this morning."

Gerald started twisting me back and forth with his arm around my neck.

"Cut it out," Father said. He stepped over and grabbed Gerald's arm and jerked it loose. I jumped away and turned around. Father was still holding on to Gerald's arm and he was bending down into Gerald's face. My neck hurt.

"Just got to keep on 'til somebody makes you stop, don't you?"

"Turn loose," Gerald said, still mad.

"I'll turn loose when I'm ready. I wouldn't have to grab a holt in the first place if you knew when to stop."

Gerald wouldn't look at Father. Father kept holding on to him the way Gerald kept holding on to me. Finally, Father let go and said, "We've got work to do. Get up there and get that post off the pile."

"I will when I'm ready," Gerald said.

Father pushed Gerald toward the pile and he stumbled against a post. "Well, get ready," Father said.

I looked at Gerald and felt sorry for him. Father was just as stubborn as Gerald was and I knew neither one of them would give in.

"I'll do it," I said, walking over to the pile.

Gerald looked at me. "If you had done it in the first place—"

"Damn," Father said. He went back over to the tractor and took a hammer off the foot rest. He opened the tractor's toolbox with the end of the hammer and pushed it in. It didn't go all the way in, but he slammed the lid down on the handle anyway. Then he pushed the hat back on his head and looked at us. "Get goin'," he said.

Gerald and I got on the same end of the post and lifted together. We carried the end to the edge of the pile, then dropped it and let the post roll off by itself. Gerald's shoulder touched mine. I looked at him, but he was mad. He looked the way he looked the time he had held my little Easter duck in his strong hands and had squeezed slowly down until something in the duck broke. Then he had given it back to me, dead.

Father came around and rolled the log with his boot. He kicked it a few times to see if it was rotten. "We'll have to cut the long end off," he said. "Ricky, go up to the shop and bring the crosscut saw back."

"Okay," I said.

I jumped up and ran along beside the tractor, then up the gravel road past the fig tree and around the corner to the shop. The inside of the shop looked dark after the bright sun on the gravel. I crossed over the doorstep and went to the cage where our rabbits were. They were crouched down in a corner. I tapped the wire and looked at them. Something made me think of Rebecca. She had a quarter that she carried that she never spent. It had 1945 on it, which is the year we were born, but that isn't why she never spent it. I found quarters all the time with that date on them. She never spent it because one of her grandfathers had given it to her. He had stamped an R on it for her. He was dead now.

I got up from the cage and dusted my pants off and went to the workbench. There were two saws there hanging on nails. I got the one that me and Gerald always used when we had something to make. I carried it around to Father and he took it and said, "This is the rip saw."

"What's the difference?" I asked, looking at my heel again.

Gerald was standing by the edge of the shed in a little

patch of shade. He was chewing his lip and looking away from Father. For a minute I thought of the man on top of the hill, but then I felt better being around Father.

"You saw the end of that post off and I'll tell you the difference."

"Let Gerald cut it off," I said. "I went and got it."

Father didn't look at Gerald. "I want you to do it."

"I have to do everything," I said.

Father looked at me with one of his you're-wasting-time looks. That's when his forehead wrinkles up and his eyebrows go up and the muscles in his jaw stick out.

I took the saw and knelt down by the post. Father walked over and kicked it with his boot where he wanted me to cut it. I moved down to the spot and started sawing. The old wood around the outside split and squealed against the side of the saw.

"This saw needs to be sharpened," I said.

I looked up at Father. He was staring at Gerald, then he looked at me and spit. "No it doesn't," he said.

I sawed. I got hot and stopped for a minute. The shade where Gerald stood looked cool. I went on sawing.

"Now you know the difference?" Father said.

I sawed and got hotter. "We can break it now," I said, after a while.

"I don't want it split on the end. It has to be strong. Gerald, go get the chain. It's on the wagon yonder."

Gerald was looking away and chewing on his lip. He pretended not to hear what Father said.

"*Boy*," Father said.

There was another minute, then Gerald pushed away from the shed and went to get the chain.

By the time Gerald came back with the short chain over his shoulder, I had cut through the post. I could smell the cedar and see the dark rings in the wood. Father took the chain from Gerald and wrapped one end around the crossbar on the back of the tractor. He let the chain trail over to me and wrapped the other end around the post. His strong brown fingers put a loose knot in the end of the chain.

"Bring the saw," he said to me.

He walked around and climbed up on the tractor. He grabbed the fender with one hand and the steering wheel with the other hand and pulled himself up. I got up on the crossbar and held on to the fender while Father cranked the tractor. After a minute, Gerald got up too, but he didn't look at me. The tractor started up with a puff of black smoke and Father put it in gear. It jumped, and I held on tighter.

On the way past the shop, Father stopped and I got off and ran inside to put the saw back on its nail. Father started up again before I got back. I ran after the post and tried to sit down on it, but it kept rolling over and throwing me off.

The loading chute and the rows of posts with no wire on them were to the side of the barn and easy to get to. I could remember Father and the Mexicans running calves through there for some reason, but I had been too little to know why. Now the fence was gone and the posts were standing in rows like army men waiting to go somewhere. Father drove along side the chute and then past it to where the first bare post stood. He turned the tractor facing away from it.

"Untie the post," he said.

Gerald jumped down and began working on the chain. The knot was tighter now and the links on the bottom had dirt in them. I walked over and helped him. The chain was heavy and rusty and hard to unwrap. I lifted one end of the post and Gerald managed to get some slack. He slipped the chain loose.

"You get the post," he said. I looked at him. His eyes were sharp. To Father he said, "All right."

I rolled the short piece of post on the ground up to the base of the standing post. Gerald followed, holding the chain off the ground while Father backed the tractor. I stood the post up in front of the other one, between it and the tractor. Gerald went around me and the tractor came back until it was almost touching me. It was loud and smelled like burning oil.

"Tie it tight," I told Gerald.

"Who you tellin'," he said without looking up. He wrapped the end of the chain around the base of the rooted post several times, then swung the hook around to the front and hooked it in one of the links. I stood the sawed-off post close in against the other one and in line with it and the tractor. Gerald ran the chain up over the top of it, in the middle, and Father eased out on the clutch until the tractor pulled the chain tight. We stood back and watched. When Father started forward again, the force of the pull off the top of the sawed-off post lifted the other post straight out of its hole. They both fell over. We untied the chain and moved over to the next post and did the same thing. Some of the posts broke off because they were so rotten. Father said that Grandfather had put the posts in himself years before, with nobody to help him. Most of the posts lifted right out though, and we laid them in a line like fallen soldiers.

An hour or two later, when we had pulled up all the posts and were riding back to get the wagon, Father was smoking a new cigar. The wind blew the smoke back on us and the smell mixed with the hot smell of the tractor. I couldn't tell if Gerald was still mad or not, but I thought he was. At the sheds, Father turned outward and backed up to the tongue of the trailer. The tongue was lying in some dry grass and the sun had made it hot as fire.

Gerald got off without saying anything. I helped him untie the chain. We threw it on the ground beside the trailer, then lifted the tongue of the trailer. Father backed into it. Gerald dropped the bolt through the hole. We stepped back and sat on the trailer. Gerald punched me when we started moving.

"Cut it out," I said.

"Make me."

The ground around the chute looked strange and empty without the posts. Even without the wire, the posts had made a kind of fence. Now there was nothing but a bunch of holes in the ground that me and Gerald would have to cover up. The lot beyond looked bigger and emptier, as if we had cut down a bunch of trees that had blocked our view of the barn and now we could see the barn clearly. I had a sad and scary feeling and something made me think of what Carol had said about growing up.

Father pulled the trailer to the middle of one row and stopped. Gerald got off right away and began throwing posts on the trailer. I got off and threw seven on before I came to a post that looked too heavy to lift. I asked Gerald three times to help me, but all he said was "Shut up." Then Father came over and said, "What's the problem?"

"Nothin'," I said.

"Well, it ain't quittin' time yet," he said.

Finally, I lifted the post by myself and threw it on the trailer, but it wasn't easy.

That night, me and Gerald sat up in our room and played cards. We had a small table set up under the window with a chair on either side of it. We could sit at the table playing cards and look out the window and see the yard and the elm tree and the driveway and the barn and, beyond the barn, the dark fields and the lights of the houses at the bottom of the hill. The lights in Rebecca's house seemed the brightest. The window faced the southeast, and while we sat there, feeling the slight breeze, I could see the moon coming up. It was a big, red moon and I watched it coming up and listened to the crickets and the cows and sometimes, very far away, the howl of a coyote.

"Your turn," I said, straightening my cards.

After a minute, Gerald drew and held his card apart while he looked for one to put back. Then I drew the ace of clubs. I knew Gerald was collecting aces because I had seen the torn corner of the ace of diamonds between his fingers, and he had never put it down. I threw back a four of spades, knowing Gerald was watching me.

"Queer," he said.

"How do you know what I drew?"

"I know," he said. "You'll never build your books trying to keep my cards."

He was right. I lost that hand and the next. Gerald shuffled the cards. I leaned my chair back against my bed. Mama had washed sheets that morning and hung them on the line to dry. I could smell them behind me on the bed. I looked out the window at the moon. It grew brighter while the sky got darker; then it was high and bright and the sky was pale. We played crazy-eight for a while, and I had to draw and draw.

"I thought you shuffled these," I said.

"I shuffled them. Keep drawing."

We played. Carol came upstairs and went into her room. I could hear her record player. She was playing a song I liked. I had to remind Gerald it was his turn. He was holding his cards in front of him, but he wasn't looking at them. I had to remind him again.

"Come on," I said.

"Keep your shirt on," he said, looking over the tops of his cards to see what suit we were playing. "Keep your pants on," he said without playing. "Keep your underwear on. Keep your arms on. Keep your face on."

"Come on," I said.

Gerald threw down his cards.

"Aw, come on," I said.

"Shut up," he said. "I'm tired of playing. It's just a kid's game anyhow."

"No, it isn't."

"It is too, and I'm tired of playing kid's games just to keep your stupid face happy."

"My face isn't stupid."

"Oh yeah? Get a mirror."

"Yours is," I said. "Yours would break a mirror."

Gerald shoved the table toward me with his hip and it caught me in the stomach.

"Hey!" I said. "Cut it out."

"You asked for it, queer."

"You started it!"

"Shut up."

"You shut up yourself."

Carol came out of her room and stood in the hall with her hands on her hips. She was wearing her rolled-up blue jeans and a white pullover.

"Would you two mind holding it down? I can't even hear my records."

"Nobody asked you," Gerald said, without turning around.

"Well, I didn't ask you, either, buster. I'm telling you."

"Go to hell," Gerald said. He turned and looked at Carol. She had started into our room, but she stopped when she saw Gerald's face. He was looking at her and his face wasn't really mad, but Carol could tell something about it because she turned around without saying anything and went back to her own room and closed the door.

"That wasn't very nice," I said.

"Oh shut up. Don't you start tellin' me what to do. I'm sick of people tellin' me what to do."

"Who does?"

"Everybody does. I'm sick of it. I'll tell you one thing, though. Soon as I get old enough, I'm leavin' this place and I ain't never lookin' back. There ain't goin' to be nobody tellin' me what to do all the time."

Gerald leaned forward and looked out the window, his forehead against the rusty screen. I straightened my chair and pushed the loose cards into a pile. Some of Father's cows were moving around the barn, restless. A calf bawled. It was probably just thirsty, but it sounded scared and lost.

"I wish it would rain," Gerald said. "It's too hot and dry. I feel sometimes like I'm tearin' up inside with the heat."

I looked at Gerald and saw the sweat circles under his arms. I looked over his head and saw the moon, small and white. Sometimes I was afraid of the moon. Sometimes it looked like a face.

"That stupid girl," Gerald said suddenly.

"What girl?" I asked, leaning forward beside him and looking out the window.

"There's no one out there, queer," he said, bumping me with his shoulder. My head hit the window frame and hurt.

"Ow," I said. "Stop it."

"Can't you quit cryin' for five seconds?"

"I wasn't crying," I said. "How was I supposed to know there wasn't anybody out there?"

"You're not supposed to know nothin'," Gerald said, still leaning out the window, his head against the screen. With our light on, that was the only way to see into the yard. I rubbed my head. I knew Gerald was thinking about the girl on the hill, and I didn't like it.

"Did you see how skinny she was?" Gerald said, kind of low, like he was talking to somebody outside. "Those apes probably never feed her."

"She was ugly," I said. I pushed the cards around on the table until I found the ace of clubs. I looked at it, trying to figure out how Gerald had marked it. Gerald was quiet. His chin was resting on his hands and his forehead was still pressed to the screen.

"I wonder what grade she's in," he said.

"Maybe she's in your grade," I said.

"Maybe," Gerald said after a while, as if he had been thinking about it. "They looked pretty poor, didn't they?"

"They were cedar choppers," I said. "That girl probably stinks."

"She was sure skinny."

"Like a post," I said.

"She had long hair," Gerald said.

"Like a long-haired, skinny monkey."

Gerald was looking out the window. The moon was high.

"Like a skinny gorilla," I said. "With her eyes bugging out and stringy hair and black lips and hairy legs—"

"Shut up," Gerald said.

"And smells like a big pile of doodoo."

Gerald looked back in the room at me. "Shut up," he said again. I looked back at him. He wasn't smiling.

"All right already," I said.

He turned and looked out the window again. I looked past him and saw a white cloud near the moon. A car went by out on the road. I put the ace of clubs back in the pile.

"You think she's goin' to tell, don't you?" I said.

"Don't worry about it," he said. Then he said, "I don't know. I wish I was goin' somewhere right now."

"We never should have gone up there," I said.

"We didn't do anything to get in trouble for."

"Then why are you so grouchy?" I said. "Is it because of Father?"

"I don't care about Father. He can die tonight for all I care."

"Don't say that."

"Why shouldn't I? It's true."

"You're just mad," I said. "I've seen you mad before."

Gerald dropped his eyes so that he was looking down into the yard. He was chewing on his lip. "I never felt like this before," he said.

"What is it?" I asked.

"I don't know. That girl."

"What about her?"

"I don't know."

"What did you do after I left?"

"Nothin'."

"Did she say something to you?"

"No."

"What about her, then?"

Gerald shook his shoulders and rubbed his forehead on the screen like it was itching and he was scratching it. Carol came out of her room and went down the stairs. Her feet made a fast skip on the wooden steps.

"It's what she did that bugs me," Gerald said.

"What did she do?"

"She smiled at me."

When I passed Carol's room, I saw that she was already up and out of bed. The sheet was twisted in the middle of the bed and the sun was coming in her windows. The pink curtains were blowing in with the morning breeze. Her closet door was open, but she wasn't in the room.

I went downstairs and into the kitchen. Mama was just getting up from the table and coming into the kitchen with a coffee cup in her hand. Carol was talking on the telephone. I listened to what she said as I went by. It sounded like the kind of stuff she said to her girlfriends. She touched my shoulder as I went by her.

"About time you got up," Mama said.

I went over and stood by the cabinet. I could see Father sitting at the table, but Gerald was not in there. I looked out the window.

"Why?" I said.

Mama poured coffee into Father's cup and put the coffee pot back on the stove.

"Because it is running out of today," she said.

"No it isn't," I said. "It's still early."

"You're kidding!" Carol said behind us. I turned and looked at her. "When? Today? I'll see." She put her hand over the bottom of the telephone and looked at Mama. "Chris says they might need someone else at the grocery store as a checker. Can I take the car in and apply, Mama?"

Before Mama could answer, Father said, "You can take the tractor in, if you want to."

"I guess so," Mama said, turning back into the dining room.

I looked at Carol. She was talking to her friend again. She was sitting on the stool under the little shelf where the telephone was. Her back was to the water heater. The kitchen light caught her hair and made it shiny as she tucked pieces of it behind her ear. She was talking fast and she was smiling. I scratched my nose and went into the dining room.

"Where have you been?" Father said, as I sat down.

"Upstairs."

There was a cold egg and a piece of bacon and two biscuits on my plate. I picked up my fork and started to cut the egg. The yellow part was hard. Father was tasting his coffee and looking at me.

"Is it still dark upstairs?" he asked.

"No sir."

Father was wearing his blue shirt and his jeans like he was going somewhere. He leaned forward with his elbows on the table.

"What do you think?" Mama said, softly, ignoring me.

"Sounds like a good idea to me," Father said. "She can take care of herself."

Mama looked down at her plate. I started eating. My egg was cold.

"Do her good to have a job," Father said, sipping his coffee.

"She'll be lucky to find one," Mama said, after a minute.

"Oh, I don't know," Father said. "People seem to like Carol. She'll get along just fine."

"I hope we do," Mama said.

I looked at her and took a bite of my biscuit.

"Cotton looks better than it did last year," Father said.

"It won't do us much good if we have to keep feeding the animals," Mama said. "That crop will be spent before it's ever picked."

"Same as last year."

"But we had some savings last year."

"It'll rain," Father said, putting his cup down. "Got to."

"Have you called Elmer back?" Mama asked.

"No. But I will," Father said. He looked at Mama.

"I know you don't want to," she said.

"Got to, I guess," Father said. "It's either those sheep or the cows. Can't feed 'em all."

"Is Mr. Ketchum mad at you, Father?" I asked.

"Why would he be?"

"I don't know. Mama said you had to call him."

"Eat your breakfast," Mama said.

Carol hung up the telephone and came into the dining room. She stood behind Father's chair and put her hands on his shoulders. "Can I go in as soon as I get ready?" she asked, looking at Mama.

"You know how to add and subtract?" Father said.

"Maybe," Carol said, pinching his shoulders.

"Well, it takes more than good looks to keep a job. If a boss just wanted pretty, he could hang a picture on the wall."

"A picture of Carol?" I said.

"Let me make out a list before you go," Mama said.

"Can I go see Chris, before I come back home?"

Carol was still rubbing Father's shoulders. He was looking at Mama. Whatever had been bothering him a minute ago was gone now.

"Now let's get something straight right now," Mama said. "Getting a job does not mean running around all over the place just because you can."

"I know that, Mama. That's what you think, isn't it? You think all I want to do is run around."

"Now, now," Father said. "It's too early in the morning to start that business. Your mama just wants you to understand that she expects you to come home after work unless you make clear plans otherwise." Then Father's voice changed again. "That is, providin' you get the job in the first place."

Carol pinched Father's shoulders again, and Mama set her face. Father was looking at her. Past him, through the window, I could see Gerald coming up to the house with the milk bucket in his hands. The cats jumped off the cistern and surrounded him. He started yelling at the cats and running for the back door. Carol and Father turned and looked out the window. Mama stood up and picked up her plate.

Seeing Gerald with the milk reminded me of mine. I took a drink from the glass. It was warm and thick tasting. Father stood up and put his arm around Carol. She slipped her arm around his belt for a minute, then went into the kitchen. I heard the screen door slam on the back porch, and Gerald started hollering again.

"What now?" Father said.

I got up and followed Father to the door between the dining room and the kitchen. Gerald came around the corner of the back porch by the sink. He was holding the bucket up and kicking at one of the gray cats that had run in the door behind him. He was yelling at the cat and kicking at it too, but that cat was only watching the milk bucket. Milk was starting to slop over the edges onto the kitchen floor.

"Watch that milk," Mama said, raising her voice over the noise Gerald was making.

Carol started calling the cat, then she told Gerald to quit kicking at it. Gerald was still yelling and kicking, then his foot hit some of the milk that had spilled on the floor. The linoleum was slick and Gerald went down with the milk bucket. Milk sloshed everywhere and the cat started licking it up. Gerald saw that cat and tried to hit it with the milk bucket. More milk went all over the kitchen floor.

By then everybody was yelling except me. Carol finally caught the cat and stepped over Gerald to throw it out the back door. Gerald was so mad he was about to cry.

"Get up off the floor," Father said.

"Damn damn damn," Gerald said.

"Get up," Mama said. "I won't listen to that kind of language in my house. Get up!"

"I'm trying to," Gerald said. "Can't you see I'm trying to?"

I turned and went through the dining room to the living room, then out the front door. I went around to the side. Carol was standing by the car looking at the house. Gerald and Mama and Father were all yelling inside. Carol turned and looked at me and started laughing.

I was sitting in the shop holding my little rabbit when Gerald came out the back door calling me. The little rabbit was very still and light in my hands and I held her up next to me. I could feel her sides moving quickly with her breathing. After a few minutes, I answered Gerald, and in a minute he stood in the doorway of the shop.

"I might have known you'd be hiding out somewhere," he said.

"I wasn't hiding out."

Gerald came over to the cage and hit the wire with his hand. His rabbit was knocked halfway across the cage. He didn't try to run or anything. He just rolled back upright and sat there shaking.

"They don't look like they're eatin' much," Gerald said.

"Maybe they aren't hungry."

"Maybe not," Gerald said. He straightened up. "Come on. We got work to do."

"Not again."

"Tell Father that."

I walked over to the cage on my knees and put Becky carefully back inside. She just sat there where I put her.

"Come on," Gerald said.

I looked at the little rabbit again, then stood up. "What do we have to do?"

"What do you think? We have to fill in all those post holes."

"The dirt is too hard," I said, following Gerald out of the shop.

"Father doesn't want us to fill them in with dirt. He wants us to fill them in with rocks."

"Rocks?"

"That's what he said. He said to pick them up out of the lot."

We turned in the lean-to at the end of the shop where we kept the hoes and rakes and shovels and bushel baskets. Gerald got two old buckets off nails in the wall and gave me one. We went down to the loading chute. One good thing about it, there were plenty of rocks. I put my bucket down and knelt down beside it and started putting rocks in it. They made a clang at first. I thought of the little boy at the top of the hill.

"Hey Gerald," I said.

He was picking up rocks about twenty feet from me. "What?"

"We ought to get that kid on top of the hill and let him do this. He would like it."

"Shut up."

"He would fill the holes up with dead lizards," I said.

I loaded rocks for a while, and Gerald did the same. He was still mad from that morning. He didn't take a bath. He just changed his clothes. He smelled a little bit like old milk.

"Maybe those people will move away again," I said.

"Why would they? They just got here."

"I don't know. I wish they would."

"They haven't done anything."

"I didn't like the way they talked."

"You don't like anything," Gerald said. He stood up and

carried his load of rocks over to the nearest hole and poured them in. He kicked some dirt in after them and came back.

"Anybody can talk," he said.

"Why are you so much on their side?" I asked.

"Because they aren't on Father's side," he said.

I carried my bucket over to a hole and poured the rocks in. They made a dull drumming sound in the hole. It was hot.

"I'm going back to the house to get my hat," I said.

"Get mine too," Gerald said.

I dropped my bucket and went up to the house. Carol was coming out the back door. She was all dressed up and had makeup on.

"Wish me luck," she said.

She walked by me to the car and I could smell her. I turned and watched her get in. She was wearing stockings. I didn't want her to get the job. I wanted her to stay home all the time and be the way she always was. I didn't want her to be pretty for anyone else ever. She started the car.

"Want me to bring you something?" she asked.

I looked at her. The sun was reflecting off the car and getting in my eyes.

"No," I said. I turned around and went in the house.

After dinner, me and Gerald went outside and sat on the back porch. One of the cats came over and smelled of Gerald. He kicked it away. Grasshoppers crackled close by in the dry grass. Up under the eaves, the sparrows were chirping. I was tired from hauling the rocks. We had worked until dinner, but the rocks kept getting farther away from the holes and we didn't finish.

"We been out of school two weeks and already I'm sick of summer," Gerald said.

"I like summer. It's my favorite time of the year," I said.

"Oh shut up."

"We do more in the summer than we do any other time," I said.

"More work," Gerald said.

"At least it ain't school."

Gerald stood up and started walking away from me. I watched him a minute, then I stood up and followed him. As soon as I stepped out of the shade, I could feel the hot sun on my shoulders and back. Me and Gerald were both wearing our hats. Father was doing something at one of the sheds behind the shop, so we crossed through the garden to get to the pasture.

"Are we going swimmin'?" I asked.

"I'm not," Gerald said.

I looked past Gerald's shoulder at the pasture. Mario's truck was parked at the bottom end of the cotton field beside another one. They were almost finished chopping the cotton. There hadn't been that many weeds in the first place.

"Are we going to spy on the new people again?"

"Maybe."

"I don't want to, Gerald."

"Then don't."

"Let's don't, Gerald. They might be waiting for us."

"Shut up."

We came to the fence and crossed through it. The wire was hot to the touch. I didn't want to go, but I didn't want Gerald to go by himself.

"You know? I bet that one guy has a prison record," I said.

"What kind of prison record?"

"A bad one."

"You don't know what you're talking about, I swear."

Looking up, I could just barely see the top of the old house on the hill. The closer we got to it, the less I liked it. Then we were in the washout and there wasn't any breeze and it was hot.

"Let's rest," I said.

"I'm not tired."

Gerald kept going, so I followed him up to the spot where we had been watching the first day. We climbed up the bank and looked at the house. There was no one outside at all. Both of the trucks were gone. After a while, we heard the scratchy sound of a radio.

"They're all gone," I said, ready to leave.

"Sure. That's why they left the radio on."

"Look at all the trash piled around already," I said.

A piece of paper blew across the yard. I was hot. When I closed my eyes, I could see red spots. Gerald slid back down the bank. I slid down beside him. It was still hot.

"Guess nothin' much is goin' on," Gerald said. He sounded disappointed.

"I'm glad," I said.

"Oh shut up."

"I wish they would all move away again."

"Quit sayin' that. They aren't hurtin' you."

"I don't like the way they look."

"They just look like everybody else."

"They look poor."

"What are we? Rich?"

"We don't look like that. Besides, Mama wouldn't like the way that man talks."

"Mama wouldn't like nothin'."

We were sitting on the edge of the washout, at the bottom. It turned sharply going uphill, and neither of us saw the girl until she came around the bend and stood there in the sun. We both turned and jumped. I was ready to go.

"Gerald," I said.

"Shut up."

I looked at the girl. She had a plain, brown dress on with a man's belt around her skinny waist. The long end of the belt had been raggedly cut off. Her legs and feet were bare. Her face was freckled and thin and her hair was tied back in a ponytail. She just stood there looking back at us. I was ready to go.

"I heard you talkin'," she said, finally.

When she moved her hands, I saw a long, jagged cut on the back of one of them. There was a long, jagged scab there against her white skin, as if it had been drawn on there by a crazy person. She was looking at Gerald.

"So what," he said.

"I heard you talkin'," she said again. Her voice was tinny and sharp.

"People can talk if they want to," Gerald said.

"I know that," the girl said. She began pulling at the belt

around her waist as if it were too tight. Something bothered me about her face, but I didn't know what it was.

"I seen you the other day," she said.

Gerald looked away, then looked at her again. "So what?"

"I seen you layin' up yonder by the fence. You was listenin'. Him too," she said, tilting her head up at me.

I was ready to go.

"Yeah? I bet you told your old man," Gerald said.

"I never told nobody nothin'," the girl said.

"I don't care who you told," Gerald said. He put his hands in his pockets.

The girl was still pulling on the belt. "I said, I never told nobody nothin'."

"I don't care what you did," Gerald said.

"Listen, boy, I said—"

"Don't call me boy."

The girl looked around and shook a few pieces of hair out of her face. She was still tugging at the belt. "I want to know why you was listenin'," she said.

"None of your business."

"I reckon it is."

"It ain't."

The girl looked at Gerald and squinted. I wondered if Gerald thought she was pretty. There was something wrong with her mouth, but I couldn't tell what it was.

"I suspect I could tell, you know," the girl said. "My pa wouldn't like it much."

"Your pa ain't nothing but trash," I said.

The girl looked quickly at me and her eyes were enough to give anybody nightmares.

"Shut up," Gerald said.

"He ain't neither," the girl said. "You take it back."

I looked at her. She didn't look quite right to me. I was starting to get scared of her.

"He didn't mean nothin'," Gerald said. "He doesn't know what he's talking about."

The girl looked at Gerald and pouted a little. "Then why did he say it?"

"He's just stupid," Gerald said.

"No I'm not. You're the one that's stupid. Let's get out of here."

"Shut up," Gerald said.

"Now that little boy said you was stupid," the girl said. "I wouldn't let nobody talk to me that-a-way."

"Come on, Gerald," I said.

"Now he's tellin' you what to do," the girl said.

I looked at her and I knew what it was about her face that bothered me. She had a scar over her lip. It made her mouth look dirty. Gerald turned and looked at me. He had the look on his face that he got when he was showing off, but he didn't do anything.

"Let's go, Gerald," I said.

"He done it again," the girl said.

"You shut up," I said.

"Don't start tellin' me what to do," the girl said, walking up to us.

Gerald turned and looked at her. He looked back at me. His face was still the same. I didn't like the way he was looking.

"Come on, Gerald," I said.

"Go on, yourself, boy, and don't be tellin' us what to do. Maybe we don't want to do it."

I looked at the girl and looked back at Gerald. She was standing close to Gerald now. She had some bumps on her face. Gerald was looking the same, then his eyes narrowed.

"Go on back," he said.

"Come with me," I said.

"No."

"Don't act so stupid, Gerald. That girl doesn't mean anything."

"I don't like that," the girl said.

Gerald stepped toward me and pushed me. I had been waiting for that. "Shut up," he said.

"Don't push me."

Gerald pushed me again. Then he pushed me again until I fell down. The girl laughed.

"I'm going to tell," I said.

"We don't care who you tell," the girl said.

Gerald laughed, and I stood up. I was so mad I didn't know what to do. I didn't want them to see me crying, so I turned and ran back through the washout. When I heard them laughing behind me, I started crying, but by the time I had reached the tank I had stopped. Then I was mad. Then I just felt cold and sick.

When I passed the shop, I saw that Father had pulled his truck up to the door and he was bent over the motor. The hood was bright and shiny in the sun even with the layer of dust that it had. I stopped for a minute and watched him pulling out the plugs and cleaning them. He saw me and gave me one to hold while he pulled another one.

"What have you been up to?" he asked, bent over the motor.

"Nothing," I said.

"See how dirty that plug is?" he asked.

"Yes sir."

"A plug gets fouled up with filth like that and all the spark goes out of it. It's just as sharp and hot as it can be when it's clean, but when it's fouled, the spark is mighty weak. You know that?"

"Yes sir."

After a while I put the plug down and went up to the house. Carol had not come back from town and Mama was lying across her bed reading a magazine. I went up the stairs to my room. It was hot in the room, but I didn't feel it. I sat in the chair by the window looking out at the empty sky.

The Sheep

I HEARD GERALD roll over in his bed and raise up on his elbow. I was lying very still. Gerald turned the radio down until it was just a quiet buzz in the room.

"You asleep?"

I didn't answer him. I shut my eyes.

"Ricky."

"What," I said.

"Nothin'. I just wondered if you were asleep."

"Leave me alone."

"Why?"

"You know why."

It was quiet in the room. I could hear the buzz of the radio.

"You shouldn't have just kept on," Gerald said.

I didn't say anything. Even though it was hot, I pulled the sheet up around my chin.

"You just kept on until I had to push you," Gerald said. "You always do that. You never let anything go, even when you know I'm not going to like it."

I closed my eyes and pushed my head down on the pillow. It was hot and still in the room and the moon was shining in the window. It was late.

"You always take somebody else's side," I said.

"I don't like people tellin' me what to do."

"I'm not people."

"That's for sure."

"Why don't you just leave me alone. I'm sleepy."

I heard Gerald move around on his bed. Then I heard him flapping his sheet up and down to cool himself off. Then it was quiet for a while and I opened my eyes. I could tell Gerald was lying on his back, but I couldn't see his face.

"That was Ruby Lee," he said.

"I saw her."

"She's not too bad."

"I thought she was ugly."

"So are you."

I didn't say anything. A dog was barking somewhere. I moved my hand a little bit and it was in a patch of moonlight on the edge of my bed.

"We talked for a long time," Gerald said. "They moved from Gonzales. She said her father had gotten into some trouble over there, but it wasn't his fault."

"Did you believe her?"

"Why not?"

"You saw her father."

"So what? Don't be stupid. She was all right." Gerald was quiet for a minute, then he said, "She's sixteen."

"I didn't like her," I said.

"You don't know anything about her."

"Neither do you."

"I talked to her for a long time."

"I'm sleepy."

"She said she never met anybody like me before. She said she could have told her father, but she didn't want to."

In my mind I could see her father. He was big and mean and I didn't like him.

"I might go up there again tomorrow," Gerald said after a while.

"Well, I'm not going," I said.

"Who asked you?"

We filled in holes while it was cool, but when it was hot, we quit. I had been wanting to see Rebecca, so I asked Mama if I could go to the store. Gerald wanted to go too, but I told him he couldn't come with me to Rebecca's house.

"So who wants to?" he said.

We walked down the driveway and got on the road. The Mexicans had finished chopping the cotton above the house and now they were in the patch across the road. Mario looked up as we walked along, and he waved for us to come out and help them. Gerald shook his head and Mario shot him the finger. Gerald shot it back and he laughed.

I walked on the other side of the road from Gerald when we started down the hill. I could see Mr. Ketchum's fields beyond the dry loop in the creek. His cotton was about the same as Father's, but from the hill, it looked smaller and a little bit browner. At the bottom of the hill, Gerald threw a rock at the fender of the old car in the yard of the empty house. It made a loud bang and left a dent in the green paint.

We crossed the barrow ditch and went up to the store. Mr. Norman was on the other side of the door with a broom. He was pushing a little pile of dust and dirt toward the door.

"Look out there, dadblame it," he told Gerald.

Gerald jumped over the pile, but I backed up and held the screen door open for Mr. Norman. He bunched the dirt up at the very edge of the door, then gave it a hard sweep and swept it out onto the porch. Some of it went on my feet.

"That's a way, boy," he said. He reached a skinny arm and caught the door above my head and I went on in. Mr. Norman spit, then let the door slam shut behind him.

The inside of the store was dark and cool. The only lights were bulbs hanging down from the high ceiling. There were six of them down the middle of the store with chains hanging down that Mr. Norman pulled to turn them off or on. In the middle of the store was a long, wide table where the men sat and played dominoes sometimes on Saturday afternoons. The wood of the table was dark and scratched around the edges and there were round circles where the men had put their sweating soda water bottles. On either side of the table were glass cases with medicines and pocket watches and sewing stuff and canned goods and bread and candy. There were barrels with nails in them and cotton sacks and hammers and fence pliers and leather harnesses and pieces of black stove pipes, all down at the far end of the store where the meat freezer and the soda water cooler were. Mr. Norman had just about everything in that store that anybody could want, but nobody wanted much of it.

I followed Gerald down to the soda waters and reached in behind him for an orange Nehi. It was cold and more orange than any orange I ever saw. We pulled the caps off and went back over to the counter. Mr. Norman sat on a high stool behind the counter and put his coffee can on a shelf under the cash register.

"Are them cash sales or charge sales, boys?"

"Cash," Gerald said.

"Big spenders, eh?"

"Can I open the register?"

"Eh?"

"Can I open the register?"

I went around the counter and pushed the five cents button. Mr. Norman reached for his coffee can as the drawer came out. He spit and said, "That's a bad habit, but I reckon it don't hurt any."

Gerald came around and dropped his nickel in and looked in the drawer. "Got any silver dollars?" he asked.

"Eh?"

We looked in the drawer. He had a lot of change, but not very many bills. In one slot were some charge tickets. I saw Rebecca's name on one of them.

"That's enough lookin'," Mr. Norman said. He reached over and slid the drawer shut. "Too much lookin' at that stuff don't do any man any good."

"Do you let Rebecca charge stuff here?" I asked.

"Girl that pretty can write her own ticket," Mr. Norman spit. "I don't care if she is only ten."

"You never let us charge," Gerald said.

"Man ought to pay cash. Makes him more of a man. Boys too. In a girl's nature to charge."

Me and Gerald walked over to the candy case. Mr. Norman picked up his coffee can and followed us. He had boxes of Double-bubble, Chum-gum, jaw breakers, licorice whips,

Snickers, Three Musketeers, and M & Ms. I pulled a penny out of my pocket and told him I wanted some Chum-gum.

"Eh?"

Gerald got two chocolate Tootsie-Roll Pops. I opened the cash register again and put the pennies in. Mr. Norman spit.

"Have you seen them new folks moved in past y'all?" he asked.

"Not really," I said. I looked at Gerald.

"Eh?"

"We've seen 'em," Gerald said.

"Just heard about them day 'fore yesterday," Mr. Norman said, spitting. "Don't know nothin' much. Harry Wheeler stopped by for a sody and told me about them. Said they were down on their luck a little, but had cash for that place."

Gerald looked at me. He had an I-told-you-so look on his face.

"They looked like cedar choppers to me," I said, cutting Gerald a look.

"Eh?"

"They looked like cedar choppers to me."

"Shut up," Gerald said.

"What would cedar choppers be doing out here? There ain't no dadblamed cedar out here. And just as well. I can't abide that stuff in the winter."

"Ricky's just stupid," Gerald said.

I took a long drink of my orange Nehi and looked at the tobacco posters on the high walls of the store. Nearly all of them had cowboys on them lighting up on the trail. One of them had a girl in a white shirt and pants who reminded me of Carol.

"These are hard times for the growin' folks, like your father," Mr. Norman said, spitting. "I just hope it goes to rainin' pretty soon or it will be hard times for the sellin' folks, like me."

"It's always dry in the summer," Gerald said.

Mr. Norman leaned back against the candy counter and crossed his arms. "It's been dry in more than just the summer," he said. "Dry spell like this happens only once in a long stretch, and this is as bad as I've ever seen. 'Twenty-five was dry, but not like this."

I tilted the bottle up and finished my orange Nehi. I burped, and my nose burned and my eyes started to water.

"I'm through," I said, looking at Gerald.

"Eh?"

I looked at Mr. Norman and shook my head. Gerald shrugged his shoulders.

"So?"

"So, I'll see you later."

"Maybe."

I walked by Gerald and Mr. Norman and took my bottle to the back where the wooden cases were stacked along the wall. The wooden floor creaked under my feet in a couple of places. If I looked at the floor just right, I could see the shiny heads of nails polished by being walked on all these years.

Mr. Norman shuffled back over to his stool. He was tall and skinny and he had white whiskers along his jaws from not shaving. The cracks in his chin were stained with tobacco juice.

"So long," I said as I passed him.

"You come back, boy. Bring lots of money with you next time."

"All right," I said. I didn't look at Gerald when I passed him. I don't think he looked at me either. He was taking a big drink of his orange soda water.

There was a chicken in Rebecca's front yard when I walked up. He was pecking around under the pecan tree where some of the leaves had already fallen. I didn't know whose chicken it was, but it was probably Mr. Norman's. I picked up a rock out of the driveway and threw it at the chicken just as Mrs. Brown came out on the porch with a rug in her hands. The chicken squawked and flew up and Mrs. Brown nearly jumped off the porch. She threw up the rug and gave a little yell.

"Hi, Mrs. Brown," I said.

"Ricky, you just about scared the life out of me."

She came forward on the porch, and I started to feel bad

because she really did look scared. Rebecca said one time that her mother was always getting scared. I asked her what she was scared of, but Rebecca didn't know.

"That old chicken was pecking around in your yard," I said. "I think it's one of Mr. Norman's."

We both looked at the chicken that was running across the road in a zigzag with its wings tucked up beside it like it was carrying something.

"I'm sorry it scared you," I said.

Mrs. Brown leaned against the porch railing. Her hair was the same color as Rebecca's, and sometimes a look on her face reminded me of Rebecca, but their eyes were different.

"Never mind," she said, straightening up.

"Is Rebecca busy?"

"She's supposed to be cleaning out her closet, but you can come on in and see."

I went up the steps and opened the screen door. It squeaked like ours did. Mrs. Brown started shaking the rug. The inside of Rebecca's house always had a strange smell that I only noticed when I first walked in. I think it was because Mr. Brown smoked cigarettes instead of cigars like Father did. There was something else too. It made me think of Carol's room. It was a smell like Carol's room has sometimes when Carol is getting ready to go somewhere.

Rebecca was sitting on the floor in her room by the closet door. She was wearing shorts and her legs were crossed in Indian style. She had a pile of stuff all around her, mostly shoe boxes and papers and stuff. There was stuff on her bed too, and her desk had a pile of books and magazines on it.

"What's going on?" I said.

"Ricky," she said and looked happy. "Can you stay?"

"A little while. I have to go home for dinner."

"Why?"

I walked into her room and sat on the edge of the bed closest to her. "I don't know. Mama said." I looked all around the room. "What's going on?"

Rebecca shifted a pile of school papers without answering me, then she said, "Nothing."

"Why is stuff stacked everywhere?"

"We're cleaning up, that's all."

"Oh," I said. "What are you going to do with all of this stuff?"

Rebecca sighed and scratched her cheek. It was hot in her room, but she had lots of windows.

"Get rid of it, I guess."

"All of it?"

"A lot of it."

I heard the screen door slam and Mrs. Brown came to Rebecca's door. She stood there a minute folding the rug, then she said, "What a mess."

"I'm working on it, Mother."

"How can one person collect so much junk?"

I looked at Rebecca. She said, "It's not all junk."

"It looks like junk to me."

Rebecca looked at me, then looked down. I could tell she was getting mad at her mother. I didn't say anything.

"Are you ready for that big box?" Mrs. Brown asked.

"I guess so." Rebecca started to get up.

"I'll get it," I said.

Rebecca sat back down again and looked at me. "Thanks," she said.

I followed Mrs. Brown down the hall and through the kitchen to the back porch. There was a big box back there that had Westinghouse written on the side of it in big, blue letters. There were other boxes back there too. Some of them were full of stuff and were taped shut.

"You sure have a lot of boxes," I said.

"We have to do something with all of these things."

"Yeah," I said.

I dragged the box back through the house to Rebecca's room. She was standing by her bed, looking at a blue dress. I remembered the dress. It was a pretty one.

"Here's the box."

"Bring it over here. We'll start with the bed. Do you mind helping?"

"I don't have anything else to do," I said.

Rebecca leaned over the bed and moved the six dolls she wanted to keep into a pile of other things like the blue dress that she was going to keep. I was close enough to smell her and I thought again about the way Carol's room smelled sometimes. I looked at the side of Rebecca's face. I felt the way I had the night I walked her home. She suddenly seemed so special to me that I wanted somebody else to come into the room so that I wouldn't be the only one who thought so. Rebecca was different from anybody I ever knew. She never acted like anyone else, or talked like them. I never knew what she would do or say next, yet, in a way, I did know.

She lifted a pile of brightly colored paper-doll cut-out dresses and dropped them in the box.

"That's the first load," she said, but she didn't say it like it meant anything to her. She said it as if she wanted to make her mother happy. I looked around the room.

"Why throw that stuff away if you don't want to, Rebecca?"

"The same reason you have to go home to eat dinner," she said, going through some old *Weekly Readers* and letting them slip through her fingers into the box.

"Hide it," I said.

"That wouldn't do any good."

"Want me to hide it?"

"Where?"

"Me and Gerald hide stuff in the barn all the time."

"What about rats?"

"Rats?"

"Sure. If you put stuff like this in the barn, the rats would get it."

"Hide it under your bed."

Rebecca dropped the last of the *Weekly Readers*. There was a little bit of dust in her dark hair. I wanted to pick it out, but I thought it would be dumb, then I picked it out anyway and dropped it in the box. She looked at me. Her eyes were brown and sharp and sad.

"Why don't you just hide me?" she said.

"Okay."

I looked at Rebecca. Her face was starting to look different to me. Sometimes she seemed like a magical person from a story book who could change her face, but her eyes always stayed the same. Mrs. Brown sucked in her breath in the kitchen, then said something that sounded like "bird." Probably a sparrow had landed on the screen over the sink. They did that sometimes. Rebecca looked down again.

"In a way, it's hard to decide what to throw away, but then I look at this stuff and I just want to throw all of it away and never think about any of it again."

I looked around her room. There was a little brown stuffed dog in her rocking chair. She must have thrown it there because it was slipping off. It looked like the dog was watching something on the floor.

"Do you want any of it?" Rebecca asked.

"Like what?"

"I don't know."

"Okay," I said. "Let's start a new pile. But all I want is magazines and school stuff. I don't want any paper-doll stuff."

That seemed to make Rebecca happy. We made a new pile together and went through all of her school papers and magazines. It didn't take very long, but it was fun. She found a map of Egypt with some of my writing on it and showed it to me. I had drawn a picture of an ugly, crazy-looking old woman with flies buzzing around her face and had written Mrs. Clingingsmith's name under it.

"Want to keep that?" Rebecca asked.

"Sure," I said. "I'll put it on my wall at Halloween. You can come see it."

"I hope so."

"You can," I said.

Rebecca said, "I hope so," again, only different, and then I knew why she was going through all of her stuff and why there were boxes on the back porch and why she stopped by the house to tell me something and never did. I put down the picture of Mrs. Clingingsmith and didn't look at it. I felt like I was deep under water and it was dark. I looked at Rebecca. She was looking down and her fingers were playing with the edge of the blue dress.

I got up off the bed and stood by the end of it. I looked all around the room. I looked at all of Rebecca's furniture and at the pictures she had on the wall, the silhouette of two people with the mirror behind it, the waterfall picture, and the picture of a stupid-looking clown that I never liked. Then I looked at Rebecca.

"You're going to move away," I said.

"We aren't sure yet."

"Then what about all this?"

"Daddy said to get ready anyway. He wants to move, but we aren't sure if he'll get the new job. I was going to tell you."

"Where do you think it will be?"

"Daddy wants to go to Waco."

"Waco!"

"There is a position at the college there. Daddy could start teaching this summer if he gets the job."

I felt good again. "Nobody teaches in the summer," I said.

"At the college they do, Ricky."

"But he hasn't got the job for sure?"

"Not yet."

"When will you know?"

"I don't know."

For a while neither one of us said anything. I was trying to think, but I couldn't. I kept hearing Mrs. Brown move around in the kitchen. She was fixing dinner. She started to hum a song. There was always the chance that Rebecca's father wouldn't get the job. I wouldn't hire him if it was up to me. I told Rebecca.

"Maybe not," she said. She looked up at me.

"Well," I said. "Anyway. What's next?"

We both looked at the box. It wasn't very full, but it seemed to be too full. It seemed to be too big and too full.

I was late for dinner, but I didn't care. Everybody was sitting at the table when I walked in carrying an armful of stuff from Rebecca's. Father was chewing a piece of bread and looking at me.

"You gettin' in the habit of bein' late for meals?" he asked.

"No sir."

"Looks like it to me."

"When I say be home for dinner, I mean be home for dinner," Mama said.

"Yes ma'am," I said.

I put the stuff in the green chair in the living room and went up to the table.

"Go wash your hands," Mama said.

For some reason I looked at Gerald. He stuck a piece of fried squash with his fork and ate it. He looked back at me like I was on television and he was waiting for me to be over. I went into the bathroom and washed my hands and dried them and went back to the table.

"I'm afraid there isn't a whole lot left," Mama said, giving Gerald a look.

Father was watching me. Then he said, "Did you see Mario and the others out in the field when you came by?"

"No sir."

I reached for the squash. There were three pieces left.

"Were their trucks in the field?"

"No sir."

"How about down at the store?"

"No sir."

"You sure?"

"Yes sir."

"I guess they finished that patch across the road," Father said, looking at Mama.

"Didn't you expect them to?" she asked.

"I suppose so."

"Then?"

Father picked his fork up and put it down again. There was only about a spoonful of gumbo left in the bowl.

"Then that's it," Father said.

"What do you mean?" Mama asked.

"I mean no more work. That was all I had for them to do."

"Well, I don't see that you're under any obligation to keep them in work."

"I'm not," Father said. "I wasn't thinking about that. If

there isn't any work here, they can go on. They always have."

"Well, let them," Mama said, still not getting Father's point.

"I will, Jean," Father said. "But I'll also have to pay them."

"But before—"

"It's not like before," Father said. "I can't guarantee them work the rest of the summer any more than I can guarantee a crop at the end of the summer. I'll have to pay them now."

Everybody was quiet at the table. I was thinking about Rebecca. After we were through putting things in the box, I pushed it over to the door. When I turned around, Rebecca was right behind me almost touching me. She stepped back quickly and went to get the pile of stuff I was going to keep for her.

"With what?" Mama said, finally.

Father picked up his fork again. He traced a pattern in the tablecloth. Then he looked up. "The sheep," he said.

"Did you call Elmer?" Mama asked quickly as if it wasn't too late.

"You know I did," Father said.

Mama looked down and pressed her lips together like she did when she put on lipstick. "I was counting on that money for some other things, Mac," she said.

"So was I," Father said.

I looked at Carol. She was looking down, but I knew she wanted to say something. She looked up and said, "If I get that job, it will help out, won't it?"

Father gave Mama a look, then said, "Don't you worry about it. I don't intend to start borrowin' money from my own girl."

Before Father even finished saying that, I heard a truck coming down the driveway. It stopped out under the elm. The horn honked a couple of times and Worthless started barking.

"There they are," Father said, pushing back his chair.

"Can't even come to the door like anyone else," Mama said. "Just sit in the truck and honk. I certainly wouldn't hurry out there."

"I've got it to do. Might as well do it."

Father got up and went through the kitchen to the back

porch and got his hat off the nail by the door. I heard the back door open and shut again. Worthless was still barking. Dust from the driveway drifted by outside the windows. I watched until Father passed. He was walking leaning forward like he always did when he had something to take care of.

Mama looked at me. "Are you through?"

"I guess so."

"Next time don't be late. Whose turn is it to clean off the table?"

"Gerald's."

"No it ain't," Gerald said.

"Oh hush," Carol said. "I'd rather do it myself than listen to you whine about it."

"I wasn't whining," Gerald said in his low voice with his teeth together.

"You always whine," Carol said, pushing away from the table. "It's your middle name."

"Blow it out your nose!" Gerald said.

"Stop it! Stop it! Just stop it," Mama said, standing. "I don't want to hear another word from anybody."

Gerald and Carol looked at each other. Gerald was giving Carol the hate face. I pushed away from the table and went outside on the porch. Father was standing beside the elm tree with one hand propped high on the rough bark and the other on his hip. Mario was standing in front of Father with his hands in his pockets. The other Mexicans were sitting in the back of the truck except for Rosie, Mario's wife. She sat in the front seat and was looking at me. Worthless walked up and smelled the back tire all around, then lifted his leg and peed on it.

I didn't want Father to get mad at me for hanging around, so I eased off the porch and came up behind him where I could hear. Worthless came over to me, but I pushed him away. He went over to Father and Father pushed him away with his boot. Then Worthless went over to Mario. Mario spit on his head. He turned away and went off to find some shade.

"How about that other patch?" Father was saying.

"Oh, no so bad," Mario said. His teeth were yellow and

several were missing, but I liked Mario because he let me and Gerald cuss around him.

"Still plenty low, though," Father said.

"Sí, Mac. Very short. Take a lot of back to pick that cotton if she don't grow."

"Well, old men like us don't have to worry about it, then," Father said.

"Oh shit no," Mario said. "Is for young ones, like Ricky."

Mario laughed and Father turned around and looked at me. I smiled at Mario. He rocked back and forth on his feet like he was waiting.

"What about these boys?" Father asked, nodding at the back of the truck. A few of the Mexicans looked at him.

"Them too," Mario said. "First we try the Valley. You know they irrigate the shit out of stuff down there. Then maybe up north. We been up north before, but I don't like it much."

"A long ways off," Father said.

"Yeah, but it's okay. I mean, some people, they like it, but it ain't like home."

"No, guess not," Father said.

They stood there for a while, and Rosie said something in Spanish from the front seat of the truck. Mario turned and looked at her, then looked quickly at Father.

"Hell, woman," he said. "You know Mac speaks better Spanish than me. Cut that shit out."

Father stood straight, away from the tree. The men in the truck got quiet.

"Sometimes women don't understand the way a man does business," Mario said.

"She's right, Mario," Father said. "If you're goin' to do any good, you'd better get on down there or up there, wherever it is. Mr. Ketchum is comin' over this afternoon with his truck to load the sheep. He's takin' some of his own over to San Antonio, and he's takin' my sheep with 'em."

"Not those damned sheep, eh Mac?" Mario turned and looked toward the barn.

"It's them or the cows," Father said. "Mr. Ketchum will bring me a check back here tomorrow when the sheep are sold, and I can have the money for you by tomorrow evenin' or Monday."

"That sounds—" Mario said. "That sounds okay, Mac."

"Y'all plannin' to leave tomorrow?"

"I don't think so. We got to get our stuff together."

I was looking at the ground and digging in the dirt with my toes. A slight breeze blew hot wind through the top of the elm tree. Everything was quiet. I could hear the engine of the truck ticking with the heat, and when any of the men in the back shifted, the springs squeaked.

"Listen, Mac," Mario said, finally. "You need some help with those sheep?"

"I don't guess so, Mario. I've got the boys and Elmer will be there. You know how he is. No more sheep than I've got—. No. We'll get it."

"Those are good sheep, Mac. Would have brought top dollar in 'forty-seven."

"Not now," Father said.

"No. If we knew this, we could have sold them then, eh?"

"A man never can tell," Father said. "Just have to do what needs to be done."

"Sí. Well, Mac. I guess we be goin' on now."

"All right, Mario. I'll take care of the bills at Mr. Norman's, but remember, no more tickets from this moment on or it comes out of the cash."

"No problem."

Mario turned to me and raised his hand. "You tell Gerald he a mighty tough hombre, but very bad," he said and laughed.

"All right," I said.

Mario turned to the truck and opened the door. Father was looking past the top of the truck to some other place. Just when I thought Mario was going to get in his truck, he stepped away from it and held out his hand to Father. Father caught it and they shook hands for a long time.

"It's this weather, Mac."

"Yeah."

"I want to stay, but there is no work."

"Not now."

"But maybe it will rain."

"Will one of these days."

"It's a mighty crazy thing, Mac, when you got all this good land and I got nothin' and I in better shape than you."

"You take care of yourself," Father said. "If it goes to rainin', come on back."

"I will, Mac. If you need me—oh hell, I don't know where I'll be."

"I'll see you tomorrow," Father said, stepping back from the truck.

"Okay, Mac. Adíos."

Mario started the truck and shoved it in gear.

"Adíos," Father said.

Mario waved as he started away. They pulled up toward the shop and turned around. Father stood in the yard watching them. The engine clattered as Mario put it in second. They went by and Father still stood watching as the truck went down the driveway toward the road. All of the Mexicans in the back of the truck were looking at Father, then, just as the truck got to the road, one of them raised his hand and waved. Father just looked at them.

When they were gone, he turned and looked at me.

"Shouldn't you be doin' somethin'?" he said.

"I don't know," I said, but Father didn't listen. He just walked away and went into the house. The screen door slammed behind him.

We went down to the shop to play with our rabbits. It was after nap time and everybody was doing something but us. The heat made my skin feel tight just before it made me start to sweat. In the shop it seemed dark and cool. When I first walked in, I couldn't see anything.

"I'm blind," I told Gerald.

"No you're not. You're just stupid."

We went over to the cage and knelt down beside it. The rabbits were over in a corner, sleeping on their sides. Gerald hit the wire a couple of times, but they didn't wake up.

"They're sleeping," I said.

"So? They can wake up. It ain't nighttime."

He undid the catch and raised the lid and reached inside and grabbed his rabbit. He started to bring it out, then he dropped it. He closed the lid. The rabbit didn't wake up. Gerald looked at me.

"What's wrong?" I asked.

"They're dead."

"Not mine," I said. I reached for the lid. Gerald stopped me.

"Yours too."

"They can't be."

"They are."

I sat back on my heels and looked at the little rabbits in the cage. Gerald looked too, and we didn't say anything. Then I said, "Carol will be sad when she finds out."

"Who cares about Carol?"

"Rebecca, then."

Gerald didn't say anything. I started to feel really bad. I didn't know if it was just the rabbits or them plus everything else. I felt bad.

Finally, Gerald said, "Come on, Ricky. Quit thinking about it. All we can do is bury them."

I was looking into the cage. The two little shapes began to blur.

"I know how you feel," Gerald said.

"No you don't," I said. "Leave me alone."

"Do you always have to act like a queer?" Gerald said.

"And quit calling me a queer!" I shouted. Then I picked up a chip of wood and threw it at him as hard as I could. It hit his leg and bounced off and hit the cage.

Gerald's eyebrows went up and as quick as thinking about it he socked me in the chest. It took some of my wind away and I started to cry. Gerald started saying some stuff, then he got up and went outside. He came back in and said some more stuff, but I didn't listen to him. I didn't want my little rabbit to be dead. Then Gerald left again and I sat up and started thinking about every sad thing that I could remember since I was born.

After a while, Gerald came back and sat in the doorway of the shop. "I got a box," he said.

I looked at him. The box he had was red.

"That's Rebecca's shoebox!" I said. "It had her stuff in it."

"Don't worry. I put it on your bed."

Gerald got up and came over to the cage. "Here. Hold it."

I took the box from him and he opened the cage and lifted the rabbits out. He put them in the shoebox one by one. I could hear his knuckles scraping in the box when he carefully put them in. I reached in and touched the fur along the back of my baby rabbit. Its back was hard and stiff.

"Move your hand," Gerald said.

"Don't tell me what to do."

I moved my hand and Gerald put the lid on the box and picked it up. For a minute we stood on either side of the box and looked at each other. Gerald's eyes were blue and hard and he was chewing on his lip. I wanted him to tell me something about the rabbits. He knew why they died, but I didn't. He kept chewing his lip, then he put the box under his arm like a football.

"Let's go bury them," he said.

I followed him out of the shop. We went around to where the holding pens used to be. Now there was only the holes left by the posts. Gerald stopped at one of the holes.

"Are we going to bury them in there?" I asked.

"Why not? We have to fill them up anyway."

He knelt down and shoved the box in the hole. He had to smash the box a little to get it in. I helped him scoop dirt and rocks to put in on top of the box. The chunks made little drumming noises on the cardboard. When we had it covered over, Gerald stood on top of the mound and it flattened out a little.

"That's that," he said.

"No it isn't. We have to say a prayer."

"Not for rabbits," he said.

"I'm going to."

"All right. Go ahead."

"Dearly departed, we are gathered here—"

"That's not how you say it."

"Yes it is. I heard it somewhere."

"That's what Father says when he makes fun of weddings."

"Our Father who art in Heaven—"

"That's the Lord's Prayer."

"I know it is," I said, getting mad.

"Well, you don't say the Lord's Prayer at funerals."

"Why not?"

"Just because."

"Well. What, then?"

"Like this. Dust to dust. Ashes to ashes."

"What's that?"

"That's what you say at funerals."

"I don't like it. Our Father who art in Heaven—"

"I'm tellin' you that's all wrong."

"No it's not."

"You want these little rabbits to go to Heaven, or not?"

"Yes."

"Then you have to say it right."

I looked at Gerald. He was watching me. Behind him, a blackbird landed on the fence and looked around. Gerald started saying some stuff that didn't make any sense. I looked at the little pile of dirt and said the first part of the Lord's Prayer. Then I stopped and started thinking about Rebecca.

Father was coming out of the house when we walked into the yard. He was putting on his hat and he was taking big steps like he did when he had something to do and was on his way to do it.

"Where you two headed?" he asked, not stopping.

"In the house," I said, feeling sad still.

"It's not supper time. Come with me."

Father walked on by and Gerald said, "Now what?"

Father was walking down toward the barn. Me and Gerald crossed the driveway behind him. I was suddenly scared that he had found our cigar boxes. Then I remembered what he had told Mario about the sheep.

Father opened the gate into the barnyard and pushed it all the way back against the fence. He crossed the barnyard and opened the other gate that led to the last pen he had left. We had put the sick cow in that pen last winter. It had died anyway. Father had had to drag it down into the field with the tractor, then pile old boards on it and set them on fire. The smoke had been black and greasy. Father opened the gate to the pen and waited for us.

"What are you going to do?" I asked when we stepped through the gate.

"We're going to round up all the sheep. You and Gerald go get them. They're at the lower end of the field. Drive them up here into this pen."

"All of 'em?" Gerald asked.

Father looked at him, then turned and closed the gate. We crossed and opened the other gate that led to the field. I stepped on a piece of barbed wire and it stuck the bottom of my foot.

"Never mind what it feels like now," Gerald said. "Just wait until lockjaw sets in."

I started to turn back to Father, but he just waved his hand at me to go on, he didn't have time to mess with me. The sheep were already moving up in the field toward us. The field was bare of anything but rocks. The sheep thought we were going to feed them.

"I hate sheep," Gerald said.

"How come?"

"Shut up. Go around over there and just stand until they get up here. Don't scare 'em."

"I'm not."

"Then don't. Go on."

I walked away from Gerald, limping a little bit. Most of the sheep had seen us by now and were moving up toward the pen. Gerald moved over and started walking along the fence. The sheep moved away from him and looked at me. They knew that if we were both out in the field, something was going on. They stopped and looked from Gerald to me. Gerald was still walking along the fence. He was saying something about the sheep, but I couldn't hear what it was. I could just see his lips moving and see him shaking his head. I didn't like the sheep either except when they were little. Sometimes we got to feed the little ones with a bottle.

"Bring 'em on up!" Father called.

Gerald had gotten around behind them now and started moving them by waving his arms and saying, "Get those woolly butts moving." The sheep kind of jumped forward and looked back and jumped forward again and looked back. Some of them were running in little circles around the others. There were about a hundred of them coming my way and suddenly I didn't like it. Then it was all right. I picked up some rocks and waited.

The sheep were coming up now and dust was rising all around them. Sometimes I couldn't even see Gerald. Father came out into the field with me to help turn the sheep into the pen. When the sheep saw Father they thought they were going to be fed and broke out running into the pen. When the last one had turned in, Father stepped forward and shut the gate behind them. Gerald walked up waving his hand in front of his face to clear the dust. It was hot, and there was almost no breeze.

Father leaned on the gate and looked at the sheep. Most of them were standing near the water trough. The rest were waiting to get fed.

"What are you going to do with them now?" I asked, walking up beside Father.

"Sell 'em," Gerald said. He spit and Father looked at him, then back at the sheep.

"All of them?" I asked.

Father looked at the sheep. The dust was drifting away from us. There were some dying sunflowers on the other side of the pen, and in the heat I could smell the sticky-sharp smell of them.

"There's the truck," Father said.

He opened the gate and we all stepped into the pen. Father closed the gate and walked across through the sheep. They were making a lot of dust and they looked nasty. They smelled bad too.

When we got to the other gate, I saw the truck pulling up by the house. Then Mr. Ketchum saw the open gate by the barn and turned in. The ground was rough and the truck swayed from side to side. Father moved some sheep away from the fence with his knee and opened the other gate. He didn't wait for us, so we just climbed up on it and sat down. Before Father got to the truck, Gerald turned and spit on some sheep and said, "No more watering and feeding these nasty old things."

"Yeah."

"What do you mean, yeah? You never did anything."

"I did too."

"Forget it. It's too hot to hear your lies."

"I did."

"Shut up."

I looked at Father. He walked up to the cab of the truck and stepped up on the running board. He held on to the mirror that stuck out at the side and pointed with his other hand. Mr. Ketchum nodded and swung the truck around almost under the loft of the barn. Then he backed it around so that the tailgates were aimed right at me and Gerald. Father jumped down and stood to the side waving his hand until the truck was right up against the gate. I could see Mr. Ketchum's sheep through the red boards of the trailer. They were crowded behind a gate that shut the front half of the trailer off from the back. Some of them were moving around like they were scared, but most of them were just standing in there looking out.

Father and Mr. Ketchum both came around to the back of the truck. Mr. Ketchum was wearing a khaki shirt and khaki pants with a big, brown leather belt. He left the top shirt buttons undone and I could see the thick, black hair of his chest. His face was big and sunburned and he had a Band-Aid over his left eye and something red like Merthiolate on his bottom lip. Father crossed behind the trailer. His shirt buttons scraped on the tailgate.

"Two blackbirds on a fence," Mr. Ketchum said, looking up at us. He reached for a latch on the tailgate and slid a long bar all the way up and out. Father did the same on his side.

"Ready?" Mr. Ketchum called.

Father nodded. Mr. Ketchum gave a yank and the gate broke loose from the trailer. They let it slide down, then Father pulled it toward him and out of the way. While I was watching Father, Mr. Ketchum reached up and jerked me off the top board of the pen as if I had been a towel on the clothesline. He swung me around twice so fast I saw red and blue lights, then he put me down on my feet, but I was so dizzy I sat down.

"Look out there, boy. You're in my way. Get up off that ground. What's the matter, you tired?"

Before I could say anything, Mr. Ketchum turned and looked at Gerald. Gerald swung his legs over the other side of the gate and jumped into the sheep pen. He stood in there looking through the boards.

"How do you want it?" Father asked, coming back behind the trailer.

"Open the gate and shove 'em in!"

Father looked at the gate with Gerald standing behind it. I got up and moved away from Mr. Ketchum along the fence.

"Got a chute?" Mr. Ketchum asked. "I know you do, but this ain't the pen, is it?"

"Chute's over there," Father said. "But the pens are gone."

Mr. Ketchum spit and said, "Don't matter. Ramp's there in the bed. If we can open the gate and move them sheep back, we can slide the ramp down and run 'em up. How many you got?"

Father looked over the sheep, then looked down again like he was thinking. "About sixty, last time I checked. Don't take that for a final count."

"Never do," Mr. Ketchum said. "No way to run a business."

Father gave Mr. Ketchum a look, then turned his eyes on me. "You and Gerald open the gate back and keep the sheep from getting out until we get those boards down. Gerald! Get the sheep away from the gate and pull it back." Father looked at me. "Go on. This doesn't have to be hard."

I went along the edge of the trailer until I came to the gate. Gerald was untying the wire that held the gate closed. The sheep kept moving around and stirring up dust. Gerald jerked the wire away from the gate and I pushed it toward him. The bottom edge of it caught the top of his foot.

"Not yet, Ricky, dadgummit," he shouted.

I pulled the gate back and Gerald hopped a little bit.

"Sorry," I said.

"Get the sheep back, Gerald, so we can get the gate open."

"You will be," Gerald said to me, then he turned and started pushing the sheep back. If they didn't move, he yelled at them or hit them with a rock. Father was watching over the top board of the fence.

"Don't get 'em all stirred up, Gerald. Just keep 'em back!"

"I'm tryin' to," Gerald hollered.

I pushed the gate open and behind me I heard Mr. Ketchum pulling the boards out of the trailer bed. Father helped him. When the gate was pushed back, I turned and saw that they had the ramp down already and one was standing on either side.

"Get over here, Gerald, and help me keep them on the ramp," Father called. "Ricky, you stay in the pen and drive them up. But do it slowly, you hear? You get them to jumpin' and I'll get you to jumpin', understand?"

"Yes sir."

"Gerald, get over here."

Gerald walked up the ramp, then jumped off beside Father. Since he was shorter, he stood at the lower end of the ramp.

"Don't scare 'em when they come through," Father told him. Then he said, "Bring 'em on."

I turned and looked at the sheep. They were all watching me or looking over each other's backs at nothing. There was a small group of them next to one of the empty troughs, so I got behind them and turned them toward the ramp. They went but bunched up at the bottom of the ramp. They could smell the other sheep, but they weren't sure what to do. Then one of them ran up the ramp and four followed it. One of them turned and ran at me, then jumped to one side.

"That's it," Mr. Ketchum called. "Get the rest up here just like that. Best damn little sheepherder I ever saw."

I cut out another group and ran them up the ramp too. Two of them tried to cut off the ramp where Gerald was standing, but he and Father waved their arms and the sheep turned. Mr. Ketchum whistled like a freight train and the sheep ran on up. The pen was getting dusty. I could taste it in my mouth and it scratched my eyes. I could barely see where I was stepping. Once I stepped into some sheep pellets that mushed up between my toes. Another time a sheep peed on my leg as I was cutting a bunch out.

The sheep were following each other up the ramp. I never would have thought they would go that easy, but more than half of them were loaded before there was any trouble. I cut a bunch of scary sheep and ran them at the gate three times. Each time they cut away and I had to chase them back. Then they went up the ramp and one of them jumped over Gerald and knocked him down. Another followed and they both ran off toward the barn. One tried to do the same thing on Mr. Ketchum's side, but he doubled up his fist and hit that sheep square in the face with a noise like a rock on wood. The sheep made a funny sound and backed up and almost sat down on his haunches. Then Mr. Ketchum reached over and swatted it. It jumped up the ramp into the trailer.

"Bring them on!" Mr. Ketchum yelled, rubbing his fist.

We got the rest of them in with only the last one breaking away over Gerald again. The last one was a hard one to get up the ramp because it had so much room to run around in. When it finally jumped over Gerald and ran off, I went to the water trough and sat down, trying to get my breath. I was so hot I could feel the blood beating in my head. I spit out dust and waited.

Mr. Ketchum went up the ramp into the trailer and tried to pry the sheep apart that were bunched toward the front. Then he came back and pulled up the boards and slid them along the floor. He tripped one of the sheep and laughed. Gerald and Father came around the trailer driving the three sheep that had gotten away. They were headed into the pen, but Mr. Ketchum grabbed the first one fast as he had grabbed me and he threw it into the trailer. The other two backed up, but Gerald drove them forward again. Mr. Ketchum grabbed both of them at once and tossed them in. Then we were through.

"Get those rods, son," Mr. Ketchum told Gerald.

Gerald was hot and mad. He looked at Mr. Ketchum.

"I only say somethin' once," Mr. Ketchum said.

He and Father got the gate and lifted it up into position and Gerald brought the rods over. Mr. Ketchum took his and slid it into place. Father fixed the other one. The hooves of the sheep were scratching around on the floor of the trailer. Several of them were bawling.

"I sure appreciate you comin' over and helpin' us with these," Father said, slapping his hands on his pants.

"I get my mileage out of 'em, don't forget," Mr. Ketchum said.

"I hadn't," Father said.

"Boy-howdy," Mr. Ketchum said then. "I could use somethin' to drink."

I stood up and walked over to the rest of them. I left the gate pushed back where it was. There was no need to close it now.

"I can send the boys to the house for some ice water," Father said.

"Don't stand by me," Gerald said. "You smell like sheep."

"You should have been in there," I said.

"No need," Mr. Ketchum said. "I've got the very thing up in the cab."

Me and Gerald stepped back and Father and Mr. Ketchum walked around the end of the trailer and up toward the front. Near the cab there was a little shade, so me and Gerald went up there and crouched down by the big front wheels.

"Can't you move downwind a little bit?" Gerald said.

I moved. Father took off his hat and wiped the sweat from his forehead with the sleeve of his shirt. The sheep were moving around in the trailer and bawling. Mr. Ketchum backed out of the cab with a little ice chest in his hand. He set it on the running board and threw back the lid. It had some iced Pearl beers in it. He reached in and took one out and offered it to Father. Me and Gerald looked at Father because we knew he didn't believe in drinking. For a minute, Mr. Ketchum held the beer, then Father took it and looked at it. Mr. Ketchum laughed and got himself one and closed the lid.

"Could I have a piece of ice?" I asked.

"Take a beer if you want it," Mr. Ketchum laughed.

Father looked at me. I got up and got a big piece of ice.
Mr. Ketchum looked at Gerald. "You want one, boy?"

"No thanks."

"Suit yourself," Mr. Ketchum said.

"I always do," Gerald said.

Mr. Ketchum turned and looked at Gerald while he dug in his pocket for a bottle opener. Then he looked at Father and handed him the bottle opener. Father flipped the cap off the bottle. It landed near my foot. I picked it up and smelled it. It had a funny, sharp-sweet smell like a kind of vinegar or rotten maize or something. Mr. Ketchum took the opener back and clicked the cap off his beer. He caught it in the same hand as the opener. He raised it to his mouth and licked it, then dropped it. He took a big drink.

"Ahh. Now you know that's some purty good stuff there. Ain't it?"

"Yeah," Father said.

Gerald was watching Father. He had a mad look on his face. I sucked on the piece of ice. It made my lips cold, but it tasted good.

"That didn't take too long," Mr. Ketchum said. "Got plenty of daylight yet." He took another drink. "Say, Mac. I seen your boys down at the store a while ago. Gonzales says they're pullin' out."

"Yeah," Father said. "Can't make money sittin' around waitin' for it to rain."

"From what I hear, you can."

Father looked at Mr. Ketchum. "What do you mean?"

"Hell, you've heard about that Soil Bank old Ikey and the boys signed last month sometime. They'll pay you to plow under your cotton and leave them fields settin' for a couple or three years. Fifteen cents per pound on the cotton and up to fifty percent of your land. How does that sound?"

Father shook his head.

"Now, imagine that. The government payin' a man to do nothin', to plant nothin', 'cept maybe coastal or somethin', and to raise nothin'. Sounds about like a government, don't it?"

"Yeah, I guess so," Father said. He took a slow drink of the beer. Gerald was watching him.

"If they come around askin' me about it, I believe I'll say hell yes and plow all that cotton under. Wouldn't you?"

"I don't know, Elmer. It might rain."

"Yeah, but even if it does, what good could it do this late? June's almost over."

"Yeah," Father said.

"Farmin' is hard enough to where if somebody comes along offerin' me a little rest with pay, I believe I'd take it."

Father looked toward the back of the trailer. I put the piece of ice in my mouth and pushed it around. It was big and cold and made my teeth hurt.

"I ain't as well off as you," Mr. Ketchum went on. "Hell, Mr. Wesley had this place paid for before you took it over. I still got the land bank breathin' down my neck, not to mention every other thing that needs takin' care of." He stopped and took a long drink. "But I know you're bound to be hurtin' to get rid of these damned sheep. Hell, you started that bunch when you were in high school. I remember how proud you were of them damned things."

Father laughed once, a short laugh like when you hit your elbow on the side of the door.

"Anyway we got 'til July twentieth to sign up," Mr. Ketchum said. "It might be one way to get my seed money back."

"Once the government gets you," Father said like he was thinking.

"Huh?" Mr. Ketchum said.

Gerald was looking at Father. "Nothin'," Father said. Then he said, "What happened to your face?"

Mr. Ketchum finished off his beer and burped and looked at Father. "What's the matter? Don't you like it?"

I laughed. Mr. Ketchum kicked out with his boot and knocked me over and laughed. "Somethin's wrong with that boy, Mac. He cain't stay up straight for nothin'. I believe his gyros is messed up." He turned and opened the ice chest again and put the empty bottle in it and got out another. He opened it and licked the cap and dropped it on the ground.

"You know a fella by the name of Haufmann? Lives over close to New Braunfels?"

"I don't think so," Father said.

"Sure you do, Mac. He's a big mouth in politics over there, a damned Republican. Thinks San Antonio ought to get water from that new dam on the Guadalupe. Been in the paper and everything."

"Yeah," Father said.

"Well, he come into the bar last night with his mouth open."

Father looked at Mr. Ketchum.

"Well. You wanted to know what happened."

"Did he jump you?"

"Hell no. But listen. That damned German can move around a table as fast as any man I ever saw. He come in spoutin' that crap like some election was comin' up and I told him San Antonio could dry up and blow away to hell for all I cared. Then he called me an ignorant goddamned farmer and it took me nearly five minutes to catch him."

Mr. Ketchum laughed and Father laughed and shook his head. He took another slow drink of his beer and Gerald was watching him.

"Elmer, I swear to God, but I think you must be a crazy man."

"What the hell do you mean by that?" Mr. Ketchum said, pushing away from the truck. Father laughed, and Mr. Ketchum looked at him. I thought Mr. Ketchum was going to hit Father.

"Gettin' in fights and all," Father said with a smile. "I guess I'd be dead by now if I was you."

Mr. Ketchum took a drink of his beer. He shrugged and laughed. "You're the only man I ever knew who never made me mad," he said.

Father finished his beer and held the bottle down beside his leg. He looked down at the ground and took a deep breath. Then he let the air out in a big sigh. Gerald looked at the ground. I stood up.

Father and Gerald went through the big gate and I pulled it closed and looped the chain around the upright and hooked it on the nail. Out at the road, Mr. Ketchum's big truck was turning out of the driveway. Mama came out of the front door and called to us so we went up to the porch.

"Did you get them all?" Mama asked.

"Yep."

"Any trouble?"

"Nope."

"I have some cold water for you."

Father pushed his hat back and looked at Mama. She was standing by the door with a tray. On the tray were three glasses of water with ice in them.

"What's the occasion?" Father asked.

We stepped up on the porch and each took a glass. Mama let the tray hang by her side. She had a look on her face that was almost a smile, but kind of sad, too.

"It's a hot day," she said.

"It is that," Father said. I didn't think he would be thirsty, but he drank all the water out of his glass at one time. "That was good," he said.

"Want some more?"

"Nope. That was fine. I'll get some more when I finish mowing."

"I thought you were through with that," Mama said.

"I still have that patch of sunflowers to cut."

Mama's forehead wrinkled and she said, "I wish you wouldn't mess with those sunflowers. I'm always afraid the tractor will slide off into that gulley."

"Now, Jean."

"I can't help it," Mama said. "You know that's dangerous."

"I won't cut that close to the edge," Father said.

"What if you can't see the edge?" Mama said.

Father took his hat off, then put it back on and looked around. I finished my cold water and sat down on the edge of the porch. Gerald sat down too, but not close to me. I knew Father was going to mow whether Mama wanted him to or not. Mama knew it too.

"Oh, never mind," Mama said. "Are you sure you don't want another drink?"

"No thanks. I'd better get on with it."

Father walked out of the yard and Mama leaned on the rail and watched him. The wind blew her hair and when Carol came out the door behind her, I thought how much they looked alike sometimes.

"I'll take another drink," Gerald said, holding up his glass.

"You know where it is," Mama said.

Gerald made a pooty noise and got up and went into the house.

"What's going on?" Carol said.

"Nothing," Mama said.

"Guess what, Carol," I said. "Our baby rabbits died."

"Oh no," she said. She came over and sat down beside me and put her arm around my shoulder. I heard the tractor start and we all turned to watch Father drive past the shop with the mower bouncing behind him.

"Oh Lord," Mama said.

"What is that smell?" Carol asked, taking her arm off my shoulder.

"Sheep," Gerald said, coming back out the door.

Carol got up again and Gerald laughed. I told him to shut up. Mama was watching and listening. It sounded like Father was coming back up to the shop. We all looked.

Father came around the corner. The tractor was smoking and it sounded like it wanted to die. When Father got in front of the shop, it did die. He sat on it a minute and tried to restart it. It turned over, but it didn't start. He got off it and stood beside it, then he walked around it. We could see his face. He took off his hat and slapped the tractor with it. His lips started moving. We couldn't hear the words, but we all knew what he was saying. He was saying, "Damn damn damn."

At supper time, Mama asked me where Father was.

"I don't know."

"Well go look for him and tell him supper is ready."

I went outside and looked around. I stood near the station wagon and called Father. Mama looked out the window and said, "I could do that myself. Go find him."

I walked down toward the shop, but only the tractor was there where he had left it. Then I saw him down at the pen where we had loaded the sheep. Supper was a little later that night than usual and the sun was going down in the west with a red haze. It was still hot, but it wasn't anything like it had been earlier. The breeze from the south was picking up. I climbed over the big gate and crossed the barnyard. I was walking in the ruts Mr. Ketchum's truck had made.

Father was standing with his back to me. He was leaning on the top board of the pen. His arms were crossed and his chin was resting on his arms.

I climbed up and sat down beside him. For a minute the wind blew around us and Father didn't say anything. I looked over at the barn and scratched my knee. The loading window was in deep shadow. Even sitting beside Father, I didn't like to look in there.

"Our rabbits died," I said, after a while.

Father moved his chin a little on his arm like the whiskers were itching him. "They always do," he said slowly. His voice sounded tired. "Boys always got to catch 'em, and they always got to die."

"Yeah," I said. "But I don't see why. We gave them plenty to eat and drink."

"That ain't enough, sometimes," Father said. "It's a lot, but sometimes it ain't enough."

I wasn't sure what Father was talking about, but I didn't want to ask him. His hat was pushed back on his head and his face was sunburned and a little bit dirty. I sat there for a while without saying anything. I scratched my knee again. It felt like I had a redbug bite there.

"Mama said it was time for supper," I said.

Father didn't say anything. He looked down and took a deep breath. After a while I jumped down and walked back through the barnyard, staying in the wheel ruts of Mr. Ketchum's truck. Then I climbed over the big gate and jumped down. When I was at the edge of the driveway, I turned around. Father was still down there, leaning on the top board of the fence, looking at nothing.

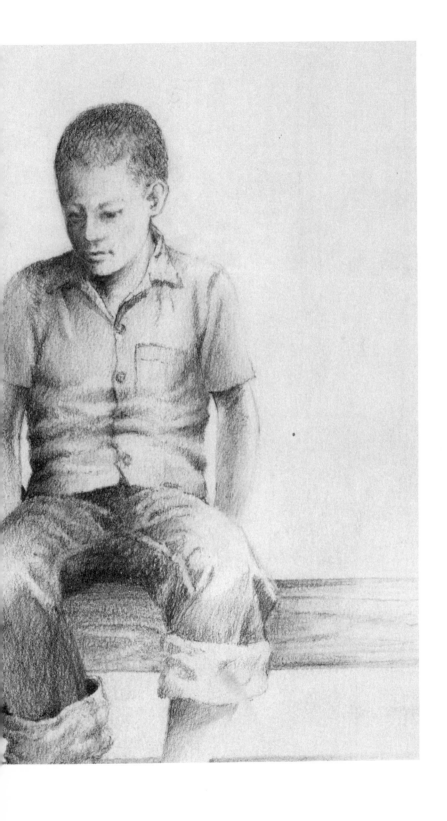

Grandfather

I DIDN'T WANT TO VOMIT. I tried for almost an hour to keep from vomiting, but finally I rolled off the bed and ran down the stairs bent over. I just made it to the bathroom, but I didn't have time to turn on the light. The lid was up on the commode, so I leaned over and out it came. The worst part was when it came through my nose. I hated that. There isn't anything that burns worse than that. On the third time, the light came on and Mama walked over to the cabinet and got a washrag out. She ran cold water on it and handed it to me. I tried twice more, but that was all. Tears were running down my nose and my whole head was burning. I put the rag over my face and half cried. I hated vomiting.

"Flush the commode," Mama said.

I flushed the commode without looking at it. Mama opened the little cabinet over the sink and pushed some bottles around until she found the one that had some flesh-colored medicine in it that you had to shake up and that tasted like chalk. She shook it.

"Do I have to take that?" I asked.

"This or castor oil."

"I'll take that," I said.

"What's the matter with you?" Mama asked, coming over and sitting on the edge of the tub. Her hair was long and loose and her nightgown was so light a yellow that it looked white. She unscrewed the cap on the bottle and poured it full of medicine and gave it to me. "Too many hotdogs?"

My stomach turned over. I took the medicine and shivered and gave the cap back to Mama. She filled it again, and I took it again.

"I guess so," I said.

"Do you feel better now?"

"My stomach does, but my head burns."

"It'll go away."

Mama put the cap back on the bottle and sat by me for a minute. Her shoulder touched mine. I wiped the rag over my face, then blew my nose in it. It burned even more.

"What time is it?" I asked.

"Almost morning. Do you feel like going back to bed?"

"I guess so."

"Flush the commode again."

Mama stood up and put the bottle back in the cabinet. I flushed the commode and stood up. I felt cold and sweaty. My legs were a little shaky.

"Can you make it?"

"I think so."

"Wash the rag out before you go and take it with you."

I ran cold water over the rag and squeezed it out. Mama followed me out of the bathroom and down the hall. She turned on the light over the stairs and waited until I was at the top to turn it off again. I went down the hall in the dark and got in my bed. I lay down on my back and my head got big, then little, then big again.

"Next time, close the door," Gerald said.

I stayed in bed while everybody got ready for church, then I got up and put on my bluejeans and my shirt. I felt a little better, but my mouth was dry and my head hurt. I went down the stairs.

"Do you feel like breakfast?" Mama asked.

"No."

"Well, we're all going to church, so you'll have to ride over to Raisin's with us."

"Why?"

"Because."

"Aw, Mama."

"It's not my fault you ate too many hotdogs," she said.

"Next time you have an emergency in the middle of the night, close the door," Father said, coming into the kitchen. He was pulling his tie tight.

"I couldn't help it," I said.

"And I see you're late for another meal," Father said.

I looked down. I didn't want to go to Uncle Raisin's.

"Mac," Mama said. "You know he doesn't feel well."

"I didn't have to guess, either," Father said.

Me and Gerald and Carol sat in the back seat. I sat in the middle because Gerald didn't want to sit by Carol. Carol smelled so sweet that my stomach turned over twice before we got backed around to head out the driveway. She opened her Bible and was looking over the passages for that week. Gerald was trying to keep his socks up.

"I don't see why Ricky gets to goof off when the rest of us have to go to church," he said.

"I'm sick."

"I'm sick too. Sick of you."

"Behave," Mama said.

Carol reached down between us and put her hand over mine. Her hand was cool and soft. I leaned against her a little bit and watched Gerald trying to keep his brown socks up.

Uncle Raisin's farm was just off the road on the way in to town. It had been Grandfather Clark's farm before he got too old to work it and moved to town. He was dead now. Grandma Clark lived in a house in town with another woman named Mrs. Parsons. Mrs. Parsons took care of Grandma Clark because she was too old to take care of herself. We hardly ever went to see her, but I wasn't sure why. Mama knew but I didn't want to ask her.

Uncle Raisin had been a farmer ever since I remembered. He had never been married. He lived in the house all by himself, but he had an old colored man named Uncle Shed who lived in a little house behind the barn and who helped him with the cows. All of Uncle Raisin's cows were black Angus and mean and I never liked them. Uncle Raisin also had some good fields. Father said once that the land had been a good section when Grandfather Clark had farmed it, but since Uncle Raisin took it over, it had gone to hell.

"These socks ain't worth crap," Gerald said.

"Please remember that we're going to church," Mama said.

Father turned in at Uncle Raisin's mailbox. He never said very much when he was driving. He liked to hang his elbow out the window and to look at everybody else's cows and fields as he drove by them.

"I see Raisin's mailbox is on the ground again," he said.

"He should get that fixed," Mama said.

"Shed might do it, but Raisin never will. He'll wait 'til the highway boys notice it."

Just then I wished I was going to church. We pulled up at the back door of Uncle Raisin's. I looked at the screen expecting to see him standing there, but all I saw was a rusty brown screen door full of holes.

"I don't see him," Mama said. "But we don't have time to get out. Ricky, you behave yourself. Raisin will bring you back to the house at dinner time."

"Can't I just wait in the car?"

"No. Now go on or you'll make us late."

I started to climb over Carol, but she told me to watch her dress, so I climbed out over Gerald.

"Queer," he said.

I stood by the car and Father pulled the door shut. He looked at me long enough for me to see his eyes, then he backed around and they left. The tires made a crunching sound on the gravel.

I looked around. There was an old tin building in front of me that Uncle Raisin used for a garage. The doors no longer slid opened and closed. The runners had broken and the doors were hanging open at an angle. There were old inner tubes and hubs and an old bumper piled along one side of the garage with at least two seasons of baling wire. Then the gravel led around the garage to two equipment sheds and on to the barn and Uncle Shed's house. I looked down there, but I didn't see

Uncle Shed's car. Uncle Raisin's truck was parked in front of the first equipment shed.

I still felt a little funny, so I went over to the screen door and knocked. When Uncle Raisin didn't come out, I sat down on the steps and put my chin in my hands to wait. It suited me just fine if Uncle Raisin didn't show up until dinner time. It was then that he came walking around the corner of the house.

"Hello, Mr. Richard," he said taking off a pair of gloves with holes in them.

"I don't feel very good," I said.

"So I hear. Let's go inside out of the sun."

I followed Uncle Raisin into the house. It was dark and cool in the house and I noticed the funny smell Uncle Raisin's house had. It was something to do with his painting, but I wasn't sure what it was. It smelled like paint thinner in a way, but I didn't think that was it. Uncle Raisin took off his cap and put it on the cabinet by the sink. He picked up a pair of pliers and turned on the water. Then he got a glass and let it fill up. He turned the water off with the pliers too, since the faucet handle was broken.

One thing that Uncle Raisin had that I liked was a water cooler in his living room. He kept it running all the time and I liked standing in front of it. Even on the hottest day I could get cool.

"Make yourself at home," Uncle Raisin said as I went into the living room.

There was a settee and two chairs that had sides made of wood to look like wagon wheels. I liked them. When I grew up and got my own place, I was going to have furniture like that. I sat down in one of the chairs. There were some strange paintings on the walls. I looked at them for a while. Uncle Raisin came in and sat down. He had a bowl of chocolate ice cream in his hand.

"Want some?" he said, holding the bowl up.

"No sir."

I sat there. Uncle Raisin ate the chocolate ice cream slowly, letting each big spoonful melt down in his mouth. After a while I heard his spoon scraping the bottom of that bowl. I looked over at him. His tight, curly hair was sticking straight up on his head.

"So," he said. "Ate too many hotdogs, eh?"

"I guess so."

Uncle Raisin laughed and put the empty bowl on the table beside his chair. He licked his mouth.

"Did you paint all of these pictures?" I asked.

"Sure did."

"Why do they look so weird?"

Uncle Raisin cut me a look, then sat up in his chair. "Impressionism," he said.

I looked at the floor. "Is it dinner time yet?"

"What's the matter? You in a hurry to go?"

"I still feel kind of bad," I said.

"Oh."

We sat there in the house listening to the water cooler. I could hear water gurgling under the noise of the fan.

"Since your land is leased, are you going to paint all the time?" I asked.

"Can't. Not enough money in it," Uncle Raisin said. He leaned back in his chair again and yawned and scratched his belly.

"What are you going to do?"

"I don't know."

"Why don't you paint houses?"

"Paint houses?"

"Sure. You like to paint and you wouldn't need a ladder."

"Ha ha. Some kind of joke, right? Jack Benny couldn't have done it better."

Uncle Raisin got up and went into the kitchen again. I got up and followed him. He sat down at the table and pulled the rubber band off a Sunday paper. He unrolled it and bent it back several times to take the curl out of it.

"Can I have the funny papers?" I asked.

"Why? You out of jokes?"

I stood by the edge of the table. The sunlight was coming in the kitchen window through a little hole in the screen.

"Sure," Uncle Raisin said. "Sit down. I'll find them."

I pulled a chair out. It was metal and had a shiny blue plastic seat. Uncle Raisin opened up the paper and went through it looking for the funnies.

"I don't feel too good."

"You already said that. Here's the funnies."

I took the funnies and opened them out in front of me. Right away I saw Superman flying over a building. Some of the red from his cape was down over the top of the building and some of the blue of the sky was in his cape. Newspapers always did that. I looked up at Uncle Raisin. He was reading something, then he looked at me.

"Are you mad at me for what I said about painting houses?" I asked.

"No," Uncle Raisin said. He put his elbows up on the table. "People say things like that all the time. I'm used to it. I guess I'm just worried about the way things are going."

"Me too."

Uncle Raisin looked at me. "Mac having trouble?"

"I don't know."

"You said you were worried."

"Yeah. Stuff doesn't seem like it used to."

Uncle Raisin went back to looking at the newspaper. "Like what?" he said.

I thought about all the things that had been going on since summer started, about the way Carol was acting, about the new people and how touchy Gerald was getting, and about Rebecca. There were too many things bothering me and I couldn't think straight about any of them. It was like trying to read the Spanish newspaper me and Gerald took out of Mario's truck one time. I knew what all the letters were, but none of the words made any sense. It was starting to seem like the older I got, the more mixed-up things were. I thought it should be the other way around.

Uncle Raisin turned the page and looked at me. He had eyes like Mama's.

"I don't know," I said. "Just stuff."

"It's the drought."

"I don't think so."

"Why not?"

"I don't know," I said, skipping down to Alley Oop. Alley Oop was a pretty neat guy. He always said stuff that showed he wasn't afraid of anything and he smoked cigars.

"Well," Uncle Raisin said. "Things change. You know that. We all have to face it sooner or later. When I was your age, things were a lot different around this old table. Daddy would be sitting over there and Mama over there. Jean and I would be sitting over on that side with Patrick. I never knew then that I would be the last one to leave this place."

Uncle Raisin turned another page and I thought about Uncle Patrick. He was Mama's oldest brother, but he died in World War One in France. I saw a picture of him one time in a book Mama kept in her underwear drawer. They were all sitting on the front porch of the house. Uncle Raisin was just a baby then. Mama was about four and Uncle Patrick had his hand on her shoulder. There was a shadow in the picture that was probably Grandfather Clark's.

"Did you ever know Patrick?" I asked.

"Only for a little while, it seemed like. He could do anything, I remember that, figure anything out. I guess it should have been me that got killed in that war instead of him. This place would look good as the old days if Patrick were still here."

"You could fix it up," I said.

Uncle Raisin shook his head and turned another page. "No. Not me. I'm no good at this stuff, even with old Shed helping me."

"Sometimes I mess stuff up too," I said.

Uncle Raisin laughed. "Yeah. Sometimes I think you're a lot like me."

"Maybe I'll grow up to be a painter," I said.

Uncle Raisin looked over at me for a minute. His blue eyes reminded me of Mama's when she looked me in the eye to see if I was lying or not. Then Uncle Raisin looked down and shook his head. "I hope to God not," he said. "For your sake."

Grandfather and Grandmother were already there when me and Uncle Raisin drove up in his pickup. Their '51 Ford was parked in the shade of the elm tree with the windows rolled down. It made me think of a big turtle trying to get out of the sun. Uncle Raisin drove on down toward the shop and parked. I waited until some of the dust from the driveway blew by before I got out.

"Somethin' a matter with the tractor?" Uncle Raisin asked, standing by the truck and looking at it. It was parked sideways to the shop just as Father had left it, and the top was raised.

"I think so, but I don't know what."

Uncle Raisin started for the house. "That would be the first time I ever saw somethin' of Mac's that wasn't working just right."

We went in the back door. Mama was in the kitchen at the stove. She was making roast gravy. Carol was reaching glasses down from the cabinet. She was still wearing her dress from church, and when she reached up, I could almost see the tops of her hose. Uncle Raisin looked at her, then pinched her side. She squealed a little bit.

"Cut it out, Uncle Raisin. You'll make me drop these glasses."

"I believe you get prettier every day," he said.

Mama turned around and looked at us. She had her hand on her hip where the apron strings were tied. Grandmother was standing in the doorway to the dining room watching Mama get dinner ready.

"Hello Raisin," Mama said. Then she looked at me and said, "How are you feeling?"

"Okay."

"Come here."

I went over to Mama and she put her hand on my forehead. Her hand was warm and had some flour on it.

"Go wash your hands," she said.

"Hi, Grandmother," I said.

"Oh hello, Ricky. I didn't see you at church this morning."

Mama poked my shoulder from behind. "No ma'am," I said.

"I told you he was sick," Mama said.

"He doesn't look sick," Grandmother said with a little laugh.

"I feel a lot better," I said.

"Bad little boys usually do, once church time is over," Grandmother said.

Mama grabbed my shoulder again and turned me in the direction of the back porch. "Go wash your hands now," she said.

"Good afternoon, Mrs. MacAllister," Uncle Raisin said.

"Oh, now, Raisin, we know each other better than that," I heard Grandmother saying.

I washed my hands and went into the living room. Father and Grandfather were in there, but Gerald wasn't. I went over to Grandfather and he sat up a little, still holding on to his cane, and turned and looked at me. He was still wearing his summer church hat with the red and blue band, but he had loosened his tie and unbuttoned the top button of his white shirt. His face was thin and sharp and had dark blotches on it that I never thought about when I looked at him. He put his old hand out to me and I shook it.

"Well, now. Your mama says you ain't been feelin' too well," he said. "Does that come from workin' too hard in the hot sun?"

"No sir."

Grandfather laughed a little bit. Father was watching us. "Well sir, don't admit it. Sounds better if you say hard work put you down. Sounds more like a man. Hard work puts a man down ever' time. Just like me."

Grandfather was holding on to my arm. He let it go and put both hands on top of his cane. He looked at the floor.

"If hard work is what's goin' to get 'em," Father said, "they ought to live forever."

Grandfather laughed and looked at me. After a minute he said, "Your mama says you ain't been feelin' too well."

I looked over at Father. He was watching me. Uncle Raisin came into the living room. I felt the floor shake.

"No sir," I said.

Gerald was up in our room. I sneaked up the stairs and along the hall until I saw him. He was lying on his bed facing the other way. He was propped up on his elbows doing something, but I couldn't tell what it was. I moved along the wall so

148

the floor wouldn't creak. Gerald was so busy that he didn't hear me until I was right behind him. I looked over his shoulder. He was writing something on a piece of notebook paper. I couldn't see what it was, but the first two words were *Ruby Lee.*

"What the hell you doin'?" Gerald said when he heard me start to laugh. He swung up off the bed and shoved me hard onto my own bed. I was laughing.

"Shut up," he said. "You ever do that again and I'll throw your sorry butt out that window."

"Leave me alone," I said, trying not to laugh. "Mama says it's time to eat dinner."

"You'll be lucky if you ever eat again," Gerald said. "Lockjaw always starts with vomiting."

I sat up on the bed and looked at Gerald. He sat down on his bed and folded the piece of paper until it was little enough to put in his shirt pocket.

"No it doesn't," I said.

"You'll see."

"Shut up."

"Talk while you can."

"Dinner is ready, boys," Mama called from the bottom of the stairs.

Gerald got up and went out of the room. For a minute I sat on the bed listening to the wind in the elm tree. I swallowed. My throat did seem a little sore.

After dinner Gerald disappeared. I was helping clean off the table when he got up. I thought he went into the living room with Father and Grandfather and Uncle Raisin, but when I was through, I couldn't find him in there. I went upstairs, but he wasn't up there, either. Carol came up while I was up there. When I passed her door, she called me in.

"What are you doing?" she asked.

She was standing by her dresser with one hand on it for balance while she kicked off her white shoes.

"Nothing."

"Well, come here. I want you to unzip me. I've got a crick in my neck that'll kill me if I have to do it myself."

I walked over to Carol and she turned around and bent her head forward. She reached up with one hand to get her hair out of the way.

"Ow. Hurry. That hurts."

I reached up and caught the zipper and pulled it down. Her slip was white and soft-looking. She straightened up and turned around.

"Thanks. How are you feeling?"

"Okay."

"That's good." Carol slipped the dress forward off her shoulders and then down until she could step out of it.

"Carol, do you know anything about lockjaw?"

She shook the dress out, then went into the closet for a hanger. "What are you talking about?"

"I stepped on a piece of barbed wire the other day and Gerald said I had lockjaw."

"Oh, Gerald."

"He said it starts with vomiting."

Carol laughed and hung up her dress. She put it in the closet. When she came out, she went over to the bed and sat on the edge of it. "Come here."

I went over and sat down beside her. She looked pretty in her slip. This time the way she smelled didn't make my stomach turn over, but it was nice.

"Show me your foot."

I showed her my heel. She caught it with her hand and looked at it.

"I don't see a thing. Are you sure it was this foot?"

"Yeah."

"Well, there isn't even a spot. Besides, you've stepped on so many things before, you'd be the last person in the world to ever get lockjaw."

"You think so?"

Carol pulled her slip up on her leg and unsnapped her stocking. "I'm sure of it," she said.

"That Gerald," I said.

Carol ran the stocking down her smooth, brown leg and pulled it off. She undid the other stocking and pulled it off. Her legs were long and brown.

"I wouldn't pay much attention to anything he said," Carol laughed. "He just needs a good whipping."

"Yeah," I said. "Thanks, Carol."

I stood up and Carol got up too. She went over to her dresser and pulled out the top drawer and put the stockings in it. She took one of the straps off her shoulder and turned around. "I'll see you later," she said.

"Okay."

I went down the stairs and through the kitchen to the back porch. I got my old straw hat off a nail and put it on and slipped out the back door. I think Mama said something to me, but I pretended not to hear anything. She was washing the dishes and Grandmother was drying them. They were talking.

I had an idea where Gerald was and it made me mad. I went down to the shop and looked there first to make sure. He wasn't there. I stood in the hot shade of the shop and looked down in the pasture. Heat waves made everything look blurry, and the dry crackle of grasshoppers made me sleepy. I wanted to just go back to the house, but I didn't. I stepped out of the shade and headed for the pasture.

Any time I walked somewhere by myself, I felt different about everything I saw. I felt that everything was somehow pointed at me, for me to notice and think about. Even a redwing blackbird sitting on the fence down near the tank seemed to be there for a reason, to tell me something, if I only could know what it was. When I started up the washout, a cloud went under the sun and threw a running shadow over me. I stopped and shivered. That was the way it was every time I went somewhere by myself. I didn't like the feeling. I didn't like the sudden movements or the wind blowing the leaves of the sunflowers. It sounded like something was in them, watching me.

I walked up the washout slowly. In places the dirt was fire under my feet. The soft, black dirt was the worst. Clay wasn't too bad. At each bend in the washout, I stopped and listened. Mostly all I heard were grasshoppers and the wind. Sometimes I heard a bobwhite quail. I got more careful the farther I went. Then I heard Gerald's voice and I stopped. I listened for a minute, but I couldn't understand what he was saying. If I went any farther, they would be able to see me. Ruby Lee was with him.

I crawled back down the washout a little ways, then crossed it and climbed out on top. The sunflowers were thick right at the very edge of the washout. That was why Mama never liked Father to mow the sunflowers. Sometimes it was hard to tell just where the edge was. I crawled into the sunflowers. They were hot and sharp and sticky and the ground under them was thick with little dried leaves and dead grass. I got up off my knees finally and went through the sunflowers bent over. Once I saw a yellow jacket nest on the branch of a tall sunflower. The yellow jackets bristled at me, so I turned off. I was starting to get hot in there, and dried bits of stuff was getting under my collar and itching my back. I turned again so that the wind was blowing in my face and I walked real slow. Then I got down on my hands and knees again and crawled. I could hear Gerald and Ruby Lee talking. I got close enough to see the tops of their heads through the sunflower stalks.

"Sometimes I do too," Ruby Lee was saying in her high, whiny voice. "I get so sick of 'em, I just want to walk away and never come back."

"I'm goin' to, one of these days," Gerald said. "When I get old enough to drive, I'm goin' to get a big red pickup and drive away from here so fast there won't even be any dust."

"Oh, I'd like to see that," Ruby Lee said.

"I'm goin' to do it. I'm not goin' to be no farmer all my life."

"What you goin' to do?"

Gerald was quiet for a minute. Some sweat rolled out from under my hat and got down in my eyes.

"Somethin' important, you can bet on that."

"Like what?"

"I don't know, but it won't be workin' on a farm."

"I'm goin' to marry me a rich man. I'm goin' to marry some man who owns his own beer joint. Then I can walk in any time I want, smokin' me a long cigarette, and order me a beer."

"My father doesn't go in for drinkin' very much," Gerald said.

"I thought you didn't care what your father did."

"That's right. I don't give a shit what he thinks."

"Course it don't have to be a beer joint. It could be a big department store with all kinds of fine clothes. Then I could go in any time I want and pick me out somethin' to wear."

"I don't know about a department store," Gerald said. He hated it when we had to go into one to buy clothes for school.

"You think about it," Ruby Lee said, looking all around. "You could just walk in there and choose anything at all and say, 'Charge it.' Just like that."

"Yeah."

"I ain't goin' to live on no farm all my life neither. The first man comes along, I'm gone."

"But not just anybody," Gerald said, looking at her.

"Well, I guess not. I been asked before, but Pa wouldn't let me go. He said I was too young. Do you think I'm too young, Gerald?"

Gerald looked at her. She raised her arms and put her hands behind her head. Gerald didn't say anything.

"I mean, I may be only sixteen, but I ain't no kid. Do you think I'm a kid?"

"No," Gerald said. I tried to see his face.

"I ain't been a kid for a long time, seems like," Ruby Lee said. She brought her hands down and smoothed the front of her shirt, making it tight against her.

When the sun got low enough to make some shade in front of the shop, Father and Uncle Raisin and Grandfather went down there. Grandfather found an old wooden box and pulled it out of the shop to sit on. Father and Uncle Raisin were looking at the tractor. I sat down in the doorway of the shop. Gerald had been back from the pasture for a long time, but he went up to our room and told me to stay out of it. He even closed the door, hot as it was.

"What happened to that John Deere you had, son?" Grandfather asked.

"Sold it two years ago. You know that, Papa."

"Oh yeah. Keep forgettin'. Well, it wasn't any good was it?"

"No sir. Not any more. That's why I sold it." Father pointed at the front of the engine block where the fan was. "See there?" he said to Uncle Raisin.

"Water pump?" Uncle Raisin said.

"Acts like it, but it got so hot on me it liked to quit, did quit. I never had one do that and the water pump not be tearin' all to pieces."

"You goin' to take it off?"

"Guess I'll have to, much as I hate to."

"Why?" Uncle Raisin asked.

"Too much trouble for one thing. Afraid of what I might find, for another."

"You could leave it and see."

"Can't do that. It got so hot on me the other day the engine was singing."

"Well," Uncle Raisin said. "Want to start now?"

Father wiped his hands on his pants and looked around. "May as well," he said.

Father stepped by me and went into the shop for his big tool box that held all of his wrenches. The box was metal and greasy and it took both me and Gerald to carry it very far. Father brought it out and set it on the ground by the tractor. Uncle Raisin was rolling up his sleeves another turn.

"What you goin' to do?" Grandfather asked.

"Take a look," Father said. He squatted down over the tool box and opened it. He pushed wrenches back and forth looking for the size he wanted.

"What did he say?" Grandfather said, looking at me.

"Father said they were going to take a look. Said it might be the water pump."

Grandfather nodded and rested his hands on his cane. For a minute he turned and looked over at the barn. A gnat landed on his cheek, but he didn't pay any attention to it.

"Barn looks mighty empty," he said.

Father handed a wrench to Uncle Raisin and watched while he fitted it on a nut. "You see any hay stacked up around here on your way out today?" Father said.

"Mighty dry," Grandfather said. "How is your place doin', Wilfred?" Wilfred was Uncle Raisin's real name.

"Burned up," Uncle Raisin said. "I'm liable to put it in the Soil Bank and plow it all under."

Grandfather looked at him sharply. "Got it planted?"

"Yep. Give me a nine-sixteenths, Mac."

"You can't go into the Soil Bank if you've signed a lease," Father said. "Daniels doesn't plan to just collect that money."

"I was just kidding," Uncle Raisin said. He put his weight on the nut and it cracked loose. "Rusty buggers," he said.

"Ain't no sense in plowin' up land that's already been planted. Ain't right," Grandfather said.

"I'm not," Uncle Raisin said. "But I bet a lot of people do before this summer is over."

"I don't believe a program like that will go over. People won't stand for it. Too big a waste of money."

"They've wasted money before, Papa. That's the last thing that bothers 'em."

"Well, the farmers won't go for it, then," Grandfather said.

"You'd be surprised," Father said. "Farmers are hurtin'."

"Farmers are always hurtin'," Grandfather said. "It comes with the land."

"How's that?" Father said.

"Five more on the other side," Uncle Raisin said.

"What say?" Grandfather asked.

Father turned and looked at him. "People are hurtin' bad. It's too dry. Can't make nothin'."

Grandfather shook his head. "It was dry, by God, in 'twenty-five, and folks made it. Had to haul some water and sell a few mules, but we made it just fine seems like. Didn't have to sell no land to the gov'ment."

"This isn't like 'twenty-five," Father said.

"That's what Mr. Norman said," I said.

"By God, it was dry in 'twenty-five," Grandfather said. "Had to sheaf maize for mule feed. Wouldn't make no heads."

"That was one year, Papa. It's been dry around here for six years now."

"It hasn't been that long."

"Yes it has. Everybody around here has just about had it. Me included."

"You got cotton up," Grandfather said. "I seen it when we come in."

"It's up, but that's all."

"Well, I wouldn't think of plowin' up cotton that was up, and this bein' only June."

"I'm not plowin' it up," Father said. "I sold the sheep. I can sell some of the cattle next. We might make it."

"You sold the sheep?"

"I told you that."

"What kind of price did you get for 'em?"

"The worst kind."

Uncle Raisin looked up from the other side of the tractor. Father looked at him, then shook the nuts he had in his hand as if they were dice he was about to roll.

"You should've kept 'em," Grandfather said. "You've had sheep since you was a boy Gerald's age."

"How?" Father said. He sounded a little mad. "How am I goin' to keep 'em? What could I feed 'em?"

"Keep back some of your crop, son. That's what we always done in the past. If the market is bad or the crop don't make, put it in the barn and use it for feed. Sit tight until next year. That's what I built that big barn for."

"Cotton makes a lousy feed," Father said.

"You tellin' me the stock can't eat cottonseed?"

"If that cotton makes enough to have seed, I'm not goin' to feed it to a bunch of sheep. I need the cash."

"What for? It ain't like you live in the city where you got to buy ever'thin'. It's all right here, ain't it? It was when I was here."

"That's it," Uncle Raisin said. He came back around the tractor and gave the nuts and bolts to Father.

"We'll have to take the fan off and get that out of the way," Father said. "Ricky, find a can to put these in. I'll get it, Raisin."

I got up and went in the shop and found a coffee can. Father dropped the nuts and bolts in it and I sat back down.

"What size is that?" Uncle Raisin asked.

"Half inch. I've got it."

Grandfather said, "Any good farmer can make it if he lives off his own crop. Don't sell the damned stuff if you can't get your price for it."

"Tractors aren't like mules, Papa," Father said, working a nut loose on the fan. "Raisin, could you hold this fan for me. It keeps wanting to turn."

Raisin went to help Father. My arms were itching where the sunflowers had scratched them. I would be glad when Father got around to mowing those sunflowers. They weren't good for anything at all. Grandfather was watching them work. The sleeves on his white shirt puffed out when the breeze blew.

"In 1925," he said, "we had eighteen mules on this farm and we kept ever' one of them. The only thing we lost that year were some worthless hands that hung around wastin' time instead of workin'. And they weren't no great loss. Most of 'em had to go nearly to Amarillo to find cotton to pick. That was the year your Uncle Abner took four wagons up north to pick cotton."

Father's wrench slipped off the nut and he cut his hand on the fan. "Damn," he said. "I guess some of these nuts haven't ever been taken off."

"You listenin' to me, son?"

"Yeah, Papa," Father said. He was starting to sound mad again. "I'm listenin' to you. But what you're talkin' about has been over for nearly thirty years. Farmers don't use mules anymore like they used to. They got these damned Ford tractors that don't eat corn or maize or Johnson grass. They take cash to run. Lights cost money to run; trucks cost money. Back when you were farmin', nobody had any money, and it didn't matter. We got along just fine, like you said. But now money matters. Like it or not, things have changed."

Grandfather shook his head. "Well, it's a damned shame, then."

Father bent and put the wrench back on the nut. "Maybe it is," he said. "But the plain fact remains. Outside of hay, what farmers grow now, they sell. Hell, they go to the store for most of their food just like everyone else."

"Damned machines," Grandfather said. "Don't mean nothin' to people. Come and go and no sire or dam to remember, no sickness or injury. Just damned machines."

"Things change," Father said. He didn't sound very mad anymore.

"Well, maybe so. I wish I hadn't lived so long as to see it. Just promise me one thing, son," Grandfather said. "Just promise me you won't plow up nothin' you got planted."

Father didn't turn around. "I'll just have to see how it goes, Papa. I don't want to do it."

"Ain't no way to face hard times. There's something sinful about it, I believe."

I was looking down at the ground. It was dry and dusty looking and the only plants were stunted and hard with little leaves. Father took some nuts off and called me over with the can.

"How long have you had that Ford, son?" Grandfather said after a while.

"About eight years," Father said.

"Whatever happened to that John Deere you had?"

The sun was going down when we carried the watermelon out on the front porch. Father and Uncle Raisin and Carol and Grandfather were already out there. The men were sitting in the red lawn chairs in the yard where the shade of the elm tree made a long circle in the heat of the day. Carol was leaning on the arm of Grandfather's chair and he had his arm around her waist and was patting her. Mama came out behind us with pie pans and knives and a shaker of salt. Grandmother was carrying the napkins and telling Mama the best way to eat a watermelon.

Me and Gerald set the watermelon down on the edge of the porch, and Carol came over and looked at it and said, "That's an awfully big one."

Gerald said, "Carol, you don't know the half of it."

I wiped my hands on my pants. The watermelon was dusty from lying around on the back porch where it was always cool. I heard Father tell Grandfather to move around more into the shade of the elm tree, and Carol turned quickly to help him, but Grandfather said the sun was going down anyway and he never saw the man yet that was hurt by a little sun. Father unwrapped a new cigar and put it in his mouth. Uncle Raisin started telling about a man he knew in the army who was from Louisiana and who had skin white as a woman's and couldn't stand the sun. Grandfather poked at the ground with his cane and said Louisiana was the sorriest place on earth—nothing there but mosquitoes and alligators. The people weren't sober long enough to be worth a hoot.

"Hand me that knife," Gerald said to Mama.

"Just settle down."

Gerald looked at her and chewed his lip for a minute and said, "I'm ready to cut it, Mama, when you give me that knife."

"Do you think—" she started to say.

"Come on, Mama," Gerald said, chewing his lip.

"Boy," Father said, looking around with the cigar in his mouth. "You wait on your mama and settle down."

"Yes sir," Gerald said, then he leaned over toward me and said, "We're liable to starve to death before that watermelon ever gets cut."

Grandmother was standing behind Mama telling her the best way to cut a watermelon. Mama was spreading the pie pans out on the porch and putting a knife on the edge of each one. Worthless walked up from somewhere and started putting his wet nose on everything. He came over to me panting, and dripped on my bare feet, so I kicked him.

"I'll cut it, Mama," Gerald said when Mama stooped over the watermelon with the butcher knife in her hand.

"Now Gerald, that's a little bit overripe and the best way to cut it is to start with the far end."

"I know, Grandmother," Gerald said, reaching for the butcher knife.

"Well, it don't hurt to think about things before you do them," Grandmother said. She was holding the salt shaker with two fingers like it was a tea cup.

Mama looked at Gerald and Gerald said, "Yes ma'am." She gave him the butcher knife and he pretended to test the edge with his thumb. He grinned at me. Gerald with a butcher knife was a happy person.

"You going to cut it or not," Mama said, watching him, her hair blowing in the breeze.

"Right now," Gerald said.

"No gov'ment at all," Grandfather was saying when Uncle Raisin finished his story about the man who died of a heat stroke. "That Huey Long, built all them bridges, was part alligator. Fella had to shoot him with ev'ry bullit in the gun 'fore he would go down. Then they say he went down mad as a hornet in a hailstorm."

"Carol, let that dog alone and help me with these pans and knives," Mama said.

Gerald stuck the watermelon on the end because Grandmother was watching, but we both knew the best way to cut a watermelon was to stab it in the middle and let it split apart from pure goodness.

"I've got the salt, now," Grandmother said, shaking it.

"Gerald, just cut the watermelon and stop making those noises," Mama said in her flat voice. Gerald was making noises like the watermelon was dying, and then he made pooty noises as the knife slid along the hump. Carol had come over and was standing beside me. She reached over and ran her fingers around the back of my neck. She always did that. Worthless walked over to Gerald to see what he was doing, and Gerald said, "Go on Worthless before I cut your guts out."

"Gerald give me that knife before you cut somebody."

"I know not to stick nobody," Gerald said, bending back over the watermelon. He cut the halves in half, then cut those into halves so that there were eight pieces. We stood around watching him. Carol moved over to let Gerald put the pieces in the pans.

"Who wants some?" Mama called to the men.

Uncle Raisin raised his head and nodded. Father took the cigar out of his mouth and looked at him.

"Mac?"

Father shook his head. Grandfather turned around and raised his cane off the ground. "You bet!" he said.

Grandmother looked around Mama and said, "You know better than that, Wesley. You'll be up all night."

Me and Carol looked at Grandfather and saw him turn to Father and heard him say, "Be damned." Grandfather was a little deaf and he said things louder than he meant to, but Grandmother was a little deaf too. Mama wasn't. She caught our eyes with her frown when we glanced at her. We always looked at Mama when anybody cussed because we knew how much she hated it.

"You going to eat any?" Grandmother called.

"Yes I am, by God," Grandfather said.

"Give him half of one of those, Gerald," Grandmother said.

"You feel like eating watermelon?" Mama asked me.

"Sure," I said.

Gerald cut one of the pieces in half and Carol scooped it up on a bent pie pan and carried it to Grandfather. He hung his cane on the arm of his chair and took the pan into his lap. Carol stood beside him with her hand on his shoulder. For a minute I thought Carol was going to run her fingers around the back of his wrinkled old neck.

"Gerald, if you don't quit playing with that knife—just give it to me."

"Aw Mama," Gerald said, handing over the knife, hilt first. Mama took it and set it down on the porch beside her.

"Man, don't that look sweet," Grandfather said. "Thanks, honey."

"You're welcome, Grandfather," Carol said, letting her hand slide off his thin shoulder.

"I don't need no pan," Gerald said, watching Mama lift one of the red slices onto a pan.

"This is for your uncle," she said.

"This is for Uncle Raisin," Gerald said, passing the pan to me.

"Take this," I said, giving the pan to Carol.

Mama looked hard at us both. "You two want any watermelon or not?"

"Yes ma'am," I said. Gerald frowned.

Mama put another slice onto a pan for herself and one for Grandmother. "Oh, not that much," Grandmother said. Mama picked up the knife and cut the slice in half. "Oh, more than that," said Grandmother. Carol had come back and was looking at Mama. "I'll take those two pieces," she said. Mama gave them to Carol, then she leaned over another slice and put the knife across it. "Here?" she asked. "Oh, that's more than enough," Grandmother said, and Mama cut the slice holding the knife just past half. Grandmother took the slice, still holding on to the salt. Mama put herself a slice on a pan and they went back to the porch chairs and sat down.

Me and Gerald looked at the slices that were left. "This is mine," I said, reaching.

"Wait," Gerald said, knocking my arms down. "You take this one."

"It's smaller."

"That's right," Gerald said, picking up the bigger slice.

I picked up my slice and followed Gerald to the edge of the porch closest to the men so that we could listen to them talk.

"I ought to have brought my apron," Grandmother said behind us.

"I'll get you one," Mama said.

"Oh, I don't want to be any trouble."

"No trouble," Mama said, but she said it in her flat voice.

When Gerald ate watermelon, he didn't use a knife. He put his whole mouth down onto the slice and took a big, sucking bite and pushed it around in his mouth and chewed carefully on it so as not to swallow any seeds. Then he spit. I ate mine the same way. Carol and Mama cut theirs into little slices with butter knives and then picked the seeds out before they ate the slices. That took forever. Uncle Raisin ate his that way too, but he was already finished and going for another slice.

Father watched Uncle Raisin pick up another slice and Father moved his cigar from one side of his mouth to the other. Uncle Raisin went back to his chair. All that was left of the first slice was white rind. Gerald spit a seed out as far as he could. Worthless got up from behind Grandfather's chair and went to look at it, then walked back to the chair and fell over. The sun was gone now, but it was still pretty hot.

"Seed on your chin, Papa," Father said, watching Grandfather.

"All right. No problem," Grandfather said.

The screen door opened and closed and Mama came out with an apron. Grandmother lifted the pan from her knees and Mama spread the apron out on her lap.

"They don't make aprons very big anymore, do they?" Grandmother said.

"Let me get another one," Mama said, but when I looked around, she wasn't getting up.

"Oh, no. This will do," Grandmother said. "I guess."

Gerald was trying to hit Worthless with seeds so I tried it too. Carol watched us. I hit him.

"You're closer," Gerald said.

"Boys," Mama said when a seed hit Grandfather's chair.

"I 'member a story 'bout watermelons," Grandfather said. For a minute nobody said anything, then Carol said, "What was it, Grandfather?"

"There was this old fella settin' by the side of the road and some city fellas pulled up in this great, long car, you know. You know what they drive—don't drive no pickups."

"I've got salt if anybody wants any," Grandmother said.

Gerald spit. "Beat that," he said.

"Go on, Grandfather," Carol said.

"And they seen this old fella just a-settin' there and they thought, well now, we'll just fool this ol' boy, because he looked like a hick to them anyhow."

"Wesley, you want some salt?"

"What say?"

"Mother wants to know if you want some salt," Father said.

"Do you want any salt, Wesley?"

"No, by God," Grandfather said, turning part way around.

"I have it if you want it."

"No!" Grandfather shouted, turning all the way around. His face was red and blotchedy looking.

"All right, but it's here."

"Nothin' in the world ruin good 'melon faster than salt," Grandfather said, turning back around.

"You pick up that harrow?" Father asked Uncle Raisin.

"Yeah. Got it Saturday."

"Need any weights?"

"Has plenty," Uncle Raisin said. "Concrete blocks."

"Anyhow these fellas had this big watermelon in the back of the car there, you see. So they pulled up to this ol' fella settin' by the road and made some talk."

"Iron's better," Father said. "Heavier."

"What say?" Grandfather said, looking up and wiping his chin.

"Nothing," Father said, chewing on his cigar.

"Well, then these fellas, thought they was smart, you see, they told this other fella they would give him fi' dollas if he could eat that whole watermelon—great big thing, bigger'n this one."

"Want some more salt?" Grandmother asked.

"No. I'm fine," Mama said.

"How about you boys?"

I bit a piece of bitter rind and spit it out. "*Ricky*," Mama said.

"Well that ol' fella looked in the winda of that car there, and studied that watermelon, and them city folks was doin' all they could not to laugh, you see. Directly that fella said he thought maybe he could eat it if they would wait while he ran up the hill to the house. Well, they said he could, so he went at a run and was gone maybe fifteen minutes 'fore he come back down again."

"Is Wesley telling that silly story again?" Grandmother asked. "I guess we've all heard it a hundred times."

"I don't know," Mama said to be polite.

"Well them fellas was curious about why this hick run up to the house, but he come down again and said, sure, he could eat it all right."

"Wesley?"

"I don't want no salt," Grandfather said, turning and looking back up on the porch. Gerald burped and I laughed.

"Are you telling that story again?"

"Maybe I am," Grandfather said.

"Ketchum say he was through harrowing?" Father asked.

"No, but he said he wouldn't be doing it this week. Too dry to make any difference," Uncle Raisin said.

"We have all heard that story a hundred times," Grandmother said.

"I haven't," Carol said suddenly. Gerald looked around me at her and raised his eyebrows. "Liar," he said where no one else could hear him.

Grandfather turned around and fumbled with the pan in his lap. "Be damned," he said, wiping his chin. Father looked at him.

"The hick said he could eat it," Carol said.

"Oh yeah," Grandfather settled down. "Come back from the house and said, sure, he could eat it. So them city fellas helped him lift the watermelon out on to the side of the road there. There was a shade tree there or somethin' the ol' fella was settin' under, and he went to eatin' that watermelon. Must have taken him 'bout a quarta of an hour and them city fellas had mighty big eyes by the time he was finished. Well sir, they was beat; that was for sure."

Gerald dropped his rind on the ground and Worthless came over to smell of it. "Worthless, you old hog," Gerald said.

"They paid up all right. Give the fella fi' dollas, one at a time, and got back in the car. Wasn't either one of them laughin' then, but one fella got curious and asked the ol' hick why he had gone up to the house like he did. Well, he told them, I had me a watermelon bigger'n that up at the house under my bed. I run up there and ate it because I knew if I could eat that one, I could eat yours for sure!"

Grandfather finished and slapped his leg and laughed and the pie plate fell off his lap.

"Look at Wesley," Grandmother said.

Carol set her pan on the porch and jumped up to help Grandfather. He was bent over trying to put the rind and the butter knife back on the pan. He knocked his cane off the arm of his chair. Father was watching him. Gerald shook his head, trying not to laugh.

"Dad blast it," Grandfather was saying.

"Don't worry about it, Grandfather," Carol said. "Nothing is hurt."

"Jigger slipped right off."

"It's all right." Carol stood up. When I saw her face, I

didn't feel like laughing anymore. "Would you like another piece, Grandfather?"

"Never used to do stuff like that," Grandfather was saying. "Huh? No. Don't believe so. I was through anyway. It was mighty good though."

Grandfather sat back in his chair and grabbed the handle of his cane. Carol stepped around his chair and came to the porch with his pan. I was watching her, but she didn't look at me. She put the pan on the porch and stepped up and went into the house.

The sun had been down half an hour when me and Gerald carried the rinds in a bucket across the driveway to throw over the fence. When we got back to the house, Grandfather and Grandmother and Uncle Raisin were getting ready to leave.

I went into the house to look for Carol. She was upstairs in her room sitting on the edge of the bed in the dark. I stood in the doorway looking at her until she saw me.

"They're leaving," I said.

She looked at me and looked down again. I didn't like the way I felt. I felt as if I was beginning to know something that Carol already knew. I went into her room and stood by the end of the bed.

"What's wrong?"

"Grandfather isn't going to live much longer," she said.

I reached out and touched the end of the bed. Carol looked down again. Through the windows I could hear the car starting and Mama calling goodbye.

Rain

I HATED DREAMS SOMETIMES. Sometimes I had good dreams about things we all did. Sometimes I dreamed about Carol. Sometimes I dreamed about Rebecca and school. Those were good dreams. We always did a lot of stuff that nobody can really do except in funny books. But sometimes I dreamed dumb things like I didn't have any pants on and I was at school. Nobody ever seemed to notice, but I knew about it and I didn't like it. But the worst dreams were when something would happen to Mama or Father or anybody else I knew. I hated those dreams.

Sunday night I dreamed that me and Father were going to town in the pickup and it turned over on the side of the road. I got out by climbing up through the door, but I couldn't find Father. I looked all around the truck and up and down the road, but he was gone. Then I saw the man called Wilbur sitting on the back of the truck pulling feathers off a dead chicken. I asked him where Father was. He just laughed and said, "Summer ain't never been this cold." That was when I woke up. For a while I didn't believe it was a dream, then I heard the radio going softly and I knew where I was.

The next morning, me and Gerald and Father were down at the shop. Father was working on the tractor again. Gerald was helping by getting the wrenches Father needed. He was bored, and I saw him look toward the top of the hill more than once while we were down there.

Then a pickup turned in the driveway and we all looked up. It was a light blue pickup that squeaked and clattered as it came down the driveway. Dust was rising all behind it. I looked at Gerald, but he was just standing there holding a crescent wrench and watching the truck. One of the gray cats that had been down at the barn ran across the driveway in front of it and I saw the front wheel of the truck hit it. The truck came on down to the shop where we were and stopped. The dust followed it and swirled around us. Father stepped around the tractor and stood with his eyes squinted until the dust passed.

The door of the pickup squeaked open and the man called Wilbur from the top of the next hill got out. I looked back up the driveway. That cat was lying there in the white dust.

"Howdy," Father said. Whenever a stranger came to the house, Father always spoke first. If it was someone he knew, he just looked at them until they said something.

"Mornin'," Wilbur said, walking up to Father. "Name's Wilbur Rutts. Just moved in last week down the road a ways."

"Sure," Father said, shaking his hand. "Been meanin' to get by and say hello, but things kept gettin' in my way. What can I do for you?"

Me and Gerald were still on the other side of the tractor. I stood up and went over to him. My stomach felt cold and I was scared.

"I bet Ruby Lee told on us," I said.

"Shut up. She didn't tell. You don't have to worry about that."

"Well, now," Wilbur said. "Man at the store, crazy-lookin' goddamned son of a bitch—"

"Mr. Norman," Father said. "Good friend of mine."

Wilbur cut Father a look. His hair was long and he needed a shave. His face looked dirty. He was wearing a long-sleeved checked shirt and greasy-looking jeans. His boots were scuffed and the left one had a cut across the toe.

"Yeah, hell. I reckon he's all right. He said you had water over here. Well water."

Father looked over at the windmill for a second, then looked back at Wilbur. "Gettin' mighty low," Father said.

"Hell, I spect so. Anyway, I was wonderin' if maybe I could haul a little of that water up to my place. I got a cistern, but she's drier than Aunt Bessie's cow."

"How much?"

"Hell, I don't know. A hundred gallons or so."

Father looked down, then looked up.

"I can't pay for it," Wilbur said, in a mad sort of way. "If that's what you're thinkin'."

"How about fifty gallons? This time of summer, a hundred at once is too much."

Wilbur looked at Father. "Hell, I guess the old woman can do with fifty for a while."

"You have somethin' to haul it in?"

Wilbur shook his head. "Didn't figure on needin' anything."

"I have a two-hundred gallon tank on a trailer," Father said. "Might be a little rusty inside, but it'll hold water."

"Hell, I'll take it."

For a minute, neither of them said anything. I didn't think Father wanted to give Wilbur the water. I wished he had said no. I didn't like the way Wilbur was talking, either. He wasn't acting like he had that day me and Gerald had been spying on them. Wilbur looked over at the tractor.

"Got problems?" he asked.

Father shrugged. "Been gettin' too hot. Got a water leak around the water pump, but I don't see how it leaks enough to get as hot as it does."

"What's the son of a bitch sound like when you got it runnin'?" Wilbur said, walking over to the tractor and leaning down to look.

"Doesn't sound bad," Father said. "What are you thinkin' about? Bearin's?"

"Hard to say," Wilbur said. While he was talking, his eyes were going from one thing to another like he was counting.

"Can't see replacin' bearin's. Not right now."

Wilbur straightened up and pushed his beat-up old hat back on his head. He looked a lot like the bad guy in a movie we saw one time called *Shane*.

"I know what you mean, goddamn," Wilbur said. "This dry weather is like to break all our asses."

Father looked around Wilbur at me and Gerald. "Yeah," he said. Then he said, "These are my boys, Gerald and Ricky."

Wilbur turned and looked at us. He looked at me for only a second, then he looked at Gerald. When he looked at Gerald, a smile came on his face and he squinted his eyes a little bit.

"Tell you what," Wilbur said, still looking at Gerald. "I could replace them bearin's if that's the problem." He looked at Father.

"Doesn't sound like bearin's to me," Father said.

"They might not be too bad yet. If they was, then shit, your whole engine's liable to be screwed up."

"I'd just have to do without a tractor," Father said.

"I'm talkin' about a deal here," Wilbur said.

Gerald moved around until he was out of the sun. Father was standing by the back wheel of the tractor, wiping his hands on an old piece of shirt.

"I'll work on this tractor for you for forty dollars, no matter what the hell is wrong with it."

"I can work on it myself for nothin'," Father said.

"Huh," Gerald said.

Father looked over at him. He turned and threw the rag on top of the tractor wheel.

"I'll be honest with you, Bud. Me and my fam'ly just moved here and spent all our goddamned cash on the house— and paid too damned much too, I can tell you. That son of a bitch sold us that place must of thought we had money growin' out our asses. I need the work, I tell you."

Father looked at the tractor. Wilbur cut a look at Gerald, then looked back at Father. I tried to know what Father was thinking, but I wasn't sure. He had the same look on his face he had when the sheep were gone.

"I understand all that, Mr. Rutts. But you have to understand that I'm not doin' much better myself just now."

"You mean to tell me with all them fields and shit you got, you can't afford to pay a man a cheap wage to fix your machine? God*damn*. These *are* hard times."

"Let him do it, Father," Gerald said.

Father didn't look at Gerald.

"What can you do without no tractor?" Wilbur said.

Father shook his head.

"Thirty-five, hell," Wilbur said.

After a minute, Father said, "No. Forty is a fair price. If you help me break it down, I'll give you twenty. If it can be fixed without costin' too much in parts, then I reckon you can go ahead."

"Well that would be mighty damned fine with me," Wilbur said, then laughed.

Father shook his hand. Gerald looked over at me with an I-told-you-so look. I just looked back at him. I didn't care what he thought. He was only thinking about Ruby Lee anyway. He didn't care what Father felt about it.

A piece of hair was tickling Rebecca's nose. She reached up and pushed it back behind her ear.

"And then he said that all the dean had to do was to make his recommendations to the president."

"How long does that take?" I asked.

"I don't know. Daddy seemed to think he would know something before the end of the month."

"That's only two weeks."

Rebecca sat back and brought her knees up and wrapped her arms around them. She put her chin on her knees and didn't say anything. We were sitting in the big pipe that went under the road down past Rebecca's house. The creek had been dry for so long that me and Rebecca had started going to the pipe so that we could be by ourselves. It was cool and dark in there and we could almost stand completely up to walk through it. Besides us, only spiders ever came there.

"Maybe he won't get the job," I said, after a while.

"I thought that too. Then when you told me the rabbits died, I knew we were going to move."

"What are you talking about?"

Rebecca looked at me. Behind her I could see out the end of the pipe. The sun was bright on the rocks and dirt of the

creek bed and on the brown and green leaves of the sandbar willows that grew along the creek.

"It was a sign," Rebecca said. "When that little rabbit died, it was a sign that I would have to move."

A car went by over us. The pipe vibrated behind my back. "Maybe not," I said.

Rebecca looked out the end of the pipe. Her hair hid her face from me, but her arms wrapped around her jeans that way looked sad. Ever since her father had started talking about moving away, Rebecca had been hard to talk to. Used to, we could talk about anything for hours, and laugh, too. But now it seemed like there wasn't anything we could say to each other.

"Did I tell you about Gerald?" I asked to change the subject.

Rebecca didn't look at me. "What about him?"

"He's been sneaking off into the pasture to see the girl that moved here."

Rebecca turned and looked at me. "Did you go with him?"

"The first time. He made me go home. Another time I spied on them."

"What were they doing?"

"I don't know. Just talking."

Rebecca looked at her knees. I heard a redwing blackbird nearby. "I saw them at the store the other day. They don't look very nice."

"Gerald thinks they are."

"Do you?"

"No."

I picked up a little stick and drew in the soft dirt with it. Rebecca looked out the end of the pipe. After a while, I wrote Rebecca's name in the dirt with capital letters.

Mr. Ketchum's pickup was parked in front of the store, so I went inside to see him. I liked Mr. Ketchum, even though he was rough and loud. I was curious about him and I liked to watch him.

He was sitting at the table with Mr. Norman. They were talking about things. Mr. Norman had his coffee can on the seat of the chair next to him, and Mr. Ketchum had a beer on the table in front of him.

"Well, looky here," Mr. Ketchum said. "Say, boy, we don't 'low no niggers in here."

"I ain't no nigger," I said.

"Well, be dog. Come over here. You know? I believe he's right."

I started around Mr. Ketchum and he swung a boot out and tripped me. "Damnedest thing about this boy," he said. "Can't stand up. Always fallin' down."

Mr. Ketchum laughed a little and Mr. Norman spit.

"What's your daddy doin'?" Mr. Ketchum asked.

"Working."

"Workin'? What has he got to be doin'? By God, he's the *only* one workin'. What's he doin'?"

"I don't know."

"You ain't hidin' out, are you boy?"

"No sir."

"Well, if you ever have to, come over to my place. Nothin' like havin' an outlaw around the house for pickin' things up durin' a slow time."

Mr. Ketchum laughed and drank down the rest of his beer.

"Want a beer, boy?" he asked.

"No sir."

"Why not?"

"Father doesn't believe in drinking," I said.

"He did the other day."

"He didn't like having to get rid of the sheep."

"Go get you a sody water, Ricky. Don't pay any attention to Elmer. *I* never do," Mr. Norman said and spit.

"By God, old man, you'd better watch yourself. I'm liable to jump over this table and knock you ahead six weeks."

Mr. Norman moved his chew and spit again. "Be one way of findin' out what the weather is goin' to do."

"That ain't no bad idea. I might just do it," Mr. Ketchum said. Then he called to me as I walked away, "Say, boy, bring me another one of them Pearls."

"Okay."

"And don't be drinkin' none of it, neither."

"I won't."

I could hear them go on talking from the end of the store. I went around behind the cooler and pulled the door open. On the bottom shelf were rows of orange Nehi's and 7-Up bottles. The top shelf had some smoked bacon on it. I could smell it when I pulled open the door. I got an orange Nehi and one of the Pearl beers and opened them. For a minute I thought about sipping the Pearl, but I didn't. I carried it to Mr. Ketchum.

"Thanks, boy. I didn't think you'd *ever* get back."

"I'll put a nickel in the register," I said to Mr. Norman.

"Here," Mr. Ketchum said. "Put this nickel in there."

He dug in his pocket and pulled out a nickel and threw it to me. I was holding my orange in my right hand and tried to catch the nickel in my left hand. I missed it and it rolled away along the floor.

"Good kid, but mighty careless with money," Mr. Ketchum said.

I found the nickel and went over to the cash register. Out the side door, I saw Wilbur coming down the road in his truck. He wasn't working for Father yet. He told him he wouldn't be able to start until Wednesday. I didn't care if he never started. I turned and punched the five cent button and pulled down on the crank. The drawer slid out. I looked around, then dropped my nickel in and pushed the drawer back.

Mr. Ketchum was laughing real loud about something, then I heard him say, "By God. What was that?"

I walked up toward the front of the store. Mr. Ketchum was sitting up straight and looking out the front door.

"Eh?" Mr. Norman said, leaning forward.

Just then, Wilbur stepped up to the screen door and pulled it open. It was darker in the store and, for a minute, all we could see was his dark outline. He seemed taller to me. I stepped over to the table and waited. Mr. Norman stood up.

"Yes sir?" he asked.

Wilbur's boots sounded loud on the floor as he walked by us. Mr. Ketchum swiveled around and said, "Say, neighbor, what was that noise outside just now?"

"I ain't your neighbor," Wilbur said. "Old timer, I need a goddamned loaf of bread."

I looked at Mr. Ketchum. His face was turning red. His eyes were big and his lips were pushed together. He still had a little scab on his bottom lip from fighting that German.

"Listen, fella," Mr. Ketchum said. "You're new around here, so I'll take it easy. But I asked you a question."

"I ain't new anyplace," Wilbur said. He didn't look around at Mr. Ketchum. He went to the shelf and got himself a loaf of Butter Krust bread and took it over to the counter.

Mr. Norman was hurrying over there with his can. Mr. Norman always wore long-sleeved shirts with the cuffs buttoned. His shirt was white and wrinkled in the back. I looked at Mr. Ketchum. He was still staring at Wilbur. Then he got up all of a sudden, leaving his beer sitting on the table. He went to the front door and shoved the screen open so hard that it slammed shut after he had stepped through it. It slammed shut and bounced three times.

"How much?" Wilbur said.

"Twenty-five cents," Mr. Norman said.

"Twenty-five cents, hell. It don't cost that much in town."

"Go to town then."

"Why you old son of a bitch. You can't cheat people just because your store's stuck way out here all by itself. I'll give you fifteen cents and you can take it or leave it."

The screen door banged shut again and I turned to see Mr. Ketchum walking back in. He was taking big steps and he was looking nowhere but at Wilbur.

"Hey, there, you goddamned cedar chopper," Mr. Ketchum said.

Mr. Norman looked old and skinny behind the counter. He caught my eyes and nodded his head toward the door, but I didn't want to leave just then.

"What the hell you call me?" Wilbur said, turning. His voice sounded like a snake's hiss.

"You ran into the side of my truck out there," Mr. Ketchum said. He walked right up to Wilbur. Wilbur still had one hand on the counter.

"What are you talkin' about?" Wilbur said.

"You done scratched up the side of my truck, that's what the hell I'm talkin' about."

"Well, you're a goddamned liar," Wilbur said.

Then, quick as that, Mr. Ketchum reached over and grabbed the poker propped against the wood heater and raised it and swung it down on Wilbur's head with a sound like dropping a bale of hay on the barn floor. Wilbur flew back against the counter and his hat rolled down his chest to the floor and

Wilbur fell on it. Mr. Ketchum stood with his legs apart look-ing down at him.

"Shit," he said. "Come see if I killed him."

Mr. Norman came around the counter and knelt down. I was thinking I had never seen a man killed before. I was a little afraid Mr. Ketchum would turn and try to hit me, but I was too scared to move.

"No sir. He ain't dead. Just out cold."

"I could just as well have killed him," Mr. Ketchum said.

Mr. Norman stood up. They both looked down at Wilbur.

"Probably should have," Mr. Norman said. "Somebody's goin' to have to do it someday. He'll have a good-sized pump knot when he wakes up, but I'll wager it won't be the first he ever had."

Mr. Ketchum put the poker back by the heater. He didn't set it up straight and it slid along the edge of the heater and clanged to the floor. I looked at it and shivered.

"Be better if you weren't here when he comes to," Mr. Norman said.

"For him," Mr. Ketchum said.

"For me," Mr. Norman said. "I don't want no killin' in my store."

"All right," Mr. Ketchum said. He turned and walked by me without even looking at me and went out the front door. I heard him get in his truck and start it up, then I heard the sound of his tires on the gravel.

I walked over to Mr. Norman and stood by him, looking down at Wilbur. A thin line of blood was running out of his hair and down past his ear. I shivered again.

"Mr. Ketchum left his beer," I said.

"Go on home," Mr. Norman said.

I looked at Mr. Norman, then turned around to leave. When I got to the door, I heard him say, "Hey you." I turned around and saw him. He was kneeling beside Wilbur again.

After supper I followed Father down to the windmill. It was down past the barn and over to the side of the pen where we had loaded the sheep. The sun was going down behind some dark clouds in the west, and the wind was blowing more than usual.

Father slid the heavy concrete lid over to one side and we looked in. The water was way down in the bottom of the well. I could see our heads reflected in the water, and, behind our heads, some high pink clouds.

"I see the water," I said.

"What there is of it," Father said.

He stood up straight and looked up at the fan. It was turning pretty fast in the wind and squeaking.

"Wouldn't hurt to grease the gears up there," Father said. Then he said, "I guess I'll get around to it one of these days."

"Do you think the well will go dry?"

"It might."

Father slid the lid shut again and we stood by the windmill looking at the sky. The day had a good feel to it, but I wasn't happy.

"Looks like it might rain, doesn't it?" I said.

"Yeah. It might."

"That would be good," I said. "I don't remember when it rained last."

Father looked down at me. He took a cigar out of his pocket and unwrapped it. He looked at it a minute, then put it in his mouth.

"Been too dry ever since you were old enough to remember *any*thing," he said.

"I remember lots of times when it rained," I said.

"Yeah. It's rained, all right. Showers."

"They help, don't they?"

"Sometimes. Depends on when and how much."

Father lit his cigar and we stood looking around at the sky.

"If it rains tonight, it'll help a bunch, I bet."

"Be better than nothin'," Father said, blowing smoke out.

For a while we didn't say anything. The clouds rolled and changed while we watched them and the sun went down.

"You ever think about livin' in town?" Father asked.

"No sir."

"I have. I've thought about it a lot. I've lived and worked out here all my life and look at what I've got."

"What's wrong with it?"

Father was quiet a while, puffing on his cigar. Then he took his cigar out of his mouth and spit.

"Nothin' is, I guess," he said. "I just get tired sometimes."

"So do I," I said.

Father looked at me for a minute, then he smiled. A cow bawled and a bobwhite answered.

The thunder woke me up. I rolled over and saw a streak of lightning, and it scared me. Then I knew what was going on and I rolled on my side away from the window. It wasn't raining yet, but there was plenty of lightning and thunder and the wind was blowing. I tried to go back to sleep, but I had to go to the bathroom.

I rolled over. The wind was coming in the window and going out again, sucking the screen in and out each time it passed. When it came in, it whistled like a water kettle. In the next flash of lightning, I saw Gerald's shoulder half under the sheet with the rip in it. The rip had been mended with part of an old rag sheet, and the long patch looked like a centipede made out of flour. Gerald was sound asleep.

I needed to pee harder when I sat up. The hall was long and dark and quiet. A gust of wind hit the elm tree and swashed through the limbs. Thunder rumbled and the screen was sucked in with a *tump* and the wind began to whistle.

Finally I stood up, trying to see into the darkness of the hall. When lightning flashed, I could see flickers from the open door of Carol's room and from the little windows on the landing of the stairs where the stairs made a turn. I walked out the door, feeling along the wall until I got to the stairs. The breeze was chilly on my back and legs. Lightning flashed when I reached the landing. In the light I could see strange shapes in the back yard that I didn't remember ever being there. The shapes made me think of strange humped animals like armadillos, only much larger, out in the yard waiting for someone to come along.

I ran down the last steps with my hand along the wall. In the bathroom, I sat down so as to make as little noise as possible. I sat looking at the lightning through the bathroom window. When I was through, I stood up and started to flush the commode, but I knew that would wake Mama up so I didn't.

Thunder rumbled as I hurried around the corner of the stairs. I tried not to look out the windows, but I did anyway. The shapes were still there.

"Who is that?"

I froze outside of Carol's door until I knew it was her voice.

"Ricky, is that you?"

"I had to go to the bathroom."

I was standing outside her door. Lightning flashed, but her bed was in shadow along the wall away from the windows. I heard the sheets move, then the springs squeaked.

"Ricky."

"It's me, Carol. I had to—"

"Could you come in here a minute?"

I walked into her room and could smell her. It was dark. Carol's room made the thunder seem louder because it was a big room with a high ceiling. When lightning flashed again I could see the outlines of the windows and the narrow curtains Carol had made lifted out and away from the outlines like the arms of ghosts. The cool air made me shiver like I was scared. I stopped at the end of her bed. She was a darker place on the white sheets.

"Where are you?"

"I'm right here," I said. "Do you want me to turn on the light?"

Lightning flashed and she saw me. I could hear her breathing. She began to scare me.

"What is it?" I asked. I was whispering.

"Will you close my windows?"

"Okay."

I stepped around the bed and went to the windows. I stood on tiptoe and grabbed the bottom of the first window and pulled down. The wind blew the curtains out. I tried not to let them touch me. Lightning streaked down and I could see the driveway and the road and way across the hill to where the clouds were dark. The curtains touched my arm and I twisted away, shivering.

"What's the matter?" Carol asked, watching me.

"Nothing."

I pulled the other window down and looked at the closet door. It wasn't closed all the way. Gerald used to tell stories about monsters that lived in closets. I didn't like closets at night.

"Ricky?"

"Yeah."

I heard her move on the bed again. The springs under the old cotton mattress were old and loose. Sometimes Carol would knock one out from under her bed when she was sweeping. Me and Gerald used to save them and tie them to our tennis shoes so that we could jump over fences with a single bound, but they never worked right. They always twisted away and finally bent.

"Come get in bed."

I went over and caught the sheet and sat down on the edge of the bed. I swung in and stretched on my back. Carol had moved over to the other side of the bed. My head was down flat on the mattress. It felt funny. I thought about going to get my pillow.

Carol was leaning up on one elbow, facing me. She smelled nice and not sweaty at all. I began to feel warmer.

"What's wrong?" I said.

Carol didn't answer. She was still leaning up on one elbow. Her hair fell down around her shoulders. I could just barely see it, like the end of a rainbow. I heard her hand on the sheets, then felt it on my arm. Her soft fingers curled loosely around my muscle. I felt them tighten and she pulled me closer to her where her smell was warm, like leaning my nose over a gas heater and smelling the burned butane and feeling the hot smell all over my face. I slid over until I was touching her legs and her stomach, and her hand was still tight on my arm. I rolled over on my side facing away from her. She didn't say anything, but I felt her ease down onto the bed and then her pillow slid toward me until I had something to lie on. I hated to sleep without a pillow.

Lightning flashed and I counted five before I heard the thunder. It was getting closer, but the rain had not started. The thunder sounded farther away with the windows closed. The air in the room became still.

"Are you all right?" Carol asked.

"Sure," I said. "Are you?"

She didn't say anything. I started to roll over and try to see if she was crying, but her grip on my arm tightened when I tried to move. Carol had strong hands. I lay back down, trying not to look at the closet door. Gerald said one time that closet doors led straight to hell at night, and that if you didn't keep them closed, all the demons would come out in the dark.

Carol got closer to me from behind and she let her arm fall across my chest like she was hugging me. I could feel her cheek against my head and her breath was warm. Her legs found mine and pressed along them, smooth as her nightgown all the way down past my feet. Carol had long legs.

"Did the thunder scare you, Carol?" I asked.

Just then it began to rain really hard on the tin roof. I thought about our open window, but I knew Gerald would close it and the screen wouldn't go tump and whistle anymore.

Carol didn't answer. I was beginning to sweat where she was touching me. I thought about one of the times when I was smaller and the owl from the barn would come and sit on the peak of the roof and hoot. The sound would be so close that it would seem like it was under the bed. It would scare me so bad that I would wake Gerald up and he would cuss and bang on the wall, trying to make the owl go away so that he could get some sleep, but he would be scared too. The noise would wake Carol up and she would come into the room with her nightgown on and hear me crying and sit on the edge of my bed and shake my shoulder. Gerald would get out of bed and come across and sit on mine by Carol and he would whisper, "It's the owl."

Carol would say, "Of course it is."

"I don't like it, Carol," I would say. "Make it go away."

"If I had Father's gun, I would shoot it," Gerald would say, sitting close to Carol's shoulder.

"Would you rather have rats and mice all over the place?" Carol would ask in her flat voice that Mama used whenever she was tired of messing with us.

"Oh no," I would say because I was so little and stupid.

Carol would shake my shoulder and say, "Don't worry about it. The owl is only telling other owls that this is his home and that he thinks it is a nice home because of us. He wants the other owls to know it."

"Can owls really talk?" I would say, feeling better.

"Crap," Gerald would say, trying to sound like Father.

"You just cut that out this minute, young man," Carol would say, turning so fast on Gerald that her yellow hair would blur in the light. Gerald would crouch lower on the bed and look away. His hand would touch the edge of Carol's gown and she would know that he was just being Gerald. She would put her arm around his hard shoulders with her other hand still on mine. I would always be asleep before she left, and in the morning, the first thing I would remember was the yellow blur of her hair above me.

When the rain hit the window glass, it made a rattle sound. The room began to fill with the smell of the rain and of Carol and her breath. I was getting warm and sleepy. Carol's fingers stretched off my shoulder and settled there again. She lifted her cheek and shook back her hair, then lowered it again. The thunder was too fast to count, as close as the mailbox.

"It's just rain," I said, but I couldn't hear myself, so I said it again, louder.

"I know," Carol whispered, very close to my ear.

"I knew it was going to rain tonight," I said.

Carol shuddered really hard and hugged me tighter and let me go a little, then slid her head down and kissed my shoulder where her hand had been.

"How did you know that?" Carol said after a while. The wind was blowing rain against the windows. Mixed in with the smell of the rain was the smell of dust.

"Father said it might."

"Father wants it to so bad."

Carol moved her head again. I felt her take a deep breath,

like a yawn, and it left her very still. I felt her bosoms push against my back and they were as soft as her legs. Once, a long time ago, she had let me touch them. We were riding in the back of the station wagon, lying down behind the seat. We were going to the coast. Carol was facing me, lying on her side, with her hair spread out like sunshine on the old quilt. I was lying with my head near the wheel hump and I could hear the sound of the tires on the road and feel it in my ear. Every time I closed my eyes, Carol reached over and poked my ribs to wake me up. It hurt sometimes, but she would laugh. Then she would close her eyes and I would poke her. She was wearing a blue shirt and the top two buttons had come undone. I could see the round tops of her bosoms and the lacy white bra she wore. She saw that I was looking and her whole face changed. She looked into my eyes and then reached over and caught my right hand and put it inside her shirt over her bosom and pressed it there.

"That is where my heart is," she said, looking into my eyes, whispering close to me with the road noises in the other ear. She took my hand away and I watched her redo the buttons. We both lay on our sides watching each other. Then she smiled and I went to sleep with the road noises in my ear.

When the lightning flashed, I thought I saw the closet door move. Carol never should have gone to bed with it open.

"Are you asleep, Carol?"

"No. Are you?"

"No," I said, then I knew she was teasing me. That made me feel better. "Did the rain scare you?" I asked.

She was quiet so long that I started to roll over to look at her.

"Yes."

"Why did it scare you?"

"I don't know."

"It never did before," I said, remembering all the times I had run to get in bed with her. Gerald used to come too, and lying on either side of Carol we would talk. Gerald would make up crazy stories to make Carol laugh, and I would listen with my eyes closed tight. I could still see the lightning on my eyelids. Then one time, two years ago, I had run into Carol's room and Gerald had followed, walking. When we were in Carol's bed, it wasn't the same. Gerald lay on the very edge of the bed, not touching Carol, and all the muscles in Carol's arms and legs were straight and hard like she was lifting something heavy. For a while none of us said anything.

Then Gerald said, "This is stupid." He got out of her bed and went to the door. Carol called to him. In the lightning, I could see him standing there in his underwear. "What?" he said. Carol never answered him, and after a second he went back to our room. I felt Carol's muscles soften, but she still didn't say anything. Then she turned and kissed me and told me to go back to bed. I went, but that night the lightning and thunder had scared me more than they ever had before.

"The rain never scared you before," I said.

"How do you know?" she said.

"You never acted like it did."

"Maybe I'm a good actress."

"I would know it if you were acting," I said, not really knowing how I would know.

"It's not the rain," she said then.

I was scared again and looked at the closet door.

"Was it the thunder?" I asked.

"No."

"Did you have a bad dream?"

"You're asking too many questions," she said like she was getting mad. "I hate it when you ask so many questions."

I was quiet, feeling bad.

"Ricky?"

I didn't answer. Her head moved down to my shoulder again.

"Don't sulk," she said.

"I'm not."

"You're too old to sulk."

"I said I wasn't."

"It's what a baby would do," she said, keeping on.

I moved away a little. My shoulder felt cold where she had

been touching me. It was raining hard and thundering and lightning. She didn't have to keep on after I told her I wasn't sulking.

"I'm sorry," she said, after a while.

I was trying not to look at the closet door. "You didn't have to keep on," I said.

"I know. I'm sorry."

"I don't like you when you're like this," I said, to make her feel bad.

"I don't like me like this either," she said.

"I didn't mean it," I said.

"Yes you did. I don't blame you."

"I didn't."

"It doesn't matter."

"I like you just fine," I said. "But sometimes I don't know what's going on."

"You're not supposed to."

"Why not?"

"Don't start asking questions again."

"Do you feel bad?"

"Not really."

"But a little?"

"Yes."

"Are you sick?"

"No."

"Then what is it?"

"Ricky," she said, but softer this time, as if she wanted my attention to tell me something I had to listen to very closely. I barely heard her say it.

"What?" I said.

"Please, please, *please,* don't ask so many questions."

"I only want you to be all right," I said, trying not to sulk.

"I know, Ricky."

I was quiet, listening to the rain. The wind was still blowing hard like the time me and Gerald had been down in the pasture climbing the tall willow that grew next to the tank. The storm had come up so fast that the wind was blowing hard before we could get down out of the tree. I was higher up than Gerald because I was lighter, and when the wind hit, the limb began to sway back and forth and I closed my eyes and hung on, too scared to let go. I could hear Gerald down behind me hollering for me to come down, then the lightning flashed and the thunder boomed. The next thing I knew, Gerald was right behind me, higher up than he should have been, and he grabbed the back of my pants and yanked so hard that I had to let go, sliding backwards down into his arms. When we were on the ground and cold and wet, Gerald pushed me up against the fence and hit the side of my head with his fist.

"You're shaking," Carol said.

"No, I'm not."

"Are you cold?"

"No," I said, shutting my eyes tight, but not very sleepy any more.

I could feel Carol's chin on my shoulder by my neck. Her face was always soft. She didn't have any of the bumps that Gerald did. Gerald didn't use to have them either. Mama told him it was because he didn't wash his face, but Gerald thought that was baloney. He made pooty noises whenever she told him that.

"You're not scared, are you?" Carol asked.

"No," I said, opening my eyes and looking at the closet door.

"Do you want to go back to your own bed?"

I started to answer, but I felt Carol move suddenly behind me. Her arm and hand grew tight and hard and I knew she was holding her breath. Then she let her breath out and her arm and hand relaxed.

"What is it?" I asked.

"Nothing, Ricky," she said, but I knew because she said my name that something was wrong.

"Do you hurt, Carol?" I asked, saying her name so that she would tell me the truth.

"Yes."

"Where?"

"Only a little."

"Where?" I asked, trying to turn, but she held me still. I lay listening to the rain a while and Carol started breathing easier. When she had held me down, I heard her voice in her breath.

"My stomach," she said finally.

I looked straight ahead at the closet door. My shoulder was starting to hurt, but I didn't want to move away. I shifted my eyes from the closet door to Carol's dresser.

"Did you eat too much squash?"

"I wish that was all it was," she said.

"What do you mean?"

"I would be all right sooner," she said, but not really to me. I barely heard her.

"Are you sick?" I asked, worried, thinking of the time I had the measles and it snowed for the first time in my life, but Mama wouldn't let me look at it because she said the bright sun on the snow would make me go blind.

"No," Carol said when a roll of thunder died down. It wasn't raining very hard now, but sometimes the wind blew hard rain against the window and the window rattled and bumped.

"Why does your stomach hurt?"

"I think you can go back to bed now, Ricky. Thanks for coming in."

"Wait a minute," I said. "I want to know."

"No you don't," Carol squeezed my shoulder.

"Stop doing that," I said.

Carol pulled her arm away and moved over in the bed and that whole side of me was as cold as ice. I turned over on my back and needles ran up and down my arm.

"Carol?"

"Just go, Ricky."

"I'm sorry," I said.

She was still and quiet.

"I'm sorry, Carol," I said again. I was feeling strange. I

looked over at the closet door. A flash of lightning seemed to make it move.

"Carol?" I whined a little bit.

"Please don't do that," Carol said, quietly.

"But I want to know what's wrong."

"You wouldn't understand."

"You're scaring me."

"I could scare you more, don't you see?" she said, turning her head toward me. Her face was pale as her hair in the dark.

"Now I'm really scared," I said.

"See."

"Are you going to die?"

Then Carol started crying. I felt like crying too, but I didn't. I just lay there beside Carol waiting for her to stop.

"I wish I hadn't called you in here," she said. "But it was so bad this time. And the rain and all after so long."

"But the rain will help," I said.

"Not this kind of rain," Carol cried. "It will just be enough to raise Father's hopes, but it won't do any good. I think he knows deep down that it won't do any good. But it's not even that. It's just everything, don't you see?" Carol cried. "I don't know anymore what I should think or do. I always end up fighting with Mama and I don't mean to. I want to help so bad, but nothing I do seems to be the right thing."

"You always do the right thing, Carol."

"No I don't. I want to, but everything is changing so much. I feel like I don't belong here any more, yet I don't know where I do belong."

I was quiet. The wind was blowing outside. Carol wasn't crying loud or anything, but I knew she was still crying. I felt as if something had come out of the closet into Carol's room, but I didn't dare turn my head to look.

"I think I must be going crazy," Carol cried. "I say things I don't mean to say and do things I don't even want to do. Sometimes I just want to run away. Everyone would be better off if I did."

"You belong here," I said. "Always."

"Oh Ricky, Ricky," she said.

After a while I said, "I hope you feel better."

Carol stopped crying. She was lying very still. "I will in a little while," she said.

The wind was blowing. I listened for rain, but I only heard a few drops every now and then.

"God," Carol said. Then she said, "Will you go back to your own room now?"

"Will you be all right?"

"Yes."

"Will you tell me what it is?"

Carol was quiet for a while. "Remember last month when you and Gerald were swimming in the tank and you wanted me to come in too, and I told you I couldn't?"

"Yeah."

"And remember later I slapped Gerald so hard his eyes started to water?"

"He wasn't even doing anything for a change."

"I know."

"I remember," I said.

Carol was quiet. Then she said, "Ricky, you know how boys and girls are different?"

"Yeah."

"Well—" and then she stopped. She started again. "Sometimes, pretty often," she said slowly, just above the noise of the wind, "girls, being different from boys, start to hurt inside. It's nothing really bad, but it makes a girl remember that she is a girl. And then she feels all sorts of feelings from sad to mean, and she does strange things, like those things I told you about."

"Why?" I asked.

"Because, well, there's a time every so often when a girl needs to be noticed by a boy, you know, to take care of her. It's so everyone will remember what their part is. Sometimes girls forget and sometimes boys don't remember. And sometimes a girl just needs to be taken care of so she doesn't hurt so bad."

"Like tonight?"

"Yes."

I was quiet and sleepy again. "I'm sorry I was mean to you a while ago," I said.

"You were nice to come in at all," Carol said. "But now I feel very sleepy and I think you'd better go back to bed."

She raised up on one elbow and bent over me. Her hair surrounded my face. She leaned down and kissed my nose. When she raised up again, the wind was softer.

"Goodnight," she said. "My little love."

I looked at her for a minute, then I sat up and got out of bed. I heard her lying back down. The sound was soft in the room. The smell of the rain was mixed in with Carol's smell. Before I left, I went over and closed the closet door.

Dust to Dust

THE FIRST THING I did was look out the window. Except for a few leaves and dead limbs in the yard, everything looked the same. I got up and got dressed and went down to Carol's room, but she was already up again. When I got down to the kitchen, Gerald was straining the milk.

"Is that all she had?" Mama asked.

"She's goin' dry, I keep tellin' you," Gerald said.

I went through the kitchen to the dining room. Father was eating his breakfast. So was Carol. I slid into my seat and Father watched me.

"Not late today," I said.

"Humph," Father said, chewing. I looked over at Carol and she smiled at me. I picked up my fork to cut my eggs.

"Guess what?" Carol said, still smiling. I thought she was probably the prettiest girl in the world just then.

"What?" I said.

"I got the job."

I put my fork down and looked at my half-cut egg. I looked up at Carol. She was still smiling.

"When?" I said.

"They called this morning. I'm starting today."

I looked over at Father. He was watching me. He was shaved and wearing his good shirt.

"Guess what," he said, using the same tone Carol had used.

I looked at him.

"It rained last night," he said.

193

"Did it do any good?"

"Nope."

I looked over at Carol. She wasn't smiling any more.

Carol took the station wagon into town right after breakfast. I went around to the front porch to watch her leave. When she passed the elm tree, she waved. I just looked at her.

"Ricky!" Father called.

I jumped off the porch and ran around to the back. Father was standing on the back steps looking around.

"Yes sir?"

"I'm goin' into town to see Papa."

"Okay," I said.

"No. Listen. He hasn't been feeling too well. Do you understand?"

I thought about what Carol had said the other day about Grandfather. "Yes sir."

"If Mr. Rutts comes today to start work on the tractor, you or Gerald show him where the tools are."

I thought about telling Father about what Mr. Ketchum had done to Wilbur, but I knew Father was in a hurry.

"Yes sir."

Father straightened his hat. "And it wouldn't hurt to stick around and help him, if you aren't too busy."

"All right," I said.

Father stepped off the porch and went to his pickup and got in. He slammed the door, then sat there a minute while he unwrapped a new cigar. He put the cigar in his mouth and started up the truck. As he put it in reverse he looked at me. Then he backed around and left. The driveway was already turning to dust again.

I waited all morning for Wilbur to come, but he didn't. Gerald stayed out of sight until almost dinner time, then he showed up chewing on his bottom lip. I asked him where he had been and he looked at me like I was a dishrag.

"Thinkin'," was all he said.

Then, about one o'clock, a man drove up in a shiny new

Ford pickup. We all looked out the window, but none of us knew who it was. Mama told Gerald to go see what the man wanted. I went along too. When we got out there, the man was closing the door of his truck.

"Howdy," Gerald said, speaking first like Father did when a stranger came to the house. "Can I help you?"

"Is your name MacAllister?" the man said.

"Yes sir."

"Is your father around?"

"Not right now," Gerald said.

The man pushed his hat back on his head. He was tall and thin and slow talking. He was wearing a gray khaki shirt and gray khaki pants and he had about six pens in his shirt pocket.

"Do you know when he'll be back?" the man asked.

"Not really," Gerald said.

"He's gone into town," I said.

"That right? Well, will you tell him that Ben Madden from the Texas Farm Bureau stopped by. I sure would like to get in touch with him."

"All right," Gerald said.

The man started to say something else, but we heard a truck and looked to see Father turning into the driveway. He was driving slowly with his arm sticking out the window. When he passed us, he looked at the man and his truck, then turned his head straight until he stopped. Dust rose and fell. Father got out and walked over.

"Howdy," he said.

The man stepped forward to shake Father's hand. Father was chewing on a cigar like always, but something looked different about him. He was holding himself taller than usual or something.

"Mr. MacAllister? My name's Ben Madden. I'm from the Farm Bureau, and I'd like to talk to you just a minute if I might."

"Go ahead," Father said. Since he had walked up, he hadn't looked at me or Gerald.

"Mr. MacAllister, I represent the Farm Bureau in its efforts as a member of the Texas Drought Emergency Committee. We're holding a final hearing in Austin all next week in an attempt to obtain agricultural relief for farmers like yourself who have been hit hard by this drought. This relief will be in the form of low-interest loans and so on, that is, if we can convince Washington that most of this state could qualify as a disaster area."

Mr. Madden paused and Father switched the cigar from one side of his mouth to the other. "Go on."

"Well, Mr. MacAllister, myself and other representatives like me are trying to enlist the aid of farmers like yourself in this area, who would be willing to go up to Austin and speak on behalf of the committee, to give, in other words, their testimony as to the extent of hardship this drought is putting on us all."

"I see," Father said.

"Well, we would like you to speak for us as one of the more respected farmers in Guadalupe County. We would also like to invite your father, who, I understand, started this farm before the turn of the century."

For the first time Father looked over at us. He took the cigar out of his mouth and shook his head. He started to say something, then shook his head again.

"I'm afraid that won't be possible," he said, finally. "My father had a major stroke this morning. I don't reckon he'll be speaking anywhere again."

Mama sat down at the table when Father told her the news. Father sat down too. Gerald sat on the arm of the green chair in the living room and I stood by the table.

"Does Carol know?" Mama asked, after a while.

"I stopped by the store and told her," Father said. "I would have called, but, I don't know."

"Her first day at work," Mama said. "Well, what is she going to do?"

Father took his hat off and put it on the table. He blew out a heavy breath. "I told her just to stay until time to get off. That would be the best thing, seemed to me. Then she can take the station wagon over to Mother's and we can meet her there."

"That will help her get through the day," Mama said. "How is your mother taking it?"

Father shrugged.

"And you?" Mama said, softer.

I looked at Father. The muscles in his jaw were working and he was looking at his hat on the table. He nodded his head.

"Well, we'd better go ahead and get ready to go in. What did the doctors tell you?"

"He might regain consciousness, but they doubt it."

Mama shook her head. "I knew when your mother called this morning that he sounded awfully sick. Well, let's go. Boys, y'all get in the bathroom and get cleaned up. Even if we don't go to the hospital, I don't want you looking like beggars."

Gerald got up and went down the hall. Mama looked at me.

"Well?" she said.

I started to say something, then I looked at Father. He was looking down at his hat and tracing a fine layer of dust around the brim.

Carol was already there when we got to Grandmother's. Father looked hard at her.

"I took a late lunch break," she said. "I'm going right back."

Grandmother didn't act very glad to see us. She was wearing the same dress she had worn to church the other day and there were lines in the heavy powder on her face where she had been crying. Right away, she started saying stuff about how messy the house looked and stuff like that. Father patted her on the shoulder once, then sat down and let Mama do all the talking. Me and Gerald had to just sit on the couch and listen to all of it.

"I'm sure it doesn't matter what the house looks like right now," Mama was saying.

"I just didn't have time to get it cleaned the way it should be. I kept telling Wesley he'd best go to the doctor. If he had been more careful, it wouldn't have happened so sudden like this. But what could I do? I kept telling him to go to the doctor, but he wouldn't hear of it. So here we are."

"I'm sure he never thought this would happen," Mama said.

"It's so like him," Grandmother said, dabbing at her eyes. "He only thinks about himself, never gives any thought to anybody else."

Father pulled a cigar out of his pocket and unwrapped it and put it in his mouth. He put the paper in his shirt pocket. Right then, I wished I had a cigar myself.

When Carol got off work, we all ate something that Mama had made. Then Mama and Carol and Grandmother got in the station wagon and me and Gerald and Father got in Father's truck. On the way out to the hospital, Father didn't talk at all. He struck a match and lit his cigar and smoked.

I had never been in a hospital before except to be born. I didn't like the way it smelled when we went inside. It smelled the way the doctor's office did when he was giving polio shots.

"Down here," Father said.

Mama stopped and said, "What about Ricky?"

"What about him?" Father said.

Mama pointed to a sign that said no one under twelve was allowed past that point.

"He can't read," Father said. "Come on."

We went quietly down the hall. Some of the doors were open and people were lying in beds with all kinds of stuff around them. A nurse passed us in a white uniform. She had very black hair. Her shoes squeaked on the floor.

When we got to Grandfather's room we stopped. Father took Grandmother's arm and led her into the room. I didn't look up until the door swished shut. Mama turned on all of us.

"Listen," she whispered. "We are just going in for a second, then we're coming right back out again. I want you boys to be very quiet and not to ask questions. Carol, I don't want to see you crying until after we leave. Understand?"

Carol nodded her head and Mama looked at us. I nodded my head and Gerald shrugged.

In a minute, Father came to the door and opened it for us.

Mama pushed us in and followed with Carol. Grandfather was lying on a high bed with his arms on the sheet. His eyes were closed and a tube was running out of his mouth. Another tube ran down from a bottle to his arm. Grandmother was sitting across from us. Carol went to the side of the bed and looked at Grandfather. I looked at Carol's back. Her pretty shoulders were slumped a little like she was tired and her hair lay like gold on her collar. Her left leg was bent and the heel of her shoe was in the air. Gerald was staring at Grandfather like he expected him to open his eyes and say something.

After a while we left. Nobody said anything, not even the nurse at the end of the hall who held the door open for us.

Mr. Ketchum's pickup was in front of the house when we got home that night. Carol stayed in town with Grandmother and kept the station wagon, so me and Gerald had to ride in the back of the pickup. On the way home I looked at the stars and tried to say a prayer for Grandfather. Gerald just sat with his back up against the cab not saying anything. I wanted him to say something, but he didn't. He just sat there with his back to the cab chewing on his bottom lip.

Mr. Ketchum walked over to us when we stopped. Then I saw Mrs. Ketchum was with him. She was walking behind him like a shadow. She wasn't very tall and was thin and worried-looking. Mama said one time that she was an orphan who had been raised by nuns in Kansas and that was probably why she seemed a little strange to people. I liked her because whenever we went fishing down by her house, she gave us cookies and a glass of water before we started home.

"Hello, Mac, Jean," Mr. Ketchum said. "I hope we ain't just steppin' in without an invitation, but we heard about Mr. Wesley and thought we'd come by."

"How is he, Mac?" Mrs. Ketchum asked.

"Not too good," Father said, unwrapping another cigar. "The doctors don't expect much."

"Come on inside, Ida," Mama said. "I think I'll put on a pot of coffee."

Mama and Mrs. Ketchum went in the house. Gerald

jumped out of the truck and stood by it watching Mr. Ket-chum. I climbed up on the side and just sat there. Lights came on in the house. Father lit his cigar. Sometimes, smelling that cigar was like hearing Father's voice.

"Hell of a thing," Mr. Ketchum said.

"He had a good life," Father said.

"He was always one of those who would do anything in the world for anybody, but wouldn't take no crap, either. He'd do it himself if he didn't think anybody else could do it. Hell, I remember him nailin' tin on that shop there when he was near to seventy. Remember that time you were laid up?"

"I remember."

"I come by and he was up there nailin' tin and Mex'cans standin' all around watchin' him. I told him to let some of them have a chance and all he said was, 'They'd mess it up.' And I remember that time he like to beat a Mex'can to death with a hoe handle. They were out choppin' and that Mex'can give him some hard talk and finally Mr. Wesley went after him with that hoe handle."

Mr. Ketchum laughed, and Father blew smoke out.

"That's the kind of man he was, all right," Mr. Ketchum said. "When it come time to do somethin', he did it. Yeah. Always hurts to lose a good man."

They stood by the truck a while. I was starting to feel pretty sad. Gerald kicked at rocks with his shoes.

"Fella named Madden stop by today?" Mr. Ketchum asked.

"Yeah."

"Stopped by my place too. That's when I heard."

"What did you tell him?"

"I told him I didn't think I'd have the time."

"What's got you so busy?" Father asked.

"Plowin'."

"Plowin'! You mean you're turnin' under your cotton?"

"Yeah, hell, Mac. I didn't want to, but that shower last night kinda finished me off. We didn't have no more than an inch and a half penetration. Under that, it's dry as hell, and the top is dry again already by tonight."

"The Soil Bank, huh?"

"Yes sir. Signed up for three years. Next spring all them fields is goin' to coastal."

Father was quiet a minute. "Well, I don't blame you," he said.

"You ought to think about it yourself, Mac. Ain't no use in bein' stubborn just because. Hell, I know you're hurtin'. We all are. All you'd be doin' is lettin' that land rest for a few years. Hell, it's got to go to rainin' sometime. When it does, you can put those fields back in cultivation or just graze 'em out."

"I don't know, Elmer. The cotton looks good."

"Sure it does. It looks damned good. But June ain't over yet. How you think that cotton is goin' to look by the end of July?"

"I don't know," Father said.

"I don't either," Mr. Ketchum said. "Damn. Look at me actin' like I got all the answers."

Mr. Ketchum shook his head. Father smoked. The night was dark and quiet around us. Gerald kicked a rock that hit the hub cap on Father's truck with a clang. We all looked at him.

"What the hell makes you so mean, anyway?" Mr. Ketchum asked Gerald.

Mama called from the house to say the coffee was ready.

The next morning I went down to see Rebecca. Gerald was supposed to stay around the house in case Wilbur came by. Father and Mama went in early to stay with Grandmother. Grandmother had two sisters but they both lived in El Paso and nobody knew whether they were going to come down or not.

At the top of the hill, I stopped and watched Mr. Ketchum's tractor plowing through his first field of cotton. He had four sweeps behind the tractor and they were breaking up the black dirt in big chunks. Dust rose like smoke behind him and drifted away toward the road. There wasn't much of a breeze.

I walked on down the hill and past the store to Rebecca's house. I could tell before I even walked up on the porch that nobody was home. All of the windows were down and latched and the front door was locked. Even the screen was latched. I sat down on the porch and looked around. I had a feeling inside me like I had swallowed a balloon and somebody was blowing it up. I kept trying to get my breath.

I rested for a while on Rebecca's porch, hoping she would come back from wherever they had gone. A mockingbird was chattering and whistling at me from the top of the pecan tree by the driveway. I got to thinking that this was what it would be like if Rebecca had to move. There wouldn't be anything here at all except a noisy mockingbird. I hated mockingbirds.

I got up and walked out of the yard and along the road. The mailman was just pulling up at the store, so I didn't go in. The mailman reminded me of that mockingbird. He always made a lot of noise, but it never came to much.

The road was hot and empty as I walked back up the hill. In a way, I didn't want to walk back up the hill. There wasn't anybody home except Gerald and maybe Wilbur, and I didn't want to talk to either one of them, especially not Wilbur. At the top of the hill, I stopped and watched Mr. Ketchum plowing again.

His tractor was out in the field and it was running, but Mr. Ketchum wasn't on it. I looked through the dust again to make sure and something else caught my eye. It was Wilbur. He was running through the unplowed cotton toward the other road where I could just see the blue of his truck through the trees that grew beside the road. I looked back at the tractor. No one was on it. It was turning and twisting and bouncing across the field whichever way the rows happened to send it. The dust followed it.

I looked back at Wilbur. He was still running. His hat flew off his head and he stopped and went back for it. For a minute he looked up in my direction. Dust blew across him and he stood looking up at me. He turned and looked at the tractor. He looked back at me and started running again. A feeling as cold as ice went through me. I looked back at the field and saw what I didn't see the first time. Mr. Ketchum was lying in the dry plowed dirt. He was twisted around the way no man could ever be and still be alive. The tractor had run over him.

I shook my head, then I shook my head again, then I started running back down the hill. I felt the hot road under my bare feet but I didn't feel the gravel the way I usually did. I ran. Wilbur had crossed the field, but I couldn't see him anymore. All I knew was that I had to get to the store before he did.

At the bottom of the hill, I saw his truck coming out of the road that curved past the empty house on the corner and led to Mr. Ketchum's house. Dust swept around the truck as Wilbur changed gears and started across to the store. I cut through the barrow ditch and jumped up on the porch. The mailman was coming out the door. Wilbur's truck pulled up in front of the store and dust covered us.

"Hey there," the mailman said. "Where's the fire?"

I looked at Wilbur's truck and saw that the door was open, but the white dust was so thick I couldn't see Wilbur. I pushed past the mailman. Mr. Norman was just inside the screen door, spitting into his coffee can.

"Mr. Ketchum!" I tried to say.

"Eh?"

Behind me, I could hear Wilbur saying something to the mailman. I was trying so hard to talk that I started to cry.

"Mr. Ketchum!"

"He ain't here, boy. What's a matter?"

"Mr. Ketchum!"

"Hey old man!" Wilbur called from behind me. I sucked in air and ran around Mr. Norman.

"What's a matter?"

"You got a goddamned telephone here? There's a man been run over by his tractor."

"What?"

Wilbur walked up to Mr. Norman who turned and headed toward the back of the store where the telephone was. He saw me and looked after Mr. Norman, then he grabbed me by the arm and lifted me off the floor. He brought his face down close to mine and his lips curled back from his yellow teeth and his eyes were as cold and mean as snake's eyes. The mailman came back inside and Wilbur let me go. He went back to where Mr. Norman was.

"You know the number for the hospital in San Marcos?" Wilbur asked, picking up the telephone.

Mr. Norman told him the numbers and he dialed them.

"What did he say?" the mailman asked.

I shook my head. I was starting to shake. I wanted to run away, but the mailman put his hand down on my shoulder.

"Hello? Yeah. We got a man out here bad hurt. Cotton-wood. There's a goddamned store there. We'll be waitin'."

Wilbur banged the telephone down and looked at Mr. Norman.

"Is it Elmer Ketchum?" Mr. Norman asked.

"I don't know his damned name," Wilbur hissed. "Big fella. Was in here the other day when I come in mindin' my own business."

"Where?" Mr. Norman asked.

"Just up the road in that sorry patch of cotton."

"Oh Lord," Mr. Norman said. "We'd better go see."

He started walking up toward the front of the store. His face was red and his voice was tight and shaky.

"Ain't no need," Wilbur said, coming after him. "I done been there. He's dead. Them sweeps 'bout cut him in half."

"Reckon we ought to call Ida," the mailman said.

Mr. Norman shook his head. "Not yet. Let 'em get him cleaned up first. You sure he's dead?"

"Mister, I know what dead looks like."

Mr. Norman started to say something twice. The mailman was still holding on to my shoulder, but he wasn't looking at me. Only Wilbur was. His eyes were cutting mine like razor blades.

"Reckon we ought to called Sheriff Burns," Mr. Norman said.

"What for?" Wilbur cut in. "I'll tell you what happened. That big guy had some kind of stroke in this heat and fell off that tractor. I come along the road and seen that tractor cuttin' along with nobody ridin' it, so I stopped to check and found him run over dead."

"Burns will want to know that," the mailman said.

Wilbur cut him a look, then they all looked at me. Mr. Norman stooped over a little. "What did you see, Ricky?"

"He didn't see nothin'," Wilbur said. "He was walkin' along the road and I seen him and told him to run ahead to put in that call."

Wilbur burned his eyes into me and stepped closer. I could still feel his hand on my arm and the easy way he had pulled me off my feet.

"Is that true, Ricky?" Mr. Norman asked.

"Yes sir," I said.

Wilbur showed his teeth again in a smile that made me scared sick to see. The devil himself would have a smile like that. Mr. Norman straightened up.

"We'd best go see what we can do," he said. "That ambulance will be a few minutes."

"I'll take you in my car," the mailman said to Mr. Norman. He let go of my shoulder.

Mr. Norman went to his coffee can and spit, then he looked at me. "You go on home, Ricky. There's no need you bein' here now."

"I'll take him home," Wilbur said. "I'm workin' for his pa, anyway."

"All right," Mr. Norman said. He and the mailman went out the front door.

I was so scared then, I felt sick to my stomach. Wilbur caught my arm and pulled me along to the door. I tried to say let me go, but nothing would come out. When Wilbur pushed me through the door, I saw the mailman backing his car around. Mr. Norman was looking at me through the windshield with a strange look on his face. They left.

Wilbur pulled me over to his truck and opened the off door and pushed me in and slammed it again. I watched him walk around the front of the truck, then pull the door open on his side. The inside of the truck was dirty and smelly. Wilbur got in and started the truck up. He backed it around and drove out onto the road. Up ahead, the mailman's car was already pulling over and stopping. We went by it up the hill.

Wilbur never even looked at me until he stopped the truck in front of the house, then he turned and grabbed my arm again and pulled me right up into his face.

"I seen you watchin', you little son of a bitch," he said. "I seen you watchin' and I don't care what you think, I come along that road and seen that tractor goin' along without nobody on it, so I stopped, you see? I stopped. I didn't even know whose goddamned tractor it was. Then I seen that son of a bitch lyin' in the field so I went to the store to get help, see?"

Wilbur shook me until I said yes. His yellow eyes were right in front of mine.

"You goddamned well better see. There's goin' to be questions and if someone asks you, I want to make sure you answer 'em right. 'Cause if you don't, your purty big sister is goin' to have somethin' happen to her, see? You think I ain't seen her, don't you? Well, I've seen her all right. You understand?"

Wilbur shook me again. I said yes again.

"Okay. I'm goin' back down there to he'p out. You just keep your little damned mouth shut. I'll be checkin' on you."

Wilbur pushed me against the side of his truck. I jerked on the handle and opened the door and got out. Wilbur put the truck in gear and drove off without looking at me again. I started shaking and crying. I went to the edge of the porch and vomited my breakfast. Then I went in the house and got a rag and wet it. I sat down on the bathroom floor with the rag over my face, and I cried and cried.

When Gerald showed up for dinner, I was sitting in the living room. I heard him come in the back door. He got a glass out of the cabinet and opened the icebox and filled the glass with ice. I heard him turn on the water and wait while the glass filled up. He came into the living room with the glass in his hand.

"What are you doing?" he said.

I looked down at my hands.

"What was that siren while ago?"

"I don't know."

"Damn. You look awful. What's the matter?"

"I don't feel good."

"You don't look good either."

Gerald took a big drink of water and headed for the kitchen. "Of course, you never did," he said.

I heard Mama coming up the stairs. The house was hot and quiet. She came along the hall and into the room. I was lying on my bed with my face to the wall. She sat down on the edge of the bed and put her hand on my shoulder.

"Ricky?"

"Yeah?" I said, but I didn't look at her.

"How do you feel?"

"I don't know."

"Is it your stomach again?"

"I guess so."

Mama didn't say anything for a little while, then she said, "I don't know what we're going to do with you."

I started to cry again. I didn't want to, but I never could be brave when Mama was talking to me in her soft voice. She made me sit up and hugged me while I cried.

"There now, Ricky. Grandfather wouldn't want you to cry like this. He would want you to be a man about it."

But I wasn't crying for Grandfather. I was crying for Mr. Ketchum and myself and Mama and Father and Carol and Rebecca and Gerald.

I didn't eat any supper. Carol came home and came up to see me for just a minute. She looked tired and her hands were cool when she put them on my cheeks.

"How do you feel?" she asked.

"Okay. How do you feel?"

"I'm fine now, thanks to you."

"Do you like your job?"

"Yes, I really do. I'm good at it too, but it makes me tired."

"What do you do?"

"I work the cash register. I'm a checker."

"Mr. Norman lets me open his register all the time."

"Sure," Carol said.

She moved her thumbs next to my eyes and caught the tears that were rolling out. She was starting to look blurry to me.

"I don't like to see you so sad," she said. "You're the one who always cheers me up."

"Carol?"

"Yes, Ricky."

"Did Grandfather die?"

"No, but he hasn't changed," she said, catching the tears.

"Did Mr. Ketchum?"

"Yes, Ricky. It was a horrible accident. I still can't believe it has happened. So much bad news at once."

"Did I kill him?"

"What a terrible thing to say!" Carol said. She dropped her head down beside mine and hugged me tightly. All I could see was her hair.

I was already dressed and ready to go. I was sitting on the bottom step of the stairs watching everybody else get ready. Mama was in the kitchen putting aluminum foil over a plate of ham and a bowl of potato salad. Father was in the bathroom shaving. Gerald and Carol were upstairs getting ready. We were going over to see Mrs. Ketchum and go to the funeral.

I didn't want to go, but I didn't feel very bad anymore, so I had to. All the day before, I had stayed in my room looking out the window. I saw the same old things I always saw, but I began to see how they were different now. The land was burning up and the wind that blew in the elm tree was a strange wind, both hot and cold. I kept thinking of Uncle Raisin, for some reason. All my life I had been scared of him, but now I wished he would come over to the house so that I could see him and watch him walking around with his big hands swinging at his sides.

All day I felt outside myself. I felt like I was looking into a window instead of out of one, and what I saw was me. I thought of every stupid thing I ever said or did. I thought about how I still wet the bed sometimes and how I always cried first when I got mad or scared. I thought about Carol and some of the silly things I had said to her. And I thought about Father. I saw Father standing by the windmill with the cigar in his mouth over and over. Then I lay down on my bed and shut my eyes and I began to feel better.

Late in the night sometime I woke up and thought I heard a noise on the stairs and I got scared. I slid out of bed and crawled across the floor to Gerald's bed. I lay down there on the floor by his bed for a long time. He never knew I was there until in the morning when he saw me sleeping on the floor by his bed. He said, "What are you, my new dog?"

Father came out of the bathroom. I was sitting on the step so that I could see him. He didn't know I was watching him, but I was. I wanted to see him doing all kinds of things so that I would know how to do them someday. His face looked older, and his eyes looked sharp as an Indian's eyes. His face was sunburned and brown as a pecan, but I could tell that he wasn't feeling very good either. The difference was that Father could hide it when he wanted to and I couldn't. I knew that if I really wanted to be like him, I would have to hide the way I felt. I had to hide it so that I could keep on doing the things I had to do. I wasn't sure yet what those things would be, but somewhere in my mind I must have had an idea about them. I could tell they were going to be hard.

When we were in the station wagon, I leaned over toward Carol and smelled her. Her eyes were very blue and far away.

"What are you doing?" she asked.

"I'm smelling you," I said, quietly, so only she could hear me.

"Smell this," Gerald said. He farted.

Carol turned to the window. I think she wanted to say something, but she knew how much it would upset Mama. I thought about what she had said the other night about fighting with Mama.

"It just smells natural for you," I said to Gerald.

"Shut up, queer."

Mama heard that and looked over her shoulder. She

looked tired. She looked like she could either be mad or sad. She turned and faced the front again without saying anything. Gerald looked at me, then looked out the window.

At the top of the hill, I looked out the window at the cotton field that Mr. Ketchum had been plowing. I thought I would see the tractor, but it was gone. Part of one fence was dragged down though. Only half the field was plowed.

"Look there," Gerald said, leaning over me. "That's where it happened."

Carol shuddered beside me and I sank back in the seat a little. I looked at the back of Father's head. He was wearing his good felt hat. I saw him look quickly to the right, then look straight ahead again.

"I wish I could have seen it," Gerald whispered.

I looked at my hands.

At the bottom of the hill, we turned off on the gravel road that led to the Ketchum place. I could feel the gravel under the tires and smell the dust right away. Someone was in front of us. We drove through their dust until we got to the house. Father swung in over the cattleguard. There were already about a dozen cars parked beside the driveway leading up to the house. We drove past them until we were close to the back door.

"Carol, I want you to carry the potato salad," Mama said as Father turned off the ignition. "Boys, you stay close and don't get dirty."

"Do we have to go inside?" Gerald asked.

Father looked around at him as he opened the car door. Mama said, "It wouldn't hurt you to come inside for a minute."

We got out and Mama handed the potato salad to Carol. Then she slid the ham over on the seat and picked it up. Some of the men were standing outside under the pecan trees where the wind was blowing. Some of them had taken off their coats and their ties were blowing across their chests like flags. Father waved to them, and they waved back.

We went up to the back door and Mrs. Wille opened it for us. She was a lady who lived past Uncle Raisin on the way into town. When Carol had been my age, Mrs. Wille had given her piano lessons. She was supposed to have given Gerald lessons too, but Gerald had run down to the barn and hidden each time he was supposed to go.

"Why, hello Carol," she said. "Congratulations. I've been meaning to send you a card, but I just haven't gotten around to it."

"Thank you," Carol said.

Then Mama and Father said hello and we were inside. Mrs. Wille closed the door softly behind us. Gerald was trying to get past me, but Father was standing in the doorway of the kitchen.

"Well, young man," Mrs. Wille said. "When are you going to start your piano lessons?"

"Never."

Mrs. Wille laughed and touched Gerald's shoulder. Mama was talking to another woman I didn't know. Father was waiting to get by. He was holding his hat in his hands.

"Hello Jean, Mac," the woman was saying. "You just can't imagine how sorry we were to hear about Mr. Wesley. How is he?"

"Not too well," Mama said. "All we can do is wait and see."

"Our prayers are with him, you know that, don't you?"

"Thank you," Father said.

We moved into the kitchen. It was full of women. I knew some of them and didn't know some of them. I saw Rebecca's mother there and started looking for Rebecca. All of the women said something to Mama and Father about Grandfather. It made me feel good, but it made me feel sad, too. Gerald punched me in the side. When I turned, he showed me a handful of cookies he had swiped off a plate on the cabinet.

"How is Ida doing, today?" Mama asked.

"Oh Jean," Mrs. Wille said, wiping her hands on a cup-towel. "It's the saddest thing you ever saw. She won't admit that Elmer is gone."

"What?" Mama said.

I looked away from the cookies to Mama's face. Carol was standing behind her by the stove. She was looking too.

Mrs. Wille lowered her voice. "She absolutely won't admit that Elmer is gone. She thinks someone is playing a joke on her. She's sitting in the living room as patient as can be, but you can't make her believe Elmer is dead."

In my mind I saw the tractor again and Mr. Ketchum lying in the field. I shivered. Gerald looked at me and said, "You got to go pee?"

Mama looked over at Father. He shook his head. For a minute, the kitchen was quiet, then a woman moved over to Carol and told her how pretty she had looked in the paper and everybody started talking again. Gerald slipped a cookie in his mouth and looked around.

"I guess we'd better go in and at least say hello," Mama said.

"Yeah," Father said, still holding his hat.

We followed them into the living room. Carol was still talking to the woman by the stove. The living room was crowded with more women and men dressed like Father. They were standing around in their dark suits talking about the drought and the little bit of rain we had the other night. When they saw Father, they stepped forward and shook hands and asked him about Grandfather.

"Look at her," Gerald whispered beside me.

I turned and looked across the room. Mrs. Ketchum was sitting on the settee between two other women. One of them was the wife of Elmer's brother Horace. I didn't know the other one. Mrs. Ketchum was wearing a neat black dress and was sitting up very straight on the settee. When I saw her face, I knew why Gerald had said something. Her face was brightly made up and she was smiling.

"She must have gone crazy," Gerald whispered.

Just then I saw Rebecca. She was coming toward me from across the room. She was wearing a light blue shirt and a dark blue skirt and black shoes. Her hair was long and brushed and fell down to her shoulders. When I saw her, I wanted to cry for some reason, then she was right there beside me, smelling nice and looking pretty, and the feeling went away.

"I'm glad you're here," she said. "I was beginning to think y'all weren't coming."

"Fat chance," Gerald said.

"Are you going to say something to her?" Rebecca asked.

I looked at Gerald. He slipped another cookie in his mouth. "Not me," he said with his mouth full. "I'm going back outside."

I watched him go through the room. Mr. Norman stepped out of the kitchen just as Gerald got there. He looked down at Gerald, then looked around the room quickly until he saw me. He was wearing a bow tie with his suit, and his coat looked too big for him. When he saw me, he looked at me for a minute, then nodded and turned back into the kitchen.

"It's so sad," Rebecca said. "I heard your mother say your grandfather was in the hospital. I'm sorry. I like him."

"Yeah," I said.

Rebecca looked down at her shoes. "This reminds me of the last day of school when everybody leaves."

"Are you leaving?"

"I don't know."

Mama came up behind us. She put her hand on my shoulder while she talked to somebody else. It was another one of the women I didn't know. Then she looked down and said hello to Rebecca and told her how pretty she looked. Then she saw Mrs. Ketchum. "Oh Lord," she said.

We moved across the living room toward her. The two women who sat on either side of her were looking at the floor. Mrs. Ketchum was smiling and nodding at another woman when we came up. She turned and looked at me and smiled. I think I smiled too.

"Well, look who's come to see me," she said. "Don't you know, since the creek went dry these boys don't come around much."

I looked at her and remembered the other night when she and Mr. Ketchum had come over. I looked at her eyes. They were a light green and the light from the windows was in them like little fires.

"I'm so sorry, Ida," Mama said, still holding on to my shoulder.

"Sorry, Jean? Why should you be sorry? It isn't your fault the creek went dry, now is it?" Mrs. Ketchum said. She looked at me.

"The boys could come down anyway, sometime," Mama said, after a minute. Horace Ketchum's wife looked up at Mama, then over at Mrs. Ketchum.

"That would be nice," Mrs. Ketchum said. "I'll tell Elmer, soon as he gets home."

I felt Mama's hand close on my shoulder until it started to hurt me. I wanted to twist away, but then her hand relaxed and she just left it there. Hearing Mrs. Ketchum say that made me think Mr. Ketchum wasn't dead after all, only in the hospital like Grandfather. The room grew quiet all around us, but Mrs. Ketchum still sat there smiling and looking at us.

"He's not dead?" I said.

"*Ricky*," Mama said, gripping my shoulders with both her hands.

Mrs. Ketchum laughed. "Everybody thinks so," she said and winked at me. "But we know different, don't we? We'll show them."

"Excuse us, Ida," Mama said. "I left a ham in the car."

Mama pulled me away and I saw Rebecca standing nearby looking at me. From behind us, Mrs. Ketchum said, "Oh thank you, Jean. You know how Elmer likes a good ham sandwich."

As we went through the kitchen, I heard people saying things like, "Poor Ida," and "Such a shame." Carol looked at Mama and her mouth opened like she was going to say something. At the back door we stopped. Mama wasn't holding on to my shoulders anymore. She stood near the screen door looking out at all the cars and the trees and the sheds and the fields. Her arms were crossed like she was cold. Father came up behind her and looked at me. He asked Mama if she was all right. Mama shook her head, but didn't say anything. Then she said, "I would be the same way if it had been you."

I found Gerald outside. He was standing along side the station wagon in the shade of one of Mr. Ketchum's pecan trees eating cookies. Some of the men had found lawn chairs and were sitting in them. Mr. Norman was sitting in one. He looked around and saw me and spit, then went on talking to a man named Elton who raised hogs. Elton was a big German man. He smoked cigarettes one after the other. His suit was black and looked new and he was wearing a black hat. I went up beside Gerald. Gerald's suit made him look older, but the pants were a little short.

"What are you doing?" I asked.

"Waiting for a train. What does it look like?"

"Yeah, but hell, Norman, people just don't do things like that. They just don't. Not out here," Mr. Elton said.

"You don't know the kind of man I'm talkin' about, I'm tellin' you. Besides that, you just can't make me believe Elmer Ketchum could let no tractor run over him."

Mr. Norman spit, and Mr. Elton took out another cigarette. I pushed away from the car and looked around. All of Mr. Ketchum's barns and sheds and pens and equipment were sitting there in the sun, waiting for him to come back and take care of them. There was even a pen of turkeys that Mr. Ketchum kept and sold during the holidays.

"Let me have a cookie," I said.

"Go get your own."

The back door opened and Rebecca stepped outside in the sun. I looked at Gerald, then went over to her. We walked a little way across the driveway to the first shed where Mr. Ketchum had parked his big truck. It was a high, open shed, and under the roof it was cooler. It smelled like oil and dirt. Dust was on everything.

Rebecca pushed her hair back off her shoulders. "I don't like funerals," she said.

"Me either," I said. "I wish we were back home again."

"You look kind of funny. Is anything wrong?"

I shrugged my shoulders, trying to think what Father would say. I kept remembering the way Wilbur's face had come down close to mine.

"I don't guess so," I said.

Rebecca looked around. High up, next to the tin, was a yellow jacket nest as big as a softball. Some people came out of the house and walked over to their cars and got in.

"Think I can come up to see you tomorrow?" she said.

"I don't know. We may have to be gone."

"Oh."

"We might have to go in to the hospital," I said.

I saw Carol come out of the house, then Mama, then Father. Rebecca looked around, then she looked down and took a deep breath.

"All right," she said.

I had never been to a funeral before. Gerald had told me one time about funerals, but he always added so much stuff when he told me about something that I didn't believe any of what he said. He said you had to listen to the preacher for a while, then you had to go look at the person in the coffin. He said that if you had been bad or were a criminal or something, the dead person would open his eyes and look at you. Then he said everybody would go to the cemetery and help put the coffin in the grave and cover it up. That's what he said, but I didn't believe him.

On the way to the church, I listened to Mama and Father talk. They were talking about the people they had seen and about what Mrs. Ketchum was going to do now.

"The first thing she has to do is realize that Elmer isn't going to come back to take care of her," Father said.

"Oh, I know," Mama said. "That's so pitiful. Such a terrible thing to happen to somebody like Ida. She's always been the sweetest person."

Father shook his head. "I don't know how she ever wound up with Elmer to begin with, the way he is, was."

"He was always good to her, though."

"Yep," Father said. Then, after a while, he said, "I reckon she could lease that land out, like Raisin is doing his."

"I guess so," Mama said. "I just hate to see that horrible Mr. Daniels get all the land around here." She turned and looked out the window.

At the church, I followed Gerald along the sidewalk to the big doors. Rebecca was standing on the steps with her mother. She was waiting for us. When we got up there, we all went in. The church was dark and cool and the sunlight came in the stained glass windows, making strange colored patterns on the pews. At the front of the church were all kinds of flowers and a big, silver-looking coffin. Rebecca reached over and grabbed my hand. I was glad because if I had to think about her, I didn't have to think about myself.

We walked about halfway down before Father stopped. He stood in the aisle looking toward the back of the church while each of us turned in and sat down. Rebecca's mother sat with Mama next to Father. Gerald had to sit next to Carol. He told her to move over a little and she bent down and whispered for him to just shut his mouth and sit still. I was holding Rebecca's hand down between us. Gerald looked around and made a face at me, but I didn't think about him.

When everybody was in and sitting down, the organ lady started to play the organ soft and deep. Everybody turned their heads and looked at her. Horace Ketchum and his wife were sitting down front with Mrs. Ketchum. Horace looked a little like his brother, but he was nowhere near as big as Mr. Ketchum.

Then Brother Dowell came out with the Bible in his hands and went up into the pulpit above the coffin. He put the Bible down and opened it and then looked out at Mrs. Ketchum. "Let us bow our heads in prayer," he said. "'Then said Jesus unto his disciples, If any man will come after me, let him deny himself, and take up his cross, and follow me. For whosoever will save his life shall lose it; and whosoever will lose his life for my sake shall find it. For what is a man profited, if he shall gain the whole world, and lose his own soul?' Amen."

We looked up. I looked at Rebecca. Her eyes were wet. Carol was sniffing a little. Gerald was chewing his lip. Father had his chin raised like he did when he got mad. I raised my chin a little too.

Then, as Brother Dowell went on with his sermon, a movement caught my eye. There was a shadow on the last stained glass window on the left. It was the shadow of a man. When I looked at it, it stopped moving, then it started again. It moved out of the first window and into the edge of the second one. It stopped again. That's when I thought it looked like Wilbur's shadow. I ran cold inside when the shadow moved again, going from window to window as if Wilbur was out there, trying to see in, looking for me. I started to sweat then. Rebecca reached down with her other hand and pulled at mine. I was squeezing her hand too hard. I looked at her, then looked back at the windows. There was no shadow on any of them.

Later, when the service was over and we were leaving for the cemetery, I looked at the outside of the church. The lowest window was fifteen feet off the ground.

It was hot in the cemetery. Cicadas were in the cedar trees and dust blew around the headstones. A tent had been set up over Elmer Ketchum's grave. Under the tent, green carpet covered the ground. We got out of the station wagon and stood at the edge of the tent behind Mama and Carol. I wished Rebecca had been there, but they had gone on home. I tried not to look at the coffin. I was looking at Mrs. Ketchum. She was sitting on a folding chair under the tent directly in front of the coffin. Horace Ketchum and his wife were sitting beside her along with other relatives that I didn't know. Mrs. Ketchum's eyes looked bright compared to everyone else's. She was staring at the coffin and holding a black purse in her hands.

Brother Dowell stepped up to the coffin and opened his Bible and said, "Let us pray."

I bowed my head and looked at my shoes. After a while I heard Brother Dowell say, "Dust to dust, ashes to ashes."

Gerald poked me and leaned over toward me. "I told you that's what they say at funerals."

I looked at him without raising my head, then I looked over at Mrs. Ketchum. She didn't have her eyes closed either. She was opening her purse. While nobody else was looking, she pulled out a long screwdriver with a red handle. Then she jumped up and ran over to the coffin and started stabbing at the edges of it. The noise made everyone look up. Brother Dowell stopped talking in the middle of a word and just looked. For a minute the only sounds were Mrs. Ketchum stabbing the coffin and the wind whipping a loose corner of the tent. Horace Ketchum's wife screamed twice and fainted. Horace jumped up and he and Brother Dowell tried to stop Mrs. Ketchum. Brother Dowell dropped his Bible and I saw it slide under the coffin and drop in the grave. A little puff of dust caught in the wind.

"Let me go! Let me go!" Mrs. Ketchum wailed. "You know well as I that Elmer isn't in that box. Let me go!"

They got the screwdriver away from her, but when they turned her hand loose, Mrs. Ketchum threw a punch at Horace that sent him stumbling backwards. He fell over his wife's legs and hit the ground. That's when Father stepped forward and had to help. Mama's face was white. She pulled Carol away and waved us in front of her toward the car.

Gerald ducked under a cedar branch as we hurried away. He looked over his shoulder once and said, "I guess she didn't live with old Mr. Ketchum all those years for nothin'."

On the way home, Carol cried a little bit. Gerald leaned his head out the window to catch as much of the hot wind as he could. He had already taken off his tie. I sat in the middle looking at my hands, then looking at Mama. Father said something to her once, but all she did was shake her head and look out the window. I looked at Father and saw the muscles in his jaw working. I made the muscles in my jaw do the same thing. It started making me feel mad instead of afraid. I guessed that was why Father did it, because it was easier to do the things you needed to do if you were mad than if you were afraid.

When we turned in the driveway, Mama looked around at us. "I suppose you'd better change, but don't get dirty. We'll be going in to see Grandmother in a little while."

Carol said all right for all three of us.

I looked out the window at the house. It looked funny to me, like no one had lived there in a long time. Father drove around to the back and stopped. Dust rose around us.

"The phone's ringing," Gerald said.

Mama was already out of the car. "I'll get it," she said. She put her hand up to her hat and ran up to the back door and went inside.

I followed Carol out of the car. Father slammed the door and reached in his pocket for a new cigar. Gerald pushed Worthless away and slapped at him with his tie. When we came around the front of the station wagon, Father turned and looked at Carol.

"How are you doing?" he asked in his tired, deep voice.

Without answering him, Carol went over and put her arms around him. Father put his big hands on Carol's shoulders, then slid them around her back and hugged her tightly. I couldn't see Carol's face, just her yellow hair like gold under Father's cigar.

The back door opened and Mama came out on the porch. She stood on the steps holding her hat in her hand. "That was your mother," she said. "Grandfather died about half an hour ago."

Carol's shoulders started to shake.

The Golden Chain

I BUTTONED MY SHIRT and went down the hall and stopped at Carol's room. It was Tuesday, but she had the day off. She had the next day off too, because it was the Fourth of July. She was still in bed and looked asleep, so I went in quietly and sat down by her dresser which was tall as me and painted white. It was an old dresser and Carol liked to write things on the side of it. They were mostly things that had happened to her on dates. There was a picture of a flower about halfway down that was kind of pretty.

I was between the dresser and the bed, with my back to the bed, but Carol looked asleep so I started to read what she had written. It was hard to read because Carol wrote very small and in cursive. Finally I gave it up and looked at the wall where she had pinned a wilted white flower and some pictures and other things from her senior year at school. Behind the flower I saw a thin golden chain that I had never seen before. I stood up and looked at it. I tried to pull it out.

"What do you think you're doing?" Carol asked suddenly.

I jumped and turned around. Carol was raised up on her arms and looking mean at me. Her hair fell forward beside her cheeks. "You scared me," I said, standing by the bed looking at her. Her face and arms and shoulders were a dark brown from the sun, and her lips were pink. I watched them, wanting her to smile.

"What were you doing there, then?" she asked. She rolled on her back and the bed squeaked. She pulled the hair out of her face.

I sat down on the edge of the bed on the white sheet. "I wasn't doing anything," I said.

She was wearing a little golden ring with a tiny blue stone on top of it. I picked up her left hand and looked closely at the ring. I looked at her fingers too. They were long and thin. Mine were short and knotty.

"You're a scamp," she said.

"I'm not either," I said, pushing her hand down. "I was just looking at the dumb stuff on your wall."

"And reading," Carol said. She pulled the sheet up around her waist. It was a little crooked on my side, so I straightened it for her.

"Why do you write it then, if you don't want anybody to read it?"

"Because I like to remember," she said.

I scooted up against the headboard and caught at the ends of her hair. "It's just dumb stuff."

"Not to me."

"Why is Mark's name all over it?" I asked.

Carol sat up suddenly and the sheet fell away from her waist. She was wearing her pink gown that didn't have any sleeves. It looked pretty, like a dress. I looked toward the door.

"You have been reading, then."

"Only that," I said without looking at her.

"What else?"

"I just saw the dumb name."

"That's private," she said. She leaned against the headboard and I looked at her. She was scratching an eyebrow with a long brown finger. Father said one time that Carol looked like Ann Blyth in the movies, but I never saw Ann Blyth in any movie.

"It's not very private if you put it where everybody can see," I said.

"It's private until somebody sneaks in here and reads it."

"I didn't sneak. You were just asleep."

"That's worse," she said. She was pulling the hair out of her face again and tucking it behind her ears.

"Why is Mark your boyfriend?"

"What?"

"I bet he's dumb."

Carol hit me with her pillow. "You don't know what you're talking about," she said.

"Stop that," I said. "You hurt my eye."

Carol put her pillow under her head and lay back on it. Her eyebrow was still itching. She scratched it lightly, then wet one finger with her tongue and smoothed it down. She yawned.

"Mark is a very nice young man," she said.

"He doesn't want to marry you, does he?"

Carol looked at me and her eyes were very blue and close. She looked me in the eyes, one at a time, with both of hers, and I couldn't tell from them whether she was being serious or not. I looked down.

"He might," she said finally.

"I don't see how," I said, looking at her quickly.

"Scamp."

"I'm not either, Carol," I said and hit her in the stomach. She jumped up and grabbed me around the neck before I could move. She put her arm in a death clinch around my neck and pulled me halfway across the bed.

"Cut it out," I said. Her arm smelled sweet and was brown and soft, but strong.

"You started it."

"Let me go!"

"Only if you behave yourself. I've told you before not to hit me in the stomach."

"Let me go or I'll break your arm," I said, trying to scare her.

She laughed and kissed me and let me go. I punched her on the arm and she hit me back. I punched her on the arm again and she hit me back.

"Why are you being so hateful?" she said, dodging my fist.

"I don't want you to get married."

"So now it comes out," she laughed. "Why not? You want me to be an old maid, I guess."

"You aren't an old maid."

"Why don't you want me to get married?" she asked again.

"Have you seen Gerald this morning?"

"Tell me," she said, grabbing my shirt at the shoulder.

"Because you'll go away and never come back again," I said.

She let go of my shirt and looked at me. "I wouldn't do that. What makes you think I would never come back again?"

"You just wouldn't, that's all. You would go away and live with somebody else in a far away town and I would never see you again. If you tried to get away like at Thanksgiving or Christmas or sometime, he would drag you back and beat you up and pull your hair and tie you in a closet and never feed you or give you water—"

"Stop that!" Carol said, catching me and shaking me. She was sitting up again. "You have some strange ideas," she said.

"They're all true."

"They're not either, Ricky. Now don't be stubborn. You don't understand anything about it. If and when I ever get married, we'll both be seeing each other."

It was quiet in Carol's room. I could hear the sparrows outside her window. She was sitting up in bed with her arms crossed over her knees. She had tucked her hair back behind her ears. Her arms were smooth and brown next to the pink of her gown, and for a moment she uncrossed them and lifted the edge of her gown just enough to uncover a small black bruise just above her left knee, on the outside of her leg. She pressed it with her fingers and the skin around it turned white for an instant, then turned brown again.

"I don't care if you get married," I said.

She flicked the hem down again and said, "Now you're acting like a little kid instead of a ten-year-old."

"Don't tell me how I'm acting."

I stood up and looked at her.

"Now what are you?" she said. "Mad?"

"Maybe I am. It's a free country."

"Sit down and behave yourself. I'm not getting married, and I'm not going anywhere."

I sat down again on the very edge of the bed. "I don't care if you are," I said.

"Not at all?"

"Maybe a little."

Then Carol made me laugh by the way she looked and it spoiled what I was trying to do. From downstairs I could smell coffee and what I thought were pancakes. I could hear Mama in the kitchen.

"You had better be nice to me or we won't take you to the carnival tomorrow."

"I'm nice enough," I said.

"You could be nicer without straining any," she said. "But at least you're nicer than Gerald."

"Is your boyfriend going to take us?"

"His name is Mark."

"Marko Dumbo."

"Too bad you won't be able to go to the carnival."

"I don't have to be nice to him, do I?"

"Of course."

"Wait a minute. Who says I have to be nice to some dumb guy?"

"I do," Carol said seriously. I thought she would take my side as she always did, but she meant it.

"He's just some dumb guy," I said, trying to make her agree with me.

"His name is Mark," she said, firmly.

"All right, all right."

She had put her chin down on her arms and now she closed her eyes, probably thinking of Mark. I sat beside her worrying a hole in my shirttail, trying to look as left out as I felt, but she didn't open her eyes or look at me. The sun came in her windows and fell in two bright sheets across the floor and the wall. I thought about the way she had felt when she grabbed me and kissed me.

"Carol—" I started to say, but Gerald was standing in the doorway at the edge of the sunlight. He rubbed his nose with one of his strong hands and looked at us. He had a red bump on his nose.

"Mama said it's time for breakfast," he said.

"Come on in," Carol said. "We're having a party."

She raised her head and shook back her hair again and

pushed her legs out on the sheet. I could just see the edge of the bruise on her leg, and I wondered how she got it.

Gerald pushed away from the door jamb and stood straight. "Some party," he said. He left.

Carol turned and looked at me for a minute, then shoved me off the bed. "That's you in two years," she said, nodding at the empty doorway.

Father wiped his hands on his pants and leaned forward with his elbows on the table beside his empty plate. He was wearing his heavy green shirt, and the sleeves were rolled up to his elbows. He picked up his coffee cup and I felt he was looking at me.

"What are you doing?" he asked.

Gerald was eating and Carol was in the kitchen talking to Mama. I heard them talking and Gerald eating and I felt Father staring at me from across the table. I put the syrup down.

"My pancakes are dry," I said.

"No they aren't. Your plate is full of syrup. You're wasting it."

"They hang in my throat."

"No they don't."

I didn't feel like eating anymore. I pushed my pancakes around on the plate until I could see all of the wheat design. Mama and Carol came out of the kitchen. Mama had on the dress she always wore on wash days. It was an old, faded yellow dress with large pockets on the hips. They sat down. Father was watching me again.

I ate a lump of pancakes and tried to swallow them. Father was watching me. I coughed and tried to make my face turn red. It would serve Father right if I choked to death.

"What's wrong with you?" Mama asked. She poured her coffee into a saucer to cool it.

"My pancakes are too dry," I said and coughed again, a little louder. I didn't look at Father, but I knew he had put his cup down.

"Drink some milk," he said.

"What do you mean, your pancakes are too dry?"

"He's just faking," said Gerald.

"Shut up," I said.

"Leave Ricky alone, Gerald," Mama said. "What do you mean, your pancakes are too dry?"

"Father won't let me put any syrup on them."

Father cut his eyes over to Mama. "He has plenty of syrup," he said.

I didn't look at him. I looked at Gerald's plate, then at Carol because I knew she would stick up for me. She was the only one who ever knew how I felt.

"It's all soaked in to them," Carol said. "Try another bite and see."

I ate another lump, and they didn't stick in my throat. Carol smiled at me, then turned to Father and said, "He's been like this all morning." The pancakes stuck in my throat.

Mama sipped her coffee. "Have you made up your mind about going in yet?" she asked.

Father shook his head. "Guess I ought to. It wouldn't hurt the cows any to have some feed."

"I wouldn't imagine," Mama said.

"Never thought I'd be takin' disaster relief money," Father said.

"It's not like you'd be taking any money," Mama said. "Those certificates just provide for partial payment, don't they?"

"Same thing," Father said.

"What are y'all talking about?" Carol asked.

Father didn't answer her. He put his coffee cup down and moved the fork beside his plate. He looked at Mama.

"Something your father got at the mill yesterday," Mama said.

"What?" Carol asked.

"Haven't you heard?" Father said then, still looking at his fork. "The whole state of Texas has been declared a disaster area by the federal government."

Gerald looked up. "The whole state?"

"What does that mean?" I asked, watching Father.

"It means we might make it out of this drought without sellin' the farm," Father said. "Maybe."

"It would never come to that," Carol said.

Father looked at Mama and shrugged. "If the cotton makes, it won't. Otherwise—"

"It's not that bad," Carol said.

"I'll be honest with you," Father said. "The way things look now, we'll be lucky to last 'til the end of the month without ever' one of us goin' in to town to look for work. We just don't have the cash."

"I'll go to work in town," I said.

Gerald looked at me. Everybody looked at me.

"Doin' what?" Father said.

"But it's not that bad," Carol said again.

My pancakes were all cold.

After breakfast, Mama told me and Gerald to pick beans, so we took the buckets out in the garden to start before it got too hot. The beans were planted in long, green rows behind the house. The rows ran almost out to the road and were still green because Father had watered them every Sunday night since May. The sun on the dirt made it hot, and as I crawled along the dirt got into the cuffs of my pants and rolled down to my knees and made them itch and hurt. I found one bush that had eleven beans on it. I counted them and told Gerald.

"Pull it up," he said. "No bush like that deserves to live."

I pulled it up and set it back in the row to look like it had just died there.

"Hey Gerald," I called. "Are you going to buy firecrackers at the carnival?"

"I don't know," he said, picking. "Maybe."

"We bought firecrackers last year."

"So what? They didn't stop making them."

"I was thinking about something different this year."

Gerald stopped picking and turned around where he could see me. I went on picking. "Like what? A stuffed banana?"

"I was thinking of buying something for Carol, maybe," I said.

"For Carol?"

"Sure."

"What for, when you could buy firecrackers?"

"I don't know. She does lots of stuff for me."

"I do lots of stuff for you, too. Why don't you buy me something?"

"It's not the same thing. She's a girl."

Gerald turned and went on picking. "She's a girl, all right, and she has other boys to buy her stuff. She probably does a lot of things for them too, ha ha."

I didn't like what Gerald said, but I went on picking without saying anything. I was sure that if I bought Carol something nice, she would forget about Mark and pay more attention to me like she had before the summer started. Then I wouldn't have to be nice to some dumb guy, and Carol wouldn't go away. I remembered the chain I had seen on the wall in her room. It had seemed to be broken. I could buy her a new one, a pretty new golden chain. Then she wouldn't go away.

When we had finished the rows, I stood up and shook the dirt out of my pants. Gerald pushed the beans down in the bushel basket at the end of the rows. I put the empty buckets on top of the beans and we each grabbed a side and lifted the basket. Gerald's side went higher than mine.

"Listen," he said as we went back to the house. "I wouldn't worry about Carol so much, if I was you. I'd get somethin' for myself."

"It's my money."

"Sure it is. That's why you ought to spend it on yourself."

"What if I want to spend it on Carol?"

"Let her queer boyfriends buy her stuff. They get goodies for it, I bet."

"Shut up," I said.

"That's how it works, Ricky. They buy her stuff and she kisses them."

"Shut up. You're just thinking about Ruby Lee."

Gerald set his end of the basket on the ground and looked at me.

"What do you know about it?"

I looked at him. "Nothing."

He looked at me with his hard eyes. "Then shut up."

We started walking again. "I just wanted to buy Carol something," I said.

"Then go ahead and do what you want. You're just a little dumb-ass queer, anyway."

We put the buckets on the ground by the back door and went into the house. It seemed dark after the bright sun in the garden. Mama was piling clothes on the back porch. She looked up and said, "Take them right on to the dining room and get busy."

"I'm tired," I said.

"You can sit while you snap them."

"I'm thirsty."

"Then get a drink."

It was the middle of the morning and it took us until dinner to snap all the beans. Carol helped us. What Gerald had said about her made me mad, but when I saw how nice she looked, I knew that Gerald was just being dumb. He found a worm on one bean and threw it on Carol's arm. She acted scared, but I didn't think she really was. Anyway, it made me mad again. I told Gerald to keep his dirty worms to himself.

"What are you crying about now?" he said.

"I'm not crying."

"Then shut up before you make me sick," he said.

I didn't say anything else, but I felt bad in front of Carol. I thought she would say something, and I waited for her to, but she never did.

After dinner the house was very quiet. I never remembered the house being so quiet in all the years I had lived there. It seemed like ever since Mr. Ketchum and Grandfather had died, everybody was waiting for something. One time I thought everybody was waiting for someone else to die, but I didn't want to think of that now.

I was lying across one end of my bed with my head on my pillow, thinking. Gerald was twisted up on his bed reading a funny book. He started making wet pooty noises with his mouth. I listened, but the only sounds were the grasshoppers in the yard, Gerald making pooty noises, and the far away sound of a tractor. I was propped up where I could look out on the driveway. Heat waves shimmered off the bright gravel, and an occasional breeze moved the dry grass beside the road and the leaves in the elm tree.

Gerald turned a page, and I heard the dry sound of the grasshoppers out in the yard and the hot tuck-tucking sound of the tractor somewhere moving up and down in the hot July sun. My hands under my chin smelled like the beans we had picked and snapped, but I wasn't thinking about them. I was thinking of the carnival that was set up every Fourth of July in town along the river. I thought of the cars and the tents, the games, the rides, and the big dance platform near the river where you paid to get in, then got all the orange drinks you could drink free. I opened my eyes once and saw the heat shimmering off the driveway. I fell asleep.

When I woke up, I was hot and sweaty and my body felt numb and tired. I had had a dream about Grandfather. He had given me his cane, but when I went to get it, it was gone. Wilbur had it. I sat up on the bed and saw that Gerald was gone. I leaned toward the window, wondering if he was in the yard, and I saw Rebecca walking up the hill in the bright sunshine. She was wearing a white dress and the wind blew the skirt of it and blew her hair around her head. She turned at the driveway and I watched her coming slowly toward the house with something in her hand.

Carol came into my room and I turned away from the window. She had just washed her hair and it was wrapped in a white towel on top of her head. It made her face look thinner and paler, and the neck of her bathrobe was wet. She came in and I watched her, still feeling strange. She sat on the bed near the window with one long, brown leg under her, and she leaned away toward the window.

"What is it?" I said, looking at the tight, brown bunch of

muscles in her bended knee. She reminded me of the ladies advertising shampoo in the *Saturday Evening Post*.

"Rebecca's coming down the driveway," she said.

I didn't want Carol to think I liked Rebecca more than I liked her, so I said, "So what?"

"She's coming to see you."

"Maybe not."

"You know she is, Ricky, and I want you to be nice to her."

"Why should I?"

"Oh be quiet. Now that's why I came in here. You've been acting like Gerald all day, and you're not Gerald at all."

Carol patted the towel around her wet hair. A little drop of water rolled down her cheek like a tear. After Grandfather's funeral, she had cried and cried. She had gone to her room and closed the door and stayed in there all afternoon and that night without even turning on her light when it got dark. After some of the company had gone, I went up to her room and opened the door. She was lying on her stomach on her bed with her face in her pillow, crying. I walked over to the side of the bed and looked at her. It seemed like all the gold had gone out of her hair.

She leaned toward the window. "She's almost here. Rebecca is an awfully pretty little girl," she said.

"Not as pretty as you," I said.

"That's sweet," Carol said. "But don't be silly. She's in the yard. Go downstairs and meet her so she won't have to knock."

I looked at Carol for a minute, then I stood up. There was something about that dream that I was forgetting, and it was bothering me, but I didn't know what it was. I went down the stairs and through the living room, and I saw Rebecca standing at the door about to knock.

"Come on in," I said.

"I can't stay," she said, and she stepped back.

I opened the door and went out on the porch with her. It bothered me that she was so dressed up. She was even wearing shoes. Her hair was brushed long with little curls at the ends and her eyes were big and brown. I could tell she was hot from the walk up the hill, but she never paid any attention to things like that. She put whatever she was holding in her hand behind her back.

"What are you doing?" I asked.

"I came to see you."

We sat down on the steps on the porch and the south wind was blowing across the yard and in the tall elm tree at the corner of the yard. The sound of the wind in the elm tree was sad.

"I haven't seen you for a while," I said, thinking that was the reason we felt so shy, but that had never made any difference before.

"Not since your grandfather's funeral," Rebecca said. "I wanted to come see you, but there was always something I had to do. So I wrote you letters instead."

"I never got them," I said.

"I have them right here. They weren't those kind of letters."

"Oh."

We sat there for a while listening to the wind in the elm tree. I had a headache, but I was starting to wake up.

"Why are you so dressed up?" I asked her.

"Do you like my new dress? Mother didn't want me to wear it, but I wanted you to see me in it."

"It's nice," I said. "Want to go to the carnival with us tomorrow?"

"I won't be here tomorrow," Rebecca said.

That was when I looked at her. The wind was blowing her hair across her face, but I could still see her eyes. She was crying. She didn't cry like other people. I just looked at her, and if I saw her eyes were wet, I knew she was crying.

"What's wrong?"

"I won't be here tomorrow because we're moving. I'll be gone."

"What?"

"I wanted to tell you before, but I just couldn't. I couldn't even come up here to see you."

"When are you leaving?"

"Today."

I slapped the knee of my jeans. "Today! You mean this afternoon?"

"Yes."

"You'll be coming back, won't you?"

"I don't think so."

I reached off the porch and pulled a stalk of dry grass. I felt like I had a balloon in my chest again, only now it was so big I could hardly breathe.

"Your father got the job," I said.

Rebecca nodded.

"Why? Why couldn't he stay here?"

"I don't know, Ricky."

"Well, listen, why can't—"

"What?"

"I don't know either," I said.

For a minute, neither one of us could think of anything to say. I looked all around the yard and down to the barn and tried to imagine what Father would do or say. There were so many things that I didn't know how to do.

"I don't know what to think," I said. "I mean, here you are like always, but tomorrow you'll be way off somewhere."

"Waco."

"When school starts, you won't be on the bus anymore. I can't think about it. It seems to me like you'll just be gone forever the way Mr. Ketchum and Grandfather are gone forever."

"It's not my fault," she said. She was crying. I felt like crying too, but I couldn't while Rebecca was crying. It was something only one of us could do at a time.

"Listen," I said. "Maybe you could run away."

For a moment she smiled with her lips pressed together. She looked at me. I was beginning to feel how much I would miss her.

"You could hide me in the barn," she said.

"The rats would get you."

"You could be my pirate, like you always wanted to be."

"Yeah," I said, but her smile went away.

"I wish I really could. I've dreamed about it every night," she said. Then she said, "Ricky?"

"Yeah?"

"You could write to me sometime, couldn't you?"

"I guess so."

"You could tell me what you're doing and things. If you had time."

"Yeah."

"Ricky, you have been the best friend anybody could ever have," she said then.

I was looking down the hill, toward the store, toward her house where she wouldn't be anymore. "So have you," I said.

"Whenever I needed something or was in trouble or anything, you always made me feel better or helped me. I think you're about the most wonderful boy in the whole world."

I was looking down. I didn't feel very wonderful.

"Will you miss me?" Rebecca asked.

"Yeah," I said.

The balloon inside my chest was about to explode. I felt older. I felt older than Gerald even. Rebecca stood up. I looked up at her and stood up too. She put her arms up around my neck and hugged me as tight as she could. She was crying into my shoulder. I bent down a little until my cheek touched her hair. Then she pulled away.

"Goodbye," she said.

She put the little package she had been holding in my hand and ran across the yard and down the driveway until she was near the road, then she slowed and just walked. I watched the wind blowing her dress out behind her. She got very small as she started down the hill. She went on and I was thinking she would look back. She just kept going. She went out of my sight.

I opened the tissue paper and saw that she had wrapped something in several sheets of notebook paper. I unwrapped the letters and saw that she had given me a harmonica. It was shiny and the wood was red on the edges. I blew on it. It made a tiny sound like a hurt animal. I went into the house.

Carol was in her room combing out her hair. I went in and sat on the edge of the bed and looked at the harmonica and the letters. Carol stopped combing her hair and looked at me. I didn't ever want her to go away. I held out the harmonica for her to see.

"What does it mean?" I said.

"It means she loves you."

After supper, we went back outside and threw rocks at the nighthawks and bats that were chasing the bugs around the big light on the shop. They were too fast to hit. Gerald said he hit one.

"Where is it, then?" I asked.

"It kept flying, queer."

"I bet you never hit it at all."

"I bet I can hit you," he said.

Then he chased me all around the yard and down beside the shop. I ducked around the corner and hid behind a barrel that caught rain water. Gerald threw rocks at the side of the shop and said to come out, but I wasn't going to unless I could make it to the house before he did. I could hear the crickets and the bullfrogs down at the tank from where I was hiding. I was used to the crickets, but the bullfrogs sounded strange. Then they all got quiet at once and I looked over toward the barn. I thought I saw a man standing down there looking at me, but it was too dark to be sure. I looked around the barrel at Gerald, then looked back, but there wasn't anything there. The bullfrogs started up again.

Gerald said, "Aw come on out. I'm not going to stay down here all night while you wet your pants."

I came out and Gerald pretended he was throwing a rock at me, but he didn't have anything in his hands. We went back up to the house in the warm summer night. Carol was sitting alone on the front porch just outside the glare of the yellow porch light.

"There's Carol," I said.

"So what."

"Let's go see what she's doing."

"You go. I'm going to go watch Red Skelton."

I watched Gerald for a minute as he turned away and went up the back steps, then I went around to the front and spread out on my back on the cool porch near Carol. A warm breeze was blowing in the elm tree and across the yard, a little stronger than it had that afternoon. The sky was clear and the stars were so thick overhead that the sky looked like a black umbrella shot through with pinholes. I thought about what Rebecca had said about being up there, but since Carol was close by it seemed like Rebecca had not really gone away.

"What have you been up to?" she asked quietly.

"Nothing," I said, after a while.

Carol didn't say anything.

"There must be a jillion stars up there," I said. "I wonder where they all came from."

Carol looked up. Her hair fell back from her neck. "They've always been there," she said. "I suppose they always will be."

"Imagine that," I said, losing interest.

"Sometimes it seems like I'll always be here, too," Carol said. "Just like this. Just like the stars."

Carol was quiet for a while and I rolled over on my side and looked at her. She was thinking about something and it made her act different and not happy. I looked past her down the hill where a set of lights should have been, but were not, and I did not feel happy either.

"Listen to the whippoorwill," Carol said. "It must be the loneliest sound in the world."

Something made me think she wasn't talking to me anymore. She was looking out into the darkness. I could see down the hill, but there was nothing there. Something was bothering me.

"I've lived out here on this farm all my life," she said. "It's all I know—this house, the barn, the animals, the fields."

"And all of us."

"Yes," she said, but it wasn't a happy yes.

"What's wrong with it?" I asked, sitting up.

Carol crossed her arms over her knees and was quiet. I

was quiet too, listening, smelling the night smells of the yard and fields. The whippoorwill called and was quiet too, and it was dark and lonely.

"What's Gerald doing?" Carol asked then.

I was thinking of something I could say to her to make her feel better and forget all the stuff that was bothering her. "Watching television, I guess."

"Why aren't you?"

"I thought I would stay out here a while. With you." I was still trying to think of the right thing to say, but Carol wouldn't look at me.

"Maybe you'd better go in and get ready for bed, Ricky. You'll want to be wide awake for the carnival tomorrow."

"Yeah," I said.

I got up and went to the door. I stopped and looked at Carol's back. She was still looking out into the darkness. Everything would be all right when we got to the carnival. I would buy her something really nice and she would forget all this other stuff. The whippoorwill called from somewhere out in the field, and I opened the door and went inside.

Everybody got the day off on the Fourth of July except me and Gerald. Father kept making up things for us to do until dinner, and then Mama made us clean up our room. By the time we had done everything and bathed and dressed, we still had an hour to wait around before Mark came. When Gerald was ready, he went downstairs to see if he could get Mama to let him have some of his birthday money that she was saving for him in a little iron box at the back of her closet. I looked in Carol's room and saw her sitting in front of the mirror putting her makeup on. I went in and fell across the bed and watched her. All she had on was her slip.

After a while, she turned around and said, "What are you doing in here, anyway?"

"Waiting," I said.

"Well go wait in your own room. I'm trying to get ready."

"Go ahead. It isn't bothering me."

I rolled over on her bed and looked at the ceiling. There

were water stains up there where the roof had leaked. The brown stains made strange, scary designs on the wallpaper. Then I looked at the wall where she had pinned the dried-up white flower and all the other stuff from school, and I saw the thin golden chain again. I got up off the bed and tried to pull the golden chain out from behind the flower, but Carol saw me and told me to leave it alone.

"What is it?" I asked.

"You can see what it is," she said, watching me in the mirror. "It's just a chain."

"What's it for?"

"Nothing. Leave it alone."

"I'm not hurting it. It's already broken anyway."

"I know it's broken. Why don't you go in your room and play with something?"

"I might get dirty."

Carol was brushing her hair now. From behind her, I could see her brown back and her face in the mirror. She was still watching me. I wondered why she didn't ask me to brush her hair.

"Let me brush it," I said.

"Ricky, I'm in a hurry."

She put the brush down and stood up and slipped one of the straps off her shoulder. I was watching her.

"Turn around," she said.

"Why?"

"Turn around or I'll make you get out."

I turned around and sat on the bed and looked at the gold chain. I liked the way things smelled in Carol's room.

"I bet you would like to have a new golden chain," I said.

"Who wouldn't?"

"I mean because the one you have is broken."

"It would be nice," she said.

Carol would never go away now. I was going to take care of it. I got up off the bed and went to the door, stopping for a second to look at her before I went out.

When Mark came, I was mad and hung back. Carol was ready and she went out the front door to meet him on the porch. She was wearing a pretty blue skirt with a jumper top and her new white blouse. I looked out a corner of the window and I saw Mark kiss her on the cheek as they met. It made me mad. I didn't want to go, then I thought of my plan and I wanted to go more than ever. Carol brought him in and introduced him to everybody even though we all knew who he was. She looked very happy and she was smiling.

"And you remember Ricky," she said.

Mark stepped over and shook my hand in a phony way. He was almost as tall as Father, but he didn't look as strong. He had a job driving a roadgrader for the county.

"Y'all have a good time and be careful," Mama said. To us she said, "You boys behave."

"Maybe we ought to go along," Father said. They were going over to join some people from the church for a picnic.

"I don't think so," Mama said. "I'd rather sit in the shade than walk in the sun any day."

We rode in Mark's car, with him and Carol in the front seat, and me and Gerald in the back. I was on the right side and I looked at Mark as we rode into town. Carol looked very happy. She sat beside him and talked to him in a happy way. It made me mad to see her acting so dumb.

"You cut your hair," she said to him, ruffling the short hairs at the back of his head.

"Oh, a little," he said. "How does it look?"

"Handsome," Carol said, then she leaned close to his ear and whispered, "And sexy."

Gerald was re-tying his tennis shoes and making pooty noises.

"When are we going to get there?" I asked loudly.

"What's the hurry?" Mark said.

"We're already late."

"No we aren't," Carol said without turning around.

"Want to flip for nickels?" Gerald asked.

"No."

"Queer."

There was a long line of cars and trucks waiting to get into the parking lot. It was hot in the car and there was dust in the parking lot. A man with a red flag waved us into a space finally, and we got out. Mark's car was green and smelled new and I was glad to get out of it. People in shorts and jeans and bright shirts were moving around and away from the parked cars.

"We'll meet y'all here after the fireworks," Carol said. She took Mark's arm and they walked away. Gerald was looking around and saying, "Hot dog!"

"Wait for us," I said, but Carol and Mark went on walking. Carol didn't turn her head. "They're going off and leaving us," I said.

"Big deal," Gerald said. "Let's go."

I tried to keep them in sight, but I wasn't tall enough and there were too many people. I thought we wouldn't be able to find them again, and I didn't know what we would do. I followed Gerald as he moved toward the tents where the people were who made things or painted pictures to sell.

We went into a long, green tent and got into some sort of line that moved slowly from one stall to another. I saw lots of paintings set on easels on the beaten-down grass, but I didn't want any of them. There were also pottery stalls and glassware and blankets, but I didn't want any of them either. Gerald stopped in front of a stall where a man made arrowheads with flint chips and deer horns.

"How about that," Gerald said. "Just like an Indian. How neat can you get?"

"Yeah," I said, but I was looking at the next stall where jewelry was spread out on a table. I moved over there and looked at the rings and bracelets, and older people crowded around me and reached over my head. A girl and a man sat on lawn chairs behind the table. They looked older than Carol, but not too much older. The man was drinking a beer.

After a while, the girl stood up and came over to watch me. She had long red hair that hung loose over her shoulders and back, and she was thin-looking. The man got up and stood close behind her. She jumped forward a little.

"Hey," she said, turning around. "Watch that."

The man was grinning. "I am," he said. "I am."

I looked at where the man had been sitting and saw the

beer bottle lying empty on its side. I didn't see any golden chains.

"Can I help you, little kid?" the girl asked. The man sat on the edge of the table and looked at me. His eyes were red as if he had dust in them.

"Do you have any chains?" I asked, but they didn't hear me so I had to ask again.

"You mean necklaces?" the girl said.

"Sort of," I said. "But without anything hanging from it. Just the chain."

"Sure," she said. "What kind would you like?"

She pulled a tray out and put it where I could see it.

"A golden one like that," I said, pointing. The man laughed and I looked at him. I didn't like him. He was wearing a black shirt.

"Well, that's not real gold," the girl said.

"Why not?"

"It's just not. It's only gold colored."

"How much is it?"

"How much you got, bud?" the man asked. He was grinning.

"How much, please?" I asked, putting my hand over my pocket. No one was stopping at the stall and I was afraid the man would try to take my money.

"Two dollars," the girl said, glancing sideways at the man.

"Got that much, kid?" he asked.

I gave the girl two dollars and she let me hold the chain. It was a really nice chain. Carol wouldn't have to know it wasn't real gold. It looked like it to me. I was feeling very proud, thinking how happy Carol would be. I wasn't afraid of the man anymore.

"Do you have a box?" I asked when the girl had put the money up.

"I suppose so, if you want one." She took the chain from me and looked for a small box.

"You got a girlfriend, bud?" the man asked.

I didn't look at him, but watched the girl. Then I got scared that I would make him mad, so I said, "Maybe."

"Does she give you any?" he asked and laughed.

The girl looked from me to the man. "Cut it out, Johnny," she said.

"I was only wondering. No harm in wondering if the kid is getting any."

Gerald came up beside me and I was glad. He said, "Hey, what are you doing? That man over there is making real arrowheads."

"I bought a chain," I said, pointing to the girl who was putting it on the table while she looked for a box.

"A what?" Gerald said.

"Isn't it pretty?"

"What a queer," Gerald said.

"You don't know anything about it," I said.

The girl found a small box and put the chain in it. I was happy watching her. Carol would really be surprised and she would know how much I wanted her to stay. It was a pretty golden chain, not broken like her other one. The girl taped up the sides of the little box and gave it to me. She smiled and touched my hand when she put the box in it.

After we left the green tent, we stopped at the fishing booth and gave a smiling lady two dimes. She gave us each a short cane pole with white string and a clothespin on the end of it. We swung our poles over a high sheet and waited until we felt a tug. Our catches were in little white bags that were folded and stapled on top. We gave the poles back to the lady and walked away opening our bags. I got a yellow whistle and a small, paper puzzle. Gerald got a pair of Chinese handcuffs, which was really only one thing made out of straw. I liked the little yellow whistle, but it was more fun to shake the box and hear the golden chain clink around inside. It was a good surprise, and I looked everywhere for Carol.

Gerald stopped to talk to the man who ran the cyclone machine. He walked around looking several times before he stopped beside the man who was sitting on an iron seat working the cranks. The man was big and dirty and he was chewing tobacco. Gerald said hello twice, then he said in the tough, low voice he used whenever he tried to sound like Father, "Hell, I bet that ain't nothin' to work." The man spit tobacco juice on the grass and said, "You two squirts either ride or clear out. I got work to do, see?"

We walked down the midway next, watching people trying their luck at throwing things. I bought a cherry snow-cone and watched Gerald throw baseballs at some wooden milk bottles. Gerald could throw baseballs and rocks as well as anybody ever could. He missed with the first ball and I said something to him. He made a pooty sound at me and threw again, knocking them all down.

"So, what do you want?" the man said who ran the booth. "Another chance or a prize?"

"A prize."

The man gave Gerald a plastic doll. Gerald wrinkled up his face and made it redder than it usually was. "Hey," he said. "This prize isn't for my brother, it's for me. I don't want no crappy doll."

The man took the doll away and gave Gerald a rubber knife in a rubber sheath. As we walked away, Gerald pulled the knife out and stabbed me in the stomach and shoulder and back and neck.

"Cut it out," I said finally.

"Shut up. You're deader than dirt."

Gerald wanted to watch some men at the shooting gallery, so we went over there. I didn't care where we went as long as we kept moving around so that I might have a chance to find Carol. I imagined giving it to her, and her opening the box and saying, "A chain!"

At the shooting gallery, a man in a wide, gray cowboy hat had just won a large stuffed bear. He lifted it over the counter and handed it to a pretty girl in a yellow cotton dress, which swirled around her legs whenever she moved. Gerald went up to the counter where he could see, but for a minute I just watched the girl in the yellow dress. Her happy laugh made me think of Carol. She took the bear, her brown arms reaching around it. She kissed the man in the gray cowboy hat. "You're wonderful," I heard her say, just as if she had gotten a golden chain.

When the sun started going down, we were on the ferris wheel. At the top and on the way down, we could see the bright red sun on the dusty horizon, the river between the willows, and the brown dusty tops of the tents where they stretched in a row out to the parking lot. Then we swung down backwards past the little tin shed where the man sat on a stool, up away again, the dusty ground dropping further below us, then to the top and the red-orange setting sun.

The iron bar in front of us was slick and greasy. Gerald was squirming around, trying to see as much as he could, but there wasn't that much to see, except for the river that looked white in the reflection of the sky. The rest was crowded, dusty and noisy. I was holding the white box in my hand, and I looked at it from time to time to be sure it was all right. I hoped Carol wouldn't think it was too expensive, because it really wasn't—not for her. I thought about giving it to her and how happy she would be, opening it and laughing like the girl in the yellow dress before she kissed me, saying, "It's such a pretty golden chain."

"Look down there," Gerald said suddenly. "Look at all those little people."

"Tell me if you see Carol," I said.

Gerald turned and looked at me, then dropped his eyes to the little white box in my hand.

"Are you really going to give that to Carol?" he asked.

"Sure. She'll like it, too."

"If you have your heart set on giving it to her, why don't you wait until her birthday?"

"I want to give it to her tonight. She said she wanted a golden chain more than anything else in the world."

"Ricky—" Gerald started to say, then he looked away. "Oh hell," he said. "You're just a dumb little queer."

"I'm not either," I said.

"You'll find out."

The ferris wheel slowed and started letting people off. When it was our turn, we threw back the bar and jumped into the crowd. The shadows had all gone and it would be dark before long. Gerald said he was hungry, but I didn't say anything because I was mad at him for what he had said before. I followed him to a hotdog stand, and we bought two hotdogs with chili and relish on them. I ran out of money, so Gerald had to help me pay for mine. We sat down on a bench to eat. I put the little box beside me and looked at it while I ate. One of the pieces of tape had begun to curl back. I tried to smooth it back down, but the sticky was gone.

It got dark while we ate. Pretty soon it would be time for the fireworks show. When we were through, I said, "I'm going to look for Carol."

Gerald didn't pay much attention. He had some chili on his chin. "Good for you," he said.

"Where are you going to be?"

"Watchin' the fireworks."

"I'll see you later then," I said, standing up.

Gerald looked at me and shook his head, but he didn't say anything. I walked away, looking along the midway first, then going into the tents, the big green one last.

It was dark when I got out of the tent, but there were lights strung out all along the edges of all the tents and of the separate stalls. Dust seemed to collect around the lights along with little white moths and June bugs that buzzed crazily about knocking into things and falling down. I had no idea where Carol could have been, but I thought they might be dancing, so I went over to the platform and walked slowly around the edges looking at all the couples. The dance floor was covered with sawdust and the couples went around and around to the tune of a polka. They were locked together and spun around and dipped this way, then that way, and the girls' skirts twirled around and away from their legs. There were lots of people on the floor or watching, and I circled the platform several times before I was sure that Carol and Mark were not up there.

When the polka ended, I walked slowly away from the platform to the path beside the river that was now lit with paper lanterns of different colors that swayed when the wind blew them. I could hear the men across the river announcing the fireworks display. The chain in the box was heavy in my hand. I was sure that Carol would never know that the chain was not real gold. Maybe she would pin it on the wall behind the wilted flower in her room and throw the other one away. It was broken after all.

A couple passed me walking slowly away from the river with their arms around each other. I moved to the edge of the willow-lined path and stood in the shadow of a yellow lantern to watch them go by. They seemed very happy together, and it made me happy too, to think how pleased Carol would be. "You're wonderful," she would probably say. The girl let her head fall on the man's shoulder and they went by without noticing me. Another polka started up from the band on the dance floor. It sounded very far away.

I walked down to the river feeling strange, as if running were not allowed on the path, or loud talking either. The frogs and the crickets even seemed hushed along the river. For a minute I watched the dark water, seeing the flow only in the ripples that made wrinkles across the reflections of the lanterns.

Couples were huddled close together in the dim light on the benches that had been set out along the water's edge. I looked quickly at them as I went by, looking for Carol's blue skirt. The couples didn't notice me.

Farther along, the path curved away from the river and the only benches were the ones around picnic tables set back in little clearings among the willows. There were couples at these too, huddled close together and kissing each other. In the fourth clearing I heard Carol's voice, whispering, and I was glad because I knew she wouldn't be kissing. I held the box carefully so the chain wouldn't make any noise and I walked slowly to the edge of the clearing.

In the weak light I saw just one shape on the bench, then I saw Mark move his head on Carol's chest as she sat with her back against the table. Her face was pale in the darkness and her eyes were closed. She was whispering Mark's name over and over, but that was all she said, just his name, over and over. His head moved again slightly and Carol moaned and brought her arms up and circled them around his head.

I was holding the box with the chain in it very carefully in my hand and my heart was beating fast and I was scared. I didn't know what they were doing, but suddenly I knew that I shouldn't have been there, that the chain would not make any difference. There was an explosion behind me and Carol lowered her head and opened her eyes.

"No!" she cried as the sky turned to fire over our heads. Mark sat up very straight and wild-eyed. I saw that Carol's blouse was unbuttoned and open.

"What the hell?" Mark said.

"Carol," I started to say, but as the light from the fireworks died out she jumped up from the bench and ran over to me, pulling her blouse together as she ran. I wanted to run too, but I could only stand there. Another rocket went up with a boom, and Carol slapped me hard on the cheek and nose, but before I could run away she dropped to her knees and grabbed my shoulders. My cheek was burning and my eyes were stinging. The rocket exploded over us. I looked down at Carol's blouse.

"Ricky," she said. Then she stuttered, then she said, "What are you doing here?"

She was gripping my shoulders very tightly, so tightly I could feel her nails through my shirt. Her whispers were like sharp ice in the warm night. I was still holding the box in my hand. I wanted to tell her about the chain, but I couldn't talk.

"Carol—" I started again, but I couldn't talk. I started to cry.

"Please Ricky," Carol said.

"There was a girl in a yellow dress," I tried to say. "She took the bear. Gerald said I should—"

I was crying and didn't know what I was saying and Carol couldn't understand me. I wanted to run away. I started to hate Carol, but I couldn't think. I wanted to run away.

"Ricky," Carol said. "Oh God, I know how you must feel—what you must think, but promise me. Listen to me. Promise me, Ricky, that you'll still love me."

I was squeezing the box in my hand. I couldn't get my breath or understand what was happening. The whole sky was filled with red and green and white and blue fire.

"Promise me," Carol said.

"No," I said.

I twisted away from her and ran back to the path, then along it back to the river, toward the lights and the music and the fireworks. When I got to the river, I coughed and spit to make myself stop crying, but at first it seemed that nothing could stop the sobs without stopping me altogether. Then I got the hiccups and spit again and stopped crying and looked out at the river. The lights of the fireworks mixed with the lights of the lanterns on the surface of the river, but it all looked ugly to me now. I felt very far away from it all and lonely.

I raised the small, white box to the light and looked at it blurry until I rubbed my fist across my eyes. The box looked to me as if someone else had bought it. The tape was curled up on one side where the sticky was gone. I had smudged the top with my wet fingers. There was no one to give it to now, not even Rebecca. I threw it hard into the river without looking and turned away before I heard the splash.

Summertime

WHEN SOMETHING HAPPENED to Father, he did what he had to do to get things back to the way he wanted them or he forgot about them. He didn't let it bother him and he didn't worry about it. Mama worried. Father just drank his coffee, then did whatever he could do. If there wasn't anything he could do, he just stepped back. For three days I tried to be like Father. There was nothing I could do about Carol, and I wasn't going to cry anymore, so I just stayed away from her. When she came into the room, I went out again. When she asked a question, I pretended I didn't hear.

On Saturday she came into the dining room right after breakfast all dressed up to go to work. I wanted to think she was pretty, but I wouldn't let myself. I put my elbows on the table and started drinking my milk. Me and Carol were the only ones in the dining room.

"Do you know where Father went?" Carol asked. She was standing behind Mama's chair with her hands on the back of it.

I sipped my milk and didn't look at her.

"Ricky, I asked you a question."

I sipped my milk and looked out the window. The milk wasn't very cold, but I started feeling cold down inside of me.

"Oh, you make me so mad when you act like this," Carol said in her sharp voice. "What you saw the other night has nothing to do with you and me. It never did. Can't you understand that?"

She waited. I swallowed my milk. I wanted to start crying, but Father wouldn't have, so I tried hard not to.

"Ricky, please."

The telephone rang and Mama came out of her bedroom and answered it. "Carol?" she called. "It's for you."

Carol stood there behind Mama's chair for just a minute more staring at me before she went to answer the telephone. I finished my milk and went outside.

Father honked as he drove up. Me and Gerald were chopping weeds along the back porch. They were mostly stunted ragweeds and the other kind with little flat leaves that spreads out like grass and is hard to chop in the hard dirt. My shoulders felt like they were about to fall off from banging that hoe on the ground.

"Now what?" Gerald said.

We threw down our hoes and walked down toward the barn. It had been hot in the shade, but the sunshine was not only hot, it blinded us too. Father's truck was stopped at the gate down by the barn, and we could see that the back was sagging down under a high pile of feed sacks. Father was opening the gate.

"Terrific," Gerald said. "Just what I wanted to do. Why couldn't he have gotten all that the other day when he said he was?"

"I think he said—"

"Shut up."

Father saw us as he came around to get back in his truck. He looked at us and got in the truck. He started it. The motor revved and the truck began to move slowly, rocking from side to side on the uneven ground.

"Close the gate," Gerald said as we walked through.

I stopped and swung the gate closed. Gerald walked on down to the barn. Father turned out from the barn, then backed in under the big window. The milk cow was in the shade under the barn. She looked at the truck and raised her big nose a little.

Father stepped out of the truck when we got there. "Y'all busy?" he said.

Gerald just looked at him. "Not really," I said.

"Good. We're goin' to put this feed in the long room. But first, we need to see what's in there."

Father stepped past us and opened the door to the walkway. Gerald looked at the pile of feed sacks. He pushed his hat back on his head and spit. "Crap," he said.

The long room was mostly empty except for a pile of old towsacks, some rusty baling wire, and cornshucks scattered around. Father looked at it a minute, then he turned to us.

"No use unloadin' that feed until this room is cleaned out. Let's drag all these towsacks and wire out and pile them by the truck. Then, when we get the truck unloaded, we'll pile all this stuff in it and I'll haul it off."

"There's plenty of room for the feed in here right now," Gerald said.

"I don't care. I want this room cleaned out. Now would be a good time, unless you got somethin' better to do."

"I always got somethin' better to do than crap like this," Gerald said, pushing it.

Father set his feet and looked at Gerald. I could tell he was getting pretty mad because the muscles in his jaw were working and he was looking at Gerald without blinking. I was thinking something must have happened in town to put Father on edge.

"Son," Father said, low but hard. "I'm gettin' mighty tired of listenin' to your mouth everytime somethin' has to be done around here. Now, as long as you live in my house and eat my food, there is goin' to be work that needs doin', and you're goin' to do it. When you get your own place, you can do whatever you want, but as long as you're here, you're goin' to do what I want. Is that clear?"

Gerald was chewing on his lip and looking at Father.

"I want to know right now," Father said.

"Yeah," Gerald said.

Father turned and went outside. His boots sounded heavy

on the floor of the walkway. Gerald didn't turn to look at the door, then he did. "Son of a bitch," he said.

"Come on," I said. "Let's do it."

I grabbed up a tangle of rusty baling wire and started dragging it toward the door. Several loops fell out of the tangle. I dragged it along the walkway and out beside the truck. The milk cow was standing beside the truck looking at me like somebody sitting at the table waiting for the food. Father was going through the gate toward the house.

When I went back in, Gerald was just standing there.

"Come on," I said. "This is going to take all day."

"Shut up," Gerald said. "I'll start when I'm good and ready."

I picked up more wire and dragged it out. On my way back in, Gerald passed me with a load of dusty towsacks. His face was wrinkled up and he held the bags as far away from him as he could because they made him sneeze. He didn't look at me.

It took us about an hour to clean the long room out. By the time we had finished, we had killed two rats and the room was filled with smoky dust. We went out to the water trough. The water in it was muddy-looking and the sides of the concrete trough were covered with green scum. We put our heads in the water to get the scratchy dust off. Gerald was sneezing with just about every breath. I sat there a minute dripping and listened to his sneezing.

"Why don't you stop?" I said.

"I would if I could, idiot," he said, between sneezes. "Damn," he said. "I hate this crap."

Father came back down and went into the long room. When he came out, he didn't look at us, but went straight to the truck and opened the tailgate. He let it drop free of the chains so that he could get right up to the back of the truck. He grabbed a bag of feed and turned with it and took it into the long room.

We went over to the truck when Father came to get another bag. "How does it look?" I asked.

Father looked over at me. "Dusty." He pulled another bag

off the truck and carried it inside. His boots were heavy on the floor.

"You get in the truck and roll those bags down," Gerald said. "I'll help carry them."

"You can't lift those sacks," I said.

"Watch me."

Gerald pulled a sack to the edge of the truck, got it up on his hip, and put his strong hands on it. Father came out of the room and watched Gerald go by. I looked at Father's face. I couldn't tell what he was thinking. He was just looking.

Just before dinner, Mr. Daniels drove up. He was a heavy man with white hair and deep lines in his face and eyes that made him look crazy-mean. He smoked a pipe and drove around in a white Studebaker pickup. Sometimes he passed me on the road when I was coming up the hill from the store. He would be sitting hunched over the wheel with his pipe in his mouth and his eyes crazy-mean looking. He had a big farm farther south toward Seguin with lots of big barns and silos and cattle and stuff. He had some oil on his land too.

Me and Gerald had just closed the gate and Father had just gotten out of his truck when Mr. Daniels drove up. He parked under the elm tree and watched Worthless wander up to sniff his tires. We went up there about the time Father got there. We were all hot and itchy and sweaty. Mr. Daniels was holding his pipe in one hand and the steering wheel in the other. His mean eyes covered all of us.

"Howdy, Mac," he said, hardly moving his mouth.

"How you doin'," Father said.

Mr. Daniels didn't say anything. He looked at us. "These your boys?" he said.

"Yep."

"Uh-huh," Mr. Daniels said. Then he didn't say anything for a while. Father watched him. "Workin' hard?" Mr. Daniels said.

"Stayin' busy," Father said.

"Uh-huh." Mr. Daniels looked around. "Place looks good."

Father looked around. He took his hat off and pulled his handkerchief out of his back pocket and wiped his face with it.

"Somethin' a matter with your tractor?" Mr. Daniels said slowly.

"Yep. Not sure what. Had a man who was goin' to he'p me break it down, but I haven't seen him."

I shivered and scratched my neck.

"Uh-huh," Mr. Daniels said. Then he didn't say anything. Gerald sneezed. "Who was it?" Mr. Daniels said.

"New fella," Father said. "Thought he could use the work."

"Uh-huh."

I looked at Gerald. His face was serious. He was watching Mr. Daniels. The way Mr. Daniels acted bothered me, but Father didn't seem to pay any attention to it.

"Your Mex'cans gone?" Mr. Daniels asked.

"My Mexicans?"

"Gonzales and his bunch."

"They went on. Yeah. Several weeks ago."

"Uh-huh. Sorriest goddamned race of people on the face of the earth," Mr. Daniels said.

"Gonzales is a good man. All of that bunch is. Been helpin' me and Papa for years."

"Uh-huh. Okay if you like 'em."

Mr. Daniels looked around for a while. He put the pipe in his mouth and took it out again. His crazy-mean eyes went from one thing to another like he was looking for something.

"Doin' well enough to hire a man for your tractor, huh?" Mr. Daniels said.

"Thought he could use the work," Father said, changing his voice a little.

"Uh-huh. Most farmers are takin' work themselves."

"It may come to that."

"Uh-huh."

Mr. Daniels didn't say anything for a while. Gerald blew his nose and wiped his fingers on his pants. Mr. Daniels took his pipe out of his mouth and looked at him. Then he looked at Father.

"Talked to your brother-in-law a few weeks ago," he said.

"Heard about it," Father said.

"Uh-huh. Decided this dry spell had beaten him. He's readin' meters for the light company now."

Father didn't say anything, then he said, "Lots of folks are havin' to do somethin' else. Like you said."

"Uh-huh."

Mr. Daniels knocked his pipe against the door of his truck and started to put tobacco in it. Mama came to the door and said dinner was ready.

"That your wife?"

"Yeah," Father said.

"Uh-huh."

Mr. Daniels lit his pipe and blew smoke out the window of the truck. "Too bad what happened to Elmer Ketchum, wasn't it?"

Father nodded.

"Uh-huh. Course, he had it comin'. Never liked him. Talked to the widow yesterday. Crazy as hell. Treats her cat like it was Elmer."

I could tell Mama was watching from inside the house, but neither me nor Gerald wanted to go in.

"So. You're doin' okay," Mr. Daniels said when Father didn't say anything.

"Yeah."

"Uh-huh. Cotton looks like it's startin' to burn up. You goin' in the Soil Bank?"

"Nope."

"Uh-huh. Just growin' it for the seed, then?"

"No sir, not just for the seed."

"Uh-huh. You think that cotton is goin' to make?"

"Yep."

"You wouldn't be interested in a lease arrangement?"

"Nope."

"Uh-huh." Mr. Daniels reached down and started his truck. Before he put it in gear, he looked at all of us with his mean eyes. Then he looked at Father. "Then you're crazy as Ketchum's widow."

He drove down toward the shop and turned around. When he went by, he had his pipe in his mouth and was hunched over the steering wheel. He didn't look at us.

Father turned and went into the house. We followed him. After we had washed up and were sitting at the table, Mama asked what Mr. Daniels had wanted.

"A lease arrangement,'" Father said, tearing a piece of bread in half.

"What did you tell him?"

"Not interested."

We all looked at Mama and she smiled. Dinner tasted good.

After rest time, me and Gerald went down to the shop and got both the rakes and the old pitchfork. One pitchfork was already in the barn, but this was the old one. Father wanted us to clean out the loft and to stack all the hay bales along the walls near the windows where they would be easy to get to, but the weather wouldn't ruin them. I didn't mind doing it, and after the way Father had talked to Mr. Daniels, even Gerald was willing to do something for him. Father said at dinner that Mr. Daniels was just an old dried-up man with more money than he knew what to do with and that he liked to drive around bullying people.

Father had opened the gates at both ends of the lane that led from the barnyard down into the pasture so that the cows could come up around the barn for feed but still go down in the pasture for water. Since the well was getting so low, he decided not to use the water troughs anymore. Once they went dry, that was it. Some of the cows were standing or lying in the shade of the barn when we went down there. Their ribs were showing and the flies were thick on their backs.

Gerald climbed up the ladder to the loft and I passed him the rakes and the pitchfork. When I got up there, we started on the lower level, raking the loose hay and tangled bits of wire to the edge of the window and pushing it out. The cows began to congregate under the window, so we collected the hay until there was a big pile of it, then we pushed it out and watched it fall on their heads and backs. They didn't care. When the piles dropped, the wind caught at the dust and made the piles look like they were smoking. The lower level was about as big as a basketball court and there was lots of old rotten hay on it. Some of it had gotten wet and was stuck to the floor in a moldy heap.

When the floor was all clean, we stopped and rested in one of the windows, the one that faced the road. A little bit of hot breeze blew in on us. The cows were walking around under us, eating the old hay and walking on it. Out across the road, heat waves shimmered off the cotton field. Gerald sneezed.

"I'll be glad when we're through with this," he said.

"Me too," I said, but I wasn't thinking about the barn. From the high edge of the window, I could see the top part of Rebecca's house through the leaves of the pecan tree in their front yard. The balloon started to grow in my chest again. I worked my jaw muscles to keep it down.

"What's the matter with you?" Gerald sneezed.

"Nothing."

"You chewin' on somethin'?"

"No."

"Look at the mirage over the cotton field," Gerald said. "It looks like a lake."

"I wish it was," I said.

"Yeah," Gerald said. "We ought to go swimmin' when we get through with this."

"The tank is too muddy. I don't like the way it smells."

"Then forget it."

Gerald stood up and sneezed and spit. He went over to the edge of the upper level, which was the ceiling of the long room below. The only good hay we had was piled up there, and it was old. If we had to use it for the rest of the summer, there would be no telling what we would feed the cows in the winter. I didn't care if we sold them, but I knew Father didn't want to. The price of cows in Texas had dropped so much it would be like giving them away.

The upper level was about even with Gerald's shoulders. He went up to it and put his hands on the edge and pulled himself up. I walked across to the ladder and climbed up to it.

"Let's push all these bales off first, then we can stack 'em," Gerald said. "I'll take this end."

I climbed up five bales, then walked across the top of the hay until I was near the back. The hay there was stacked up to seven bales high. It was dark and shadowy back in the corner and I didn't like it. I turned and watched Gerald roll a bale down and onto the floor of the lower level. I looked back in the corner where the shadows were the deepest. I didn't know what it was that made me so afraid of that end of the barn.

I stepped up to the nearest stack and pulled a bale down. There was nothing behind it except the wall covered with dust and cobwebs. I rolled the bale over to the edge and let it roll down. Dust flew off it like smoke and the smell of it was thick as smoke back in that dark corner. I turned back. The corner seemed even darker. I couldn't help it. I went down to Gerald's end and started helping him.

"What are you doin' down here?" he said.

"Helping you," I said.

He looked at me a minute, then looked over at the other end of the barn. He bent down and pulled another bale loose.

The hay on Gerald's end of the barn was newer and not as dusty. We rolled the bales off until there was a big pile on the lower level. We could stand on the floor now and flip the bales end over end until they hit the pile below us and tumbled on down or got stuck in the pile. One of them rolled out the side window. We ran to see if it had hit a cow, but it hadn't. It was just broken out on the ground.

The barn began to look like a totally different place at that end. Near the back wall, we moved a bale of hay and there were our cigar boxes where we had hidden them. For a minute, we stopped and just looked down at them. It was the first time the back wall had not had hay against it. Behind the boxes was the crack in the boards where we could spy on the tank. I began to feel how different everything was getting to be. I looked at Gerald.

"Well, so much for that hiding place," he said.

"We can find another one," I said.

"You can. I'm too old for that stuff now."

"You weren't too old last month," I said.

"Last month was a million years ago," Gerald said.

He rolled the bale of hay across the floor and pushed it off the upper level. It fell about a foot and stayed there, on top of the stack. All the hay was on the lower level now except the hay in the far corner. Gerald came back and picked up his cigar box. I picked up mine too, and we climbed down the pile of hay and went over to the window again to rest.

I sat down and opened my cigar box. Inside there was my old wooden pistol, some matches and a candle, and, on the bottom, a valentine that Rebecca had sent me the year before. I picked it up and looked at it. The balloon started growing again. I turned it over. In ink, on the back, in Rebecca's tight handwriting, was the note, "For Ricky. My pirate and my true love forever. Rebecca Brown."

Gerald was dumping his stuff out of his cigar box onto the heads of the cows down under us. He looked at me.

"What's that?"

"A valentine from Rebecca."

"Well, you won't be getting any more of those," Gerald said.

He stood up. I put the stuff back in my box and stood up too. We put them by the edge of the window and looked around.

"Want to stack those bales first or push the other ones down?" Gerald said.

"I don't care."

"Let's stack them first, then. These are newer, so it'd be best to put them on the bottom."

One by one, we carried or rolled the bales of old hay over into the corner of the lower level and started stacking them. They were between the windows now, where the rain couldn't get at them, but they would be easy to toss down for the cows. We stacked over thirty bales before we stopped again. Then, after a short rest, we climbed up on the upper level and went back into the farthest corner where the hay was old and dusty. Even with Gerald beside me, I didn't like being in that corner.

Gerald went all the way to the back and pulled a bale off

the top. After it fell, he forced his fingers under the tight wire and picked it up. Our hands were rough and had little cuts in them from doing that all afternoon. That's why I liked to just roll the bales, although sometimes an old grassburr would stick me in the palm of my hand.

Behind the first bale of hay I moved was the skeleton of some small animal. It surprised me. I called Gerald over.

"What is it? A cat?" I asked.

"Possum," Gerald said. He picked up the yellow skull and looked at it. It had sharp teeth. "Must have got up under here and died," Gerald said. He threw the skull down with the hay. It had an old, dead smell about it.

"This corner gives me the creeps," I said.

I thought Gerald would make fun of me, but he just said, "Yeah."

We rolled hay off until we had worked ourselves back into the corner. The top bales back there were not stacked against the wall. There was room back there for someone to hide behind them. When I thought of that, I knew why I had been afraid. I stood back and watched while Gerald pulled those bales off. There were three bales along the back wall and two along the side wall. Gerald pulled them off one by one. When he pulled the last one off, I made a dumb sound and pointed. Gerald jumped to the side like a snake was up there, but it wasn't a snake. It was a beat-up old hat like the one Wilbur always wore.

There wasn't much to do on Monday. It was always like that. Sometimes we worked until we couldn't stand it anymore, but other times there wasn't much to do. On summer days like that, the time would go by slowly and I would get bored. I was bored and restless on Monday. I finished all my stuff early and everybody else was doing something. Finally I went into the kitchen and stood around by the cabinet watching Mama. She was cleaning out the icebox.

After a while, she looked at me and said, "What?"

"Can I go down to the store?"

"Just you?"

"Yeah."

"Yes ma'am."

"Yes ma'am."

"Where's Gerald?"

I figured he was up in the pasture trying to see Ruby Lee, but I said, "I don't know."

"All right. Don't get in the way, and be back before dinner."

I got my hat off the nail on the back porch and went down to the store. At the top of the hill, I couldn't help but look at Mr. Ketchum's cotton field. Parts of it were turning a dark, rusty brown, like dried blood. Only half of it was plowed, just like the day Mr. Ketchum died. Father thought that if Mr. Daniels got the land, he would go ahead and let the crop fail and use it as a tax write-off. That meant he wouldn't have to pay much tax because he was so rich and stuff.

It still scared me to think about the day that Mr. Ketchum had died, but since Wilbur had not been around, I tried not to think about it very much. I watched Father and learned how he might do things, and I would try to make myself mad every time I started feeling scared. It helped. That, and not seeing Wilbur. Nobody had seen Wilbur.

When I walked up to the store, I saw Mr. Norman sitting on the concrete porch near the screen door. He had pulled out a chair and was sitting close enough to the edge of the porch that he could spit onto the ground by just turning his head a little bit.

"Mornin', boy," he said as I walked up.

"Good morning," I said.

"What can I do for you this mornin'?"

I walked up to him and stopped. Walking down the hill had made me hot. It was shady and there was a good breeze on the porch of the store.

"Can I get a sody water?"

"You payin'?"

"Yes sir."

"Go ahead, then."

"Can I put a nickel in the cash register?"

"Eh?"

"Can I put—"

"Yeah, yeah. Go ahead."

When I came back out of the store, Mr. Norman had just finished spitting. He wiped his mouth and looked at me.

"Drag a chair out here, if you've a mind to."

"I'll just sit on the step," I said.

I sat down and turned my head to look at Rebecca's house. It made me feel funny to think that if I went over there, the house would be all locked up on the outside and all empty on the inside.

"I know what you're thinkin', son," Mr. Norman said. "It's mighty lonely down here with them folks gone. Not that Mr. Brown was all that much company, but that little girl of his sure was."

"Yeah," I said.

"She used to come over to my house in the evenin's and sit on the porch with me. Half the time I didn't know what she was sayin' because I don't hear so good anymore, but long as I could see that happy little face, it didn't much matter. I said, happy, but you know there was somethin' sad in her face too, like she knew somethin' bad that the rest of us couldn't see. I've known that look before, but not in anybody as young as her."

I drank my orange and looked at the ground. Mr. Norman yawned and spit.

"First night they left, I come out on the porch over there at the house and just sat down waitin' for it to get dark. I was waitin' for it to get dark so's I could see their light wasn't comin' on. I sat there and it got dark and that house was dark and quiet as the grave."

"Yeah," I said. I took another drink of my orange. It tasted funny.

"Just had to see it to believe it, I guess," Mr. Norman said and spit. "Ain't been sleepin' good at night since they left, either."

"What's going to happen to the house now?" I asked.

"Oh, somebody'll buy it, I reckon. It's for sale, you know."

"Yeah."

We sat on the porch for a while. It was cool there. Mr. Norman spit and I drank my orange.

"Sure is quiet," Mr. Norman said. "I don't know what to think. It's like a storm was brewin', but there ain't no storm. I've lived a long time and ain't never felt nothin' like it."

"What do you mean?"

Mr. Norman spit. "Hard to say, boy. Hard to say. Has somethin' to do with the weather, but it ain't all the weather. People get peculiar when things stay the same way for too long a time, if it stays hot or cold or cloudy or clear too long. A few weeks ago, about the time Elmer and your granddaddy passed away, I thought all hell was about to break loose, and in a way it did, I guess, but I don't think we've got to the end of it yet. I think there's still more to happen. More that ain't good."

"Like what?"

"Eh?"

"What kind of bad things?"

"I don't know, but I'll tell you this. I'll bet whatever happens, that Wilbur Rutts will be involved. I don't care for that man at all."

"Me either," I said.

"Listen," Mr. Norman said. "You say you didn't see Wilbur and Elmer havin' an argument that day he was killed like they had in the store that time?"

"No sir."

"You didn't see anything like that?"

"No sir."

"I don't believe it," Mr. Norman said. "I never have, and I never will."

I finished my orange and thought about what Mr. Norman was saying. He knew the trouble came from Wilbur. I wanted to tell him right then what I had seen and what Wilbur said later, but I got scared and didn't. I remembered the hat we found in the barn. It could have been anybody's, but it looked enough like Wilbur's to scare me.

Mr. Norman spit. "Oh well," he said. "Summertime is

about over anyway. Another six weeks and school will start again, though Lord, it won't be the same without that little Rebecca around."

"No sir," I said.

"Eh?"

"I said, no, it won't be the same."

"It sure won't," Mr. Norman said. He leaned away and spit.

Mama was cooking dinner. Father had gone to the bank in town, and Carol was at work. I went into the kitchen and watched Mama cooking. I didn't know why I felt like watching her, but I did. She moved around like she always knew exactly what she was going to do next. If she needed a spoon or a pan, her hand started reaching for it before she would even turn to look where it was. Sometimes she would hum or sing to herself while she cooked. When she was doing that, she reminded me of Carol.

"What are you doing now?" she asked.

"Nothing."

"How is it that I work my fingers to the bone every day and you never have anything to do?"

"Is Father coming home for dinner?"

"He said he would. Where's Gerald?"

"I think he's fishing."

"He sure does a lot of fishing these days. Why doesn't he ever bring any fish to the house?"

"I don't know."

"Well, go get him. Dinner will be ready in about thirty minutes."

I put my hat on again and went down into the pasture. Gerald had been going down there with his pole and sticking it in the mud of the tank. Then he would slip off up the washout and see Ruby Lee for a little while. If anybody wanted to know where he was, he would say he had been fishing.

When I got to the tank, I saw that his pole was there, stuck in the mud, but he wasn't. I went up through the washout, going slow and listening. This time I turned the bend and

268

walked right up on them before I saw them. They didn't see me, so I ducked back out of sight. They were kissing and both of them had their eyes closed. I got down on my stomach and looked through a clump of dry grass at them.

Ruby Lee was wearing a pair of blue jeans and a brown shirt. She was barefooted and her feet were dirty. Gerald was leaning back against the bank of the washout and Ruby Lee was leaning across him, kissing him. Gerald brought his hand up and put it on Ruby Lee's little tit. Ruby Lee wiggled around when Gerald did that. My heart was beating as fast as a bird's heart.

Ruby Lee pushed away and sat back. She shook her hair out of her face and looked at Gerald. Gerald was grinning at her. He sat up.

"My oh my, but I believe you feelin' kinda serious," Ruby Lee said.

"Yeah," Gerald said.

"Well just calm yourself. I don't plan to drop my pants in no gulley."

"Why not?" Gerald said.

"Because. Why not do you think?"

"I don't know."

"Because I'm not, that's all."

Ruby Lee rubbed the back of her hand across her mouth and looked at Gerald. After a minute, she smiled and smoothed her shirt down.

"Did you like what you felt?" she asked.

"Sure," he said.

"You give me a dollar and I might let you do a little more than just feel."

"I don't have a dollar," Gerald said.

"Ever think about gettin' one?"

"I might."

"Well, if you might, then I might," Ruby Lee said and laughed.

I scooted backwards and ran down the washout for a little way then stopped and started calling Gerald's name as I walked slowly along. I had gone about fifty feet before he came around a bend in the washout with his hands in his pockets.

"What do you want?" he said.

"Mama said it was time for dinner. Where have you been?"

"Lookin' for grasshoppers," he said.

"How many did you find?" I asked.

Gerald looked at me as we walked along. Then he looked at the ground.

I was in the shop when Wilbur drove up. I went to the door to see who it was. He was already too close for me to run to the house. He came to a stop by the tractor and got out of his truck before the dust had time to settle. I ducked into a corner of the shop and crouched down to hide, but he came right in there and saw me and came over to me, licking his lips.

"Well, boy," he said, reaching out and grabbing me by the arm and pulling me up. "Long time no see. What you been sayin' 'bout me, huh? You been a good little son of a bitch or a bad one?"

"I haven't said anything," I said, shaking.

Wilbur's face was just the way it was in my worst dreams. It was dirty and ugly, and his skin was rough and scaly, and his eyes were little and sharp like the eyes of a snake.

"It's a damn good thing, boy, because I been watchin' you. I been watchin' ever' step you make. You better never get in my way. Not ever."

Wilbur turned me loose and looked out the door of the shop. Father was walking up.

"Well, hello there, Mr. MacAllister," Wilbur said, stepping out of the shop into the bright sunlight. "I bet you thought you'd seen the last of me, goddamn."

I looked around the corner and saw them shaking hands.

"I thought you'd changed your mind," Father said.

"Oh hell no. I just got so damned busy with some movin' in business that I couldn't make it, but I'm just fine now. Just fine. Son of a bitch in Gonzales took me to court was the problem, but I straightened him out. Just fine."

"Good," Father said. He looked around Wilbur into the shop.

"Uh, I was just askin' your boy there where the tools was so I could get started this afternoon. That is, if you still want me to."

"Job's yours," Father said. "I've been savin' it for you."

Father and Wilbur walked into the shop. Father blinked in the shadow of the shop. Then he saw me.

"You helpin' Mr. Rutts?" Father said.

"Oh sure," Wilbur said, licking his lips. "He's a good boy. He's he'pin' me a lot."

After supper, Father stood between the dining room and the living room staring at the television without really looking at it. It was about seven-thirty and still hot, but a good breeze was blowing in the south windows. Mama looked at Father each time she went from the table back into the kitchen. It was Gerald's turn to wash dishes and he was plenty mad about it. What really made him mad was that since Carol had started working, she didn't have to wash dishes anymore. She was upstairs, but I didn't care about her.

"We work just as hard as she does," Gerald said.

"Oh be quiet," Mama said. "And remember: whatever you break is coming out of your allowance."

That settled Gerald down. He wanted as much money as he could get, and I knew why.

After Father had stood there a while, Mama said, "What's the matter?"

Father shook his head and shrugged.

"Are you still hungry?"

"No. Supper was fine."

"What is it, then?"

Father shrugged again. Then he said, "I think I'll take a ride back up on the hill."

He turned and went through the kitchen. Mama called me from the dining room. I was watching "The Adventures of Robin Hood."

"What."

"Don't you 'what' me. I want you to go with Father."

"Where's he going?"

"I don't know, but I want you to go with him. Hurry now. He's already outside."

"All right."

I got up and went out the front door. Father was walking over to his truck. I could hear his boots on the gravel. I jumped over Worthless who was lying on the porch and ran around to the back. Father was pulling open the door of the truck on his side. I went around to the other side. He looked across at me.

"What do you think you're doin'?" he said.

"I'm going with you."

"You are, huh? How come?"

"Mama told me to."

For a minute, Father turned and looked back at the house. It was still a lot lighter outside than it was in the house and Father couldn't see in the screens. But if he could have, he would have been looking right at Mama.

"All right. Get in."

We both got in and Father started up the truck. I liked the inside of Father's truck. On the sun visor on his side was a clip with feed tickets and envelopes stuck under it. Some of the envelopes had writing in pencil on them, figures and telephone numbers. On the dash were old papers, cigar packages, a package of chewing tobacco, a tape measure, some pens, string, a pair of pliers, one of Carol's plastic rollers, a bent piece of wire, and some nails. There were always cigar butts in the ash tray, and they made the inside of the truck smell like Father.

Father backed around, then drove past the shop. I looked over at the tractor. Ever since Wilbur had said he would work on the tractor, I didn't like it. It seemed to just be sitting there like some animal sleeping. Sometimes I would turn and look at it and it would scare me in a way I didn't understand. We went past the sheds and the pile of old fence posts down to the first gate. When Father stopped, I got out, opened it, and closed it behind him.

We drove up on the tank dam and Father slowed down to a stop and looked at the muddy water. Some fish hit the top and made little circles in the water.

"It's going dry," I said.

"Yeah."

"Think it will last until winter?"

Father let up on the clutch. "I don't know."

We drove over the dam and then around to the next gate that opened on Father's biggest field of cotton. I got out and opened the gate and Father drove through and turned along the edge of the field. I closed the gate and went over to the truck, but Father was getting out. He reached back in and got a cigar off the dash, then closed the door. I went around beside him while he unwrapped the cigar. We were at the very edge of the field. The rows of cotton wound away from us toward where the sun was getting low in the sky. Father started walking. The cotton brushed against his boots as he stepped through the rows. The dirt was still hot under my bare feet. Every now and then there was a crack in the black dirt that ran like jagged lightning across the field.

Father stopped and knelt down beside a low bush of cotton. He broke off one of the little green bolls and cracked it open with his thumbnail. The skin was thick and the cotton inside looked wet like baby chicken feathers when they first break out of the shell.

"How does it look?" I asked.

"Small," Father said. "Small and burned up."

"When will it be ready?"

"A few more weeks. Never."

We walked on a little bit until we were at the top of the hill in the middle of the cotton. I could see where the rows ended at the fence. I had to squint my eyes against the sun.

"I don't know," Father said.

"Don't know what?"

"I don't know if I did the right thing not plowin' this cotton under, not turnin' this land over to the Soil Bank."

"It doesn't look too bad," I said.

"The plants don't," Father said. "They're small, but cotton is hardy. It likes hot weather."

"What, then?"

"It ain't makin', that's what. It just ain't makin'. This old drought has burned down to the very bottoms of their long roots. It's all getting ready to die now instead of yield."

We stood there a while. It seemed like the wind wasn't blowing and I was starting to get hot.

"Papa just didn't understand," Father said. "Things have changed so much since I was a boy like you out here, but Papa just didn't understand that. I guess if I had been smart like the others, I would have plowed this cotton under."

"Grandfather didn't want you to."

"I know. And if he could speak to me now, he'd say the same thing. A man's got an obligation to both the living and the dead. It should be the same thing, and most of the time it is. But now, I just don't know. I've got all Papa's raisin' inside of me, and at the same time I've got my own family to think about. I'm not sure I've been thinkin' too straight on this."

I looked down at my feet then looked sideways at Father. He was standing with his legs apart and his thumbs hooked in his belt on either side of the buckle. His cigar was in the corner of his mouth, and his hat was pushed back on his head. He was looking around.

"I don't think you should plow it under," I said.

Father didn't say anything for a minute, then he said, "That's Papa's raisin' goin' through me to you. Papa was right for his age, but I'm not sure Papa is right for now. I'm not sure I'll be right for you when you're my age."

"Why not?"

"I don't know. And Papa didn't know either. I just wish I could have told him more about all this so he could have understood it better. Or I don't know, maybe he already knew all about it, but there wasn't anything he could do about it."

"Knew what?" I said. From somewhere in the cotton, a bobwhite called.

Father took a deep breath. "Knew that any man has to go by what he believes, whether it is wrong for the times or not. That doin' all right doesn't matter as much as doin' things according to how it is in you to do them."

I didn't say anything. I didn't think Father was really talking to me anyway, but to Grandfather or himself or someone else. And it sounded like Father was saying he was sorry. I had never heard him do that before.

"Your grandfather used to work all this hill and across the road with a pair of mules. Used to get up early and work all day and go to bed tired to his bones. He never took less than was his due from any man, least of all himself. He never made excuses or complained. He worked hard and he was honest. He knew above all that anything you got in this world, you got with your own hands doin' hard work. . . . Damn," Father said then. "But sometimes you work and work and don't get nothin' at all."

The wind was blowing in the field now. The leaves of the cotton were making a sound like rain falling on green grass. The sun was going down. It was a big red ball on some far away hills toward town and it was turning some high, thin clouds red. The sun always went down like that in the summertime. It looked almost the same as every other sunset, and yet it was different. It was different because of what Father was saying, and because Carol got a job in town, and because Gerald kissed Ruby Lee, and because Rebecca was gone to some place that didn't even have sunsets probably.

Father was standing the same way as when I had last looked, but I knew he was through talking. I stood beside him waiting until he finally said, "Let's go back."

We walked down through the cotton with the south wind in our faces and the bushes rubbing against our ankles. For some reason Father put his hand on my shoulder. I didn't think he had ever done that before.

Rebecca

GERALD WAS STANDING on the edge of the tank peeing out into the water as far as he could when Mama started calling me from the house. I scrambled to the top of the dam and looked at the house. Mama was standing on the back porch calling me.

"We better go," I said.

"She's calling you," Gerald said, looking toward the washout. "You go."

Mama called again and was waiting, so I hollered back as loud as I could and waved my arms. I thought she heard me, but she didn't go back in the house. She stood on the back porch with her hands on her hips.

"Rats," I said.

"You did it now," Gerald said.

I picked up my pole and started wrapping the line around it. There wasn't much line. When I got to the cork, the line kept slipping with the weight of the cork, so I had to hold the hook and pull the line tight to wrap it.

"What did I do?" I said.

"Who cares?" Gerald said. He leaned back and slid his hat over his eyes.

"Aren't you coming?"

"Why should I?"

I ran up the bank and looked back at Gerald. He had turned his head in the direction of the washout again. His feet were in the edge of the muddy water.

"Queer," I said.

Gerald sat up and turned around. He felt on the ground for a rock to throw. I ran down the other side of the dam toward the house.

Mama was in the house when I got there, so I put my fishing pole against the wall by the door and went in. The inside of the house seemed dark after outside. I checked the bottoms of my feet for mud. They were dry. There was just a little dried mud on my cuffs.

"Mama?"

"In here."

Mama was in her bedroom sitting on the edge of the bed. Carol was in there too, leaning against the dresser and looking out the window. She looked like she had been crying. Right away I was suspicious and mad at Carol.

"I didn't do anything to her," I said.

"Oh be quiet, Ricky. I never said you did."

I looked at Mama and I said, "I didn't, Mama."

Mama looked at me for the first time and I knew by her face that I was going to get a whipping, but I had not done anything. It must have been Gerald.

"Hush both of you," Mama said, looking at me. "I didn't call you up here so that you could fight with Carol. Something's happened to Rebecca."

"When? What?" I looked at Carol again and she was beginning to cry a little and I felt cold in my stomach. "What did, Mama? When?"

Mama looked at me. "About a week ago a man came to their house while she was alone. Evidently the man was trying to steal something and Rebecca screamed, so he hit her to make her be quiet. No telling what would have happened if something hadn't frightened the man off."

"I just can't believe it," Carol said.

"I can't believe the Browns left Rebecca alone in the city like that," Mama said.

I backed up a little bit and looked at Carol, then looked at Mama. For some reason I thought of Wilbur.

"Is she all right? How do you know?"

"Mrs. Brown told me. She just called. She said Rebecca had been hurt pretty bad, but that she was getting over that."

"Did they catch the guy that did it?" I asked.

"Oh Ricky," Carol said, crying.

"Hush that, Carol, or leave the room," Mama said.

"But it's so awful."

Carol looked pretty standing by the dresser crying, but I didn't care. I wished that she would leave so I could talk to Mama.

"Why don't you go somewhere else," I said. "Nobody told you to stay. Rebecca's my friend, not yours anyway."

"Ricky don't say another word," Mama said.

I looked at Mama and wrinkled up my face. Carol went out of the room, and I was glad. I heard her going upstairs.

"Aren't you ashamed?" Mama said.

"Nobody asked her—" I stopped and looked at Mama.

"Listen," she said. "What would you think about going up to see Rebecca for a little while?"

"To Waco?"

"For about a week, maybe."

"Is she in the hospital?" I asked.

"No. She's at home. But Mrs. Brown thought it would be good for her if you went to see her. It would make her feel better. In fact, it was Rebecca that called."

"What did she say?"

"She—" Mama stopped. "She didn't say anything. I answered the telephone and there was no sound until Mrs. Brown came on the line."

"Can't she talk?"

"She hasn't said a word to anybody since it happened."

I looked at the floor, remembering Rebecca's brown eyes.

"Mrs. Brown says all she does is sit and stare."

I looked at Mama. The way she looked reminded me of the time I had pneumonia and Mama sat on the side of the bed with me all one night.

"Will she be all right, Mama?"

"I don't know."

"When am I going?"

"There is a bus that leaves right after dinner."

"You aren't going to take me?"

"Can't you go on the bus?"

I thought about it.

"Go take a bath and get your clothes ready. We'll talk about it at dinner."

I walked out of the room and upstairs. Carol was in her room sitting on the edge of the bed.

"Ricky," she said.

She was looking at me with her head tilted a little to one side and her yellow hair was hanging down. Her eyes were red and a tear was sliding off her cheek. She looked pretty and sad.

"Leave me alone," I said.

After dinner, Mama took us all in to the bus station. Father had gone to Seguin and wouldn't be back until later, so I didn't get to say goodbye to him. The grocery sack I had put my clothes and funny books in was on the seat between me and Gerald.

"I wish I was going," Gerald said.

He was still wearing his muddy jeans and the same shirt he had been wearing down at the tank. He had a little smear of mud by his ear, and he was chewing on his bottom lip.

"Someone has to stay and take care of the animals," Mama said.

Gerald looked over at me and said, "I'm going to remember this, queer."

"It's not my fault," I said.

"Everything is your fault," Gerald said.

Carol was riding in the front seat with Mama. She didn't say anything the whole way in to town. She looked out the window and her hair blew back toward me. I wished it wasn't her day off. It was better when she wasn't around.

At the bus station in town, we all got out. There were two buses parked at the edge of the street and some people waiting around. The station was so small that it only had about five chairs inside, but it had a long rack of funny books and men's magazines. Gerald picked one up right away and opened it to a picture of a girl having her shirt ripped off by a bear. The name of it was *Big Adventure*. Carol went with Mama to buy the ticket, so Gerald and I stood by the magazines. There were some funny books that looked pretty good, but Gerald kept saying, "Hey boy, look at this." When Mama came back over with my ticket, Gerald hid the magazine behind a funny book and said, "Mama, can I have an advance on my allowance?"

Mama didn't look at him and said, "No."

Carol snatched the *Big Adventure* magazine away from Gerald and held it up. Gerald got mad and wanted to fight, but he didn't want Mama to see the magazine, so he just gave Carol the hate face while she slipped the magazine back in the rack. Mama stood in front of me and gave me the ticket. It was in two pieces. Mama opened her purse and started talking.

"I don't know how long you'll be up there, but it doesn't matter to us if it doesn't matter to Mrs. Brown. We didn't talk about that, so you have to ask Mrs. Brown when you've been up there a day or two. I expect you to behave yourself and help around the house if you can. Tell Mrs. Brown that we're all thinking about her and Rebecca and we will call later in the week. Do you understand?"

"Yeah," I said.

Mama gave me a ten dollar bill. "And don't say yeah when you get up there. You say yes ma'am. Understand?"

"Yes ma'am."

"That ten dollars is spending money for you to pay your own way if you go anywhere."

"Wait a minute," Gerald said, stepping over to me.

I put the ten dollars in my pocket away from Gerald's eyes.

"You just hush, young man," Mama said.

Gerald gave me the hate face he had been giving Carol, then he just stood there chewing on his lip.

"I guess that's all. The bus is already here, so you may as well get on it."

Carol was standing just behind Mama when Mama straightened up. Two men in army jackets came in the bus station and Gerald dropped back to look at them. They were talking together. One of them was smoking a cigarette. Then, as we started to go out, Mama saw Gerald pick up a nasty magazine and she went over to him and grabbed his arm and led him past us out the door. Just Carol and I were standing there.

I went over and picked up the magazine from the floor and put it back. I could see Mama and Gerald outside and Mama was letting him have it. I was trying not to look at Carol, but it was quiet in the station all of the sudden and Carol was standing right beside me.

"I better go," I said, even though I was feeling a little scared about riding the bus with all those people I didn't know.

"Can I kiss you goodbye?" Carol whispered.

I looked at her and knew she didn't mean it, so I said, "No."

"Ricky, listen."

I wouldn't look at her. Gerald was chewing his lip outside. Carol didn't say anything, so I looked at her.

"I know what you think of me. I don't blame you, even though I think you're wrong."

Mama and Gerald were coming back toward the door. I looked down.

"Please be nice to Rebecca, the way you used to be nice to me. I believe she really needs you now. You can help her Ricky."

I didn't want to go. I looked up at her. She looked about as pretty as I had ever seen her. Her eyes were so blue and her hair was bright as a light around her face.

"Going somewhere?" someone said behind me. It was the soldier with a cigarette in his mouth. He was looking at Carol and smiling.

"No," Carol said, smiling a little, which made me mad.

"Too bad," the soldier said. I looked at him and he took the cigarette out of his mouth and blew smoke out through his nose.

Gerald and Mama came back to the door, Mama first and Gerald lagging behind, red-faced and mad. I dodged past Carol, holding my sack, and went to the door. I heard Carol call me and start to follow, but I went on outside.

"Here you are," Mama said. "Now get on the bus and be good and we'll call you."

Mama bent over and caught my chin and kissed me on the cheek. Gerald had his hands in his pockets and was looking at the bus. I heard Carol come up behind me.

"So long, Gerald," I said and started toward the bus.

Gerald looked at me as I passed him and said, "Queer."

I went to the bus and got on it. All the people were looking at me and my sack. I held it tighter and went toward the back of the bus. I could see an empty seat back there. I got to it and sat down and looked out the window. Mama and Carol and Gerald were all standing there. I waved at them and Mama waved. Carol stepped forward a little, but I turned my head before she waved. The soldier was standing behind her in the doorway of the station, looking at her.

After about five minutes, the bus started up. I could feel the motor through my seat, but that bus was a lot better than the school bus. As we were leaving the station, I looked back and saw everybody getting in the car. Carol was standing by the front door, watching the bus, but I don't think she saw me. Then we were moving and I looked at the town through the window of the bus.

I knew the ride was going to take a long time, but I looked out the window. All the land and fields were brown and open and the trees seemed to hang their limbs down. Father said once that all of Texas would blow away if the drought lasted one more year. Everywhere I looked, things were brown and dead. Cows stood in the shade of little trees and looked hungry.

On the other side of Austin I began to think about Rebecca and I imagined what I would have done if I had been there with her. I imagined a big fight and I was the hero and nothing was wrong with Rebecca. Then I thought about Carol and looked down.

Mr. Brown was in the bus station in Waco when I got off the bus. He was smoking a cigarette and looking for me. He was wearing a pullover shirt which showed how big his stomach was getting, and for a minute I didn't want him to see me. The other people kept crossing back and forth in front of me, and I thought about just walking away behind one fat lady and never going with Mr. Brown. Then he saw me. He looked mad.

"The bus was late," he said when I got up to him.

"Hello," I said.

"Is that all your stuff?"

I looked at my sack. It was a big sack. "Yes sir."

"Well come on. I have other things to do this afternoon."

I needed to pee really bad, but Mr. Brown just turned and started walking away, so I followed him. I was beginning to wish that I had never come. I didn't see why Rebecca couldn't have come down to our house just as easy. We could have played there and everything. I passed some of the people who were on the bus with me. They all looked different standing up.

It was bright outside and hot in Mr. Brown's car. I rolled down the window when I got in and put my sack on the seat beside me. My arm was sweaty where I had been holding the sack. Mr. Brown got in and started the car. He took a pack of cigarettes out and shook them down. Several cigarettes popped out the end of the pack and he pulled one out with his teeth. He put the pack in his pocket and lit the one he had in his mouth with the dash lighter.

During the drive to their house, Mr. Brown never said anything to me at all. Once or twice I told him about something back home, but he just smoked his cigarette, then lit another. I started looking at the buildings in the city and how the people dressed. They dressed pretty much like they did at home, but some of them were fancier looking.

The house was on the corner of two streets filled with other houses. I liked their house right away because it was two stories like ours and it had lots of big trees around it. I was afraid it would be new and little like a lot of other houses. Mrs. Brown came out the back door after the car had stopped and she seemed glad to see me. She even put her hand on my shoulder. For a minute, I thought Rebecca was all right.

When Mr. Brown came around the car, he said, "Well, here he is."

"Was your trip all right?" Mrs. Brown asked me as we walked up the sidewalk toward the back door.

"There were lots of people on the bus," I said.

As soon as we were inside, I looked around for Rebecca, but the house was quiet and still.

"The bathroom is right through there," Mrs. Brown said. "Make yourself at home, then I want you to go upstairs to see Rebecca."

When I came back out of the bathroom, Mrs. Brown was in the kitchen and Mr. Brown was gone again. I was glad. I went into the kitchen and stood by the table. I was still holding my sack.

Mrs. Brown looked at me for a long time. The icebox motor came on. "Ricky," she said.

My knee began to itch. "Yes ma'am?"

"Something very bad has happened to Rebecca. You know that is why you are here, don't you?"

"Yes ma'am."

"Rebecca has been very sad for a while and we are worried about her. We thought if she saw you again she might not be so sad."

I remembered the way Rebecca had hugged me the day she left. I rubbed my itching knee against the other one to make it stop itching.

"Oh," I said.

"I just wanted to tell you that Rebecca might seem a little different at first, but I want you to act just like you always do."

"Yes ma'am."

"You can go see her now."

I turned out of the kitchen toward the stairs and Mrs. Brown followed me to show me where I would sleep. I hoped it would be upstairs with Rebecca because I liked sleeping upstairs. Mrs. Brown took me upstairs. The first door we came to was closed.

"That's Rebecca's room," Mrs. Brown said. Her voice was tight like she was saying it at the end of a breath.

There was another bathroom, a big closet and another bedroom. "This will be your room while you stay with us. I want you to act like it is your own room at home."

"How long will I stay?" I asked.

Mrs. Brown sat down on the bed and looked at me. "Your mother and I decided that would depend on Rebecca and, of course, you. Ricky, we want you to help Rebecca. We don't know how long it will take."

"Yes ma'am," I said. I felt like she was on a television show that I was watching. The things she was saying didn't seem real. I was used to her fussing about noises or cats scratching on the screen door and tearing holes in it that flies could come through.

"Think you can manage?"

"I think so," I said.

"Think you can get along without Gerald for a while?"

She smiled, so I smiled. Mrs. Brown was pretty when she smiled. I felt older, more like Father.

"Sure," I said.

She stood up. "I suppose anybody could get along without Gerald for a little while," she said. She went to the door and stopped. "I'll tell Rebecca you're here, then you can go in any time you want."

"Yes ma'am," I said.

"I'll see you later."

"Okay."

I went over to a table by the window and put my sack on it. Through the curtains, I could see the limbs of a tree, the yard and the street. At the top of a pole on the corner was a street light. A car went by. I heard Mrs. Brown open Rebecca's door and call her name. Rebecca must have been sleeping, because Mrs. Brown called her name several times, then told her in a loud voice that I was here. I heard Mrs. Brown come back to the door, but I pretended that I didn't. I heard her walk away and go quietly down the stairs. Two more cars went by in the street. One was blue, the other one was yellow.

I knocked on the door to Rebecca's room two or three times, but there was no answer. I didn't know what to do, then. I was going to knock again, but I didn't want Mrs. Brown to hear me and come upstairs again. I opened the door and looked in.

Rebecca's bed was under the south windows like the one

in my room, and it had a pink spread on it that was wrinkled and pulled too far down on one side so that it hung crooked. On either side of the bed were little tables that I had never seen before. Her rocking chair and chest of drawers and little desk and chair were the same ones she had had in her other house. It was funny to see them here in this new room in a city with noises of cars coming and going instead of tractor sounds and cows ready to eat or calves lost or Gerald outside hollering that Mama said it was time to come home, you little queer.

Rebecca was sitting in her rocking chair holding a pillow over her lap, hot as it was. She was wearing the blue shirt I remembered and a pair of white shorts. Her back was to me and I knew she was awake because the chair was moving back and forth like a swing.

"Rebecca?" I said, so as not to scare her.

She didn't answer, but kept rocking. As I got in the room and closed the door, I began to smell the girl-smell of things that girls wore. Girls' rooms always smelled different from me and Gerald's room. Ours smelled like old wood and sweat. I went over by the bed and stood against it and looked out the window where Rebecca was staring. Two negro boys were walking along the street in shorts and T-shirts with the sleeves cut off. The shirts were so dirty they looked yellow. One of the boys was singing a song and the other one was picking his nose. The one singing was ahead of the other one.

Rebecca didn't turn her head to look at me, even though I was beside her. Her legs were brown and hanging down from the seat of the rocking chair and her hands were holding the pillow on her lap. I could see her face. Her left eye was still purple from a bad black eye, and her bottom lip was swollen and had a red scab on it. Her arms had bruises on them too. She just rocked and I looked at her like that was what she wanted me to do, wanted me to see what had happened to her. I sat on the edge of the bed and heard the boy singing and the curtains sliding against the bed when the breeze blew them out from the window.

I felt sad for Rebecca and I hated the man who had done it and I wanted to kill him. For some reason, I kept thinking he looked like Wilbur. Rebecca was staring out the window like she was daydreaming. Her big eyes were brown and far away. She still had not looked at me and I began to think she was mad at me, but Rebecca never stopped talking to me when she was mad at me. That time I had chosen Jenny Warren for my partner in the three-legged race Rebecca had been mad at me. She had come up to me after the choosing, but before Jenny could get there, and she said she hoped I fell and broke my leg. I didn't answer her right away and Jimmy Peters had said that I could do that without a partner. I told him to shut up, then Rebecca said she would talk to me on the bus. I still didn't say

anything and Rebecca had looked at me with her big brown eyes and her dark hair blowing. I only chose Jenny Warren because everybody else was making fun of her.

The only rug in the room was under Rebecca's rocking chair, and she went back and forth without a sound. Her hair was in braids with blue ribbons around the ends.

Finally, I said, "How do you feel?"

Rebecca just rocked and stared out the window like I wasn't even there. I moved back on the bed a little bit and looked out the window too. The boys were gone, but a car was going by. It was quiet in the house. In a way I wished Carol was with me, but when I thought about her for a while, I knew I didn't want her around ever again.

"Guess you feel pretty bad, huh?" I said.

She rocked back and forth without a sound.

"Your mother said you tried to call me but me and Gerald were fishing. I knew we wouldn't catch anything, but I was mad at Gerald and I knew if I was there, he wouldn't be able to go see Ruby Lee."

I looked at Rebecca.

"Mr. Norman said he sure did miss you. Hardly anybody ever goes to the store anymore."

Rebecca rocked and I couldn't think of anything else to say. The curtains blew in from the window and cars went by. I sat on the bed while Rebecca rocked and looked out the window. After a while, the two boys came by again. The one who had been singing was carrying a paper sack from a store, and the other one was drinking an orange Nehi. I thought of me and Gerald. I looked at Rebecca, but she didn't seem to see the boys.

When Mrs. Brown called me, I got up from the bed and looked at my tennis shoes. "I have to go now," I said. Rebecca rocked back and forth. I started to touch her shoulder, but instead I went to the door and opened it and went out. Then I thought of something and put my head back in.

"Do you want me to close the door?" I asked her. She was still rocking, but the pillow had slipped off her lap and was on the floor under her feet.

We ate supper in the kitchen at the green table with the plastic-covered chairs around it. I sat across from Mr. Brown by the macaroni dish and the bread. Mrs. Brown gave me milk to drink, but I would rather have had tea. Mr. Brown looked at me like I owed him some money. He tore a piece of bread in half and put one half on the table by his plate. He held the other half in his right hand while he scooped up some meatballs. He was left-handed. The kitchen smelled strange to me. Other people's kitchens always smelled strange to me.

"Did he see Rebecca?" Mr. Brown asked, not looking at me.

"Yes. Ricky spent quite a while with her this afternoon."

I was eating some green beans and thinking of Rebecca rocking back and forth.

"Did she talk to him?"

"No," Mrs. Brown said in a low voice.

I stopped chewing and looked at Mr. Brown. He was looking at me like I had told him a lie. It made me feel bad. Mrs. Brown was eating again, but slowly. I took a sip of my milk.

Mr. Brown turned to Mrs. Brown and said, "What good is he?"

Mrs. Brown looked up and gave me a smile that went away so quickly I thought I had only dreamed it. Mr. Brown was chewing again, but I didn't feel very hungry. Mrs. Brown's food tasted different from Mama's.

"He's only been here one day," Mrs. Brown said.

"I thought it was supposed to make a big difference," Mr. Brown said, biting off some of his bread. I felt the same way I felt when Mama and Father argued about something I had done wrong. I looked at the macaroni on my plate and thought of Gerald.

"Nobody said it would right away," Mrs. Brown said.

"Humph," Mr. Brown said.

We all ate for a while without talking. I was trying to think of something to say, but nothing would come to my mind or I would think of something stupid. I thought of Carol again and how she always understood how I felt, but then I kind of shook my head and felt mad.

"Something wrong?" Mrs. Brown asked.

"No ma'am," I said. I started eating quickly to show her nothing was wrong. Mr. Brown was watching me again.

"We ought to feed Rebecca down here," he said.

"We tried that. At least in her room, she eats something."

"She's been this way long enough."

"How long is long enough after what has happened to her?"

"The doctor says—"

"We've talked about doctors—" Mrs. Brown said.

"I have. You never—"

"Don't tell me what you've done. It's because of you we're here."

I didn't look up from my plate when the room got quiet. The icebox clicked on and I was glad because I needed to swallow, but I didn't want them looking at me. Mr. Brown pushed away from the table and left the kitchen. After a minute, I heard the television come on. "The Adventures of Ozzie & Harriet" was on.

Mrs. Brown looked at me and made a smile that looked tired. She looked a lot like Rebecca when she smiled.

I went into the living room and stood by the door watching the end of "Ozzie & Harriet." Mr. Brown was sitting in his chair and smoking a cigarette like he had to be going somewhere in thirty seconds. During a commercial, he looked around and saw me. I pretended I was just coming into the room. I went over to the couch and sat on the edge of it and watched a lady washing her dishes in Lux. I could feel Mr. Brown looking at me, but I just watched the television. I didn't want to do anything to make him mad.

After "Ozzie & Harriet" was over, Mr. Brown turned to the "Life of Riley." That was one of Gerald and Father's favorite shows. Riley was always getting into trouble, and the more he would try to get out of it, the more he would mess up. It was over before Mrs. Brown came to the door.

"You can go up anytime, Ricky. If you want to see Rebecca, go ahead. Make yourself at home."

"Yes ma'am."

I looked over at Mr. Brown and he was still watching me. Later, I got up to go upstairs. As I passed his chair, he said, "I don't know what you can do." Smoke followed me out of the room.

At the head of the stairs, I stopped by Rebecca's door. I listened, but it was quiet in her room. I heard Mr. and Mrs. Brown start talking downstairs. I couldn't tell what they were saying. I went to the door and stood there a long time with my hand on the knob. Every bad thing that had happened since summer started came back to me. Then I opened the door and looked in at Rebecca. She was lying on her stomach on the bed with her elbows propping her up and one leg was in the air. She looked just like she used to when we played marbles on the porch.

I went over to the bed and put my hand on the post and looked at her. She didn't turn her head toward me, but that was all right. I liked just standing there and looking at her.

It was hard to go to sleep in the strange bed and I lay there a long time trying not to think of Wilbur or Grandfather's funeral. It was hard not to think of them and of Mr. Ketchum's tractor bouncing off across his field of cotton. Then I wondered what everyone was doing at home. I had been away from them a few times, but never for very long. I thought about Rebecca some too, and what the man had done to her and how different she was now. Seeing her was almost like looking at a picture of her. She wasn't really there. Finally, I started counting the cars that went by in the street. A lot of them went by before I went to sleep.

Sometime in the night, I heard Rebecca screaming and the sound made me cold as the deep water in the tank before it got so low. I pulled the sheet up around my ears and I called myself a queer for not running into her room to see what was the matter. Her screams were so different and scary, I was afraid to get up. A light came on over the stairs and Mrs. Brown was running up them in her nightgown. I lay very still and pretended to be asleep.

For a while I could hear Mrs. Brown's voice talking to Rebecca, but I didn't hear anything from Rebecca. Then Mrs. Brown came out of her room and stood listening at the door. Her shadow came across the floor into my room and I waited and pretended I was asleep. Then Mrs. Brown went down the stairs and the light went off and the house got very still. I got hot and pushed the sheet back. I kept thinking the telephone was going to ring. I kept thinking it would ring and Mrs. Brown would call me and it would be Carol.

I was glad when the sun came up and it got light in the room. I got out of bed and got dressed from the clothes I brought with me in the grocery sack. I heard a car start up and I went to the window in time to see Mr. Brown backing the blue Chevrolet out of the drive into the street. I watched him turn in the street and drive by. It seemed to me that he looked up at my window as he went by. I was sorry he was Rebecca's father.

I left my room, then went to the bathroom. The bathroom was clean and smelled like perfumes and powders. It was the kind of bathroom Gerald said you always have to sit down in and flush the commode in every time you use it instead of saving it up like we did at home.

Downstairs, Mrs. Brown was in the living room reading a magazine. When she heard me, she got up and made me breakfast. While I was eating, she sat at the table reading her magazine. It was quiet in the kitchen. Before I was through eating, Mrs. Brown began to watch me.

"How are you doing?" she asked. She put her chin in one hand and looked at me in a nice way. It made me feel good.

"Fine."

"What do you want to do today?"

"I don't know. Talk to Rebecca, I guess."

Mrs. Brown sighed and shook her hair. She looked tired, but friendly.

"I wonder if we did the right thing bringing you all the way to Waco."

"I wasn't doing anything at home," I said to make her feel better.

"Rebecca's not much fun now, though."

I thought about the night before. "Mrs. Brown?"

"Yes, Ricky."

"What happened last night?"

She looked down. "A bad dream. She has them almost every night."

"Do you think she will get better?"

"I don't know, Ricky. I hope so. Don't you?"

Rebecca was wearing a pair of jeans and a pink shirt. The pink shirt made her eyes browner. Her hair was in a ponytail, and she was sitting in the rocking chair again with her empty hands folded in her lap. She was looking out the window. Sparrows were making a lot of racket in the trees outside the window. I sat on the bed again.

"I remember that clown picture," I said. "I never did like clowns all that much. Remember that clown at the circus last year who had the spotted dog? He looked stupid with those big shoes."

Rebecca rocked back and forth. Her eye looked a little better. I moved from the edge of the bed to the window and sat on the sill. Her eyes fell to my knees and she kept them there. I bent over, trying to make her look at me, but she only dropped her eyes lower. I sat up again and looked around the room. I pretended I was falling out the window, but she wouldn't look at me.

"Aren't you going to say anything to me?" I asked.

She rocked back and forth on the rug and there wasn't any sound. I looked around the room again. Rebecca stopped rocking suddenly and I looked at her. She was really very pretty. She sat still. Even the birds seemed to be quiet. I was waiting. Then she started to rock again, slowly, like she was trying to remember the words to some song. She was deep inside herself, it seemed to me.

That afternoon I stretched out on her bed and read the funny books I had brought with me. I had read all of them before, but they were the only ones I had. Gerald had some new ones, but he wouldn't let me take them because he was so stingy with his stuff. There was one Superman that was my favorite. I read it about six times that afternoon. Rebecca sat in her rocking chair and stared out the window the whole time. Finally, I got up and showed her the Superman funny book and told her it was a really good one and I wanted her to read it.

"This one is really good," I told her. "Even you would like it. Superman almost marries Lois Lane. Look," I said.

Rebecca's eyes were staring away, almost to home I thought.

"Come on, Rebecca. Look at it, please. Please? Please?" I said again and made my voice high and silly.

She wouldn't look at it.

"Please?" I said. "Please? Pleeeeze?"

She wouldn't look at it. I was standing beside her chair and I could smell her. I thought she had been faking to get attention like I did sometimes, but then I knew she wasn't faking. I let the funny book fall to the floor and I stood beside her chair looking at her hair and feeling the chair go back and forth on the rug without a sound.

After Rebecca had had time to eat her supper, I went up to her room. She was lying on the bed like she had been the night before. I went up to the bed and told her hello. She was lying on some of my funny books and some were in front of her where she could be reading them if she had wanted to, but they all looked just like I had left them. She had not moved or opened any of them.

"I went outside and looked around while ago," I said. "I kept thinking how much fun it would be if we could sit out under the trees and watch the stars get bright in the sky. I feel like I'm all by myself. I never used to feel this way, but I've been feeling it for a long time. You know the night you left I dreamed we were living together in a house by a big river."

I walked around the bed and knelt beside it facing her. She lowered her eyes to the bedspread. Her face was darkened by the black eye, but she looked more like herself than she had the day before. I slid my hand along the bed until her eyes were on it. Then I made a fist. She kept her eyes on my hand. I spread my fingers out and she watched them. I waved at her. I showed her two fingers, then four. I showed her the thumbs-up. I let her look at the back of my hand, then the front. She never took her eyes from my hand.

I got up and went back around the bed and lay across it right beside her. The mattress gave a little and her shoulder slumped against mine. She still wouldn't look at me, but I showed her my hand and she watched it. Then I reached over and took one of her little hands. It felt warm and dry. I spread her fingers out, then bent them into a fist. Her hand did not push against mine. It was like her hand had gone to sleep and she couldn't feel what I was doing to it.

I raised her hand to my chin and her eyes followed it, but when I bent down quickly, she dropped her eyes even faster. I was getting kind of tired of that, like a joke that Gerald carried too far.

"Come on, Rebecca," I said. "You can't do this forever. Can you? I know you see me. Why don't you look at me? I'm beginning to think you don't want me here."

She was looking at the bed.

"I came up here to see you and have a good time, and all we've done is sit around your room and do nothing. You could at least look at me or nod your head or something."

The bruises on the side of her face made her freckles look different, or maybe it was just that the room was getting dark.

"I know you feel bad, Rebecca. I would too, if I was you."

Rebecca was looking at the bed. Her shoulder was touching mine. She was staring so hard that her eyes were watering. A tear ran off her cheek and fell on my arm.

"Can't you hear what I'm saying, Rebecca? Doesn't it even matter that I really want you to be all right? Don't you remember all the stuff we used to do? Rebecca? Rebecca?"

I stopped talking and looked at the cover of a Batman funny book. Batman was swinging off a building. He could do anything. Robin was on the cover too, but I didn't like him because his shorts looked like fish scales. Rebecca suddenly let her elbows slide out from under her and she put her head down on the bed on my right hand. Her face was six inches from mine and I could see that her eyes were closed. Another tear was rolling along her nose. I could feel her ear and her hair on the back of my hand. I looked at her a while and started feeling really bad. Then I moved my hand so that it wouldn't press on her face.

Mrs. Brown came to the door and looked in.

"Is everything all right?" she asked, turning on the light.

"Yes ma'am." I got up and started picking up my funny books.

"It's about time for me to get Rebecca to bed. Is she asleep?" Mrs. Brown came over to the bed.

"I don't think so," I said.

Rebecca was partly lying on the Superman funny book that I had tried to get her to look at. I pulled on the pages to see if I could get it out from under her without bothering her. Mrs. Brown opened the door to Rebecca's closet. The cover of the funny book made a tearing sound and I said "Rats" to myself and half aloud. Rebecca raised up just a little and the funny book slid free. I looked at it, then looked at her. For a second I thought she was looking at me, but her eyes dropped too fast for me to be sure.

"Come on, honey," Mrs. Brown said, bringing a gown over to the bed.

I told Mrs. Brown that I liked to listen to a radio at night, so she let me take the one out of the kitchen and put it in my room. I listened to it when all the lights went out and the house got quiet. It had lighted dials so I could tell what station I was listening to. I found the numbers of the station in San Antonio that me and Gerald always listened to. It came in, but there was lots of static and the static made me feel lonely. Cars went by in the street and sometimes they were loud. I wondered what Gerald was doing and I decided to write him a letter the next day. I would be sure to tell him not to let Carol read it, even if she begged him on her knees with tears in her eyes.

I was thinking of what I would write to Gerald when the door to Rebecca's room opened and she stepped out in the hall. I turned my head and watched her. Her gown was pink, but it looked white in the blue light of the street light outside her window. She was standing by her door facing me, but she didn't move and that began to bother me.

I pushed up on my elbows and whispered her name. She still just stood there, and in the dim light I couldn't tell where she was looking.

"Come on," I said.

She started walking toward me and I moved over in the bed so that she could sit on it if she wanted to. She stopped at the edge of the bed. She was looking at the lighted dials of the radio.

"Your mother said I could listen to it," I said.

She stood by the bed looking at the radio. The song ended and a man with a deep voice came on to give the weather. As soon as Rebecca heard the man's voice, she put her hands to her mouth like she was going to call somebody from down in the pasture and she screamed.

The next day, Mrs. Brown woke me early and said that she wanted me to go up to the school with Mr. Brown. I put on my best pair of jeans and a white shirt. I brushed my teeth before breakfast and went downstairs. Mr. and Mrs. Brown were at the table in the kitchen. Mr. Brown was drinking his coffee and Mrs. Brown was taking toast out of the oven. I thought they were a little mad at me, but what happened the night before wasn't my fault.

"I still don't see what she was doing in your room in the first place," Mr. Brown said, right away.

I looked at the milk by my plate and waited for Mrs. Brown to bring me some toast. Mr. Brown was still looking at me, so I said, "She just came in there."

"That doesn't sound like her," he said.

"Can't you take that as a good sign?" Mrs. Brown said.

"I could if I believed it."

I took a piece of toast and reached for the jam. It was plum jam, but that was better than dry toast and milk. Mr. Brown was still looking at me.

"Are you sure you didn't try to take her in your room?"

"Marvin!" Mrs. Brown said.

It was quiet around the table then, and I knew what Mr. Brown was thinking. It made the toast stick in my throat.

I didn't talk to him the rest of the morning until after we were up at the school where Mr. Brown taught economics, which is money stuff. He took me to his office and showed me where I could sit, then he began working on some notes for class. Several men and one girl came in, but Mr. Brown didn't introduce me to any of them. The girl reminded me of Carol and she smiled at me as she was leaving. I raised my upper lip and wrinkled my nose like I had smelled something bad. Even if she only looked like Carol, that was bad enough.

At eleven Mr. Brown had to teach a class. He asked me if I wanted to come along, but I told him I would rather sit outside for a while. He told me not to get lost or make lots of noise or throw rocks or disturb the students. I said I wouldn't.

What I really wanted to do was find a candy machine and a bathroom. I followed Mr. Brown out of his office and into the hall. In the hall, he turned to me and said, "Remember. And be back here at twelve-thirty."

I watched him walk down the hall with a lot of students, then I turned down the stairway that we had come up. Outside the sun was bright and hot and all the grass around the buildings was dying. They must have been watering it for a while or it wouldn't have lasted this long. There were lots of people walking down the sidewalks and some were sitting in the shade of some little oak trees. I saw two guys come out of one building holding soda water cups, so I went over there.

It was a big building with open windows and venetian blinds pulled up in the windows. I went in behind a guy wearing boots made out of alligator skins. Gerald would have liked to have seen them, I thought. Inside was like a cafeteria and the students went through a line for what they wanted. Over on the side wall were drink machines, so I went over there and put a dime in the first machine. It got stuck or something and nothing would come out. That was my only dime. I pulled down on the change return lever about fifty times.

"Having trouble?" a girl asked, behind me.

I turned around and saw the girl who had come into Mr.

Brown's office and who looked like Carol. She didn't look too much like Carol close up, but she had yellow hair and a smart-alecky look on her face that could have been Carol's.

"No," I said.

"Trying to cheat the machines?" she smiled.

I didn't answer her but looked around instead. Nobody else was looking at us. I was trying to think of something to say. Nothing seemed right, so I just did what Father would have done: not anything.

"Let me try it," the girl said, stepping up beside me. She put a nickel in the slot and asked me what I wanted.

"I want my dime back," I said.

"Let me guess. An orange?"

She pushed the button and a cup slid down and ice dropped into it and it began filling up with orange Nehi. When the orange stopped, she reached in and took the cup out and handed it to me. She had the same smile on her face.

"I want my dime back," I said.

She just stood there holding the orange and smiling, so I finally took it. She was trying to make me smile just like Carol used to. I held the orange and looked around. I could smell it and it was making me thirsty. The girl put another nickel in the machine and got something else.

"There," she said, turning to me. "That's just as good as a dime, isn't it?"

"No," I said.

"Come on," she said. "Let's sit over here."

"I have to go."

She was already walking away when she looked over her shoulder and said, "No you don't. I saw Mr. Brown in the hall. You have until twelve-thirty."

I made a face and followed her over to a table and sat down across from her. She put some books and her purse on the table between us. I looked around. The room had lots of windows and some fans and it was pretty cool.

"Are you Mr. Brown's nephew?" the girl asked.

"No," I said.

"Well, my name's Carolyn and I'm going to watch you for a while, so you can just drop the tough-guy stuff."

I looked at her like she had been reading my mind and looked down. "I don't need a babysitter," I said.

"I'm not a babysitter. At least, I don't think you are a baby. Maybe you are."

She sat back and looked at me with that same smile again. She didn't really look like Carol except that her hair was yellow and her face and arms were tanned brown. She looked pretty.

"Thanks for the orange," I said, trying to sound bored.

"What's your name?"

I told her and looked around. Then I looked at her. Then I looked around again.

"Are you staying with Mr. and Mrs. Brown?"

"Yeah."

"How is their daughter doing?"

I shrugged and sipped my orange and looked down at the table.

"Such a bad thing to happen," she said, sounding really sorry. "You just don't know any more what can happen. Sometimes I think God just went away and left Texas without looking back."

"She may get better," I said.

"Did the doctors say that?"

"I don't know."

"Are you her friend?" Carolyn asked, leaning forward.

"Yeah." My nose started itching. I scratched it.

"You can make her all right," she said, leaning forward.

I looked at her to see if she was teasing me, but she looked serious. I looked down at the ice in my orange.

Carolyn took me to the library where she checked in two books. For a while, we wandered through the shelves looking at all the books. I had never seen so many books in one place in all my life. The library at the elementary school just had one wall of books and I had read all of those. Carolyn showed me where some Scribner's illustrated books were and we took them down and showed each other the pictures. Carolyn tried to get me interested in *Treasure Island*, but my favorite was *The Deerslayer*.

"You sure are a stubborn boy," she said. Then she said, "It's almost twelve-fifteen. We'd better head back."

We walked along the sidewalks back to the building where Mr. Brown had his office. It was hot. Carolyn walked slowly and I felt older walking beside her. Lots of college boys looked at her and me, but she didn't seem to notice them. There were squirrels running around under the oak trees.

"I wish I had a gun," I said, feeling older.

"Why would you want to hurt those little squirrels?" Carolyn asked, sounding a little mad.

"They don't do any good. Besides, it would be fun to shoot them."

"Little boys like you grow up to be men that hurt little girls."

I stopped walking like the sidewalk had suddenly stood up in front of me. I looked around, and in the heat across the street I thought I saw Wilbur standing there looking at me with an ugly smile on his face. Carolyn bent down beside me quickly and said, "I didn't mean you particularly. I didn't mean you."

I looked at her and she seemed more like Carol than ever.

"Leave me alone," I said.

I ran around her and down the sidewalk and through the door and up the stairs to Mr. Brown's office as fast as I could. I knew that if I could just get in the office away from everybody, I would be all right. I got in the office and closed the door and went to the only window and looked out. Down below me on the sidewalk, a man carrying too many books felt one slide under his arm and he grabbed for it. All of the books fell on the sidewalk. The wind blew the pages open.

Mr. Brown came in the door and I turned around. I thought that Carolyn would be with him, but he was by himself. He looked at me as he went to the desk and put his class notes down. I must have looked funny, because he said, "What happened?"

I tried to say something, but I couldn't.

"Now you know how I feel," he said.

That evening, we ate a watermelon under the trees in the backyard. I liked watermelon, but with Mr. Brown there, it wouldn't be like when we ate watermelon at home. Mr. Brown carried the watermelon out to the picnic table and put it down. I went with him and sat on the bench with my back to the table. A boy went by in the street on a red bicycle. When I looked over at him, he turned and watched me. When I kept looking at him, he shot me the finger and went on down the street, pedaling as hard as he could. The queer.

I turned and looked at Mr. Brown. He was sitting across the table smoking a cigarette and mashing wood ants with his finger tip. His thin hair was catching a breeze from somewhere and lifting on top. He looked at me suddenly and I kept looking at him. Then I looked down at the ants and back at him. He went on looking at me and smoking.

Mrs. Brown brought Rebecca out the back door. Seeing her from a distance, she looked small again, like I remembered her running up to the bus from her porch, holding her books and a sweater in her hands. But now she moved more like a robot. I sat up a little. Mrs. Brown was talking to Rebecca, but I couldn't hear what she said. Rebecca let Mrs. Brown lead her along. Once Rebecca looked fast at the driveway, then she looked back down.

"Well, here's my girl," Mr. Brown said. He said it like he was reading it out of a book. I turned and looked at him and he gave me a look like he had to kill all the ants because I couldn't do anything.

"That's right," Mrs. Brown said. "Oh, it may still be too hot out here."

Mrs. Brown led Rebecca right up to me and helped her lift her legs over the bench and sit down facing the table. Then she went back in the house and brought back pans and knives and forks and salt. Mr. Brown cut the watermelon and I could see that it was a good one. Rebecca just sat looking down at the table, no matter what Mrs. Brown said to her. Mr. Brown passed me a piece of watermelon cut so that all I could see was about a thousand seeds. He watched me slide the pan over in front of me and look at all the seeds.

"I hope it's not still too hot out here for you, honey," Mrs. Brown said.

Mrs. Brown kept talking to Rebecca the whole time I was trying to get seeds out of the way. It made me feel kind of bad to listen to Mrs. Brown talk and not hear Rebecca say anything. I thought it would make Mrs. Brown mad the way it made Mama mad when Gerald ignored her. When Mr. Brown put a slice of watermelon in front of Rebecca, she just looked at it. Then we started to eat and it was quiet and Rebecca's piece of watermelon just sat there. Flies landed on it and Mrs. Brown shooed them away.

"This is good watermelon," Mrs. Brown said. "Don't you think so, Ricky?"

"Yes ma'am," I said, but I was thinking about the last time I had eaten watermelon and the story that Grandfather always told. But mostly I remembered the way Father sat smoking his cigar and watching Grandfather's every move. I didn't think he had been at the time, but now it seemed that he had never taken his eyes off Grandfather.

I was quiet for a while. Cars went by in the street and sparrows played in the trees. Before long, I was down to the rind. My pan was black with seeds.

"Want some more?" Mrs. Brown asked, looking around Rebecca.

"Sure," I said. I lifted the rind off my pan and passed it across in front of Rebecca to the big tray where the rest of the watermelon was. Some seeds fell off the table and one landed on Rebecca's leg just below her shorts. It was black there against her skin, like a big tick. Mr. Brown gave me another piece crawling with seeds. He looked at me while I took it. I could feel his eyes on me. I put it on my pan and looked down at Rebecca's leg. The seed was gone, but there was a little wet spot where it had been.

Later, Mrs. Brown picked up the pieces we had not eaten and carried them in the house. Mr. Brown put all the other slices on the tray and was going to take them to the trash cans by the garage.

"Need some help?" I asked, getting up and wiping my chin.

"I think this is one thing I can do without you," he said.

I sat down again beside Rebecca and felt a little bad. I turned toward the road and thought of the boy who had shot me the finger. I felt like fighting. Then something wet hit my neck and stuck there. I reached up quick and grabbed it. It was a watermelon seed.

I took a bath that night and went to bed early so that I could write Gerald a letter. I closed the door to my room and went to the table and took out my writing tablet and a pencil. At first, I didn't know how to start, so I drew a picture of a tank blowing a hole in a wall. Then I flipped through the pages looking at other stuff I had put in there and I found one of the letters Rebecca had wrapped around the harmonica she had given me. It was my favorite letter. It said:

Ricky,

It is eleven o'clock. The light in your room has been off for almost an hour. I wish I could see more than just your light. If I had a telescope I could watch you, couldn't I? Today has been a bad day. Mother and Daddy had a fight this morning about moving. I don't think Mother minds moving, she is just tired of doing everything herself. She says I don't help her at all, but I try to. After dinner I broke the glass in one of my picture frames. Then I cut my finger and it bled all over my shorts. Mother was upset again. She acts like I hurt myself on purpose. I wanted to come see you this evening, but Mother wouldn't let me. Pretty soon I won't be able to at all. I have been in my room all night. It doesn't look like my room anymore. I think that when I leave here I will die and become someone else. I wish I could put you in one of my boxes and take you with me. You are the only person in the whole world I really love.

Rebecca

I read the letter over again, then folded it and put it back between the pages of my tablet. I picked up my pencil and wrote:

Dear Gerald,
    I am in my own room at Rebecca's. They have an upstairs like our house, but the walls are painted white. It is hot here just like there, isn't it? What has been going on around there? I have spent most of my time with Rebecca. She looks just like always, but she has bruises on her arms and a black eye. She doesn't say anything. She plays like nobody is around, but I think sometimes she isn't playing. We had water-melon tonight and after we were finished, a seed landed on my neck. I think Rebecca spit it. Do you? Also this guy on a bicycle shot me the finger. I don't know if the man who hurt Rebecca was ever caught. They don't talk about what happened at all and Re-becca won't talk as I said. Well, I hope the work is not too much for you. Don't let Carol read this even if she begs you to let her.

                                                    Ricky

When I was finished writing the letter, I read it, then added something I had forgotten. I ripped the sheet out of my tablet and folded it up. I would have to ask Mrs. Brown for an envelope and a stamp. I felt better having written to Gerald. For a minute, he seemed to be in the room with me, chewing on his lip and pulling a scab off his stumped toe.
    "Ricky?"
    I turned around and saw Mrs. Brown at the door.
    "Yes ma'am?"
    "Could I come in a minute?"
    "Yes ma'am," I said, closing my tablet.
    She came in and sat down on the bed. "Is everything going all right? Do you need anything?"
    "No ma'am," I said.
    Mrs. Brown looked down at her skirt and picked a little piece of food off it. Then she smoothed the dress on her leg.

"What do you think about Rebecca?"

"I don't know," I said.

"Has she—done anything?"

"What do you mean?" I asked.

Mrs. Brown wasn't looking at me. She was biting her lip and smoothing out her skirt. "Has she talked to you, looked at you?"

"No ma'am," I said.

For a minute, I thought about telling her about the funny book and the watermelon seed, but then I thought she would just think I was being stupid. I looked down at the floor.

"Well," she said suddenly, taking a deep breath. "I just wondered if you needed anything."

"I wrote a letter to Gerald if you have a stamp and an envelope," I said, then wished I had not.

"Of course. We'll mail it first thing."

I looked at her and she stood up. She went to the door and said she was going to wash some clothes in the morning if I had anything to put in. I said all right and she left. I followed to the edge of the stairs and looked down in time to see her reach the bottom. Mr. Brown was standing there. "Well?" he said. Mrs. Brown didn't look at him, but shook her head. Mr. Brown looked down and turned away. "It's our own fault," I heard him say. The light over the stairs went out and I went back to my room.

Before I went to sleep, I turned the radio off. But later, when the moon had come up, the sound of the radio woke me. I opened my eyes and looked at the lighted dial. I heard a man talking on the telephone to another man. They were talking about different ways to get more water for Texas.

I raised up on my elbow to turn the radio off again and saw Rebecca on the floor by my bed. It scared me so bad I thought I was going to wet my pants. Then I knew it was her and I knew why the radio was on. Her hair was loose and messed up and she was sitting on the floor with her back to the bed and her knees were drawn up. She was hugging her knees.

"Rebecca?" I said. I was scared she would start screaming.

"Shhh," she said.

"Rebecca, you can hear me," I said.

"Sometimes I can," she said. "Sometimes you're just as far away as everybody else."

I slid out of bed and went around where I could look at her. By the light of the street light that came through the window, I could see that her eyes were full of tears and that her cheeks were wet.

"You've been crying," I said, sitting down beside her on my heels so that I could watch her face.

"Yes," she said. "I woke up and started and just couldn't stop, so I came in here. I didn't want to wake you up."

"Why not?"

"Because then I knew I would have to talk to you and I wasn't sure I wanted to yet."

"Wanted to?"

"Shhh, be quiet. I know for sure I'm not ready to talk to them." She tossed her head.

"How are you?" I asked. "Are you all right?"

She was quiet for a long time, and I could see that she was crying again. I got up and went to my sack and got a handkerchief and brought it back to her. She wiped her eyes with it.

"I want to be dead," she said.

All of me went cold. I shivered. "No," I said.

She wiped her eyes again and folded and refolded the handkerchief in the dark. "That's how I feel."

I wanted to say something then to make her feel better, but I couldn't think of a single thing. I remembered when she had come up to the house to tell me she was moving. I felt the same way then. I wanted to do and say the right thing, but I didn't know what it was.

"I wrote a letter to Gerald," I said.

Rebecca was quiet. Then she said, "What did you tell him?"

"Just what we have been doing. He was worried about you."

"Gerald was?"

"Sure," I said, making something up. "He was going to climb under the bus and ride up here with me."

Rebecca started crying again. The man on the radio was

talking to a lady. The lady had a plan for bringing ocean water all over the state. I listened to the plan for a minute. It was a pretty good plan.

"Rebecca?"

"What," she said, wiping her eyes. Rebecca never sniffed when she cried.

I was quiet for a while, then Rebecca said, "Oh Ricky, I'm glad you're here. I feel so bad."

"You'll feel better," I said.

"I don't think so. I never felt this way before."

"What is it?" I asked.

"I can't tell you."

"You can tell me."

Rebecca was crying. "No I can't."

"All right," I said. "Try to stop crying."

The man on the radio was through talking on the telephone. I had missed the end of what he was saying. A song started playing. It was a soft song, but Rebecca's crying was softer.

"Your mother wanted to know if you had talked to me," I said.

Rebecca reached out fast as that and grabbed my arm. "Don't tell them," she said. "Don't let them know I was in here or that I was talking to you."

"Why not?"

Rebecca let go of my arm and wiped her eyes. "I don't ever want to talk to them again as long as I live."

I waited, then I said, "Why not?"

"I hate them," she said.

Rebecca leaned forward and started crying really hard and I was cold to hear her cry like that. I moved closer to her and started to put my arm around her little shoulders, but I didn't. I sat down beside her and she leaned against me and I could feel her shaking. It made me want to cry too, to feel her crying like that, but I started working the muscles in my jaw instead.

The radio was playing "Whatever Will Be, Will Be." I listened to it and to Rebecca crying. By the time the song was over, Rebecca was still. Her hair on my shoulder tickled and the night was quiet. I could smell her sweet girl-smell, like coming out of a shower on a cool afternoon in May and sitting on the front porch while your hair dried.

"Rebecca. I'm sorry you came way off up here and this happened to you."

"You wanted to be my pirate, remember?"

"Yeah."

"I kept thinking that if you had been here that day, you would have done something. You would have, wouldn't you?"

"Sure," I said.

"Ricky, if I died, would you remember me?"

I started to move, but something in the way Rebecca leaned closer to me made me think she didn't want me to. "Why would you die?"

"Ricky, this house reminds me of yours, you know that? Sometimes I pretend I am in your room and in a little while you'll come up the stairs and say hey, what are you doing in my room?"

"What would you be doing in my room?"

"Waiting for you. I would lie on the bed and look out the window or read a book and wait for you."

Another song came on the radio. Rebecca pushed her legs out straight and wiped her eyes. Her hair hid her face from me, but I thought she might be feeling better. She turned and looked at me for a long time.

"What is it?"

"Nothing," she said, looking down.

"Tell me," I said.

"No."

"I want to know. Tell me."

"I'll live with it."

"Tell me, Rebecca."

"You're lucky not to have moved. You have a good family."

"That isn't what you were going to say."

She looked down and started folding the handkerchief and unfolding it again.

"Tell me."

Rebecca turned and looked at me and something made me

think of the blue sweater she wore last fall and how she carried the two kittens in that sweater all the way up the hill to our house. I felt lonely and older.

I woke up. The bed felt good, and where I had not been lying, the sheets were cool. The sparrows were singing outside. Their noise reminded me of home and I shut my eyes and tried to be there, but cars started going by and I knew I wasn't there. I turned over in my bed and looked out the door and thought of Rebecca. She came out of her room and saw me watching her. She turned and went into the bathroom. I thought she would smile or wink or something, but she didn't. I got out of bed.

After I had put on my last set of clean clothes, I stacked all the rest of them together and started out of the room. When I got to the door, Rebecca came out of the bathroom. I stopped and looked at her to see what she would do. She stopped too. She looked pretty and soft, but her eye was swollen again from crying.

"Hi," I whispered.

"Not a word," she whispered back, nodding towards the stairs. She looked older.

"All right," I said.

Then she smiled and she was Rebecca again. I was glad.

"Go on," she said. "My mother will be up here pretty soon." Her face set hard like she was thinking, then she turned and went in her room and closed the door.

I carried my clothes through the kitchen and into the room at the back where Mrs. Brown's washing machine was. The floor of the room was concrete and it had an old smell that reminded me of a book I read from the library, one that was made in 1905. There were some jars of preserves on the shelves, mostly plum and some fig. On one shelf was a hammer and a box of nails. The hammer looked old and the head was rusted a little. A box of rat poison was behind it, but it was old too.

I heard Mrs. Brown open the icebox and close it again, so I dumped my clothes on the floor and walked back into the kitchen. Mrs. Brown was at the cabinet, pouring some milk in her coffee from the milk bottle. As I walked back in, she put the lid on the bottle and turned and saw me and screamed and dropped the bottle on the floor. It broke and milk went rolling away under the table.

I backed up against the wall, she scared me so bad. She looked down and started shaking her head and taking deep breaths.

I looked at all the milk on the floor and said, "I'm sorry, Mrs. Brown. I was only putting my clothes in the wash room."

Mrs. Brown was still taking deep breaths. She went over to the table and pulled a chair out of the milk and sat down. Her hand was on her chest and her face looked white and cold.

"I'm sorry," I said again.

"You mustn't ever do that again," she said.

"I won't."

"I thought you were that man—" she said, then she stopped suddenly and swallowed and looked at me.

"I'm sorry," I said again. I really felt bad and wanted to make it up to her. "I'll clean it up."

Before she could say anything else, I went back into the little room and got the mop and came back. I slid the mop around in the milk for a minute until Mrs. Brown stood up and said, "Here. I'll do it. We'll have to wet it first."

She took it to the sink and ran water on it. I knelt down and began picking the largest pieces of the broken glass out of the milk. Mrs. Brown went to the table and slid the mop under it. In a little while the floor was all clean again.

While Mrs. Brown fixed my breakfast, I looked at a newspaper that was on the edge of the table. The paper said the Waco area had now gone ninety-two days without measurable rainfall. I turned over to the funnies and started reading them. Alley Oop was the best.

Mrs. Brown put my plate on the table and said, "I guess you'll have to do without milk this morning." She made a smile and I felt sorry for her and I wondered why Rebecca hated her now.

"That's all right," I said.

After a while, Mrs. Brown said, "Well, I think we have reason to celebrate this morning."

I looked at her. "Why?"

"Rebecca went all night last night without a bad dream."

"That's right," I said, but I looked down fast.

"Listen," I told Rebecca. "Isn't there a store around here? I saw some boys going to the store the other day."

"There is one. It's down the street." She nodded out the window.

We were both sitting on the floor under the window, very close together so that we could talk in whispers.

"Let's go to the store," I said.

"Why?"

"I like stores. Besides, it will be like old times and we can talk."

"What will you tell my mother?"

"She needs milk. She broke the milk bottle this morning." I told Rebecca all about it. It made me want to laugh now, but when I looked at Rebecca, I said, "What's wrong?"

"It figures," she said in a tight voice.

"What does?" I asked.

Rebecca looked mad and ugly.

"What is it?"

But Rebecca wouldn't say anything else. She got up and went to her rocking chair and sat down and started rocking. She was staring out the window. I got up and went over to her.

"Do you want to go?" I asked her.

She rocked back and forth.

"Come on, Rebecca," I said. "Don't start doing that again. What's wrong?"

Rebecca rocked and wouldn't look at me. I backed up and sat on the bed and watched her. Then I looked out the window. Almost an hour went by. Then Rebecca stopped rocking suddenly and looked down. Tears were in her eyes, but that was all. She shook her head and looked at me.

"All right," she said. "Let's go."

Mrs. Brown said it was all right, but that if Rebecca got too tired, I was to call a taxi from the store to bring us home again. I said I would and Mrs. Brown gave me some money for the milk and a taxi if we needed it. The whole time Mrs. Brown was going on, Rebecca stood by the door staring at it like a robot. We went outside, me holding Rebecca's hand like we had decided, and Mrs. Brown called me back.

"Thank you, Ricky," she said. "You are so good."

I felt like a rat then. I just said, "Yes ma'am." I went back to Rebecca and we crosssed the yard. I could feel Mrs. Brown watching us. At the corner, we waited for two cars, then we crossed and started down a low hill. When the bushes of another house hid us from Rebecca's, she said, "Thank goodness."

"What's this store like?" I said, trying to forget the look Mrs. Brown had given me.

"It's bigger than Mr. Norman's store. It even has air conditioning."

"Does it have funny books?"

"I think so. It has lots of things."

I still held Rebecca's hand as we walked down the street. When a car passed us, I moved way over by the curb. Rebecca looked all around and seemed glad to be outside again. Before we got to the store, I looked at her.

"Why do you hate your parents?" I asked. "Because they moved up here?"

"Don't ask me about it, please, Ricky," she said.

She looked down and tried to pull her hand out of mine, but I held on to it. My hands were not as strong as Gerald's, but they were stronger than Rebecca's.

"All right," I said. "I won't ask you again, but I think you aren't being fair to them."

"What do you know about being fair to someone who has let you down?"

"Nothing," I said, but as we walked across the parking lot of the store I thought about Carol.

That afternoon, Rebecca and I played Monopoly. We were both lying on the bed. The game was going pretty good except that Rebecca had both Boardwalk and Park Place and she was wiping me out with rent. She was always buying new hotels. Everything on the board was bought out except the yellow spaces. Neither one of us bought them.

I rolled the dice on the board and looked at the numbers. It was a three.

"Community Chest," Rebecca said.

I picked up one of the little cards and looked at it. It showed the man with the moustache holding two babies looking at a nurse. I had to pay $100 in hospital fees.

"What is it?"

"It says to pass Go and collect two hundred dollars."

"Let me see it."

"Don't you trust me?"

"No." Then she said, "Yes." She picked up the dice and started to roll them.

"Wait," I said. Rebecca looked at me. "It says to pay one hundred dollars."

Rebecca watched me pay the money, then she rolled. She wound up in jail. "Ha ha," I said.

"That's where you should be, cheater," Rebecca said.

Then I said, "Did the guy that broke in ever get put in jail?"

She picked up the dice and looked at them. She rolled them in her fingers for a minute, then looked at me and handed me the dice. I took them. She was still looking at me.

"I don't know," she said.

"Didn't they catch him?"

"I don't know."

"Didn't your father come home and scare him away? Didn't your father see who it was?"

"Roll. It's your turn."

"I want to know, Rebecca."

"Roll."

"Tell me. Then I'll roll."

After a minute, Rebecca said very slowly, "*Roll.*"

"Tell me."

Without looking at me, Rebecca said, "My father didn't scare anybody anywhere."

She got up off the bed and went to the door before I could

even say I was sorry for pushing it. She went out the door and I heard her go in the bathroom. I waited for her to come back and looked at the dice. Time went by. Half an hour went by. I put all the money and hotels and cards back in the box. Mrs. Brown came to the door and looked in.

"Where is Rebecca?"

"In the bathroom."

Mrs. Brown came over to the bed and looked at me. "Playing Monopoly?"

"Not really," I said.

When Mr. Brown got home he called me downstairs. I didn't mind anyway. Rebecca had come back in the room and wouldn't talk, so I was ready to do something else. When Rebecca sat in her rocking chair, it was like she had gone to another place. Mr. Brown was at the bottom of the stairs waiting for me.

"You busy?" he asked.

"No sir."

"Come with me."

We went outside. It was almost five, but it was still hot. Mr. Brown took me to the garage and we went inside. Against a wall were some rakes and shovels and hoes. Of all the tools in the world, those were the ones I hated the most.

"What are we going to do?"

"You'll see."

He gave me a shovel and he took a rake. I didn't like that.

"You want me to rake some leaves?"

"You bring the shovel."

We went around to the front of the house and Mr. Brown stepped off the lawn into an old flower bed. He started raking some leaves and dead limbs out of the way.

"What are you going to do?" I asked.

"Louise wants a flower bed again."

"In the middle of summer?"

Mr. Brown looked at me as if he knew I had drawn two aces. "Talk to her," he said.

We were going to clean the bed out and dig the dirt up

with the shovel. I could think of a hundred other things to use for turning the dirt than a long-handled shovel. After he had all the leaves and limbs out of the way, Mr. Brown pointed at the hard, dry dirt and said, "You start."

I started, but it wasn't easy. I was glad we were in the shade, but it was hot.

"You see any change in my girl?" he asked suddenly. He said *my girl* like I was trying to get her away from him.

"What do you mean?" I said.

"You know what I mean."

"She seems older."

"That's not what I mean. Has she noticed you, acknowledged your presence in any way?"

"I'm not sure," I said, standing on the shovel blade and jumping to make it go down in the hard dirt.

"What do you mean you're not sure?"

"Well," I said, straining. "Sometimes I think she's looking at me, then I think I'm wrong and she isn't."

"You're probably wrong," he said like anybody would be crazy to look at me. That made me mad. I pulled back on the shovel handle and clods popped out of the dirt. Mr. Brown wasn't watching.

"What do you do up there all day?" he said. "You don't try to take advantage of her, do you?"

"What?"

"Nothing. But I won't have it."

"Yes sir."

Mr. Brown lit a cigarette and watched me trying to dig the rock-hard dirt. He had said more to me then than he had ever since I had known him.

"Mr. Brown?"

"What."

"Could you tell me more about what happened? I mean, I don't really know. If I knew more about what happened, maybe I could help more, you know?"

Mr. Brown watched me digging. He smoked his cigarette and acted like he was trying to hear the telephone ring in the house. I stood on the shovel again and jumped up and down.

"You know enough," he said finally.

"Did you scare the man away?" I asked.

Mr. Brown threw his cigarette butt at the small pile of dirt I had to the side. It was still smoking. He stood up and came over to me.

"Let me try a while," he said.

Rebecca woke me up again. She said she wanted to talk to me. I was sleepy, but I said all right. She sat on the floor in the same place she had the night before, but I lay on my stomach and looked down at her. I didn't want to get up.

"Turn the radio on," she said.

I reached over and turned it on. The lighted dial came on, then the sound came on. It was the news. A man had killed his family, then killed himself. The police thought the heat had something to do with it.

"What do you want to talk about?" I asked, feeling sleepy.

"I don't know."

"Oh," I said. Then I said, "How do you feel?"

"All right. My eye feels a lot better."

"It looks better."

The newsman was talking about the Korean War. I thought about that for a while. They named places over there with numbers, like on a map. I thought it might be a code of some kind. I would have to ask Gerald about it. He would know.

"Ricky?"

"Yeah?"

"How come you never kissed me?"

"Kissed you?" I said.

"Yeah. Don't you think I'm pretty?"

"Sure I do."

"How come you never kissed me?"

"I don't know."

"Would you like to?"

"Right now?"

"Sometime."

"All right."

"Right now?" she asked, turning a little.

"All right."

She got up on her knees and leaned forward and I got up on my elbows and kissed her. I could feel where her lip had been cut.

"How was that?" I asked. I didn't know what else to say. Rebecca sat back down again and didn't say anything. I lay down again and looked at her hair.

"I'm almost eleven," Rebecca said.

"I'll be eleven before you will," I said. My birthday was in October and hers was in November. We were both older than everybody else in our grade at school. I liked that.

"Have you seen where you'll go to school yet?" I asked.

"No."

"It will be big, I bet."

"I don't want to go there," Rebecca said. She looked down. "Why do things have to change?"

"I don't know," I said, thinking of Carol.

"Everything was just fine before I moved up here. Since then everything has been horrible."

"I know."

"We always used to do things together and now there isn't anyone but me all day long."

"There isn't any kids living around here?"

"Just one boy named Arthur who lives two streets over. But I don't like him. He stopped on his bike a couple of times when I was in the yard and said a bunch of dumb things."

I remembered the boy who shot me the finger. "Does he have a red bike?"

"Yes."

"I saw him the other day. I don't like him."

"We ought to fix his bike," Rebecca said.

"Yeah. We could fix it so the chain would come off when he was going down a hill."

"You could do it," Rebecca said.

"Sure I could."

"You could fix him for good."

"You bet."

"He would never stop here again."

"Yeah."

Rebecca was quiet for a while. I was thinking how to fix Arthur's bicycle. Then Rebecca turned around and looked at me.

"Kiss me again," she said.

Mrs. Brown called me and said that Mama was on the telephone and wanted to talk to me. I got out of bed, wondering what time it was, but the sun was up and I knew it wasn't too early for Mama to be calling. I pulled on my pants and ran down the stairs buttoning my shirt. Mrs. Brown was in the living room holding the receiver to her ear. She said, "I'm sure he has." When she saw me, she said, "Here he is now."

She gave me the telephone and I said hello. The telephone smelled like Mrs. Brown.

"Ricky?" It was Mama.

"Yeah."

"Are you getting along all right?"

"Yeah."

"Not being any trouble are you?"

"No."

Mrs. Brown was standing at the door watching me with a little smile on her face. It was good to hear Mama talk. I felt like things were right again.

"Are you about ready to come home?"

"I guess so," I said.

"How is Rebecca doing?"

"All right, I guess."

"Have you gotten her to talk—"

"No. Not yet," I said. "Are you coming to get me?"

"I think you can ride the bus home. Don't you?"

"Okay."

"Do you have any money left?"

"Just about all of it."

"Well, let us know when you're coming and we'll meet you at the station. All right?"

"All right."

"Behave yourself. We miss you."

Suddenly I wanted to be home and sitting on the back porch wondering what to do next.

"Just a minute. Gerald wants to talk to you." Then I heard her say, "Don't talk all day. This costs money."

"Hey queer," Gerald said. "You owe me eight dish-washings."

"I wish you were here, Gerald. There is a guy we could take care of."

"Grow up," Gerald said. "I can't follow you all your life."

I didn't say anything. I was looking at my big toe and wishing I was at home.

"Yeah, well," Gerald said. "Here's Carol."

Then, before I could say anything, Carol was on the telephone saying hello. I smiled when I heard her voice, then I remembered, and I stopped smiling.

"Ricky," she said. "Are you being nice, like I said for you to be? Is it helping Rebecca any?"

"All right, Mama," I said for Mrs. Brown to hear. "I will. Goodbye."

I was sitting at Rebecca's desk and playing with the drawer. She was sitting close by in her rocking chair, scratching her foot. Her eye was almost completely well and she looked good.

"What did Gerald say?" she whispered.

"You know Gerald," I said. I didn't really want to talk about it.

"Did you talk to Carol?"

"No."

"She must have been busy. I like Carol. She was like my big sister when I would come over and your father had you working."

"Yeah. I don't want to talk about it."

"Why not? Does it make you homesick?"

"No."

"It makes me homesick and it's not even my home." She was quiet a minute, then she said, "Neither is this."

"Carol makes me sick," I said.

"Why?"

"I don't want to talk about it."

"I don't understand," Rebecca said. "Carol is really nice."

"She makes me sick," I said again.

Rebecca looked at me. "What did she do?"

"I don't want to talk about it."

"Was she mean to you?"

I didn't say anything for a while, then I finally told Rebecca what had happened at the carnival on the Fourth of July. I told her Carol didn't have to do things like that. She could just stay on the farm forever.

"But she can't," Rebecca said.

"I might have known you'd take her side," I said.

"It's time for her to make a place of her own. It would hurt her to just keep on living at home."

"I don't see how."

"You're just jealous and you shouldn't be. Carol will always be your sister."

She looked at me. I looked down and pulled out the desk drawer I was playing with. On top of some other papers was a letter I had written to her.

"You're not making any sense," she said quietly.

"Why do I have to make sense? You never told me why you hate your parents. They seem perfectly nice to me, except your father sometimes."

I turned and looked at Rebecca. She had dropped her eyes. I didn't mean to make her feel bad, but something was turning over inside me and I didn't feel right. I felt like everybody knew what was going on except me. Rebecca let her foot slide to the floor and she sat back in the rocking chair and looked at me. Her brown eyes were like fire.

"Just forget it," I said. "I'm sorry. I don't know what's wrong with me."

"If it wasn't for my parents, nothing would ever have happened to me," she said. I thought she was talking about having to move to Waco, then she said, "You heard I was all alone when that man broke in the house—" she stopped. I was looking at her brown eyes. "I wasn't," she went on.

Rebecca did a funny thing that night. She came in my room again and turned on the radio and lay down beside me waiting for me to wake up. I must have been slow in waking up because when I did, Rebecca was leaning over me, tickling my nose with the ends of her hair. Her sweet smell was all around me.

"Hey," I said. "Are you trying to make me sneeze?"

She was lying beside me on top of the sheet. "I was trying to wake you up," she said.

"Oh."

"Were you dreaming?"

"I don't remember."

"Your eyes were moving all around."

"How could you tell?"

"I could see them."

I yawned and tried to wake up. Rebecca was watching me.

"Are you sleepy?" she asked.

"I'm used to sleeping at night."

"So was I."

"Did you have the bad dream?"

She looked down. We listened to the radio for a while. Rebecca knew some of the songs and she hummed them while they played. It made me sleepy again.

"You want to go home, don't you?"

"I guess so."

She looked at me. "I don't blame you. I'm not much fun."

"You're all right."

"I can't help it."

"You're fine," I said.

"I hate myself."

"I like you. Come on, Rebecca."

"If I could have one wish in the whole world, do you know what it would be?"

"No."

"I would wish that I was you."

"Why?"

"Because I think you're neat. And you have a neat family and live in a neat place."

"You're neat too. If you were me, who would be my friend?"

"Rebecca would," she said and shook her hair back.

"You look funny in the dark," I said.

"What do you mean?"

"You look older."

"In seven more years I'll be eighteen."

"Me too."

"Everything will be completely different and you probably won't ever think about me or even know where I am."

"Why do you think I would forget you?"

"I don't know. Because I don't want you to."

"That's not a reason."

"Let's make a pact, then," Rebecca said. "Seven years from today we will meet again."

"Where?"

"Not here," Rebecca said.

"Mr. Norman's store?"

"Okay."

"He would like that," I said, thinking of him.

"Promise?"

"I promise. No matter what."

Rebecca was leaning over me and all of her hair fell like a shadow on the left side of her face. I was happy being close to her. Sometimes she made me feel like I could do anything.

"Do you love me?" she asked.

"Are you going to kiss me again?"

"Answer me first."

"Yes," I said. "Are you going to kiss me again?"

"Do you want me to?"

"I don't know."

She looked down at me. I could feel her breath and hear her words before she began to say them.

"Well, if you don't know, then I'm not going to do it," she said.

"Are you mad?"

"No."

She leaned down and put her soft lips on mine. It was

really more of a touch than a kiss. She pushed up again and shook her hair back. We listened to the radio a while. It was late at night. One time I heard the man say it was four-twenty. I got sleepy again.

"Are you going to sleep?"

"I don't know," I said.

"You are."

"Are you?"

"Maybe."

She put her head down on the bed and I could smell her with my eyes closed.

The first thing I saw in the morning was both Mr. and Mrs. Brown standing by my bed. For a minute, I didn't know what was going on, then I felt Rebecca on the bed behind me and my stomach went cold. "Is this what he came up here for?" Mr. Brown said.

Even while I was sitting up, I felt Rebecca get stiff beside me.

"She came in in the middle of the night. I was asleep," I said.

Mr. Brown stepped closer to the bed. "Is that so?" he said.

"Marvin," Mrs. Brown said.

"Honest," I said.

Rebecca sat up, then, and tossed her head so that her dark hair flew back like a flag. They both stopped. I would have too if Rebecca had looked at me the way she was looking at them.

"Leave him alone," she said, even as ice.

Mrs. Brown's face started working with surprise. Mr. Brown straightened up a little and looked hard at Rebecca.

"Coward," she said.

Mr. Brown backed up at that. Mrs. Brown was shaking her head. "Oh Rebecca," she said.

I got up and moved to the end of the bed. I looked at Rebecca. I could hardly recognize her. Her face seemed hard and thin and her eyes were burning like Gerald's did when he made the hate face.

"Now listen," Mr. Brown said.

"No. I'm not going to listen to you ever again!" Rebecca

screamed. "When that man came in and started hitting me, I prayed you would come and save me, but when you got home and came in and saw him, you just ran back outside. I saw you! You ran away faster than he did!"

"Rebecca, I was going to get—"

"I don't want to hear it!" Rebecca screamed. "I don't want to hear it! I saw you!"

Rebecca was crying and screaming like she was living her dream. Mrs. Brown stepped closer to the bed with her hands out.

"And you," Rebecca screamed. "I knew you were in the kitchen hiding. You were hiding and didn't do anything. You didn't do *anything*!"

"I was so scared," Mrs. Brown said.

Rebecca was crying so hard that she couldn't get her breath. Mrs. Brown reached for her, but she screamed for them both to get away. When they just stood there, she got more crazy and threw my pillow at them.

"Let's go," Mr. Brown said. He could barely talk.

"Ricky," Mrs. Brown said. Mr. Brown led her out of the room toward the stairs. He looked back at me, but he didn't look mad. He looked ashamed.

I moved over on the bed and sat down beside Rebecca and waited while she cried. We must have sat there like that for almost an hour. I felt lonely and sad and clenched my jaws as hard as I could so I wouldn't cry. Finally Rebecca sat up and reached for my hand and held on to it while she cried some more. Then she started to choke, so I helped her into the bathroom and stood beside her while she vomited in the commode. I washed her face with a rag when she was through. She was as white as the bathtub.

I took her back into my room and sat beside her with my arm around her shoulders. After a while she got very still and quiet.

"How are you doing?" I asked her.

"I don't feel very good."

"Are you going to throw up again?"

"I'm glad you're here."

"Me too."

"They didn't do anything, Ricky," she said, then, and shook her head. Tears fell on my hand.

I waited until Rebecca was dressed and we went downstairs together. Mr. and Mrs. Brown were in the living room. Mrs. Brown was sitting on the couch, and Mr. Brown was standing by the windows, looking outside. Mrs. Brown stood up and came toward us. Rebecca reached out and grabbed my hand and squeezed it hard. Mrs. Brown stopped. The look on her face made me want to run and hide.

"I'm so sorry, Rebecca," she said. "I've never been a very brave person, I'm afraid. I don't know what happened. I just couldn't move. I wanted to, but I just couldn't."

Mrs. Brown looked down, then tried to smile, then looked very sad. Her eyes caught mine.

Mr. Brown walked up. "I guess," he said, "for all my knowing ways and high ambitions, I'm just what you said I was, Rebecca. But I swear to God in Heaven there was a police car at that little store and I went to get help."

Rebecca was still holding my hand tightly in hers. There were tears in her eyes again. She looked at me. "I don't feel very good," she said.

I started to take Rebecca to the couch, but Mrs. Brown put her hands on Rebecca's shoulders to help her. For a second Rebecca wouldn't go, then her hand slid out of mine and she let her mother take her to the couch. Mr. Brown watched them and then looked down at me.

"I think I'm ready to go home," I said.

The next day we all went down to the station together. It was hot in the car and nobody said anything. Rebecca sat beside me and I held her hand. Her eyes had rings under them, but otherwise she looked pretty good. At the station, Mr. Brown went to buy my ticket. After he had gone, I thought of the money Mama had given me and I went after him. I caught up with him at the counter.

"I have some money," I said.

"I'll pay for it," he said. He bought the ticket and turned around. "I guess you must think I'm—" he started.

I looked down, then looked at him. He looked back at me. Then he held out his hand. I took it and shook it. I thought he would say something else, but he didn't. He gave me the ticket and we went back to Mrs. Brown and Rebecca. Rebecca was holding my sack.

"When does the bus leave?" she asked me.

"In fifteen minutes," Mr. Brown said.

"Will you ever come back?" Rebecca asked.

I looked at her. "Sure I will."

"Thank you so much for coming, Ricky," Mrs. Brown said.

"Yes ma'am," I said.

She bent down and kissed me. Her face was soft and sad. Rebecca and I were looking at each other. Rebecca turned and looked at her mother.

"I'm walking out to the bus with him," she said.

They both nodded and we walked away from them. Outside where the buses were, it was hot and noisy and the bus exhaust filled my nose. I started to take my sack, but Rebecca said she would hold it. I found the bus I was supposed to ride and we went over to it.

"Maybe you could come down and stay with me a while," I said. Just as I thought, she was starting to cry.

"I want to," she said.

"Will you be all right?"

She nodded, then she said, "I don't know."

She looked at me and my stomach hurt like I hadn't eaten anything in about two weeks.

"I'm going to miss you so much," she said. "Will you write to me as soon as you get home?"

"Sure," I said.

It was time to go. Rebecca gave me the sack, then she hugged me so hard that I couldn't breathe. Then she kissed me. I went to the bus and got on and went toward the back and sat down. I could see Rebecca still standing there. She was still standing there when I couldn't see her anymore.

I slept all the way home. People walking by me woke me up. I picked up my sack and walked off the bus. Only Mama was there. She hugged me when I walked up to her. She wanted to hear about everything. I told her only what Mr. and Mrs. Brown knew. I didn't tell her about all the talks that Rebecca and I had.

"Such a shame," Mama said.

All the way home I kept thinking how funny everything looked, how changed it all was. When we turned in the driveway, it seemed to me that I had been gone for years. I got out of the station wagon and followed Mama in the house.

"Where is everybody?" I asked.

"One place and another. I think Gerald was supposed to help your father this afternoon."

I went up the stairs, thinking it was different than I remembered. When I passed Carol's room, I saw that she was mopping her floor. She stopped a second and looked at me like I was a dog, then went on mopping. I went into my room and put the sack on my bed and looked out the window. I could see Gerald coming up from the barn. He had probably been hiding out there so he wouldn't have to work. In a few minutes he would be to the house.

I walked back down to Carol's room and stood in the door. She made a pass by her closet and turned and saw me. She stopped mopping when she looked at my face. Then she just stood there waiting. It seemed to me that she could go either way, and so could I. I ran to her and she dropped the mop and hugged me. That was the way we went.

MAMA PUT HER COFFEE cup down and looked at me. "Do you still have that ten dollars I gave you?" she asked.

"Most of it."

"Where is it?"

"In my sack in my room."

"As soon as you finish eating, I want you to get it," Mama said.

Father looked at me, then looked over my head into the living room. He had a far away look in his eyes like he was trying to remember six telephone numbers. His mouth was open a little. I was used to seeing him with his jaw clamped tight and his muscles working, but now he looked different.

"Well, will he be through this morning?" Mama asked him.

"Who?" Father said, looking at her as if she had just come into the room.

"Mr. Rutts. Will he be through?"

"I think so," Father said. "Nothin' left to do now, but put all the pieces back and fill it with water and oil."

"Are y'all talking about the tractor?" Carol asked. She was sitting at the end of the table eating a piece of toast with jelly on it.

"Yeah," Father said.

"What was ever wrong with it?" Carol said.

"It was broke down, for one thing," Father said, leaning back in his chair. He looked like himself again. He had set his jaw and his eyes were sharp. He had a little smile on his face. He cut Carol a look, with his eyebrows raised.

"Oh really?" Carol said.

After a minute, Father said, "More than I thought, but less than I was afraid of. Both the water pump and the oil pump were out on it. That'll never happen again in a hundred years."

"I hope not," Mama said.

Father looked at her. "Anyway, it's done," he said.

"I'll be glad when that man stops coming around here," Mama said. "I don't care for the way he talks at all."

"He's a little rough," Father said. "But he seems to be a good worker, once he shows up."

"I hope I never hear a lot rough," Mama said.

For some reason we all looked at Gerald.

I was standing in the hall waiting for Carol to come down the stairs. I wanted to tell her about something Rebecca had told me. Mama came out of the kitchen and looked at me as she went into her bedroom. When she came out again, she looked at me again. I smiled at her.

"Is that all you have to do?" she said.

"No ma'am."

She went on in the kitchen to clean up the breakfast dishes. I heard the sound of Carol's shoes on the floor upstairs and then she was coming downstairs. She was brushing her hair as she walked.

"Hi," I said.

"Hello yourself," she said. She went by me into the kitchen without hardly even looking at me. "Mama, have you seen the keys to the station wagon?"

"No I haven't. What did you do with them?"

"Mama, I gave them to you. Don't you remember?"

"Don't you use that tone of voice with me," Mama said. "Try looking on the dresser."

"Thanks," Carol said like she didn't mean it. When she came out of the kitchen, she said, "Ricky, don't you have anything better to do than stand in the way?"

"Sorry," I said. I watched her go in the bedroom. In a minute she came out with the keys in her hand. "I have something to tell you," I said.

Carol kept walking. I followed her into the kitchen.

"Did you find them?" Mama asked, looking over her shoulder.

"Yes," Carol said.

I followed her onto the back porch. She put the brush on the cabinet by the door, then turned suddenly.

"*Ricky*. What are you doing? I have to get my purse. I'm going to be late if you don't get out of my way."

She walked past me and I heard her running up the stairs again. I stood by the sink and looked at the floor. I looked up. Mama was watching me.

"I don't think Carol has time for us anymore," Mama said.

When Carol came back downstairs, I followed her out the back door. She smelled nice and looked pretty, but she wasn't looking at me. When she opened the car door, she saw me standing on the porch.

"What did you want?" she asked.

"I wanted to tell you something."

"Was it very important?"

"I guess not," I said.

Carol turned and got in the car and slammed the door. As she put the key in the ignition, she looked at me.

"Tell me when I get home," she said. "I don't want to be late." She started the car. "I think I have something to tell you, too," she said. "And it is important."

She said goodbye, then put the station wagon in reverse. I stood on the porch in the sun and watched her leave. After she was gone, I still stood there, looking around. When I turned back toward the house, I saw Mama. She was standing in front of the cabinet looking out the window at me.

Father started working on the tractor before Wilbur got there, so I went down there and watched him and Gerald matching pieces to the empty places on the tractor. The tractor was covered with dust and the mower was still hooked to it, waiting.

"Ricky could do this," Gerald said, holding a handful of short, greasy bolts.

"So can you," Father said. "I don't want to hear anything else about it."

I stood in the doorway of the shop. Ever since I had left Rebecca, I felt lonely, like everybody but me had been chosen to play on a team. I could be around other people, but it seemed like it was their game, not mine. I had no part in it, but to watch it. Even though they didn't get along very well, Father and Gerald were right together, and Mama and Carol were right, but I wasn't.

The sun was hot. The ground around the tractor was stained with oil like the tractor had bled to death or something. I didn't like the way it looked. I started to go in the shop, but I saw the little cage where we had kept our rabbits and that made me feel bad, so I didn't. I squinted my eyes against the sun and looked toward the road. It was still too early for the mail to come. I wondered if Rebecca had written me a letter. She and I were right together, but she was gone.

Then Wilbur drove up.

Gerald looked around the tractor. Father straightened up a second, then went back to tightening a bolt. Dust swept over us, like Wilbur himself was the drought and carried the dust and heat and dryness with him wherever he went. I stepped back in the shop. Every time I saw Wilbur, I felt like something bad was going to happen. When he opened the door of the truck, I thought he would have a gun in his hand.

"Already at work?" he said, walking up to the tractor.

"Yeah," Father said. "No use killin' a good mornin'."

Wilbur cut his eyes at me. I had a hole in the knee of my jeans. Wilbur looked at it, then raised his eyes to mine and spit. "No sir, goddamn," he said.

I shivered and looked over at Gerald. Gerald was smiling enough to make me sick. I couldn't see how Gerald could feel the way he did when I felt so scared.

"Mornin'," Gerald said.

"Say there, boy," Wilbur said. "Gimme them bolts and let me get at that son of a bitch right now."

"I've got these started on this side," Father said.

"Mighty damn fine," Wilbur said. As he went around the front of the tractor, he looked at me again. His smile was gone. I stepped back.

"Noticed that cotton openin' up," Wilbur said. "Be time to get it picked 'fore long."

"Yeah," Father said.

"Man over in Seguin already brought in his first bale," Wilbur said.

"That right?"

"Yes sir. The son of a bitch irrigated though."

"He was lucky he had the water," Father said, straightening up and taking a bolt out of Gerald's hand.

"Rich bastard," Wilbur said. "Name of Daniels. Not a hard workin' man like us."

"Nope," Father said. He wiped his hands and looked at me, then looked back at the tractor. "You haven't seen that half-inch, have you?" he said.

"Half-inch?" Wilbur said, sliding the bolts into the oil pan from the other side.

"Yeah," Father said. "After we quit the other day, it was gone."

Wilbur straightened up and looked across the tractor at Father. He looked mean again, thin and tough.

"You sayin' I stold it?"

"Nope," Father said evenly, looking at him. "I'm just askin' if you've seen it."

Wilbur cut me a look, then his face changed. "Matter of fact, I took it with me. Had to do some work on my truck."

Father started to say something. Wilbur was watching him. "We'll need it," Father said. "You got it?"

"I said I did."

"With you?" Father said.

Wilbur's face changed again. "Sure," he smiled. "Brought it with me, what do you spect?"

Wilbur went over to his truck and came back with the wrench. He gave it to Father. Gerald was watching Father.

"Didn't think I'd keep the little rusty son of a bitch, did you?"

"Nope," Father said.

They went back to work. Gerald gave them what they needed and I just watched. After a while Mama came outside with a basket. When the screen door slammed, Wilbur turned and watched Mama. His eyes were cuts in his face. Mama took the basket to the wash-shed and went back inside.

"Say," Wilbur said, after a while. "About that cotton. You got any pickers lined up yet?"

"Nope," Father said. "But I've got the boys here and there are some workers usually make it through here every year about this time."

"I don't want to pick cotton," Gerald said.

"Goddamn," Wilbur said. "Listen to that one talk."

"He does a lot of that," Father said.

Wilbur looked over the tractor at me. "I bet that one don't," he said. A drop of sweat tickled the corner of his mouth and he licked at it with his tongue. He looked more like a snake than ever.

"Sometimes," Father said.

Wilbur cut Father a look, then looked back at me. He smiled. "I'd be glad to pick along too," he said. "If you'd have me. I still ain't found no work and the old woman and them kids ain't stopped their eatin' any."

"Sure," Father said. "There may not be much to pick, though. It's burnin' up faster than it's makin'."

"Yes sir, it's mighty dry. That's a goddamned fact."

I thought about going to the house, but I didn't. I stayed down there until they were through. By then it was almost dinner time. Father went into the shop and got the oil bucket and a funnel and Wilbur helped him pour the oil in. When that was done, Father told Gerald to take a bucket up to the house and fill it with water.

"Let Ricky do it," Gerald said. "He ain't done nothin' all mornin'."

"All right. One of you do it. It's too hot to sit around ar-
guin' about it."

Gerald looked mean at me, so I got up and took a bucket
up to the house where the hydrant was. I put the bucket on the
ground under the hydrant and turned it on. A few rusty drops
came out, then there was a gurgling sound like when water
runs out of the sink. Then there was nothing. I stood there
looking down at the bucket for a while.

"Hey!" Father called. "What's the hold up?"

"No water's coming out," I hollered back.

Behind me, I heard Mama coming out of the house. The
back door slammed. "No water in the house, either," she said.

I looked at Father down at the shop. He took off his hat
and looked at the windmill and shook his head.

"Did the well go dry?" I asked Mama.

Mama looked at me, then looked down to where Father
was standing. She bit her bottom lip. For a minute, she looked
exactly like Gerald.

We waited all that day for the windmill to pump some
water. The wind blew and the fan squeaked around and around,
but there was no water. The end of the pipe was sucking air.

After supper we went down to the windmill and looked in
the well again. Father reached up and pulled the lever that shut
the fan down. It squeaked to a stop and everything was quieter
than I ever remembered it being. I looked at Father and the
muscles in his jaw were working.

"Well. We'll turn it off tonight and see if the water comes
up any," he said. "If it doesn't, we'll have to haul water from
town and put it in the cistern."

"Why don't we just put it in here?"

"Soak in and be gone," Father said. "The water table has
dropped too low. We'll probably be using the cistern for a long
time."

"Water tastes funny coming out of the cistern," I said.

"Better than no water at all," Father said, sliding the cover
back on the well. He looked up at the fan and said, "It'll be a
good time to grease those gears, anyway."

"Can I help?"

"I doubt it. You get up there and fall off and that'd be the end of you."

"I wouldn't fall off."

"Maybe not," Father said. After a while, he said, "Papa never thought this old well would go dry." He looked around at the barn and the house and the fields. "Far as he knew, it never did."

The next day Father took the tank into town. On the side of the road near the river was a pump with a fire hose on it for people in the country who had run out of water. I wanted to go with him, but Mama made me and Gerald clean up our room, so I didn't get to. All the water we had until Father got back was in a bucket on the cabinet. We had to go outside to the old outhouse to use the bathroom. It was half-rotten and unlevel and it stunk pretty bad.

After we had cleaned our room, Gerald went outside and disappeared, so I decided to follow him. Just as I thought, he went up the washout to see Ruby Lee. I never knew whether he ever gave her a dollar or not, but I didn't think so because we were going to the movie on Saturday, and he would need the dollar for that. It was a western movie with John Wayne in it called *The Searchers*. It had been a long time since we had gone to the movies.

When I got near the end of the washout, I heard Gerald whistling some song. I thought I knew what the song was, but the way Gerald whistled made any song sound like about three different songs put together. I peeked around the edge of the washout where a pile of dirt with sunflowers still growing out of it had caved off the side. He was looking over the top and whistling louder and louder. Then he slid back down and looked the other way from me. After a while, Ruby Lee came walking slowly around the bend. She was wearing jeans and a yellow shirt.

"Hey," Gerald said. "I thought you weren't comin'."

"Why should I when you're just gonna make fun of me?"

I tried to see Ruby Lee better because there was something

different about her. Then the wind blew her hair out of her face and I saw that she had a black eye and a cut on the side of her face. I thought of Rebecca, then. I didn't understand how the same thing could have happened to Ruby Lee.

"What happened to you?" Gerald said.

"Go ahead and laugh. I don't care, but I don't have to listen to it."

Ruby Lee turned like she was going to leave. Gerald went over to her and caught her arm. He turned her around and looked at her.

"Don't that hurt?" he asked her.

"What do you think? You think it feels good or somethin'?" Ruby Lee said. I thought she was starting to cry a little bit. I couldn't tell from where I was, but her voice sounded like it.

"What happened?" Gerald said.

"Nothin' did."

"Tell me," Gerald said.

"I don't have to tell you nothin' just so you can laugh at me. I don't need nobody laughin' at me. I don't feel like it."

"I'm not goin' to laugh at you. Why do you think that?"

"People always laughin' at me. At school and around. I'm sick of it, do you hear me?"

"But we're friends," Gerald said.

"Sure, long as I let you kiss me. That's all."

"No it isn't," Gerald said.

"Sure it is. You think I don't know?"

"You're wrong."

"Don't tell me I'm wrong, Gerald. If I'm wrong, how come you never invited me down to your house? Huh? How come we always got to meet in some damned gulley?"

"My parents might not like us seein' each other," Gerald said.

"'Cause I ain't good enough," Ruby Lee said. She tossed her head and her hair blew back. Her face was pretty beat up.

"That's not it," Gerald said.

"Sure," Ruby Lee said. "I'm goin' back to the house. This sun is makin' my head hurt."

"Tell me what happened," Gerald said.

"My pa hit me, that's what happened."

"Why?"

"None of your business. But it's your daddy's fault. He give him that money and he went and got drunk and came home and liked to kill me."

"Why?"

"I told you it weren't none of your business."

"He must have been pretty drunk," Gerald said.

"He don't need to be drunk to do this. He's done it before, and I'm sick of it. See this lip? How you think I got that scar?"

"I never thought about it."

"All that kissin' we done, and you never thought about it? You sure must be dumb."

"Dumb, hell," Gerald said. "I just had other things on my mind."

"I got other things on my mind too," Ruby Lee said. "Other things than just you. I'm tired of gettin' beat like this for nothin'. I ain't the only one either. Ma said when we moved here that Pa had to change or she was goin' back to her relations in East Texas. She means it too. She's gonna take Bo and leave one of these days, but I won't be goin' with her. I got my own plans. Quick as I can find me a way out, I'm gone."

"Me too," Gerald said.

Ruby Lee laughed an ugly laugh. I was pretty sure she was crying now. She was holding her arms across her chest and she was rocking back and forth on her feet as if she couldn't be still.

"You? You talk big, boy, but you're dumber than I think if you really believe you'll ever leave your precious daddy and his big farm."

"I'm goin' to, I tell you," Gerald said.

"Sure you are," Ruby Lee said, practically screaming. "Listen. Your daddy prob'bly said the same thing one time, but the only way he'll ever leave is in a coffin."

"I'm really goin'," Gerald said. "I'm not about to stay out here all my life."

"Tell it to the wind," Ruby Lee cried. "I got a headache and I'm just sick of all this."

Gerald went up to her and put his strong hands on her shoulders, but she twisted away.

"What are you doin'?" she cried.

"I don't like to see you this way," Gerald said.

"Don't touch me," Ruby Lee cried.

She twisted away again and walked up the washout crying. Gerald just stood there and watched her skinny back as she went around the next bend in the washout. I wanted to get up and go over to him, but I didn't. He stood there a while, then I heard him say, "Oh hell."

I scooted backwards and started running back toward the house.

On Saturday morning, I could hardly wait until the afternoon. I couldn't remember when the last time was that we had gone to a movie. I was hoping that it would make me feel better and get things back more to the way they had been, but Gerald was in such a bad mood that I was afraid he would make Mama mad and she wouldn't let us go. I wanted Carol to go too, but she had to work. She went in early with Father. He was going to the bank again. Mark was supposed to pick Carol up after work.

After dinner, Mama made us go upstairs. I sat on my bed and blew on the harmonica Rebecca had given me. I didn't know any songs yet, but it was fun just to make the sounds, and it made Rebecca seem closer.

"Quit suckin' on that thing or I'll feed it to you," Gerald said when he came upstairs.

I looked at him. His face always looked like he had smelled something bad. He brushed some funny books off his bed and looked at them piled around on the floor.

"I'm too old to be takin' some damned nap like a baby," he said, chewing on his lip.

"Mama takes naps."

"Shut up. What does that prove?"

"I don't know."

"Then shut up."

"All right already."

"And another thing. I'm sick of these stupid funny books. From now on, they're all yours."

"All of them?"

"All of them," Gerald said. "Just keep them out of my way. And if Mama wants to know why they're all over the floor, it's your fault, not mine."

He plopped down on his bed and blew his breath out. He stretched out on his back with his hands behind his head and his shirt fell open over his stomach. A button was missing.

"I've never been so sick of a summer in all my life," he said.

I turned the harmonica over and over in my hands, polishing the metal where it was smudged. "What's wrong now?" I asked, remembering Ruby Lee.

"Everything. Shut up."

"I only asked," I said. I wanted to tell him I felt the same way, but I didn't.

By two o'clock we had changed clothes and were ready to go. We went out to the station wagon and got in. The seats were hot as fire. We rolled all the windows down.

"How much money you got?" Gerald asked.

"A quarter."

"Don't expect to bum off me this time."

"How much you got?"

"That's for me to know and you to find out."

Mama came outside and let the screen door slam. She was wearing a light blue dress and had brushed her hair back up from her forehead. She looked pretty like that because she had a high forehead. She held her purse in one hand and her keys in the other.

On the way in to town, none of us talked very much except once when Mama asked Gerald when he thought the movie would be over. He told her it would probably be around five-thirty or six.

"I want to see it twice," I said.

"No you don't," Mama said.

We passed Uncle Raisin's place. His truck wasn't parked at

the side and the place looked like no one had been there in a while.

"I wonder what Raisin's up to these days," Mama said half to herself and half out loud. "I worry about him. He can get crazy sometimes."

"Really?" I said.

Mama didn't look at me. She hummed a tune she always hummed. The only words she ever sang were, "There was a time."

"What is that song?" I asked.

"I don't remember the name of it," she said.

"Then why do you always sing it?"

"I like it," she said.

"What does it mean, there was a time? A time for what?"

"A time for you to shut up," Gerald said.

"Not a time for anything," Mama said, glancing in the rearview mirror. "Just a time."

"It has to be for something."

"Not really," Mama said.

"What's it about, then?"

"I don't know," Mama said. Then she looked at me. "Losing something, maybe."

"Like what?"

"Like your head," Gerald said.

"I don't know," Mama said after a hill and a curve. "There is a time and everything is one way, good or bad, then it changes."

"What does?"

"The time," Mama said. "It changes and goes away and then you know you have lost something that you can't ever get back."

"Like money?" I said.

"Maybe," Mama said and laughed.

"But that's not what you meant, is it?"

"No," she said.

In town there were a lot of cars because it was Saturday and everybody came to town on Saturday. The Palace Theater was on the main street of town and I saw it before Gerald did. He moved up to the edge of the seat and looked out the front window. Mama pulled up next to the curb in an empty place.

"I can only stop here a second," she said. "I want to see both of you on the sidewalk at six. Here is a dollar."

"Can we spend the change?" I asked.

"I guess so, but remember that it is part of your allowance."

We got out of the car and Mama drove away. At the box office was a short line of mostly kids. We got in line behind three negro boys who seemed a little older than Gerald, but Gerald knew them from school.

"Hey man," one of them said, seeing Gerald.

"Hi Bill," Gerald said.

"Look who we got here, boys. It's old tough-nut Mac-Allister, the meanest man in town."

The other two turned and looked at Gerald and grinned. Their eyes were big and brown and their hair was short and crinkled up. All three of them were wearing cut-off jeans and dirty shirts with some of the buttons missing.

"What are you doin', man?" Bill asked.

"Comin' to the movie," Gerald said.

"Us too, if we can get past that fat lady. You goin' to play football nex' year, man?"

"Sure."

"Ooooh, look out!" Bill said. "We liable to go to State."

When Bill and the other two got up to the window, the fat lady inside the little booth leaned forward and said, "What you boys doin' here? What? You know this ain't your movie house."

"We come to see the picture," Bill said.

"Go to your own movie house."

"They ain't got John Wayne over there."

"This movie house is for white people. We can't have you nigger boys messin' it up, can we?" the lady said, smiling like people do when they don't mean it.

"We got the money," Bill said, showing her the handful of coins he was holding.

"No," the lady said. "Now move on. There's other people that want in."

Bill and the other two turned away from the window. The other two looked disappointed, but Bill looked mad. I looked at them, then I looked down.

Gerald stepped up to the window and said, "Hey, I know those guys. They're all right."

"So what? Who are you? Abraham Lincoln?"

Gerald stood there a minute and I knew he was getting mad.

"You want a ticket or not?"

"Two," he said, giving her the dollar. After she had given him the tickets and the change, he said, "Maybe I ain't Abraham Lincoln. But I ain't some old fat mama cow, either."

Bill and the others laughed and me and Gerald jerked open the door into the lobby as quick as we could. Behind us, I heard the lady yelling both at us and at Bill and the other two to get out of here.

"Old cow," Gerald said, chewing his lip and looking back through the glass. The lady was looking at him, but she wasn't coming to get us. "That ain't right."

Another lady behind the candy stand called us over and took our tickets. I liked the lobby because it was air conditioned and smelled of popcorn and other neat stuff. There was just something about being in the movie house that was neat.

"You sure got Bertha stirring around out there," the lady said, looking at Gerald. She was younger than the lady outside, and when she reached over the counter to tear our tickets, we could see her bosoms swell out the front of her dress. I looked at Gerald. He was watching.

"She asked for it," he said.

"She always does. She's just an old crab."

"Yeah," Gerald said. "How much are them suckers there?"

"Them little things?" she asked, rolling her tongue along her lips.

"Yeah," Gerald said.

She bent over to look at them under the glass and Gerald and I bent and looked through the glass. We could see her bosoms again, white and swelling out of her dress like they were about to pop the buttons off onto the floor.

"These?" she asked.

Gerald was grinning. "Yeah," he said.

She picked up a roll of suckers and brought them out. She looked down at me. "What are you looking at?" she said.

I turned red and didn't say anything. The lobby was empty except for us.

"Hey you," she said, leaning over the counter again. "I'm talking to you."

Gerald was grinning. I didn't know what to do. When I looked up at the lady again, I could see her bosoms. She put her hand on one of them and started rubbing it around like it was sore. Gerald's eyes were big.

"You like what you see?" the lady asked.

I didn't know what to say. A man opened a door behind the counter and walked over to the lady.

"Picture's ready to start," he said, looking at us.

"These are a nickel," the lady said, straightening up and dropping her hand.

Gerald gave her a nickel, then I told her I wanted some too. She bent over again. Gerald gave me a nickel. When the lady gave me the suckers, she winked at me.

We went up the stairs to the balcony. Behind us, I heard the man say, "Honestly." Then the lady laughed and said, "Well, they came to see the show, didn't they?" She laughed again.

We found some seats near the back where it was highest. The balcony was empty except for a few kids from town and us. The kids from town looked at us. They were older than Gerald and had long hair. Gerald looked back at them and they turned around.

"That lady was nasty," I said.

"Yeah," Gerald said. "She had some tits on her, all right."

The movie started with some previews, then the newsreel, then a cartoon. Then the screen got dark and *The Searchers* started. John Wayne was coming home to see his brother. There was a little girl there who reminded me of Rebecca except that her hair was longer and Rebecca didn't carry around dolls. Then, while John Wayne and some other men were gone, the Indians came and wiped out the family and took the little girl and her sister who had yellow hair like Carol's. John Wayne and some other men had to go looking for them. That's why they called it *The Searchers*.

While they were looking for the girls, I started feeling a little sad. John Wayne reminded me of Father, except that he talked tough like Gerald. He had come home hoping to be with his family again and work on the farm, but then something bad happened and messed everything up. I started thinking about the way Father looked when supper was over and he had to sit down and watch television and think about the day and what he was going to do the next day or week or month or even year. As long as Father was doing something, he was all right, but when there was nothing more to do, he acted like his mind was somewhere else.

Right now, while we were watching the movie, Father and Mama were at the bank trying to take out a mortgage on the farm. Grandfather had paid the farm off, so it was clear, but now we needed the money to try to hold on until the rains came again, if they ever did.

I felt Gerald move lower in his seat next to me. I looked over at him and saw that he was watching a boy and a girl who were going down the steps looking for a place to sit. The guy was kind of rough-looking, and he was wearing a cowboy hat. The girl was shorter. She was leaning on his arm like she was sleepy or something. Then they turned in down in front of us and I saw that the girl was Ruby Lee.

"Hey," I said.

"Shut up."

Gerald had a pink sucker in his hand like he was going to put it in his mouth, but he was just holding it and looking at Ruby Lee. They sat down. The guy didn't take off his cowboy hat. Ruby Lee leaned over against his shoulder and he put his arm around her.

In the movie, the man who liked the little girl's sister attacked the Indian camp because he found out the sister had been killed. John Wayne and the other guy were just standing there on a hill listening to the shots. The Indians killed that man.

"Damn," Gerald said.

"They killed that girl and that man," I said.

"Shut up. Who cares about the movie?"

Gerald was still holding the sucker and staring at Ruby Lee. When Gerald acted like that, it made me feel bad. I wasn't having as much fun as I hoped we would. It didn't seem like anything was turning out right.

I watched the movie, but I wished we hadn't come. I was starting to think Gerald might try to start a fight or something. John Wayne and the other guy called Martin went back home, then left out again. They were looking all over Texas for the little girl. She might have been dead already, but that didn't seem to matter to them. They were going to find her or else. Then a lot of things happened. Then they met Mose Harper, the crazy guy, again. I liked him. They went out to talk to some Indians. In the teepee of the Indian called Scar, they saw a girl who was supposed to be the little girl all grown up. I was disappointed. I liked the little girl better.

The guy wearing the cowboy hat got up and walked by us without looking at us. He was putting his hand in his pocket like he wanted to see how much money was in it.

"Stay here," Gerald said.

"Where are you going?"

"None of your business."

"Gerald, don't go down there. That guy might come back."

"So what?"

"Gerald," I said, but he was already out in the aisle.

I slid over and followed him down a couple of rows, then sat on the edge of the first seat of an empty row. The town boys were across the aisle from us. Gerald went down another row and crossed over to behind Ruby Lee.

"Well hell-oh," Gerald said.

Ruby Lee sat up and turned around. I couldn't see her face very well, but it looked like she had a lot of makeup on to cover the bruise around her eye.

"Gerald!" she said.

"Yeah. Didn't expect to see me here, did you?"

"You better go before Roy gets back."

"What are you doin' here with some other guy?" Gerald asked in his mad voice.

"It ain't none of your business what I'm doin' here."

"Yes it is."

"Well you could have asked me, but I didn't hear nothin' about it."

"I can't drive yet. How could I bring you to a movie?"

"How did you get here today? Did your daddy bring you?" She looked past Gerald at me. "And him too?"

"I thought me and you were—"

I looked up at the screen. I couldn't believe what I was seeing. John Wayne was trying to shoot the girl. I couldn't believe it. It was so wrong, like everything that had happened since summer started. It was so wrong, yet so much a part of everything else.

"You and me were what?" Ruby Lee said.

"I thought you were my girl," Gerald said.

"Ha ha," Ruby Lee said in her high voice.

One of the town boys looked over and said, "Shhh."

Gerald turned his head and said, "Screw yourself to the floor, creep." He stared at them until they turned and looked at the screen again.

"Well I ain't," Ruby Lee said.

"I thought you were."

"I told you you was dumb."

"Cut that out," Gerald said.

"Hey, now. Don't start orderin' me around. I told you I wanted to get away from Pa and that old place. You can't do nothin' 'cause you ain't old enough nor brave enough."

"I was old enough to kiss you," Gerald said, mad.

"Boy," Ruby Lee said. "Anybody is old enough to kiss if they got lips."

One of the town boys laughed. Gerald cut them a look and they were quiet. John Wayne got shot in the shoulder and him and Martin just barely got away from the Indians. I didn't see what happened to the girl.

"But Ruby Lee," Gerald said. His voice sounded different

from what I had ever heard it sound like. I looked at his back.

"You better go on before Roy gets back. He's got an awful bad temper."

Just then the door behind me opened and Roy stepped through it holding a bag of popcorn and a soda water. I went cold and looked down at Gerald. He wasn't saying anything. Ruby Lee had turned back around. Roy passed me and went on down to his row. Gerald saw him and straightened up. Roy walked over to Ruby Lee and looked at Gerald.

"What's goin' on?" he said. His voice sounded dumb.

"You know what time it is?" Gerald said.

"Time for you to get lost," Roy said.

The town boys started laughing. Gerald stood up and walked out of the row. He came toward me, then he turned and walked down the row where the town boys were sitting. There were three of them and they all turned and looked at him. He stood there for a minute without moving, then he said, "You queers got somethin' to say to me?"

One of the town boys started to get up. Gerald leaned toward him. The town boy sat down again. Gerald looked them over, then backed out of the row and came up the aisle. We went back to where we had been sitting.

"I thought I told you to stay here," he said.

"I didn't want to."

For the rest of the movie, Gerald just sat in his seat staring at the screen or cutting the town boys a look. At the end of the movie, I thought John Wayne was going to kill the girl, but he didn't. He caught her and raised her up over his head, then held her in his arms. It made me cry, that or something else. He took her home. While they were getting back to the other farm, Roy and Ruby Lee stood up and came out of their row and up the aisle toward us. I looked over at them, but Gerald just watched the movie. At the very end, everybody had somebody except John Wayne. After all he had done and all he had been through, he was all alone. He just walked off by himself with the dust blowing and the door of the house closed. I knew just how he felt.

Before they turned the lights back on, the door behind us opened and Ruby Lee came back in. She came over to Gerald and sat down beside him. She reached down and caught his hand.

"Please hold my hand," she said. She didn't pay any attention to me. "I'm sorry, Gerald," she said. "It isn't your fault and you aren't dumb. But you can see how it is, can't you?"

Gerald looked at her. She was holding his hand in both of hers and her eyes were big.

"I just can't keep on livin' out there. I know you think—. If you were older, I would wait for you, Gerald. But I can't wait, don't you see. I've got to go now. Do you understand? Oh please say you do."

Gerald looked at her.

"I'll never forget you, Gerald. I hope everything works out for you."

Ruby Lee leaned over and kissed Gerald, then got up and ran up the last two steps and out the door. There had been tears in her eyes.

Gerald turned and watched her. When the door stopped swinging, he turned around and looked at the screen for a long time. I could hear the town boys whispering. Finally Gerald stood up.

"Let's go."

We went down the stairs. The lady behind the counter was gone. We went out through the lobby. The sun on the street made my eyes water, it was so bright. It had seemed like night-time inside the movie house. The fat lady in the ticket booth stared at us.

When Mama came, we ran out to the station wagon and got in. I got in the front seat again and Gerald got in the back. Mama pulled away from the curb.

"How was it?" she asked.

"Sad," I said.

I sat back and looked out the window. A car passed us. There was a dark-haired girl in the back seat and the wind was blowing her hair around her face. She looked at me. After we got out of town, I thought how good the hot afternoon smell was. Mama began to hum, then she said, "There was a time."

That night, when I went up to go to bed, I stopped by Carol's room and looked in it. I could smell her, but she wasn't there. Her light was off, but I could see by our light that her bed was made up. I didn't feel like myself looking at her room. I felt like someone else with my memories looking at her room.

Gerald was already in bed. He was lying on his back with his hands behind his head, and he was staring at the ceiling. When I walked in the room, he didn't even look at me.

"Turn out the light," he said.

Drought

FATHER HUNG UP the telephone and came back into the dining room. I was just finishing my glass of water. It was from the cistern and had a funny taste to it, like old rain water. Since the cow had gone dry, we didn't drink milk in the morning anymore.

"Any luck?" Mama said.

"All the old hands are scattered out looking for work. Nobody has any help around, not enough to make any difference."

"How will you get the cotton in?"

"I guess the boys and me will have to do it ourselves. Rutts said he would be glad to help."

"I don't like that man," Mama said.

I put my glass down. "My cotton sack has a big hole in it," I said.

"So does your head," Gerald said.

"We'll get you another one," Mama said.

Father looked at his coffee cup. "I guess I'll take the tank in again this morning. Mr. Norman asked me if I could haul him some water, too."

"It wouldn't hurt to call Ida Ketchum and ask her if she needs some," Mama said.

"I'll let you do that," Father said. "If she needs it, I'll be glad to haul it."

"Well, let me call before you go."

"All right. I'm takin' Gerald in with me," Father said.

355

"What for?" Gerald said.

"You got somethin' better to do?" Father said. He turned and looked at Gerald.

"I guess not."

"Good." Father looked at me, then Mama. "You think you can do with just him this mornin'?"

"I might be able to stand it."

I looked at my empty plate, then cut my eyes to Carol's chair. It was empty too.

Under the stairs was a little room we called the pantry. It was about as big as a closet just inside the door, but it got lower as the stairs went down. The walls were covered with pans and things hung on nails. There was no light in there. I didn't like to hang up the pots and pans at night, because it was so dark in there and scary like some place in a story Gerald would tell.

I went in there and hung the frying pan on a nail, then got very quiet. I could hear a truck pulling up to the back porch. It was squeaking and clattering—Wilbur's truck. Mama came out of the bathroom.

"Ricky? Who is that?"

With just me and Mama at home, I got scared and didn't say anything. Mama came into the kitchen and passed the pantry without seeing me. I pushed the door closed a little bit and stood there in the shadow with the cuptowel in my hand.

"Ricky?" Mama said again. Then I heard her say, "Oh Lord."

There was a knock at the back door. I heard Mama's feet on the floor.

"Yes?" I heard her say.

"Miz MacAllister? Good mornin'. Is your husband at home?"

"No. He went to get some water from town."

"That right? Usin' a lot of damned water, huh?"

"Seems that way," Mama said. "Is there something I can do for you?"

I could hear the edge on Mama's voice, like when she was

getting tired of Gerald. For a minute, Wilbur didn't say anything. Then I heard him say, "I could sure use a drink of water, if you ain't out completely."

"All right," Mama said, but I could tell by her voice that she didn't think it was all right.

Mama came back into the kitchen and I heard the screen door squeak open and close again. Wilbur's boots scuffed along on the floor.

"Sure smells like breakfast in here," Wilbur said.

Mama opened the icebox and I heard her pouring water from the jug we kept on the top shelf.

"Well, I guess it hasn't been that long ago," Mama said. "Here you are."

"Thank you, ma'am," Wilbur said. I could hear him swallowing the water. He drank like a horse.

"I'm sure Mac will be back in just a few minutes," Mama said.

"Ahh," Wilbur said. "That was mighty good. Did your boys go with him?"

"My oldest did. The other one is around here somewhere. He should be helping put away these dishes."

"Where's that pretty little daughter of yours?"

"She's working," Mama said.

"I got me a daughter too, but she ain't nothin' but trash. Tried my best to raise her the right way, but it didn't come to nothin'. The little tramp didn't come home last night."

"It's hard to tell about young people," Mama said. "Maybe she'll come home today."

"I don't care if the little bitch don't never come home," Wilbur said.

"Listen," Mama said. "If you'd like to come back a little later, I'm sure Mac will be right back."

"If he's goin' to be right back, why should I leave?"

"I thought you might have other things to do."

Wilbur laughed through his nose. "Like what? There ain't nothin' else I got to be doin'. I might as well stay here and keep you company."

"I'm sure there are other things—"

357

"I'm sure there ain't," Wilbur said. For a minute, there wasn't a sound, then Wilbur said, "Where did you say that boy was?"

"He should be right around here. *Ricky!*" Mama called.

I almost went out, but I didn't. I leaned back farther behind the door. There wasn't a sound then.

"Guess he done run off someplace," Wilbur said.

"I think it would be better if you waited outside, Mr. Rutts," Mama said.

"Friends call me Wilbur."

"I'm not one of them," Mama said.

Wilbur laughed and I heard his boots scuff on the linoleum. I looked up on the wall at the black frying pan I had just hung there.

"You ought to be," Wilbur said. "You're a mighty fine lookin' woman."

"Mr. Rutts, I don't want to hear that kind of talk from you," Mama said. "Now, I really think you should—"

Then I heard Wilbur's voice as cold as ice. "Don't tell me what you think, woman. I ain't got the ears to listen to no woman tell me what she thinks. Far as I'm concerned, don't no woman think. She just does the kitchen work all nice and good, then gets on the bed for that other kind of work."

"Oh," Mama said, like she had been bitten by a snake. I never really thought Mama would be in any trouble, but now she was and I was hiding, just as Mrs. Brown had hidden while Rebecca was being hurt. Rebecca had asked me if I would have done something if I had been there. Now I understood why she asked. I reached up and lifted the frying pan off the wall as quietly as I could. I was shaking. When I had the frying pan down and the handle was in both my hands, I got the idea that I was going to have to kill Wilbur, and it both scared me and made me sad.

"Stop that," Mama said. I heard her move across the floor to the stove. Wilbur laughed.

"Ever had a real man before?" Wilbur said. "A man that don't play by the rules all nice and easy?"

"You'll be thinking of rules when Mac gets home," Mama said.

358

"Your great and mighty husband don't scare me none," Wilbur said. "He's my good friend. Besides, I got ways of dealin' with him. With you too."

It seemed like I could see outside the pantry. I was across the room looking at myself holding the frying pan. I looked little and scared.

"Please don't," Mama said.

"Now there's a pretty word," Wilbur said.

I stepped closer to the edge of the doorway. I was holding my breath and shaking.

"There's no need for this," Mama said.

"I got the need," Wilbur said. "I got the need right here."

"Oh," Mama said again, like she was hurt.

I raised the frying pan. Just as it got to my belt, I heard another truck pulling up to the house. It sounded like Father's truck, but there was something different about it.

"You better go," Mama said.

I heard Wilbur's boots on the kitchen floor. "All right. I'm goin' this time, lady. But I can come back anytime, you understand me? There's ways to make you sorry if you make trouble for me."

"Get out," Mama said.

"Yes ma'am," Wilbur said in an ugly way and laughed through his nose. I heard his boots on the floor, then I heard the screen door open and slam shut. Mama didn't move in the kitchen. I heard Wilbur's truck start up, then back around and take off. Mama still didn't move. I wondered why nobody had come in the house. Then I heard a truck's horn. Somebody was parked outside honking.

Mario was back.

I turned and hung the frying pan on the nail, then picked up the cuptowel off the floor. Mama walked by the pantry on her way to her bedroom. She didn't see me standing in there, but I saw her. Her face was white. After she passed, I slipped out of the pantry and through the kitchen to the back porch. Mario was just about to leave when he saw me come out the door.

"Hey there, Rickito," he said. "How come you gettin' so big?"

"I'm not," I said.

"Where's Mac?"

"He's hauling some water for us and Mr. Norman and Mrs. Ketchum."

"The well go dry? Not that well."

"It did."

"Goddamn, deep as that well is. What about your *novia* and her folks?"

"She's gone. They moved to Waco. A guy broke in up there and beat her up."

"I think maybe I kill that *cabrón*. What else been goin' on?"

"Grandfather died at the end of June. Mr. Ketchum too."

"Goddamn," Mario said and crossed himself. He shook his head. He looked a lot older to me and tired. "I think next time I better stay here. Who was that man just left?"

"Wilbur Rutts. He and his family moved in at the top of the hill."

"Oh yeah," Mario said. He looked through the windshield at the tractor sitting in front of the shop. "I don't like him," he said.

I was sitting on the back porch when Father drove up, pulling the tank behind him. The sides of it were wet and after he stopped, I could hear the water sloshing in the tank. Mama came out the door behind me as they got out of the truck. Father pushed his hat back on his head.

"Have you already been to Mr. Norman's?" Mama asked.

"Yep," Father said.

Gerald went around behind the tank to the cistern. He took the little concrete lid off the cistern and looked in.

"What about Ida's?"

"There too."

"How was she?"

"Lonesome. Mixed up. Glad to see somebody."

"It wouldn't hurt to send one of the boys over there once in a while, do you think?"

"It wouldn't hurt."

Then Mama stepped off the porch beside me and crossed the yard to Father. She put her arms around his shoulders. He looked at me with a question in his eyes, then put an arm around Mama's shoulders. Gerald straightened up and looked at them.

"What is it?" Father said.

Mama broke away. She gave me a look long enough for me to see the tears in her eyes. Something rose in me, and I looked away.

"I don't know," Mama said. "I guess I'm just thinking about Ida."

"We'll send one of the boys over," Father said, looking at me again.

After a minute, Mama said, "Well. Dinner will be ready in a little while."

"Fine," Father said. "I'm just goin' to empty the tank."

Mama turned and came toward me, then passed me and went into the house. Father stood there looking at me until I got up.

"Anything happen this mornin'?" he asked.

"No," I said. "Not really. Mario came back."

"Mario! Where is he?"

"He said to tell you he would be at his cousin's house in town, but that he would be out to see you pretty soon."

"Did he say where they had been?"

"He said all over."

Father turned and looked at Gerald. "Well, let's get that tank emptied. It's almost time for dinner."

I heard the truck before it stopped in front of the house. It was late and everybody was asleep, but I woke up and heard the truck before it stopped. I thought it was Wilbur's truck at first, then Mario's, but when it stopped I raised up on my elbow and looked out the window. It was Uncle Raisin. He turned off the headlights, but I could still hear the radio.

"What's goin' on?" Gerald said, sitting up in bed.

"Uncle Raisin's here. He's sitting outside in his truck."

Uncle Raisin whooped and laughed as loud as he could.

The truck rocked on its springs and the porch light came on.

"He's crazy," Gerald said.

"Hooeee," Uncle Raisin said. "Y'all sure go to bed early 'round here."

I saw Father in the yard. He was barefooted and didn't have a shirt on, just his pants.

"Raisin, what the hell is goin' on?" Father said. He didn't like anybody to wake him up.

"Hooeee!" Uncle Raisin whooped again.

"He's drunk," Gerald said. "Uncle Raisin is drunk as a skunk."

"What is it, Mac?" Mama said. I couldn't see her. She must have been at the front door.

"Howdy Jean!" Uncle Raisin called.

"It's your little brother. I think he's had a few."

"A few nothin'. I've had a lot."

"Bring him inside," Mama said. I heard the door close.

"Come on," Father said.

"Nope. I'm just fine here. Got the radio to listen to."

"Come on," Father said. "Jean wants you in the house."

Father walked up to the truck door. Uncle Raisin leaned away from him. Carol came into our room in her nightgown.

"What in the world?" she said.

"It's Uncle Raisin," Gerald said. "He's plastered."

"Oh no," Carol said. "Mama is going to be so upset."

"She already is," I said. The kitchen light was on.

"What is Father doing?"

"Trying to get him in the house."

"I don't want to go, Mac. Let me stay here. I don't want to go in the house. Jean'll be mad at me."

"Too late for that," Father said. "You should have thought of her before you came here."

"I didn't," Uncle Raisin said.

"What's got into you in the first place? This isn't Saturday night. Where have you been?"

"Every—everywhere," Uncle Raisin said. Then he said, "Listen to this song, it's a good one."

"Turn that down, Raisin. You'll wake the kids, dadgummit."

Father reached in Uncle Raisin's truck and shut the radio

off. Uncle Raisin laughed a little bit, like a giggle, then he just looked at Father. Mama came to the door again.

"Get him in here, Mac," she called.

Father opened the truck door, but Uncle Raisin leaned away again.

"I'm not comin' in, Jean. I just came by to say hello."

"At two in the morning?" Mama said.

"Listen, Mac, I didn't even know it was dark," Uncle Raisin said, and laughed.

"Mac?" Mama said.

"I'm not about to carry him in there," Father said. Gerald laughed. "Be quiet," Carol said.

"Raisin?" Mama called again.

"No," Uncle Raisin said in his strong, serious voice. Father still had his hand on the door and was looking at the ground. "No. I'm not coming in. I don't even know why I came here in the first place."

Uncle Raisin was looking at the steering wheel. Father looked at Mama and shook his head. The front door closed. Father looked around and yawned.

"Raisin, what is this all about?" he said.

Uncle Raisin rubbed his hand across his face and went on looking at the steering wheel. "I've got a headache," he said.

"I'll bet you do."

"Damn it, Mac. I don't know. That old house was too quiet tonight. I just couldn't go back there."

"Why don't you stay here tonight."

Just like that, Uncle Raisin was crying. He made a lot of noise at it for a few minutes. Father stood by the open door looking at the ground. Then Uncle Raisin quit and wiped his face with his hand.

"Poor Uncle Raisin," Carol said. She was sitting by my bed in my chair.

"Must be something bad," Gerald said.

The door opened under us and Mama came out with two cups of coffee in her hands. She was wearing her robe.

"Here," she said, giving Uncle Raisin a cup. "I want you to drink that whether you come in the house or not."

"I'm, I'm sorry, Jean. I just—"

"I don't want to hear it," Mama said. "There is no excuse you can tell me that I want to hear. If something is bothering you, that's one thing. I'll listen to that, but I won't listen to excuses for drinking."

Uncle Raisin started to cry, then stopped again, just like anybody else would cough and then stop. Father held his cup and looked up at our window. We all ducked, but I didn't think he could see us.

"I haven't been 'round in a while, Jean," Uncle Raisin said, sniffing. "How have y'all been doing?"

"Fine, Raisin," Mama said. "We've been doing fine."

"Everything has dried up," Uncle Raisin said. "I was afraid y'all were in trouble, but I was scared to ask."

"We're makin' it," Father said. "Had to take out a lien on the place. That gave us a little more room to play."

Uncle Raisin took a gulp of his coffee and wiped his hand across his face again.

"What is it, Raisin?" Mama asked in her soft voice.

Uncle Raisin shook his head. "Everything, Jean. Seems like. I'm just tired of this drought. Everything burned up and no relief in sight. I feel like I'm not anything but a empty husk myself."

"It's just something we have to live with, Raisin."

"Live with how?" Uncle Raisin said. "It's taking everything away from us. Damn. Look at me. I don't drink. Drinking scares me to death."

"It's terrible," Mama said.

Father drank his coffee and looked at her. There was no breeze or anything. The night was quiet and still.

"I got me a job," Uncle Raisin said. "Did you know that?"

"We heard something," Father said.

"Reading meters for the electric company."

"Yeah," Father said.

"Something any moron could do," Uncle Raisin said. "I get chased by dogs, yelled at by folks, and stung by yellow jackets. And all the others think it's such a big joke."

"Well, Raisin," Mama said.

"I wanted to be a great painter," Uncle Raisin said. "Or at

least a good farmer, but I'm not either one. That's what gets me. I'm just sick and tired of all this dry and dust and—"

Uncle Raisin started to cry again. Mama stepped up to the truck and put her hand on Uncle Raisin's shoulder. Father was looking at the dry ground under his bare feet. Uncle Raisin stopped crying.

"Why don't you stay with us tonight, Raisin," Mama said. "We'll be glad to have you."

Uncle Raisin shook his head. "If it was only something I could put my hands to, something I could wrestle."

"We've all wished that, Raisin. There's been days when I'd go out this driveway to check on the fields and I just wanted to keep on drivin' and never look back."

"Oh Father," Carol said in a whisper and wiped her eyes.

"But. There isn't a thing to be done, but to stick with it and hold out," Father said.

"Stay 'til morning," Mama said.

"No, Jean, thank you. I'm, I'm going to just go on home. I have to get up and go to work tomorrow."

"All right, but let Mac follow you."

Uncle Raisin finished the cup of coffee and shook his head. "No, I think I can make it."

"I'll get my boots," Father said.

"There's no need, Mac," Uncle Raisin said, but Father had already come in the house. "I wish we got along better."

"Y'all get along fine," Mama said. "Are you going to be all right?"

"I don't know. It comes and goes, Jean. I don't know."

"Try for me, will you?"

"All right. I'm sorry, Jean."

"I love you Raisin. Take care of yourself."

Father came out of the house and said he was ready. Uncle Raisin slammed the truck door and Mama stood back. He started up the truck and ground the gears into first. Father's truck started up. Mama stood in the yard. She waved as both trucks went by.

Carol scratched her arm and yawned. She got up and went back to her room without saying anything. Gerald lay back down, then rolled over. For a while Mama just stood in the yard, then she came back in the house. She left the porch light on and the light in her bedroom on. Father was gone a long time, but the light was still on when he came back.

When supper was finished, Grandmother said, "Now comes the hard part."

"Just leave the dishes," Mama said. "It's too hot right now to worry with them."

Grandmother was holding her plate up. "Are you sure? It'll just be harder later to get them clean."

"I'm sure," Mama said.

"We'll take care of them later," Carol said from across the table. "Mark told me he just loves to do dishes."

"Not me," Mark said and laughed.

"Oh come on," Carol said.

I looked down at my plate, then I cut a look at Gerald. Gerald was looking at me and shaking his head a little like he was sure that Carol had gone completely crazy.

"All right," Grandmother said. "If you're sure, but it will be harder to get them clean later."

"You heard Carol, Mother," Father said. "Let them do it, if they want to."

"Now wait a minute," Mark said. "Carol is the one who said something."

"Well I have no intention of doing them by myself," Carol said.

"I have to," Gerald said.

"Yeah," I said.

"Thanks boys," Mark said.

Father pushed away from the table and stood up. His shirt had wet patches on it where he had sweated. It seemed like it was the hottest day of the summer.

"I don't know about you people," Father said. "But I think I'm goin' outside to see if there's any breeze."

"Sounds like a good idea," Mark said.

"Boys, y'all go get the chairs and put them up on the porch," Mama said.

"All right," I said.

We followed Father and Mark out the front door. Behind us I heard Grandmother say, "Well, we could at least put the dishes in the kitchen."

"Let the kids do it," Mama said. "Let's go outside."

We put three chairs on the porch and Father sat down in one of them. Then Mama and Grandmother came out and took the other two. Mama was sitting next to Father. Gerald and I sat down on the porch. The concrete was warm under me.

"I've seen hot days," Father said, taking a deep breath and blowing it out. "But I never hope to see one this hot again."

"Oh it has been hot," Grandmother said.

Mark was standing on the ground with one foot on the porch, waiting for Carol. His face was sunburned and the breeze was blowing his hair.

"Let me borrow one of your cigarettes," Father said to him. "I promise to give it back when I'm through."

"Sure," Mark said. "Take a couple."

"No thanks. Don't like 'em that much. Rather have a cigar, but I'm out."

Father took one and Mark lit his and one for himself. Carol came outside and he walked over to her. They sat on the steps. Carol tucked the skirt of her dress behind her knees so that it wouldn't blow in the breeze that blew across the yard. She whispered something to Mark and laughed and shook her head.

"Did you get a chance to talk to Mario?" Mama asked Father.

"Yeah," Father said, smoking.

"Is he going to help you with the cotton?" Mama asked.

"What there is of it."

"Then you won't need Mr. Rutts to help you?"

"He can if he wants to," Father said.

"I would rather he didn't," Mama said. "I'd just as soon he never came around here again."

I looked at Gerald. He was looking down and chewing on his lip.

"If he needs the work—" Father said.

"Let him look somewhere else. I don't think it's good for the boys for him to be around. You've already helped him once."

"All right," Father said. "If you're so set on it. I'll tell him next time I see him."

I looked around at Mama. She was looking at her hands. Father was looking at her.

"Listen, everybody," Carol said.

We all looked over at her. Mark flipped his cigarette out into the yard and then looked down with a smile on his face.

"I've got something to tell you."

"Well?" Father said. He flipped his cigarette out into the yard. I watched it a minute.

"Mark and I are going to get married."

"Oh my," Grandmother said.

Both Carol and Mark stood up. Father stood up too, and so did Mama.

"It's about time," Gerald said. Mark tried to hit him on the head as he went by. Gerald ducked and grinned. Father shook Mark's hand.

"I figured something like this," he said. "We welcome you to the family."

"Thank you, Mac," Mark said.

Carol went to Father and he hugged her while Mama hugged Mark.

"Well, my little yellow-haired girl is a woman now, huh?" he said.

Carol started to cry. Mark gave Grandmother a hug.

"I just wish Wesley was here," she said and sniffed.

Carol stood in front of Mama and they looked at each other for a minute, then they hugged each other. Mama had some tears in her eyes too. Then everybody started talking at once.

I got up off the porch and looked at them and smiled, but I didn't feel like smiling. It was a trick I had learned from watching Father. Then, while everybody was saying something, I turned and walked across the front yard and went around to the back porch. It was really hot around on that side of the house because it faced the west, but I didn't care. I sat on the step of the porch and watched the sun go down. It was bright and red. Then even it was gone and I was sitting on the back porch all by myself.

"What would you say to going over to Mrs. Ketchum's for the afternoon?" Mama said.

"Do I have to?"

"Wouldn't you like to? You used to like going over there before."

"That was before."

"You don't have anything to worry about. Ida is not going to hurt you or anything. In many ways she's just like she always was."

"Everybody says she's crazy."

"Do you believe everybody?"

"Sometimes."

"Why don't you go, just for a little while? For me?"

"Is Gerald coming, too?"

"Gerald's helping your father."

I looked out the kitchen window, then looked back at Mama. "All right. Are you going to take me?"

"In what?"

"Oh yeah," I said.

After dinner, I put on my hat and walked down the hill. The road was as hot as fire under my feet, so I walked along the edge where there weren't too many grassburrs. The grassburrs weren't as bad as the goathead stickers, but they were bad enough. Up ahead, on the road, I could see a mirage. It looked like a big pool of water with waves in it. Everywhere heat waves made things look blurry and burning.

At the bottom of the hill, I went over to the store thinking I would rest there a minute. When I stepped up on the porch, I saw that the door was shut and locked. Sometimes Mr. Norman took a nap after dinner before he opened his store again. Sometimes he didn't open his store at all. I sat down on the steps and thought about Rebecca. She was on my mind all the time, it seemed like.

It wasn't much cooler, so I got up and went back across the road in front of the empty house with the old car out in the yard. Even in the middle of the day, I didn't like the house. The inside was dark. There was just something about a house nobody lived in that bothered me.

When I got to the cattleguard at the end of Mrs. Ketchum's driveway, I grabbed the corner post and swung around so that I wouldn't have to walk on the burning hot pipes. The house looked shady and quiet as I walked up to it. I went around to the back and called Mrs. Ketchum. It was hot and I could feel my blood beating in my head. I heard Mrs. Ketchum move through the kitchen toward the back door. When she came out on the screened-in back porch, I heard her say, "Elmer?"

"It's me, Ricky," I said.

She pushed open the screen door and looked at me, then looked all around. "Ricky! I'm so glad to see you. Come on in."

She stood to one side and held the door open for me. As I started up the steps, I saw something white look around her legs. At first I thought it was a ghost, then I saw it was a white cat.

"Get back, kitty," Mrs. Ketchum said, pushing the cat back with her foot. "I always have to tell that cat to get out of my way. It's just the most curious thing I've ever seen, always poking its head here and there."

I looked at the cat, then looked at Mrs. Ketchum. She looked the same way she always had except that she was thinner and was getting some gray in her hair. I had heard Mama talk about the cat. He had been at the house the day they got back from the funeral and had been around ever since. Mama said that people were saying she thought that Elmer had come back as a cat.

"Could I have a drink of water?" I said.

"Oh lands, yes," she said. "After all, it was your father who brought it here in the first place."

I followed her into the kitchen. There was a pitcher on the cabinet by the sink. It was clear with slices of yellow lemons and green leaves painted on it and it was full of water. Mrs. Ketchum got a glass down and poured it full for me, then handed it to me. Her cistern was metal and stood on the south side of the house in the shade. The water tasted sweet.

"You tell your father how much I appreciate him hauling water for me while Elmer's gone. Lord, I can't imagine why the well has gone dry."

"I'll tell him," I said.

"Are you going to stay for a while?" Mrs. Ketchum asked.

"Not if you have other things to do."

"Oh no," she said. "Just a little bit of sewing is all. I caught the sleeve of my white blouse on a nail out in the shed and just about ripped it off."

"Want me to go pull that nail out?"

"I think next time I can be more careful."

"It won't be any trouble," I said. "I'll be glad to do it for you, or anything else that needs doing. I'm a good fix-it man."

"I just bet you are," Mrs. Ketchum said, and laughed. "Well, come in the living room and rest first, then you can look for that nail."

We went into her living room. It was cool in there because of the trees all around the house. I could hear cicadas buzzing in the trees. Gerald used to climb in the elm tree in our front yard looking for them, but they were hard to find.

"Sit down a while and tell me what you've been doing, Ricky. How is your Grandmother getting along?"

"Okay," I said.

Mrs. Ketchum sat down in a green chair by the window that had a little table beside it and a floor lamp behind it. The cat went in and out between her ankles, watching her. She leaned over the table and put on her reading glasses, then picked up the white blouse and a needle and thread.

"Lord knows how I'd get along if I were her," she said. "Course with Elmer being gone like he is, it gets pretty lonely around here, but at least I know he'll be coming back some day."

I was twirling my hat in my hands and watching the cat. Mrs. Ketchum smoothed the sleeve on her knees and started with the needle.

"I guess you miss little Rebecca Brown, don't you?"

"Yes ma'am."

"I remember you two were like two peas in a pod around here. She was such a sweet, pretty little thing, always happy. But, I guess Marvin just wasn't satisfied here. A man like that isn't satisfied anywhere, seems like. Oh well, people have been moving away from here ever since the war ended—more work in town I guess. It's not like it was when Elmer first brought me here. This was quite a community then with a store, a church, the gin and what have you."

The cat jumped up in Mrs. Ketchum's lap and she pushed it off again. "Get down, kitty," she said. "You'll get stuck with this needle."

"Did you come from Kansas?" I asked. The cat looked at me and half closed its eyes.

"Yes," Mrs. Ketchum said, sewing. "Years ago. I grew up there, in Hays, Kansas. There was a wonderful little school there for orphans. I didn't have any family that I ever knew of."

"What happened to them?"

Mrs. Ketchum sewed the sleeve and the cat switched its tail at her feet and watched me with its sleepy eyes.

"They both died of typhoid when I was a little girl. I didn't have any aunts or uncles and no one knew who or where my grandparents were, so I went to a little school for orphans in the center of town. I remember it had this giant tree, practically the only one in town, that all of us children climbed. It was an old tree and there was supposed to be a ghost in it."

"A ghost?" I asked. The cat's tail stopped.

"Oh yes. According to the story all the children learned by heart, a man by the name of William Rust had been hanged from that tree by some cattlemen after the Civil War. He had been an outlaw all over the state and was a particularly bad man. Some people believed that he wasn't all human, but was a kind of devil who would not only commit crimes but who could also make a well go dry or wither a crop or cause a woman to lose her baby."

Mrs. Ketchum looked at me and laughed a little. "Listen to me talk," she said. "Jean would have a fit if she knew I was telling you this."

"What happened?" I asked.

"Oh I don't know. I'm not sure this story is even true, although it seemed true to us when we were little. Some cattlemen caught this outlaw after he had stampeded a herd near Hays and they took him into town to that tree, which, I suppose, was the only one there, and they hanged him. They had to do it more than once. They say the first time they put him on a horse, the horse fell dead of a burst heart. The second time, they did the job, but those that were there said that even after he was dead, they could hear a voice coming from him saying horrible things. And to that day, no grass would grow around that tree and the limb they hanged him from never dropped off the tree although it had been dead for years."

"And y'all played in that tree?"

"You know how kids are," Mrs. Ketchum said. "But we never went near it at night."

"That's scary," I said.

"I shouldn't have told you. I haven't thought about it in years. I try not to think much about Kansas. I wasn't very happy there. The children in the orphanage were nice enough, most of them, but they weren't like a real family. I never had that until I met Elmer and came here. Oh he was something back then. Tall and so rough and strong. I think I fell in love with him the first time I saw him. I was a young woman then, with a job in a store, and Elmer walked in there one day on his way to somewhere and bought a dozen apples and ate them right there in the store, leaning on the counter, talking to me."

Mrs. Ketchum laughed and tied off the thread and bit it in two with her teeth. The cat looked up at her and yawned.

"There," Mrs. Ketchum said. "That will do, I think."

"Want me to go get that nail?" I asked, putting my hat back on.

"All right. Let me hang this up first."

We went through the kitchen to the back porch again. There was a freezer back there and an old wicker couch and some cabinets with canned vegetables and fruits.

"I have a hammer in here you can use," Mrs. Ketchum said. "Elmer is so particular about his tools that I had to break down and get my own set."

The white cat ran between us and jumped up on the cabinet above the drawer Mrs. Ketchum pulled out.

"Oh now, kitty. I've told you about getting in the way. Go on now."

She pushed the cat away with her arm while she looked in the drawer for the hammer. When she found it, she gave it to me, then closed the drawer with her hip and picked the cat up.

"What are you so busy looking at?" she asked it.

"What's his name?" I asked.

"Oh he doesn't have a name. Elmer doesn't think it's right to give an animal a name like it was a human being. But I'll tell you, since Elmer's been gone, this cat has just been the best company I've ever had. I don't think I would ever want to part with him."

"Yeah," I said. "Where's that nail?"

"It's out in the feed shed just as you get in the door. I went out to feed the turkeys just the other day and caught my sleeve. I'm just lucky I didn't hang my arm."

"I'll take care of it," I said.

"I don't know what Elmer is planning to do with those turkeys," Mrs. Ketchum said. "Do you think your mother would like to have one?"

"I don't know," I said, swinging the hammer. "I guess so."

"Well, your father was so nice to bring me some water, I feel like doing something nice back."

"A turkey would be okay," I said.

"All right. I'll do it this very day and put it in the freezer. The next time your father brings me some water, that turkey will be all ready for him to take home."

"Yeah," I said.

Mrs. Ketchum went into the kitchen carrying the cat and talking to it. I went outside.

The feed shed was behind the turkey pen. I opened the door. In the heat of the afternoon, the shed smelled dusty and the feed smell was so strong it almost stank. I felt along the wall and found a nail and hammered it in. Dust fell off the walls and a rat skittered across a rafter. If I had had a rock, I could have hit it. I found some more nails and hammered them in too. When I was through, I looked at the sacks of feed. On the floor by one of them was a piece of red ribbon, like a hair ribbon. I picked it up and looked at it, then dropped it again.

I closed the door of the shed and watched the turkeys for a minute. They were good to eat, but they were ugly to look at. I went over to the big truck shed where Rebecca and I had stood on the day of the funeral. I could still see her footprints in the dust. There was a doodlebug hole in one of them. Standing under the high shed, it was cooler and I could almost think Rebecca was going to walk up and start talking to me. When I thought about her, I thought about her brown eyes with the light in them and her hair and the way her voice filled me up with something I didn't understand. I wished she was there so I could talk to her. There were so many things that I couldn't tell anybody about. The more I thought about her and the summer, the more alone I felt.

After a while, I looked up and saw the yellow jacket nest I had seen the day of the funeral. It looked bigger and was crawling with yellow jackets. I put the hammer on a shelf where Mr. Ketchum kept his oil and transmission fluid. There were plenty of rocks on the ground, so I picked up a few that were just the right size and took aim on that nest. The first rock I threw hit a rafter and bounced down and hit the hood of Mr. Ketchum's truck. I moved around so that my next shot wouldn't do that and took aim. I threw the rock as hard as I could. It hit the tin just above the nest and bounced off and hit the nest. The nest and all those yellow jackets fell and I ran back to the house. I looked once and saw the nest on the ground.

Mrs. Ketchum was walking into the kitchen with the cat right beind her when I got there.

"Did you get the nail?" she asked with a smile.

"Yes ma'am."

"Where is the hammer?"

"Oh. I left it in the shed. I'll be right back."

There were yellow jackets on the ground around the nest and a few were flying around in the shed, but most of them were back up near the roof again, crawling around on the rafter looking for their nest. I didn't feel sorry for them. I hated them.

I ran inside the shed and picked up the hammer and turned to go when a big yellow jacket landed on my cheekbone and started stinging me. I threw down the hammer and brushed the yellow jacket away and ran for the house again. Even after it was gone, I could feel the dry, crackling, buzzing sound it made and the stinger going in my face.

"Lands, what is the matter?"

I was crying a little bit, mostly because I was mad, but I told Mrs. Ketchum about the yellow jacket.

"Let me see," she said. "Take your hand away and let me see. Hold still now," she said.

I couldn't open my eye on that side of my face and it was burning where the stings were. I felt chills on my body and shivered.

"Looks like he got you three times," Mrs. Ketchum said. "What were you doing? Throwing rocks at them?"

"No ma'am," I cried. "I just went to get the hammer."

"Well, come into the bathroom."

Mrs. Ketchum took me in the bathroom and put some calamine lotion on the stings.

"It hurts," I said.

"It will stop in a little while."

"But it hurts now."

"All right," Mrs. Ketchum said. "Just settle down. Come back in the kitchen and I'll give you an aspirin."

We went back in the kitchen and Mrs. Ketchum gave me a glass of water and an aspirin. I drank the water and swallowed the aspirin. My face still burned. It was starting to swell.

"Now come into the living room and lie down on the settee for a little while," Mrs. Ketchum said. "We have to give the aspirin time to work. Elmer is going to have to do something about those wasps."

We started into the living room, but the cat got under my feet and almost tripped me. Mrs. Ketchum fussed at it. We got in the living room. Mrs. Ketchum helped me stretch out on the settee. The stings were throbbing like I was being stung over and over again.

"There now. You lie there and rest a while. Do you think I should call your mother?"

Mama would know I had been throwing rocks at the yellow jackets. "No. I'll be all right," I said.

"Are you sure?"

"Yes ma'am."

"Well, you rest. I'll take the cat and we'll go fix a turkey up for your folks."

"Okay," I said.

She turned to go out of the room and I watched her with my one good eye. She seemed very tall and thin and alone like I was. The cat padded along beside her.

I didn't know I had been asleep until I woke up. My face burned a little still and felt stiff where it was swollen and the calamine lotion had dried. I was sweaty from lying on the settee and my mouth was dry.

The house was quiet. I listened for sounds from the kitchen, but there wasn't any. Then the back door slammed and I heard Mrs. Ketchum's steps in the kitchen. Her steps went around the room, stopping, then starting again. I heard the rattle of pans. The icebox was opened and closed, then a cabinet door. After a minute, Mrs. Ketchum came in the living room, wiping her hands on a cuptowel. Her hair had come unpinned on one side and had slumped down a little. Her face was red and her blouse was wet around her collar and under her arms.

"How do you feel?" she asked.

"A little better."

"Your face is certainly swollen," she said. "What's your mother going to think when you get home looking like this?"

"It was really my own fault," I said.

"Does it hurt too much?"

"It still stings."

"You can take another aspirin if you want."

"I don't know," I said. "Did you kill a turkey?"

After a minute, she said, "Yes, that's right. I need to clean it and put it in the freezer."

She went back into the kitchen and I got up and followed her. The headless, plucked turkey was lying breast-up in the kitchen sink. Mrs. Ketchum went over to it and poured water on it to wash the blood and feathers off. The cat should have been crouching around, but I didn't see it anywhere.

I walked over to the back door and looked out. The bright sun made my face hurt. I could see the chopping block by the well with the handaxe stuck in it, and beyond it the turkey pen and feed shed. I went back into the kitchen. Mrs. Ketchum was bent over the sink pulling the guts out of the turkey. I could smell the chicken smell of it. She put the guts in a pan and looked around the kitchen.

"Now where is that cat?" she said.

"Maybe he's eating the feathers," I said.

"No. I don't think so. I put them in the burning barrel. I was sure he came back in the house with me."

"Want me to go look for him?"

"He will show up, I guess."

"I don't mind."

"Do you feel like it?"

"Sure."

"Well, put your hat on before you go."

"Okay."

I got my hat off the back porch and went out into the bright sun. It made my face sting. The first place I looked was around the house in the flower beds and under the trees. It was cool under the trees and my head felt better in the shade. I found a quarter on the ground under the pecan trees.

I went past the truck shed, where the yellow jacket nest was still on the ground in the sun, and went down to the barn. It was different from ours and not very scary. It was open down the middle with rows of stalls on either side and two high-sided cotton wagons in the middle. I called the cat, but he wasn't in the barn. The only thing that moved was an owl that flapped suddenly out of the loft.

Mrs. Ketchum came out the back door. She was carrying a pan of water which she dumped out in the flower beds. She went back inside, then came out again without the pan.

"I don't see that cat anywhere," I said.

She met me by the chopping block. "Lands," she said. "Where could that kitty have gotten to?"

The chopping block was covered with black, dried blood and I stepped up to it and looked at it. Down beside it on the ground was a turkey head with the bill open and the tiny eyes closed.

"Look here," I said. "That cat didn't even eat this old turkey head. It must be sick."

"Oh Lands. I hope not," she said. She raised her head and began calling the cat. After a minute, she said, "Do you feel like helping me look for that cat? There's no telling what kind of trouble it might have gotten into."

"Sure," I said.

I followed Mrs. Ketchum all around the house again, helping her look while she called the cat. We went down to the barn again too, but the cat still wasn't there. Mrs. Ketchum stopped and rested against one of the cotton wagons.

"I just don't know," she said. "That cat has never gone off like this before."

"Maybe he went off hunting field mice," I said. I was ready to go back to the house. Whenever sweat got on my stings, they burned.

"You think he might have gone down toward the creek?" Mrs. Ketchum asked.

"What for?" I said.

"Let's take a look. I just can't help but worry."

When we got to the creek, I sat down on the bank in the shade of a hackberry tree. My head was hurting. It wasn't that far from the house to the creek, but it was hot. Mrs. Ketchum looked one way, then the other up and down the dry creekbed, but there was no sign of that cat. She came over and stood by me. Heat waves shimmered off everything and grasshoppers crackled on clumps of dry grass. Somewhere a bobwhite called.

"I just don't know," Mrs. Ketchum said. Her face was getting red and her voice was getting higher and higher. "I just don't know," she said again.

I got up and walked along the bank trying to see through some of the mesquite brush that grew along the creek. Then something caught my eyes. Something shiny was in the loose black dirt of the bank. I slid down the bank until I came to it. I picked it up. It was one of Mrs. Ketchum's mother of pearl hair clips.

"Mrs. Ketchum," I called. "Look here."

She stepped carefully down the bank until she was beside me. I held the clip up to her. She squinted her eyes at it. "Lands," she said, reaching up and touching her hair. "How did that get here?"

I looked down again at the soft black dirt of the bank where the clip had been when it caught my eyes. The dirt looked like a hole had been dug and covered up again. I knelt down and dug a handful out, then another and another. I could feel the heat reflect off the dirt, but I kept on digging.

"What are you doing?" Mrs. Ketchum asked.

"You put something here," I said.

"I certainly did not."

I kept digging. I scooped something out that rolled to the side with the dirt. It rolled down the bank toward the creek bed and me and Mrs. Ketchum both looked at it. It was the head of the white cat.

"What did you do?" I said.

Mrs. Ketchum sat down beside me in the sun, just staring. She looked completely different. "I told that kitty to watch out, but he jumped up there anyway."

"You chopped its head off," I said.

Mrs. Ketchum had a tear in each of her eyes. They were right at the edge, ready to fall. She looked at me.

"Elmer's really dead, isn't he, Ricky?"

"Yes ma'am."

The tears fell.

"If you want me to stay, I will," I said.

Mrs. Ketchum looked up from the kitchen table and shook her head. Her eyes were red, but she wasn't crying anymore.

"No. You go home. Let your mother look at your face."

"It really feels better," I said.

"I'm glad."

"Are you sure, Mrs. Ketchum?"

"Yes, Ricky, I'm sure. There are some things I've got to do. I've got to call some people. I don't know what I've been doing all this time. I must have been two different people. Now I've got to try somehow—"

After a while, I got up and Mrs. Ketchum followed me to the back door. She opened it and I went out on the steps.

"It's awfully dry, isn't it, Ricky?"

"Yes ma'am. It's the drought."

"I suppose so."

She let the door close quietly and went back inside somewhere.

I didn't turn at the store and walk up the hill, but went on by it and by Rebecca's house to the pipe that went under the road where Rebecca and I used to sit and talk. It was still cool and dry under there and quiet and private. I crawled until I was about halfway, then I stopped and leaned back against the pipe. My face was hurting me and I felt so bad that I just wanted to curl up in the pipe and never go anywhere or do anything else ever again.

"Rebecca," I said. "I feel so bad. Why aren't you here right now to help me think what I have to do next?"

I wanted to cry, but it made my face hurt, so I didn't. I just sat in the pipe trying to pretend Rebecca was in there with me. Even that wasn't any good, so I stopped.

Before I left, I crawled over to the place where I had written Rebecca's name in the fine dirt with capital letters. I wanted to see if it was still there. It was. And underneath it, Rebecca had written my name in capital letters.

When I passed Mr. Norman's house, he came out on the porch. He was wearing some old brown pants and a white shirt with suspenders. His hair was messed up like he had been lying down.

"Say there, boy. You goin' to the store?"

"No sir."

"Eh?"

"No sir."

I walked into Mr. Norman's yard. He sat down in a rocking chair on his porch. He had a pair of house shoes on his feet and no socks.

"What happened to your face?"

"Yellow jackets."

"Teasin' 'em?"

"Yeah. Knocked their nest down. Over at Mrs. Ketchum's."

"You been over there?"

"Yeah," I said. Then I told him what happened. He leaned forward in his rocking chair and listened to me, then shook his head.

"By God, somebody better go over there. Just when everybody else is gettin' over it, she's got it all to go through the first time."

"I'll tell my mother," I said.

"Good. You do that. She'll know what to do. Tell her to call me if she needs anything."

"I don't really understand what happened," I said.

"Never mind. Don't try to. Forget about it. You're messin' with the human heart here. There's no tellin' what it can make a body do. It ain't your worry."

After a while, I said, "How come you didn't open the store today?"

"What for? Just as easy to sit over here as it is to sit over there. Sittin' over here, I don't keep expectin' folks to come by. I know they won't. Don't see any use in openin' the store when it don't make any difference to anybody."

"Guess not," I said.

"Eh?"

"Guess not."

"Yeah," Mr. Norman said. "Times just—I don't know. Too much for me."

"I'll see you later," I said.

"Tell your mother to call me if there's anything I can help her with. That woman could use some company tonight, I'm thinkin'."

I didn't follow the road home. I didn't feel like it. It was shorter to go around Mr. Norman's house and cut up through the empty fields behind the burned-out gin. When I crossed the second fence, I could see the barn and the house and the windmill. There were two people on the windmill, on the little platform at the top. Father and Gerald were greasing the fan gears, probably.

I crossed the next fence and started up through the field toward the windmill. I was getting hot again, even though I was pretty sure it was getting close to supper time. About halfway across the field, I heard some hollering and looked up at the windmill. The sun was in my eyes, but I could tell that Father and Gerald were hanging on to each other, but it wasn't Father's voice I heard, and it wasn't Gerald's either. It was Wilbur's.

I stopped and put my hand up over my eyes to see better. They were still holding on to each other, then one of them wasn't. One of them was falling backwards off the windmill.

I ran then as fast as I ever have in my life. The other man was climbing down the ladder that ran up to the top of the windmill. I reached Father just as Wilbur stepped off the ladder. He grabbed me and shook me. I tried to get away from him.

"Listen to me, goddammit. It was an accident, an *accident*, you hear me. Don't you say nothin'!"

He turned me loose and ran up toward the house. I knelt down beside Father. The afternoon had gotten very still, like it was holding its breath. Father's hat was off and his eyes were closed. I had to keep blinking over and over before I could tell whether he was alive or not. I saw him breathing.

I raised my head and looked up toward the house. Wilbur was coming out the front door with Mama and pointing. Something inside of me got very hard and cold and I clenched the muscles in my jaw to keep from crying. The whole summer had come to a point like sunlight through a magnifying glass, and that point was cold and hard, so cold it was burning.

Then Gerald broke out of the house at a run.

All Those Things

THE DOCTOR CAME DOWN the hall with a big manila envelope in his hand. Mama stood up and waited for him. In the last hour she had not said a word.

"Mrs. MacAllister? I have the x-rays on your husband. If you'll come with me, I'd like to explain what has happened."

"Can the boys come?"

"These your boys?" the doctor said, looking at us. He wasn't as old as our family doctor and he had a friendly face. "Looks like one of them got in a tangle with yellow jackets."

Mama turned and looked at me.

"Sure. They can come. Let's step right in here."

The doctor caught Mama's arm and led us to a little room just down the hall from the waiting room. When we were inside, he closed the door behind us.

"Mrs. MacAllister, your husband has had a very serious fall, and it is something of a miracle that he is alive at all," the doctor said, opening the envelope and sliding out the x-rays. "As I understand it, he fell from a windmill tower?"

"Yes," Mama said.

"Ordinarily a fall like that—" the doctor looked at Mama and stopped. "He must have managed to get his feet under him, because he took the fall mostly on his left side. He seems to be in excellent physical condition, and that is in his favor, but there is going to have to be extensive physical therapy and great care taken during the next two weeks, and variations on that therapy for weeks thereafter."

387

Mama stood with her arms folded across her chest. Gerald stood beside her with his hands in his pockets. I was standing on the other side of Mama. The doctor slipped the x-rays under clips above some light panels, and the picture we saw was of Father's skeleton.

"You see here," the doctor said, pointing to the x-rays, "that there are numerous fractures. Five ribs here. Three cracks in the hip here, and two breaks in his left leg. His left arm is broken here and there has been some shoulder damage. These look bad, and they will be painful, especially the hip, but it is this here that has us worried. The twelfth and fifteenth vertebrae have been crushed. With surgery, we can repair some of the damage, but there will, I'm afraid, always be some residual pain and the accompanying problems and limitations. Your husband has lost a certain amount of spinal fluid, but that will replace itself. Until it does, your husband will have extreme headaches. We can't be certain at this point, but we believe that there has been no major nerve damage, and in that way, your husband has been very lucky. There may be some paralysis at first that, with therapy, will pass. There may be some lasting paralysis, particularly of the fingers in his left hand. At this point it is too early to tell, but once he has regained consciousness, we should be able to find out most of what we need to know. Do you have any questions?"

For a minute, Mama didn't say anything. Then she said, "Will he be able to talk, then?"

"Oh yes. But we can't tell how long it will be. We have stabilized him and that's good. The next step will be his."

"Will he, then, be able to walk?"

"With therapy, Mrs. MacAllister, I feel reasonably sure that he will be, but it may not be until, say, Christmas. Injuries to the spinal column are extremely sensitive and dangerous, and I want you to understand this. All that I have told you is what seems to be, but until he wakes up, we can't really say what the damage has been. We can make a lot of guesses, but we don't know for sure."

"How long?" Mama said.

"The next thirty-six hours will be critical. We have your

husband in intensive care with 'round the clock attention. We're doing everything we can."

"Thank you," Mama said.

"Now, Mrs. MacAllister," the doctor said in a soft voice. "Let me please say some things to you, not concerning your husband. Do you have a place to stay here in Austin?"

"No. The waiting room will be fine."

"Mrs. MacAllister, I'm afraid you are going to be in for a long wait. Let me suggest that you go back home tonight and return in the morning. Our nurses have your number and we can call should there be any change at all."

"I don't think I can leave," Mama said.

"Me either," Gerald said.

I didn't say anything. The doctor smiled and nodded his head. "I understand. Your husband is a lucky man, Mrs. MacAllister."

"Can we see him?"

The doctor looked at Mama. I thought he was going to say no, but then he kept looking at Mama. Then he looked at Gerald, then at me. He smiled a little.

"Only for a moment," he said. "No talking, no noise, no crying."

The doctor led us down the hall and into the intensive care unit. We passed some beds with old people who were sleeping. Then we came to Father's bed. He was lying flat on his back with no pillow and he had things hooked up to him the way Grandfather had. His face was clean and not at all sunburned. His eyes were closed.

Mama went to his side and touched the edge of the bed. I thought the doctor was going to tell her not to, but he just walked away and started talking to a nurse. Gerald went up to the bed on the other side. I couldn't. All I could do was stand behind everybody and watch. Gerald's face was strange looking. Then tears began to roll down. Mama looked up and saw him. She looked at Father again, then she went around his bed and caught Gerald by the shoulders and pulled him away.

We went out in the hall again. Down at the end, by the waiting room, were Carol and Mark. Carol saw us and ran down the hall toward us. She hugged Mama. Both of them were crying, but Carol was crying more than Mama was.

"How is he?" Mark asked when he had walked up to us.

Gerald started to answer, but he turned away before any words came out.

We had ridden to Austin in the ambulance just as we had been when it came out to the farm and picked Father up. Mark talked to Mama a long time about going home for the night. He sat beside her in the waiting room and leaned forward. His eyes and face were serious and everything he said made sense. He reminded me of Father once Father had made up his mind about something and I liked him for the first time since I had known him.

But Mama had made up her mind too. Finally she took a deep breath and looked at us.

"This is what we'll do. I want you all to go home with Mark—no, now listen. I want you all to go back to the house and get some sleep. In the morning, you can come back with a change of clothes for yourself and for me and whatever else we need. Carol, I want you to bring me my blue dress and a change of underthings. See what needs to be done around the house and do it. Grandmother will want to come up here, so you'll need to stop by and get her in the morning. Be gentle with her, please."

"I'm not goin'," Gerald said.

"Listen—" Mama said.

"I'm not going," Gerald said again.

"All right. You can stay. But the rest of you are to go, understand?" Mama looked at me.

"All right," Carol said. "What about something to eat? None of you have eaten anything, have you?"

"I couldn't," Mama said. "I may send Gerald downstairs later."

We said goodbye and got in the elevator to go. I stood over to the side at first, then Carol pulled me over in front of her and put her hands on my shoulders. Outside there was a full moon over the tall buildings of Austin. It made me feel sad and lonely.

I rode in the back seat on the way home. Mark and Carol talked a little, then they were quiet. Carol was curled up beside Mark on the seat and the way they talked reminded me of the way Father and Mama talk when they think no one else is around. By looking up, I could see the moon out the side window. It was big and full and seemed to follow us all the way home.

Something moved on the front porch. I could just barely see that it was a man. I thought it was Wilbur, but then he spoke and I knew it was Mr. Norman.

He came around to the side where Mark had parked and said, "Howdy."

"Hello Mr. Norman," Carol said. "This is Mark Coburn, my fiancé."

"Well now, by God. Heard about you. Glad to meet you." They shook hands, then Mr. Norman said, "How's your father?"

"We don't really know yet," Carol said. "He's stable, but we have to wait before we know what kind of damage has been done. I think he broke every bone in his body."

"Well, thank God. I didn't know whether he'd be alive or dead."

"Did you walk all the way up here by yourself?" Carol asked.

"Yeah. Couldn't sleep. Ida Ketchum was here for a while, then she left. Got to feelin' tired."

"Come on in," Carol said. "I'll make some coffee. It's two o'clock, but I don't think any of us feels like going to bed."

Carol and Mark went on in the house, but Mr. Norman said he would be just fine on the porch. He walked over to me. He put one of his shaky old hands on my shoulder and shook me a little bit. I started crying and he hugged me.

"Now, now," he said. "Let it out. This is the time for it. You've been through a lot today."

I cried for a while, then I stopped and pulled away.

"Tell me," Mr. Norman said. "How did it happen? Was Wilbur Rutts up there with your father?"

"Yeah. But, but I couldn't tell if he pushed Father or not."

"Did he have anything against your father?"

"Father was going to tell him we didn't want him to work for us anymore. Mama didn't like him hanging around."

Mr. Norman didn't say anything, then he said, "If Wilbur Rutts was up there, then you can bet he pushed your father."

"What can we do?"

"Nothin'," Mr. Norman said. "Not a by God thing unless we can prove it. I talked to Sheriff Burns after Elmer Ketchum was killed, and he said motive or no motive, you needed proof. Well, I ain't got none. That's what makes Rutts such a devil."

I saw a shadow pass in front of the kitchen window. The crickets were loud in the dry grass, and somewhere past the shop a whippoorwill was calling in the dark. Mr. Norman spit and looked at the moon. I wiped my face on the tail of my shirt. The stings were starting to hurt again.

"Come on, boy. I got to sit down. These old legs get to shakin' on me after a while."

We walked around to the front porch. The lawn chairs were still there against the side of the house. I looked at the one Father had been sitting in. Mr. Norman sat down in the one next to it, then waved me over to Father's chair. I backed up to it and sat down. I thought I smelled one of Father's cigars.

"Well, hell," Mr. Norman said, a little bit too loud. "For a man that ain't done nothin', I sure am tired."

I looked out across the yard and listened to the wind blow in the elm tree. The whippoorwill called again, then was quiet.

"You know, I had a long talk with Ida Ketchum while ago. She came up here after the ambulance had gone. I thought maybe the sireen reminded her of when Elmer was carried in. Hard thing, that sound in the middle of a hot afternoon. Like a tea kettle whistlin'. Makes a man want to do 'most anything to shut it up."

"Was she all right?" I asked, thinking of the cat's head as it rolled down the bank.

"I think so," Mr. Norman said. "Just kinda lonely and a little turned around. I don't know. I think she'll be all right now. She'll hurt like blue blazes for a while, but she'll be okay."

We sat without talking. I wiped my nose. The whippoor-will called again.

"By God, I hurt," Mr. Norman said quietly, like he was singing a song with the wind. "When Nancy died, I took my truck into Dallas, lived about twenty miles from there back then. Drove right down to the middle of town and parked and got out and hit the first man I saw. I hit ever' man I saw until they all jumped me and held me down 'til the police came and carried me away. By God, I was hurtin' then."

Carol slipped out the screen door with a cup of coffee in her hand. "Y'all just going to sit in the dark?" she said.

"Eh?"

"Y'all just going to sit out in the dark?"

"Guess so," Mr. Norman said. "Got man-things to talk about. Don't we, boy? Don't mean to be antisocial."

Carol gave Mr. Norman the cup of coffee and touched his shoulder.

"Don't seem right without Mac around, does it?" he said.

"No," Carol said.

Mark came out the door. He had a glass in one hand and a cup in the other. He walked over and sat down on the other side of me and held out the glass.

"Here," he said. "It's Kool-Aid. I put a couple of aspirins in it for your face. You won't be able to taste them."

"Thanks," I said. I looked at him for a minute in the dark and he looked at me. Neither one of us smiled, but I almost knew what he was thinking. He leaned back and took out a cigarette and lit it.

"Guess I ought to go on back down the hill and let you folks get some rest. Reckon you'll be needin' it."

"No hurry," Carol said, standing by his chair. "You sit and finish your coffee, Mr. Norman."

We sat still and everybody looked out at the dark. Even the full moon didn't seem to make much light. I could just make out the outline of the windmill. I felt a tear fall on my shirt.

"Your father will be all right," Mr. Norman said. "He's

been bein' tough for too long to let this stop him. If he'd been—well, anybody else'd been killed outright. Mac'll be back out here 'fore you know it, wonderin' about this and takin' care of that. It's this place and you kids and all those things a man's got to do in his life that keeps Mac goin'."

Mr. Norman was quiet for a while. Mark finished his cigarette and dropped it on the porch and stepped on it. The sparks were small and red and blew away in the wind.

The elevator opened and we went down the hall. Carol was carrying the things Mama wanted. I was carrying some of Gerald's clothes that he could change into. Grandmother was carrying her purse in one hand and a handkerchief in the other.

Mama stepped out of the waiting room and saw us. Uncle Raisin was with her. I had never seen her looking so tired before. Her eyes were bright and sharp though, and when she saw us, she smiled.

"Hello Mama," Carol said, looking at her. "Uncle Raisin."

"I was so upset when I heard," Grandmother said. "At least someone could have called me and let me know. How is he?"

Carol cut in front of Grandmother and hugged Mama. Mama turned and looked at me over Carol's shoulder. She smiled a little.

"I'm sorry, Grandmother. There just wasn't time yesterday—"

"I already explained to Grandmother about it," Carol said.

Grandmother sniffed. Mama reached out and caught her arm.

"He's doing much better," Mama said. "This morning about six, he woke up just like he always does."

"Did you get to talk to him?" Carol asked.

"Oh no," Mama said. "They wouldn't let us in. But the doctor said he was responding well—there may not be any paralysis, but he is in a lot of pain, so they are keeping him sedated. Oh, and they told me they were going to have to wait to set his hip."

"Oh Mama," Carol said. "He really may be all right?"

"The doctor said things looked much better this morning, but you have to remember that all of this is going to take time."

"Mac is too good a man to keep down long, though," Uncle Raisin said. He caught my shoulder, then turned it loose again. He looked like his old self, and I was glad.

I went around Mama and looked in the waiting room. Gerald was asleep on one of the couches they had in there. During the night, they had brought Father's clothes and Gerald was sleeping on his side with them beside him. He had one of Father's cigars in his hand. The cigar was broken.

"Look at him," Mama said, behind me. "I guess you just don't know about people until something like this comes up. He has really been a comfort to me." Mama came up behind me and put her hands on my shoulders. "I sure do have me a couple of good boys," she said.

Right then I thought she only had one, and it wasn't me.

I went outside and stood on the back porch. It was early yet, and we wouldn't be going to see Father for another hour. Mama and Carol were in the house getting ready, but Gerald was already dressed and had gone out into the fields with Mario to see how the cotton was. He didn't have to, but he wanted to. He had been doing a lot of other stuff around the place too, in the last two weeks, that he had never wanted to do before. I didn't even know he could do things like he did, but he was good at it.

I didn't feel like doing anything, though. I didn't even want to talk to anybody or be around them much. In a way, I knew why. It was like before Rebecca left. We didn't want to talk about it, but we couldn't talk about anything else, so we just didn't say anything. I knew what I had to do, but I didn't want to do it, and I couldn't do anything else, so I just didn't do anything.

I stepped off the porch and walked over to Father's pickup. It was right where he had left it the last time he had gotten out of it. I opened the door and got in and closed the door again. It was hot in the truck and a dirt dauber was buzzing against the windshield. Father had left the windows down and there was a thin layer of dust on the seat.

Wilbur had not been around since Father fell. When Father could talk, Mama tried to find out what had happened, but he didn't remember. He didn't even remember Wilbur being up there with him or anything. Mama called Sheriff Burns and talked to him on the telephone for a long time, but there must not have been anything he could do because Mama was mad when she hung up. It was all like Mr. Norman said. Nobody could do anything to Wilbur because they couldn't catch him.

The inside of the truck smelled like Father. I closed my eyes and pretended we were going for a ride together. I began to smell Father more and more. I started to think like him. There were things that needed to be done. It didn't make sense to put things off. The only time to quit was at dark or when you were through. Being tired didn't count or matter. Everybody was tired. Being finished, getting it done, was what mattered.

I opened my eyes and looked at the dirt dauber. It was beating its wings against the glass for nothing.

Father was propped up in his bed. Under his hospital gown, I could see the hard shapes of his casts. His face looked thinner and sharp and his eyes looked a little sad. His jaw muscles were working.

"You haven't quit your job, have you?" Father asked Carol.

"No. Mr. Klausen is giving me some time off. He didn't have to. It was his idea."

"I'll have to thank him."

"Today?" Carol said.

"Maybe not today," Father said and smiled.

Mama was holding Father's hand. Gerald was sitting on the other side of the bed by Father's shoulder, looking at a machine on the wall. I was standing near the end of the bed. Father's room was pretty small and there wasn't much room around his bed.

"There's no tellin' how long I'm goin' to be sittin' around in here while ever'thing goes to pieces around the farm."

"You don't have to worry about that," Mama said. "Your oldest son has been looking out for things very well."

"Who? This one?" Father said, cutting his eyes at Gerald. Gerald looked at him and smiled. Everybody was smiling. "I thought you always had better things to do than farm work."

"Sometimes," Gerald said.

"He hasn't had time for anything else, lately," Mama said.

"That right? Well, tell me about it, then," Father said.

Mama's eyebrows went together and she looked like somebody who had seen somebody else get hurt.

"How's the cotton?"

"Mario has his bunch out there pickin' it right now," Gerald said. "Mario says there ain't much, but there's too much just to let it go to waste. He thinks we can sell it or keep it a while."

"What do you think?" Father asked.

"I think we should sell it now. Lots of farmers didn't make any crop at all and some of those that did are going to hold it for a better price this fall. But the buyers know they can't hold it long on account of they're goin' to need the cash to buy feed with this winter. The price now is probably the best we'll get."

Father cut a look at Mama. Mama was smiling in a sad way. "Didn't I tell you?" she said.

"Where did you hear all that?" Father asked.

"Mario told me he had heard all that talk from one place and another. He said to tell you that he had never seen such sorry cotton."

"He did, huh? What kind of yield we gettin'?"

"Pretty low," Gerald said. "I'll ask Mario this afternoon."

"It won't be enough to pay for all of this," Father said. His face tightened up. "We might have made it before, but not now."

"We have insurance," Mama said.

"I think we can sell some of the older stock," Gerald said. "The prices won't be very good, but we'll save in feed, and the younger ones could stand eatin' less this winter."

"How many head will that come to?"

"Me and Mario counted about twenty-five."

Father thought a minute. I was watching his left hand. It was starting to bunch the sheet like he was trying to grab hold of something.

"We'll be lucky if we don't have to sell any land before all of this is over," Father said. Then he looked over at me and said, "What do you think about all this?"

I reached forward and kind of shook my head. I touched the cold metal of Father's bed.

"He hasn't said too much of anything lately," Mama said.

I looked up at Father to say something, but his eyes were closed. His hand on the bed had a fistful of sheet in it and he was squeezing it. Tears rolled out of the sides of his eyes and his mouth opened enough for me to see that he was gritting his teeth.

"Father," Gerald said.

"Mac?" Mama said. "Are you all right?"

For a minute, Father didn't move, then he nodded his head and tried to say something.

"He's having a spasm," Mama said. "Get out of the way, Ricky. I'm going to get a nurse."

I stepped away from the bed. Mama went by me out into the hall. Carol and Gerald were bent over Father watching him. I went to the window and looked out. Down below me, on a balcony, was a girl wearing a housecoat and sitting in a wheelchair. She was close to the rail in the shade of the building. When I looked, she leaned forward and crossed her arms on the rail and put her head down on her arms.

The day Father was to come home from the hospital, I didn't go with Mama and Gerald and Carol and Mark to get him. Grandmother was out at our house, and Mama didn't want to just leave her all by herself while we went to Austin, so she asked me to stay. I didn't really want to, but I said I would. After they had gone, Grandmother started fixing stuff in the kitchen, so I went outside.

It was hot outside and dry as ever, but everything seemed different to me. Everything was quiet and still the way a tank gets when you throw a rock in the water at night and all the frogs shut up. I went down to the shop. The tractor was still parked in front of it, but it was fixed and running now. Father had the mower hooked up still to mow that patch of sunflowers around the washout.

I walked past the shop and down the gravel road toward the pasture. The shop made me think of the rabbits and they made me think of Rebecca. I liked to think of Rebecca, but sometimes when I did, I felt so lonely I didn't know what to do. I crossed over the fence and went down to the tank. It was almost dry now. There was just a little water in one end. Two bass were floating upside down near the edge of the muddy water. I went over and looked at them. They had been dead a while. I could smell them.

I went back up on the tank dam and looked all around at everything. The wind was blowing across the pasture in hot gusts. I turned and walked along the edge of the tank toward the washout. It seemed strange to be going up there now, strange and a little scary. It was like a place I had seen in a dream one time, but now it was just a place and everybody was gone.

I went up to the bend where Ruby Lee and Gerald used to meet and sat down. It was hot in the washout, but I didn't care. I started thinking about how everything was different now. The farm was different. Mr. Norman didn't open the store every day anymore. Mr. Ketchum was dead. Carol was going to get married. Grandfather was dead. Rebecca had moved. It seemed to me that everything I had liked and enjoyed was gone now, yet I was still there. After a while I cried. I started feeling sorry for myself, I guess. I just sat there in the bright sunshine and cried.

I stopped finally, because I knew Father would think crying was just an excuse for not doing something else. I wanted to be like Father and I wanted him to be proud of me, but I kept thinking that it was my fault that he had been hurt. If I had just said something about Wilbur and Mr. Ketchum, none of these things would have happened. Mr. Norman knew about Wilbur, but he was too old to do anything. That's what made me feel bad. I was the only one who could do anything and I had not done it.

A clump of dirt caved in off the bank I had slid over and it rolled to the bottom of the washout. I jumped at the noise, then stood up and tried to look through the sunflowers to see if anyone was hiding there, spying on me. After a minute, I felt cold inside. I knew what I was going to do.

Wilbur's truck was parked in front of his house, but there wasn't anybody around. I lay in the dry grass watching the house for a long time, but I didn't see anybody. I got up and walked over to the fence and crawled through it.

Walking up to Wilbur's house reminded me of walking by the house at the bottom of the hill that nobody lived in. I felt like the house itself was watching me with big rusty-screened eyes that could tell all about me. The yard around the house was full of trash. Papers lifted and blew in the wind. There were car parts too, or truck parts. They lay in greasy piles near the side of the house.

When I got to the steps, I stopped and looked at the screen door. It had three big holes in it like someone had kicked it three different times. I could hear a radio going from inside the house, but no one was moving around. I was afraid that everybody might be gone.

I went up the steps and crossed the porch to the door. I could see the kitchen through the screen and a corner of the front bedroom. A smell I didn't like came through the house. It smelled like old, greasy food. I knocked on the door. The sound scared me. I knocked again and said hello as loud as I could. Then, without any other sound to warn me, Wilbur stood right in the doorway bent over so that his face was even with mine.

"Hey there, you little son of a bitch," he said. "Just what the hell do you want?"

"I, I came to see you about a job," I said, stuttering because he scared me so bad. I could feel the little hairs tickle on the back of my neck.

"You ain't said nothin', have you?"

"No sir."

"Sure was lucky your daddy didn't die, wasn't it?"

"Yes sir."

"He say somethin' 'bout me?"

"He doesn't remember what happened."

Wilbur straightened up and laughed through his nose. He wiped his mouth with the back of his hand and looked at me.

"A job, you say? You hirin' me, or you lookin' for work?"

"I'm hiring you," I said. "My father needs somebody to do something for him."

"Is that so? Well, come on in and let's talk about it."

"I need to—"

Wilbur kicked the door open and I had to jump to get out of the way of it. "I said, get your little ass in here and let's talk about it."

Quick as a snake, Wilbur grabbed my arm and pulled me into the house. The smell I had smelled before was heavier in the house. Wilbur pulled me into the front room and threw me down on a bed without any sheets on it. I sat up and looked at him. Nobody else was in the house.

"How do you like my place?" Wilbur said. He sat down in a chair near the bed and looked at me with his mean eyes.

"Just fine," I said. I wanted to rub my shoulder, but I didn't move.

"That's a goddamned lie. It makes you sick to look at it, don't it?"

"No sir."

Wilbur leaned forward and grabbed my arm again and pulled me toward him. I was scared to look at his eyes and scared not to.

"What the hell you want to lie for? Are you good at lyin'?"

"No sir."

"Shit," Wilbur said and pushed me back again. A package of cigarettes fell out of his pocket and he reached down and scooped them up. "Why for two cents I'd wring your little goddamned neck. Who'd miss you, huh?"

"I don't know."

Wilbur sat back and took out a cigarette, licked the end of it and put it in his mouth. He slipped the package in his shirt pocket and felt around in the same pocket for a match. He needed a shave and his shirt was dirty and untucked. I started to smell him.

"Nobody would miss you," he said. "Nobody gives a shit about you or anybody else but their own goddamned self. My own kids don't give a shit about me. You think they do?"

"I don't know."

Wilbur found a match and lit the cigarette. He blew smoke out and dropped the match on the floor.

"Well they don't. That goddamned little whore I had around here done run off. You think she'd do that if she gave a shit? Hell no. Then the old woman took the boy and she's gone fast as a ten dollar bill on Saturday night. What do you think of that?"

"I don't know," I said.

"You don't know shit," Wilbur said. "Well good riddance to them, I say. But if I ever catch up to them, I'll wring ever' one of their goddamned necks, you hear me?"

"Yes sir."

"Well, you'd better believe it. You know what I can do, don't you? First it was that fat man and his tractor. He told me to get out of his field, but I fixed him. I waited 'til he put that International in gear and I snatched him right off that seat by his collar. You should have seen his eyes pop out when them wheels hit him."

Wilbur laughed through his nose, then took a puff and blew smoke out. I looked at the floor and tried to think of nothing.

"And your daddy. He's just lucky I didn't kill him. But you ain't said nothin', have you boy? Now why is that? You scared? Well, you better be. I ain't done nothin' to you yet. Listen. I'll tell you a secret. I got my eyes on that sister of yours. She got some sweet little body on her, that one does. I sure would like to taste some of that."

Wilbur rolled his eyes, then rubbed his pants and licked his lips. He took a big puff and blew smoke out at me.

"And you wouldn't say nothin', would you?" he said.

I looked at him.

"Would you, goddammit?"

"No sir."

"Damn right, because that would only be the beginning. Oh boy, but that would be some sweet stuff. Wouldn't it, boy?"

I looked at him. He laughed and leaned back in his chair and looked at me. He took one last puff of his cigarette and threw it on the floor and stepped on it.

"Now what is this shit you sayin' 'bout some job?"

"Father wants you to do some work for him," I said.

"Oh yeah? Like what? He want me to service your mama?"

"He wants you to mow that patch of sunflowers up on this end of the pasture."

"When?"

"This afternoon."

I tried to eat dinner, but I kept thinking about Wilbur and the food would catch in my throat. Grandmother noticed.

"Don't pick at your food like that, Richard," she said, pointing at my plate with her fork.

"Yes ma'am."

"I worked hard all morning fixing up this dinner for you. The least you could do is eat it."

"Yes ma'am."

Grandmother ate for a while. I tried to eat. Every time a truck went by out on the road, I nearly choked to death.

"Where have you been all morning, anyway?" Grandmother said.

"Just messing around," I said.

"I could have used some help around here. Don't you think that with everybody else working so hard to help out that you could do a little something?"

"Yes ma'am."

After a while, Grandmother said, "Your mama called this morning. She said they would be a little later than they thought."

"Are they still going to let Father come home?"

"Yes, of course. They just had to wait on a doctor for something, she said."

"Oh."

I tried to eat. A truck went by on the road and I held my breath. It kept going.

"School is going to be starting in a couple of weeks, isn't it?" Grandmother said.

"Yes ma'am."

"Well, I, for one, will be glad to see the end of this summer. I never knew a summer to be as bad as this one."

I tried to eat. Grandmother finished eating and stared at me for a while.

"I do believe you look more grown up every time I see you," she said. "I just wish you'd act like it."

After dinner, I helped Grandmother clean up the dishes. Then she went into the living room to stretch out on the settee to rest. I slipped out the back door and went down to the sheds behind the shop. I climbed over the trailer we had hauled the posts in and sat down in the dirt behind it, waiting. If Wilbur didn't come today, I didn't know what I would do.

Then I heard his truck pulling up to the shop. I went cold inside, but I stood up and climbed over the trailer and ran for the pasture. When I got to the tank, I slipped over the dam and lay down on the hot dirt and looked up toward the house. The tractor came around the corner of the shop and Wilbur was sitting in the seat. I slid down the dam and ran along bent over up toward the washout.

When I got there, I stopped and looked back. Wilbur was at the gate, opening it. I turned and ran again until I got to where the sunflowers grew thick along the edge of the washout, then I climbed up into them and crouched down. I could feel my heart beating. My breath was coming fast like I had been under water for too long and had just come up. The ground was hard and dry and dead leaves from the sunflowers were crackly and sticky under my hands. It was quiet where I was sitting, about ten feet from the edge of the washout.

After a while, I heard the tractor. It sounded far away, like Wilbur was mowing in some other field. The noise of the tractor and the smell of the sunflowers and the heat all made me think of other things, other seasons, and other summers.

I remembered the time Gerald and I had caught the rabbits while Father mowed around the tank, trying to cut back the weeds enough to let the grass grow. Father had known all along that the rabbits wouldn't live, but he didn't say anything. He just let us catch them and try to raise them and find out for ourselves. I understood now what he had meant when he told me that food and water weren't enough sometimes.

I remembered sitting in the station wagon waiting for Mama when she went to the store. She always said it wouldn't take long, but it always did. Before I could read, I used to just sit and look out the window at the people and the cars. Later I used to read the signs that were taped to the big windows of the store. I would try to guess whether it was Mama or not when the doors opened and someone came out.

I thought of the stories Gerald used to tell in the winter when we would sleep in the same bed trying to keep warm. Gerald would start with some story we had seen on television or with a cartoon or something he had read, then he would make up stuff until we were laughing so much that Mama would come to the bottom of the stairs and tell us to be quiet and go to sleep. Then we would roll over with our backs touching, and under the quilts we would be just as warm as if we were in front of the fire.

The noise of the tractor went by me and I knew that Wilbur was cutting along the edge of the fence. When he got to the corner, he would have to turn and come along the edge of the washout. That was the way Father mowed. He always cut around the outside first, making big circles then smaller ones until he was through. I turned around in the sunflowers and faced the other way. I looked at the ground while I waited.

The way the dirt looked, all hard and cracked, reminded me of the flower bed in Waco that Rebecca's father and I had dug up. He had been weird all that time, but Rebecca wrote in a letter that he was changing. I thought about Rebecca and all the times we had read the same book on the bus. She would hold one side and I would hold the other. I knew she read faster than I did and would finish the page first, but she never said anything. She just waited until I looked at her happy brown eyes, then she would turn the page.

Carol used to read her books out loud to me and Gerald

when we were little. She would sit on her bed and we would lie on either side trying to see the pages even though there weren't any pictures. Carol would change her voice for each of the characters and get loud during the exciting parts and soft during the sad parts. Sometimes, listening to her, I would imagine the story in my mind. Other times I would pretend that I could read the words she was saying.

Father read to us sometimes too. His voice was always funny to listen to because he read every story with his mad voice, no matter what was happening in the story. Father never made up stories, but sometimes he would tell us about when he had been a little boy. The time he helped me carve the gun out of a piece of wood, he told me about another gun he had carved and how he had pretended to be a robber and scared Grandmother. She had given him a whipping.

I thought about Grandfather too, and how he used to try to teach me and Gerald how to play marbles. There was a time when he would hitch up his pants a little and crouch down in the dirt of the driveway and help us lay out the circle of marbles, then show us the best way to shoot. Grandfather never missed when he shot.

The tractor noise was getting louder now. Wilbur was driving along through the sunflowers, mowing them down. Suddenly the tractor stopped. I could tell Wilbur had it in idle. I raised up through the sunflowers until I could just see him. He was drinking from a bottle. He drank it down, then threw the bottle into the washout. I didn't hear it hit. I couldn't hear anything but the tractor. Then Wilbur dug in his pocket for something. When he pulled it out, I saw that it was a cigarette. He tried twice to light it, then I saw the smoke go up around his head in a thin cloud. He let his foot off the clutch and the tractor started forward again. I ducked down into as small a ball as I could make and waited. I almost saw myself from outside myself again. I looked like a little rabbit hiding in the sunflowers.

The noise of the tractor got louder and louder, but I waited. Then, when I heard the front wheels smashing through the sunflowers right in front of me, I stood up. At first, Wilbur didn't see me, then his head turned and he saw me. By that time, the front of the tractor was so close I could have spit on it. When he saw me, he jerked the wheel just enough to make the back tire catch the edge of the washout. The bank caved in and the tractor rolled over into it. Wilbur jerked at the wheel trying to get back out again, then he stood up to jump, but it was too late. The tractor turned over and threw him with it into the washout.

For a minute, the tractor was still going, like an animal on its side trying to get up, then the clanking, banging of the mower stopped and the tractor died. The blades of the mower were wet with the sap of the sunflower stalks. At first I thought everything was quiet, then I knew it was only because I was holding my breath.

I walked over to the edge of the washout and looked down. The tractor was hissing and gasoline was running out the top of the tank and staining the dirt. I couldn't see Wilbur at all. I moved farther down, then I saw him. His right leg was pinned under the steering wheel and he was lying on his stomach with his hands out on the dirt like he was reaching for something. His hat was gone and his left leg was bent back over his body with the boot in the air. The only thing moving was the smoke from his cigarette.

I slid down the loose dirt and walked around the front of the tractor. The wheels were high as my head and I could smell the gasoline and the hot oil smell of the tractor. The gasoline was running onto the clay and spreading out. If it kept running, it would reach Wilbur's cigarette and blow up.

"Hey!" Wilbur stretched his head around.

I jumped back, scared.

"What the hell are you doin'! Oh shit. I'm gonna kill you for this."

I just stood there beside the tractor staring at him. He reminded me of a snake caught under a rock. He was scratching around in the dirt and looking from side to side.

"Hey! Goddamn. Help me. Son of a bitch," Wilbur hissed with pain. There was dirt in his hair and in his mouth.

I watched the gasoline reaching for the ashes of Wilbur's

cigarette, then I kicked dirt over it and turned and walked away in the hot August sun. Behind me, Wilbur was yelling again, but I didn't listen. I walked down toward the tank, making the muscles in my jaw work. I wasn't going to cry anymore if I could help it. I passed the tank and crawled through the fence.

I didn't think where I was, I just kept walking. Someone was calling me and the sound was a long ways off like it was from another time. Once, I wanted to stop and stand in the same place forever, but I didn't. I walked across the field. The house seemed miles away in the hot afternoon sun. It wouldn't be hot much longer though. Summertime was over and everything would be different.

When I got up to the sheds I saw Gerald. "Where you been?" he said.

I looked at him, at his hard face and sharp eyes and his strong hands tucked behind his belt. He was still wearing his good clothes. I was so tired I could hardly stand there. I felt it all coming out of me.

"Wilbur killed Mr. Ketchum," I said. "He pushed Father off the windmill. I tricked him into mowing the sunflowers, then made him roll the tractor into the washout. He's up there now."

Gerald looked at me with his sharp eyes and his hands slowly slid out from behind his belt.

"Is he dead?"

"I wanted to kill him for all the things he did, for hurting and killing and drying up the land. I thought I could make everything like it had been before."

I was trying not to cry. The heat was spinning me around. There were patches of darkness in my eyes.

"Damn," Gerald said.

I wanted to go on to the house, but I wasn't sure which way it was anymore. Then Gerald was beside me. He put his arm around my shoulders and it was strong and hard and held me up.

"Don't ever call me a queer again," I said.

"Come on," Gerald said, pulling me along beside him.

We came around the shop and I saw Father's truck and the

house and the elm tree and it was still and blurred like an old photograph. Even the clouds seemed stopped and there was no breeze.

"I could have told you lots of times, but you were always so mean, Gerald," I said, shaking like it had suddenly gotten cold.

"Settle down," he said, pulling me around the back of Father's truck. "We got things to do."

Gerald took me up to the back door and the sun was bright on the back porch, but I felt like winter had already come. I could feel the icy wind cutting all around me except where Gerald's arm was.